Praise for Janet Tronstad and her novels

"Janet Tronstad's lead characters in *A Hero for Dry Creek* are charming."
—*RT Book Reviews* on *A Hero for Dry Creek*

"Janet Tronstad's quirky small town and witty characters will add warmth and joy to your holiday season."
—*RT Book Reviews* on *A Dry Creek Christmas*

"In *At Home in Dry Creek*, Janet Tronstad presents a warm, touching story that's part of the Dry Creek series, which connects the townspeople in a comforting setting."
—*RT Book Reviews* on *At Home in Dry Creek*

Praise for Susan Hornick and her novels

"*More Than a Cowboy* [is] an emotional and heartwarming story for contemporary western readers."
—*RT Book Reviews* on *More Than a Cowboy*

Janet Tronstad grew up on her family's farm in central Montana and now lives in Turlock, California, where she is always at work on her next book. She has written more than thirty books, many of them set in the fictitious town of Dry Creek, Montana, where the men spend the winters gathered around the potbellied stove in the hardware store and the women make jelly in the fall.

Susan Hornick lives in Colorado with her husband, two horses and a cat. As a child on her grandparents' farm, she loved creating stories in her head, which later translated into journals, short stories and finally novels. Her writing won numerous awards before finding a home in the inspirational market. When not writing or spending time with her family, her biggest passion is visiting historical places—especially old cemeteries—and wilderness camping with her husband and friends, where she explores old ghost towns and wide-open spaces from the back of her horse.

A Hero for Dry Creek

Janet Tronstad

&

More Than a Cowboy

Susan Hornick

HARLEQUIN® LOVE INSPIRED®

TM LOVE INSPIRED BOOKS

PLEASE RECYCLE

THIS • PRODUCT IS RECYCLABLE •

Recycling programs
for this product may
not exist in your area.

ISBN-13: 978-1-335-00667-7

A Hero for Dry Creek and More Than a Cowboy

Copyright © 2017 by Harlequin Books S.A.

The publisher acknowledges the copyright holders
of the individual works as follows:

A Hero for Dry Creek
Copyright © 2003 by Janet Tronstad

More Than a Cowboy
Copyright © 2008 by Susan Hornick

CONTENTS

A HERO FOR DRY CREEK

Janet Tronstad

Dedicated to the princess in our family,
Aurora Borealis MacDonald,
currently four years old.
May all her dreams come true.

It is a good thing to give thanks unto the Lord…
—*Psalms* 92:1a

Chapter One

Nicki Redfern didn't believe in fairy tales. Instead of glass slippers she wore cowboy boots—and not the highly polished ones rodeo riders wore. No, her boots were sturdy, working boots meant for riding horses and chasing cattle.

Her feet sweat in those boots.

Still, recently, in the early-morning hours while she was lying in her twin-size bed—as the pink sun rose over the Big Sheep Mountains and shone through her small second-story window—her dreams turned to fanciful things such as waltzing with princes and blushing with love.

In the full light of day, of course, Nicki stopped those kind of daydreams. No good would come of them.

A woman like her had no time for Prince Charming or ballroom dancing. She was a farm woman with calluses on her hands and responsibilities on her shoulders. Unless Prince Charming knew how to pitch hay bales, she had no use for him.

When her father died last year, Nicki and her brother, Reno, had inherited equal shares of the Redfern Ranch.

The ranch was four thousand acres of prime grassland, starting at the bottom of the Big Sheep Mountains and spreading south to the gully that each year guided the spring run-off into the Yellowstone River just east of the small town of Dry Creek, Montana.

The ranch had been in the Redfern family since 1890 and Nicki was fiercely proud of its history. But it took every ounce of energy from both her and Reno just to keep it going. The price of cattle dropped each year and the dry spell hitting Montana didn't seem like it would end anytime soon.

Nicki needed a hired hand, not some fairy-tale prince.

Besides, Nicki had a weary suspicion that those fluffy dreams were meant for her mother—they had just arrived over twenty years too late. When her mother had left, she'd taken the family honor and eight hundred dollars from the church building fund with her.

Nicki shook her head. There was no point in remembering the woman who had deserted them. No one got everything they wanted in life, and Nicki had learned to be content with what she had—a father, a brother and some of the best ranch land in Montana.

When her father tried to show her some newspaper clippings her mother had sent once, Nicki refused to read them. One look at the accompanying picture of her mother dressed as a Vegas dancer was all Nicki needed to see.

Nicki was half-asleep as she limped down the stairway in her old chenille bathrobe to start the coffee. She was alone in the house this morning. Reno had left yesterday with a truckload of steers. The final cattle sale in Billings fell the day before Thanksgiving each year, and the Redferns always saved their best stock for this sale because the cattle were at their heaviest by then and the buyers more inclined to pay higher prices.

Her brother hadn't wanted to leave her alone. Reno never liked going to Billings and the tumble Nicki had taken yesterday only gave him another reason to fret about leaving the ranch. Nicki had to assure him repeatedly that she was all right. Her horse, Misty, had stumbled into a gopher hole, tossing Nicki to the ground. Nicki was so relieved that Misty hadn't broken any legs that she didn't pay much attention to the bruise coloring her own thigh. Nicki's leg was sore and she couldn't walk far if the old cattle truck Reno was driving had trouble. She'd only slow Reno down if there were problems, and they both knew it.

Nicki yawned as she limped into the kitchen. She headed for the chipped enamel sink and put the nearby coffeepot under the cold water faucet. The sink in the kitchen was right under the window that looked out of the front of the old ranch house. She'd looked out that window thousands of times in her twenty-nine years of life. She always saw the same thing—the old oak tree that had the rope swing dangling from its branches and the mountains in the distance.

It was still more night than day outside. Nicki looked out the window wondering if it would be light enough to see the rope on the tree. The swirl of snowflakes made it especially dark outside. She could only see outlines and pinpricks of white snowflakes. Actually, it was the snowflakes that made her look twice.

She blinked and then closed her eyes before blinking again.

Whoa—the man didn't disappear like she'd thought he would.

He was right there, standing like a figure in a darkened snow globe. The man was looking at the house and leaning against the side of a long white limousine—a limousine so unexpected and shiny, it could as well be a pumpkin carriage sprinkled in fairy dust.

And the man! She only saw the outline of the man, but he looked…well, wonderful. Magical. A white scarf was wrapped around his neck and dangled down over a black jacket that looked suspiciously like a tuxedo. Nicki's eyes followed the man's long legs all the way to the ground and then back up again because there was Hunter, Reno's half-wild dog, standing politely at the man's side.

Nicki had to blink. *Oh, my word!* Nicki woke completely.

Prince Charming! She was looking at Prince Charming. And he was apparently there with a limousine to take her away to the royal ball.

The cold water ran over the sides of the pot and chilled Nicki's hand. She slowly set the pot down in the sink and turned the water off.

She kept staring. The man didn't fade.

She told herself it was time to sit down before she lost it all together. Limousines didn't appear in the driveway of the ranch. Neither did Prince Charming. As for Hunter, the dog would never calmly stand beside a stranger.

Nicki was hallucinating. Her mind had somehow reached into her dream and pulled out the image that had been filling her nights. That much was obvious. She couldn't remember hitting her head when she'd catapulted off Misty yesterday, but she must have done so. What else could explain this?

Nicki stumbled over to a chair.

She needed to stay calm. She'd close her eyes for a bit and wait for it to grow lighter outside. She didn't want to wake Dr. Norris this early. She'd be fine. She'd sit a minute before she tried making coffee again.

And, in the meantime, she'd try to pray. Her father had stopped going to church when Nicki's mother left, but he had still insisted on driving Nicki to services in Dry Creek. So every Sunday Nicki sat in the same pew her family had occupied before her mother left. She sang all the hymns and joined in all the congregational prayers.

But, in private, Nicki never prayed. If she thought about talking to God, no words came. Even now, instead of talking to God, she stared at the bare light bulb hanging from the kitchen ceiling and started to talk to it. *Oh, my, I think I could use some help here… It's not possible—I know it's not. But I'm seeing Prince Charming standing outside my window! Do you think I'm crazy?*

Garrett Hamilton liked the cold of the morning as the snow settled in damp patches on his face. The weather was bracing. And at least when he was standing outside the limousine he didn't feel so much as if he were in the middle of a bad prom date. Nobody but an aging Vegas dancer would insist he wear a tuxedo uniform to fill in for her sick chauffeur, especially when he was doing her a favor.

Well, technically he was doing the favor for his cousin, Chrissy. Or was it his aunt Rose who was responsible for him being here?

"Yeah, it had to be Aunt Rose," Garrett said to the dog who stood silently and watched him. He'd been talking to the dog for a good hour now, and he'd swear the animal understood. "Aunt Rose got me into this one."

Garrett had resisted Aunt Rose's worries about her daughter, Chrissy for weeks now. But that last conversation had gotten to him. She'd said Chrissy had asked him to come.

Garrett snorted. The dog whimpered in agreement and Garrett nodded. "Yeah—I should have known better."

Chrissy hadn't asked him to come, especially since she knew Aunt Rose wanted him to find out more about what was going on with Chrissy and her boyfriend. "Can't say I blame her. Don't know what Aunt Rose was thinking. Shoot, I don't know what I was thinking."

Garrett looked down at the dog.

When Garrett had cut the engine on the limousine and let it coast into the driveway of the ranch late last night, the dog had been there. When Garrett opened the window, the dog moved out of the black shadow under the tree and growled low and deep in his throat. Garrett knew the dog wouldn't give much further warning if Garrett were foolish enough to just open the door and step out of the limousine.

It was too dark for the dog to see whether or not Garrett was looking at him directly, but Garrett knew the dog could sense any fear and would use that as a trigger to attack. Even as the dog growled, Garrett admired the animal. The dog had a torn ear and a scar along its left flank. "You've had a hard time, haven't you, Old Boy?"

Garrett knew that the way to settle a wild animal's nerves was to give him time to get used to you. So he took his old leather coat, the one that he sometimes wore for sixteen hours at a stretch when he was on a long haul, and gently threw it out the window for the dog to sniff. After the dog scratched at the coat and rolled it around in the snow, the dog seemed resigned to Garrett's scent. Not happy, but at least not growling anymore.

"That's a good dog." Garrett knew how the dog felt. Sometimes, even if you got used to something, you still might not like it much.

That's how Garrett felt about this mission his aunt had sent him on. Aunt Rose meant well, but if she hadn't been able to convince Chrissy not to marry her high school sweetheart, Garrett wasn't likely to, either. Besides, Garrett would rather have a tooth pulled than see Chrissy cry. This gave Chrissy a tactical advantage that she used shamelessly.

Garrett was the last person who should give marriage advice anyway. He knew he wasn't a family man.

Garrett was even more of a mutt than the dog beside him. Garrett's mother had died when he was five. After that, alcohol had been all the family his father needed. Garrett had raised himself and, while he had no complaints, he knew less about being a family man than the dog beside him did.

Which was all right.

"I've got my life and it's a good one." Garrett was a legend among truckers. He'd set a record from New York to San Diego that hadn't been broken yet. "A man can't ask for more than that." Garrett loved all that asphalt rolling under his wheels. There were plenty of strangers along the highways and not one of them gave Garrett any grief.

Giving him grief had become Aunt Rose's job. The odd thing was Garrett hadn't even known his aunt Rose until his father died and she showed up at the hospital. She'd told him then that she wanted to adopt him and have him come to live with her and Chrissy, but the thought of being part of any real family had scared Garrett spitless. He told Aunt Rose he'd do fine on his own, and he had.

Garrett wouldn't admit it, but he had grown fond of Aunt Rose over the years. They had made their compromises. She no longer expected him to spend any holidays with her and Chrissy. But they had their own tradition. Every September after Labor Day Garrett came to spend a few days with Aunt Rose and Chrissy. He'd clean out the rain gutters and do any heavy chores they needed. Plus, no matter where he was, he made it a point to pull off the road on Saturday at three in the afternoon and make sure his cell phone was on. That's when Aunt Rose would call.

Aunt Rose didn't ask much more of him than that and so, when she'd asked him to talk to Chrissy, he'd known she was desperate. What could he say but yes?

He should have had his head examined.

Chrissy had flatly refused to talk to Garrett when he pulled into Las Vegas. All she needed, she said, was a favor. Garrett had agreed to help her before he even knew what she was going to ask.

"Bad habit of mine," Garrett mentioned to the dog before glancing back at the limousine just to be sure the woman his cousin had asked him to drive to Montana was still sleeping on the long back seat. Chrissy had met

Lillian at the casino where they both worked—Chrissy
as a waitress and Lillian as an entertainer. "I thought
she was going to ask me to move some furniture in the
back of my truck or something. I could move a whole
city block in the back of Big Blue."

Garrett had already told the dog about Big Blue. Garrett's fourteen-wheel big rig was now parked near the
casino where Chrissy worked. The dark blue cab had
Hamilton Trucking stenciled in white lettering on the
door. It wasn't the fanciest rig on the highways and it
certainly wasn't the newest, but Garrett knew Big Blue
and he had confidence in her.

Garrett looked back at the ranch house. Surely someone would be up soon. He thought he'd seen some movement at that window, but then he'd looked closer and
decided he'd imagined it.

He felt a stirring of sympathy for the poor man who
lived inside. The man had no idea what a surprise this
morning would bring. Garrett's passenger had asked him
to go to the door and prepare the man for her arrival.

From the few remarks the older woman had made
and the engagement ring she'd asked him to return,
Garrett figured Mr. Redfern had wanted to marry the
woman at one point in time and didn't know she was
coming to visit.

A visit like this could give an old man a heart attack.

Failing that, it could give Garrett one.

"Ah, here we go." Garrett relaxed.

Someone had turned a light on in the kitchen.

The morning sun still had not made its way completely over the mountains so Nicki didn't risk looking out the window this time. She focused on filling

the pot with water. Once that was done, she'd start the coffee maker and sit down again. It was a good thing she didn't have many chores to do today.

The knock on the kitchen door came just as the pot was filled with water. Nicki calmed herself. No need to panic. She told herself that the still falling snow had muffled the sound of someone driving up. It must be Lester.

Lester Wilkerson was her neighbor—and friend, Nicki added to herself somewhat guiltily. The fact that he made her nervous wasn't his fault. So far she'd managed to derail most of his hints about getting married, but he didn't seem discouraged.

Nicki figured she would eventually marry Lester, but she just needed more time to get used to the idea. She had no illusions about why Lester was interested in marrying her. His land ran along the east side of the Redfern Ranch, and he had his eye on more grazing area for his cattle.

Nicki knew some people wouldn't see that as a good reason to get married. But Nicki preferred it to some nonsense about love. Land stayed with a person. Love, on the other hand, could fly away at any time.

Lester didn't expect love and neither did Nicki. They would suit each other well. And things between them would be better once they actually got married. Nicki hadn't been able to bring herself to meet Lester's lips yet when he attempted his clumsy kisses, but she supposed she'd come to accept him before long.

In the meantime, Nicki expected Lester would continue his plodding courtship. He had started going into Dry Creek early every morning to pick up the mail for both ranches and then coming over to have coffee with her and Reno.

Yesterday morning Lester had bought her a lavender orchid in a plastic box. The petals were waxy and the flower felt artificial even though it was real. Still, it was a sensible flower for snowy weather in Montana and Nicki appreciated that. The brief yearning she'd had in her heart for roses was easily stamped down. She was a practical woman and should be pleased with a practical flower. Roses wouldn't last long here.

Nicki flipped the switch on the coffee maker before she wiped her wet hands on her chenille robe. She limped over to the door and looked out the small window. All she could make out through the frosted glass was the general shape of a man.

It had to be Lester on the other side of that door, but Nicki wasn't fool enough to just open it for anyone unless she was ready.

She looked over by the ancient refrigerator. There it was. Reno had bought a thick-handled broom at a farm auction last year. Then he had taught her how to hit with it. They were both thinking of that stubborn cow's head when she practiced her swing, but it'd stop a man as quick as a cow. She brought it over.

Nicki unlocked the door and opened it.

Her jaw dropped and she stared.

If it had been the Boston Strangler on the other side of the door, she wouldn't have been able to raise the broom in defense of herself.

It was him. Prince Charming. Flakes of snow sparkled in his hair. He sparkled everywhere. His teeth sparkled. His eyes sparkled. Even the shine on his shoes sparkled. But, as much of a fairy-tale prince as he appeared to be, one thing was clear. "You're real."

Chapter Two

Garrett waited for the woman to finish her sentence. He thought she was going for "real cold" or maybe "real lost." Even "real strange" would do, but the sentence just hung in the air.

Garrett looked past the woman into the kitchen of the house, but he didn't see anyone else there. Having a woman answer the door certainly complicated things. He'd assumed Mr. Redfern was an old bachelor or maybe an old widower. The woman he'd brought up here wouldn't welcome the presence of another woman, especially not someone twenty years younger than her.

"Good morning." Garrett cleared his throat.

The woman still stared at him.

Garrett looked at her. She seemed dazed. Maybe she was a little slow. He softened his voice. "Sorry to bother you, but I'm looking for your husband."

The woman's eyes widened and her voice squeaked. "My husband?"

Nicki began to realize something very important. Prince Charming was standing on her porch talking about husbands and she hadn't combed her hair. Or washed her face. Or put on any clothes except her ratty old robe. *Oh, my.* She was a mess.

"I can wait for him outside. I'm sure you'll be more comfortable with him around."

"He's not—" Nicki breathed. "I mean, I'm not married."

This is where the music starts, Nicki thought to herself. Her heart literally tingled. She'd been wrong all those years. Fairy tales did come true. Forget about her boots. Forget about that waxy orchid in her refrigerator. They didn't matter. Her world had shifted on its axis because Prince Charming was here. Any second now he was going to hold out his arms to her and she was going to float away into some beautiful fairy-tale land where totally impractical rose petals would softly fall on them as they waltzed together. Just like in her dreams.

The prince frowned. "I must have the wrong place," he said, and then turned to walk away.

Nicki gasped. This wasn't how the story was supposed to end. The prince didn't just leave before one rose petal even had time to fall. "It's cold. It'll only take a minute for you to warm up inside."

Nicki stepped back so the man could come into the kitchen.

Prince Charming didn't go into the kitchen, but he came close enough to the door to feel the heat. Nicki forgot to breathe. Outside, the shadows and half-light of the morning had hidden all but the outline of the man's face. But up close in the light she'd turned on in the kitchen—well, his nose and chin were classical; his eyes were a smoldering pewter; his raven hair was thick and wavy. And there—when he smiled—was a deep dimple in his chin.

Nicki was staring. She knew it. But all she was able to do was stand there leaning on the open door as the man stood on the porch. Even the cold wind blowing into the house didn't make her move.

Nothing could make her move—and then she heard the slam of a car door.

"Garrett," a woman's voice called out in exasperation. "Garrett—where are you?"

Nicki's heart sank when "Garrett" turned in response to the woman's call.

Nicki looked out the open door and saw…*her.*

The woman was wearing one of those glamorous wide-brimmed hats so Nicki couldn't see her face but, even without seeing the woman's face, there was no mistaking the fact that she was beautiful. Blonde and svelte—with enough gold draped around her neck to bankroll a small kingdom.

Why was it, Nicki thought, that when Prince Charming finally showed up on her doorstep, he had Cinderella in the car with him?

Nicki's eyes looked down at the woman's feet. Yes, the woman was Cinderella right down to her tiny little feet perched on some ridiculously high-heeled shoes that did little to protect against the snow.

Nicki expected the man to go to the woman, but he didn't. She heard Hunter's low vibrating growl as the woman walked closer, but the dog didn't leave the man's side. Garrett put his hand down and rested it on Hunter's head. The dog stopped growling. "Maybe you could tell me how to get to the Redfern Ranch. I'm looking for Mr. Redfern."

"Reno?" Having a stranger ask for her brother was almost as shocking as seeing some unknown man silence Hunter with a touch. The dog never let anyone touch him except Reno.

"No, it's Charles Redfern I'm looking for."

"My father is dead."

"Oh. Are you sure? Mr. Charles Redfern?"

"Of course I'm sure."

"Garrett," the woman from the car called out to the man.

"Your friend—" Nicki had to look around the man to see the woman from the limousine "—she sounds angry."

"I'll get to her in a minute." Garrett reached into his pocket and pulled out the diamond ring that the woman insisted belonged to Charles Redfern. The ring had found one of the holes in the pocket of Garrett's uniform and it kept falling out at the most awkward times like last night when he was talking to that kid in the café, getting directions to the ranch. Garrett wanted to be rid of it. The woman before him was the man's daughter. That was enough for him. "This ring belongs to you now, I guess."

Nicki stared at the ring. It was a delicate ring with one small center diamond and a circle of fiery opals around it. She heard the sound of the woman muttering angrily, but Nicki didn't turn to look again. She couldn't be bothered with Cinderella.

Nicki wondered how a hallucination could be this real. But it must be a hallucination. The man was wearing a tuxedo and holding out an engagement ring that he said belonged to her. And something about the memory of it made it seem as if he was right.

"It's real," Garrett said, as if sensing her disbelief.

"I—I don't think—" Nicki heard her voice squeak. *Oh, my.* "Could you—could you—pinch me?"

Garrett froze. Surely the woman didn't want him to pinch her, but she looked as if she was going to faint.

"Please."

As the woman's face went whiter, the green of her eyes grew deeper. Like emeralds, Garrett finally decided. They were like muted emeralds. Deep pools of muted emeralds. A man could be pulled into those eyes and drown before he knew it. She really was quite... unusual. But still. "I can't pinch—"

He thought she was going to faint.

He slipped the ring back in his pocket and reached out to pinch her, but found himself holding her arms instead. He couldn't pinch her if he wanted to. Not through the thick robe she wore. But he had to do something.

So he kissed her. On the lips.

He meant it to be a pinch of a kiss. Just a peck to say he hoped she didn't faint. But she gasped, and he—well, he forgot why he was kissing her. He just knew that he was experiencing the sweetest kiss he'd ever shared with anyone. He didn't want it to end.

Nicki couldn't breathe. She'd never been kissed by a hallucination, but she figured it couldn't be like this. She really thought she'd have to faint after all.

"Oh, for Pete's sake, I'll pinch her!" The woman's annoyed voice penetrated Nicki's fog just before she felt the sleeve of her robe being raised.

Cinderella used her nails to deliver a solid pinch.

"Ouch!" The fog left Nicki instantly. She was definitely not hallucinating.

Nicki looked up at the man. He looked dazed. But the

petite woman standing beside him had lifted the brim of her hat and didn't look the least bit vague.

Oh, my. Nicki suddenly wished desperately that she was dreaming after all. The woman's hair was bleached so blond, it shimmered in the faint morning light. Her lips pouted a well-penciled pink. Diamonds dangled from her ears and hung from her graceful neck. The woman looked like she was forty, but Nicki knew that she would turn fifty-five this coming May 13.

"What are you doing here?" Nicki said the words. They sounded defensive to her own ears. But then, she decided, she was entitled to be defensive. The woman hadn't even written in twenty-two years. If it wasn't for the photos in the news clippings that came in the mail periodically, Nicki wouldn't even recognize her now.

The woman's jaw lifted slightly. "You must be the housekeeper. I came to see Mr. Redfern. Would you tell him I'm here?"

Nicki wished with all her heart that she had gone with Reno into Billings. She could have crawled home if the truck had broken down. The woman standing before her didn't recognize her, but Nicki would know the woman's face anywhere. It appeared life really wasn't a fairy tale, after all.

Nicki opened the kitchen door farther. "Maybe you should come inside."

Nicki let the woman walk in front of her and enter the kitchen, but she didn't follow her. She needed to wait.

Nicki forgot she was still holding the end of the broom handle until she felt it pressing against the length of her thigh. That meant it was not only pressing into Garrett's leg, it was also resting on his foot. "I'm sorry, I—my brother makes me use this when he's not here."

Nicki and Garrett were standing facing each other in the middle of the doorway to the kitchen. The main door swung out over the porch, letting cold air come in. The screen door swung back into the kitchen, letting warm air seep out. Neither one seemed able to move.

Garrett's ears were ringing. He decided it must be the altitude. His ears felt as if they were stuffed with cotton, as well. "Huh?"

"The broom. He wants me to carry it." Nicki told herself she was barely making sense. She was feeling a little dizzy. But it was only natural. She needed more than a minute to think before she faced her mother.

"Whatever for—"

"So I can hit heads." Nicki knew she should step aside so they could close the kitchen door, but she was afraid her legs wouldn't work. She'd just stand where she was for a bit more. She needed to focus on the man's face instead of the woman in the kitchen. No, his face wasn't a good thing to look at, either. How could a man be so sexy that even his Adam's apple made her wobbly?

"You want to hit me? On the head? You'll need a stepladder."

Nicki looked up and saw in surprise that it was true. The man was a good six inches taller than herself. It wasn't often that a man was that tall. "You're supposed to be a cow."

"I beg your pardon?"

"I'm supposed to hit the cows' heads with the broom handle. Just on the forehead. To show them which way to go."

"I see," Garrett said. He seemed bewildered as he put his hands around the broom handle so she didn't drop it.

"It doesn't hurt them," Nicki added. She let the

broom fall into his hands. Now, why did she have to tell the man something like that? He'd think she was a barbarian. Not that his opinion mattered. He was only her mother's—Nicki stopped herself. Just who was the man in her mother's life anyway?

"Have you known her long?" Nicki jerked her head in the direction of her mother. She could hear her mother inside the kitchen as she walked across the floor to the counter where the coffee was.

The hostility in this woman's voice cut through Garrett's haze and reminded him the other woman was Chrissy's friend. "Long enough. And you?"

Nicki gave an abrupt laugh. "Me? I barely knew her."

The wind had blown snow across the wooden porch. Nicki could see white puffs coming out of her mouth when she talked. She could feel the goose bumps on her arms, and the frozen boards of the porch chilled her feet even though she had her winter slippers on. She was used to the weather in Montana and she was still cold. "She won't want to stay for long so you might as well go inside and get warmed up. It's freezing out here."

Garrett nodded. The cold would explain the tingling he still felt all over his body. Yes, that would be it. And his breathing. That would explain why his breath was coming hard. But as the woman backed up farther against the doorjamb, all he could think about was that she had to be even colder than he was. "You go ahead— you must be freezing. You're in your pajamas."

The sun was rising and the day was taking on a faint pink glow. Garrett couldn't help but notice how delightful the woman's face was when she blushed.

"It's a robe."

Nicki had never wished for silk in her life until now. Her chenille robe must be twelve years old. It had been faithful and warm, but it was not what a woman dreamed about wearing at a moment like this.

Not that, Nicki assured herself, it would matter for very long. The man in front of her would be leaving with her mother and, if Nicki had anything to say about it, that would be happening soon. Nicki pulled on the ties of her robe to knot it more securely. She was a sensible ranch woman. She didn't need silk. She didn't need her mother. She didn't need some fantasy prince. She had her land, her boots and her pride. That had to be enough.

Garrett looked at the woman. The cold had turned her nose red and the wind had blown strands of her hair this way and that way until they finally just gave up and tangled around her head. Her hair was neither permed nor colored nor highlighted. She kept it brown—not honey brown, not mahogany brown. Just plain brown. And she didn't have a dab of lipstick anywhere.

Added to that, she was wearing an old bathrobe that kept her shape so well hidden, a man couldn't tell if she was a woman or a fence post.

Still, she appealed to him in a crazy sort of way. Garrett wondered if the snow could have frozen his brain or something. The woman sure wasn't the usual kind who caught his eye. He liked a woman who strutted her stuff and wore her clothes tight enough so a man didn't have to strain himself wondering what was underneath.

And that robe wasn't his style. He liked the black see-through kind that was worn more for invitation than for warmth. The bulky old robe this woman wore wouldn't get her noticed in a monastery.

Besides, the robe said loud and clear that the woman who wore it was a nice woman who wasn't inviting anybody to look at her twice.

Garrett made it a policy to stay away from nice women because they always thought a man like him had promise. It wasn't true, of course, but try convincing a woman who was intent on reforming him. If he knew one thing about himself, it was that he was a short-term kind of a guy. He liked the freedom of the road. Given that, he felt it was only right to keep his dating to women who weren't interested in a long-term arrangement, either.

Granted, Garrett had grown a little tired of dating strangers lately. He told himself he was just off his game. He hadn't been out on a date in six months.

But that was bound to change soon. Somewhere, someplace, a woman in black spandex was waiting for him.

Still, if he had been the sticking-around kind of guy, there was something about this woman that interested him even more than the black-spandex ones. Maybe it was the freckles on her neck. She'd tied the belt of the robe tight around her waist and that made the collar bulge just enough so he could see the light sprinkling of freckles that scattered out from her collar bone. The bone itself was fragile and made him feel protective. But it was the freckles that were his undoing.

For the first time in his life, Garrett wished he knew a thing or two about marriage.

"I'm sorry, I—" Garrett began. He didn't know what he was going to apologize for exactly. Maybe the fact that cold air had gone into her warm kitchen. Or that he had snow on his shoes. Or that he hadn't been born into an Ozzie-and-Harriet kind of a family.

Nicki shifted in the doorway. A faint pink made her face glow in embarrassment. The man didn't need to apologize. She wasn't such a ninny that she thought he was serious. Of course, she was acting like one. The man had been making her agitated and that wasn't like her. She was usually very calm and sensible.

"I know it wasn't a real kiss." Nicki waved her hand vaguely, as though she'd experienced a million kisses that were real and so could tell the difference instantly. "You don't need to apologize."

Garrett frowned. "What do you mean it wasn't a real kiss?"

"That's what I'm saying—it wasn't like the kiss was supposed to be real, so you don't need to apologize."

"I wasn't apologizing for kissing you."

The pink on Nicki's face deepened. "Oh, well, I just wanted you to know I know it didn't mean anything. It was just because of the ring, and me asking to be pinched and you in that tuxedo and all."

"It's not a tuxedo, it's a uniform. Besides, every kiss means something."

Nicki could hear her mother's high-heeled footsteps as she continued walking from the counter that held the coffeepot to the counter that held the dishes. "Where do you keep the cups?" her mother called out.

Nicki forced herself to turn and look. Everything in the house looked shabbier than it had when her mother left. Because of her fall yesterday she hadn't even done the dishes from yesterday. Three mugs stood around the sink. "There are more mugs in the cupboard."

Every Christmas the hardware store in Dry Creek

gave away a mug to its customers with the store's name on one side of it and the year on the other. In addition to the three by the sink, another dozen of those mugs sat in the cupboard.

Nicki's mother took one look at the dirty cups. "I'm not talking about mugs. I'm talking about real cups. I always drink my coffee from a real cup. Something pretty and tasteful. Surely, Charles still does the same."

"I'm afraid the mugs are all that we have." Nicki tried to hold back the defensiveness in her voice, but she didn't succeed. Nicki wasn't sure she wanted the woman in front of her to realize that she was her daughter. The fuss the woman was making over cups that were functional instead of pretty only reminded Nicki of how critical her mother had been of her. Nicki had never been the pretty little girl her mother wanted. Nicki remembered that her hair never curled enough and the lace on her dresses always made her itch so she couldn't wait to change into her jeans.

"But these mugs don't even match."

"They don't need to match to hold coffee."

All of a sudden, Nicki realized what her mother was looking for. Nicki's mother had had a set of English bone china that served sixteen, but Nicki and Reno kept it packed away in the old bunkhouse where their father had put it. The dishes were the one thing Nicki hadn't even dreamed of replacing over the years. Her mother loved that china with its clusters of pink roses and the gold rim around each plate.

Nicki decided she needed to get the mugs so that her mother could drink her coffee and leave. She forgot about her leg, however, and her first step made her wince.

"You're hurt!" Garrett said, and stepped toward her. Unfortunately, he let go of the broom handle so that he could steady Nicki just as she moved again. Instead of falling to the floor harmlessly like it should have, the broom landed on Nicki's foot.

"Ooh." Nicki felt the pain shoot up through her leg. The broom hit her toes and her slippers weren't enough of a cushion. To make matters worse, it was her good foot that had been hit. The bruise was on her other leg and so now she didn't have one good walking foot between the two legs.

The dismay on the man's face made Nicki wonder if her face had turned white with pain. "Don't worry. I'll be fine. It's just that yesterday my horse fell and now this—"

"You need to stay off your feet," he said.

"I'm fine. Really." Nicki gathered the collar of her robe around her more closely. To prove she was all right, Nicki carefully put one foot in front of the other and started walking toward the cupboard that held what dishes they did have. She smiled to show it didn't hurt.

Her smile turned to gritted teeth as she bit back the moan. *Oh, my, that hurt.*

"It's my fault the broom fell," Garrett said as he stepped forward and scooped Nicki up in his arms.

Nicki gasped in surprise. Maybe she was still dreaming. Her cheek was pressed against the tuxedo's satin lapel. The suit even smelled of class. Nicki wished she were wearing perfume. Forget perfume—she wished she were at least wearing deodorant.

"You need to put me down. I can walk," Nicki said. But maybe she couldn't walk. Everything seemed dizzy. Her whole world was shifting. Her heart was building up to a pounding close to thunder. Being swept up by Prince Charming was a fantasy come true.

Nicki's mother walked closer to the two of them and frowned. "Are you Mrs. Hargrove's daughter? You look familiar."

Nicki kept her cheek pressed against the man's shoulder.

"Doris June? No, I'm not her," Nicki answered when she knew her mother couldn't see her eyes. Doris June Hargrove had gone to school with Nicki. She lived in Anchorage now and was working for a television station there.

"Oh, I was just wondering." Her mother didn't sound convinced. "I'm sure Charles needs someone to look after the house for him since both of the kids took off like they did on him."

"Who told you anyone took off?" Nicki asked quietly when she was finally sitting on the kitchen counter. She reknotted the tie on her robe just so she had somewhere for her eyes to focus that didn't involve looking at her mother.

"Why, Charles, of course. He wrote me a letter. Years ago. I'd written to ask about the kids, and he said they'd just up and left. I was surprised about that, but I suppose they had their reasons. He promised he'd let me know if he found out where they were. Have you worked for Charles long?" Nicki's mother smiled thinly. "I know I'm going on, but I would like a cup of coffee before I have to see Charles. Do you think he'll be up soon?"

"No, no, he won't be up soon," Nicki said. Everything seemed fuzzy. Her whole world was shifting. Her heart was pounding. She didn't know whether it was because of seeing her long-lost mother or because she'd woken up to see Prince Charming.

Nicki immediately rejected the idea that her mother could affect her like this. She'd gotten used to living without a mother and she was doing fine. The woman standing by the sink could be any woman. Nicki didn't feel anything for her.

Not that, she remembered with a start of guilt, she should be so willing to think the dizziness was from the man, either. She shouldn't be swooning over any man. She was going to marry Lester. That thought alone was enough to bring her back to earth with a thud. At least it settled her stomach.

"Oh," Nicki's mother said as she turned to leave the kitchen. "If he's not going to be up soon, I'm going to visit the ladies' room while you finish making the coffee. It was a long drive."

"The bathroom's upstairs," Nicki offered. "The first door on your left."

"I remember where it is."

Nicki didn't say anything as she listened to the staccato tapping of her mother's heels as she climbed up the stairs.

Garrett wished he could offer to clean out the rain gutters on this woman's house or something. She looked drawn and pale, and he'd always had a soft touch for any wounded being. Of course, it hadn't helped anything that he had dropped the broom that hit her foot. And the broom wasn't half-plastic like the ones they made today; it was pure oak and could do some serious damage. "Let me look at your toes."

"What?" Nicki looked up in time to see Prince Charming reaching for her slippers.

"I'm hoping no toes are broken."

Nicki was just hoping she'd survive.

Garrett had never seen more elegant feet. The toes themselves were worthy of a poem. "I like the pink."

Nicki blushed. She had never meant for anyone to see the nail polish on her toes. She didn't want to wear polish on her fingers, because someone was sure to comment on that. But she figured her toes were safe from the eyes of others and a good way to practice using nail polish just in case she ever wanted to do her fingernails. "There's nothing wrong with having good toe hygiene."

Nicki almost groaned. She was sounding like a schoolteacher. No wonder there had never been a line of men waiting at her door to date her. "I'll be fine in a minute. My foot will be better."

"I'm sorry I dropped the broom."

The man didn't need to apologize, Nicki thought. A man that good-looking—women probably flocked to him to have their toes bruised. *It must be the tuxedo*, she decided. That, and the way he had of lifting her into his arms, as though she didn't weigh any more than a feather.

Nicki wondered why Lester had never swept her off her feet like Prince Charming here had done. She might mention it to Lester. *That's right*, she told herself. It was the action that had made her heart all jumpy. It had nothing to do with the man. If Lester put on a tuxedo and swung her up into his arms, she'd feel the same breathlessness as she felt now. She might even want to kiss Lester after something like that.

Nicki heard a motor in the driveway. "I'd better get down four mugs."

Seeing Garrett's bemused expression, Nicki said, "Lester's here." She reached for the mugs and put them down on the counter beside her.

"And who's Lester?"

Nicki hesitated. "Our neighbor. To the east of here."

Nicki told herself she didn't owe this man any explanations. "He's just here for his coffee. Oh, and some coffee cake."

Nicki started to brace herself to slide off the counter.

"No, you don't." Garrett stepped over and held out his arms to scoop her up again.

"You shouldn't."

"The floor's cold."

Nicki nodded. She supposed once more wouldn't hurt. It might actually be a good thing. She probably wouldn't be dizzy this time, and she'd know it had only been a momentary thing before. It was really for scientific research that she was going to let Garrett carry her again.

Nicki slid into his arms.

Garrett was a happy man. The fuzzy material of Nicki's bathrobe brushed against his cheek and the pure soap smell of her surrounded him.

"You didn't need to carry me. I can walk if I have to."

Garrett knew that. But he wasn't fool enough to pass up the opportunity to carry her again. He'd even walk slow. The refrigerator was way across the kitchen. If he worked it right, he could almost make a waltz out of the whole thing.

Nicki heard Lester's footsteps on the porch. Fortunately, the door was already unlocked. "Come on in."

Garrett felt the cold air rush into the kitchen, but that's not what made the back of his neck tingle. Something was wrong. He heard the door slam. It was followed by the quick hissing indrawn breath of an angry man.

"What the—" The bellow coming from the doorway made Garrett turn as the man charged toward him. The man was small, but wiry—and red enough to explode.

Garrett had been in enough street fights as a kid to know what was coming, but he'd never had someone in his arms before. If he had even a second longer, he could have slid Nicki down to the floor. But the man was coming too fast. All Garrett could do was protect her as best he could. He pivoted so that Nicki was not between him and this madman.

"Lester," the woman squealed.

Garrett only had time to bend his shoulder so he could hide Nicki in the hunching of his shoulder. The man's fist caught him high on the right cheek.

"Lester!" Nicki tried to twist out of Garrett's grasp so she could slide down to the floor and get her broom. What had gotten into him? She'd always assumed Lester was shy and that was why he was so patient with her about kissing and things like that. But the man in front of her wasn't shy. He was acting like a deranged man. "Stop that! What do you think you're doing?"

Garrett's hands held her to him like steel.

"What do I think I'm doing?" Lester exploded. Garrett wondered how the vein in the man's head could throb that hard. "Just what do you think you're doing here with some man and you in your nightgown?"

Ah, so that's the way the story went, Garrett thought to himself. Well, he supposed the woman had to have a boyfriend. *Even in a remote area like this, the men would be foolish not to notice the*—Garrett stopped himself. It wasn't beauty he noticed. It certainly wasn't stylish clothes. What was it about the woman?

"I've got a robe on—not just my nightgown," Nicki corrected him. "And if you'd bothered to notice, you would see everything is perfectly innocent and—" she could hear her voice rising "—just what do you think is going on anyway?"

Nicki had lived by the rules all her life. Lester should know that.

Lester flushed. He was so red already that he actually grew less red when he flushed. Now he looked mottled as he mumbled. "Duane at the café told me some guy stopped last night at midnight and asked how to find the Redfern place. Some guy in a tux. Everyone knows Reno took those steers down to Billings and that you're here alone."

"What's Reno got to do with—" Nicki stopped and then realized what he was implying. "Lester Wilkerson, you have your nerve!"

Garrett felt the swelling start on his cheekbone. He hadn't had a bruiser like this since he'd stepped between two fighting truckers once. He supposed it was safe for Nicki to slide down to the floor now, but Garrett didn't want her to leave his arms. Some primitive part of him figured he was entitled to carry her now that he'd taken a fist to his face on her behalf.

Nicki heard her mother's footsteps as she came back down the stairs.

"Did I hear something about Reno?" Nicki's mother stood in the doorway and asked. "Reno still lives here?"

Everyone in the kitchen forgot Nicki's nightgown and the bruise on Garrett's cheek.

"Let me get you your coffee." Nicki slid to the floor

and tested her foot. Garrett let her rest against him until she was steady and then she stepped away. "I put the clean cups on the counter."

"Why would Reno be here? Charles said the kids had both left." Nicki's mother walked over to the counter. "He said he would let me know if he heard from them."

By now the older woman had picked up one of the clean mugs Nicki had put on the counter and was rubbing the side of it almost unconsciously. She had stopped smiling and her face seemed to age ten years as she stood there. "I know Charles was angry with me. But if Reno's here and he didn't tell me, that's not fair. When Charles wakes up, I'm going to have to tell him that's not right."

Nicki felt her face was so tight, it would rip. She refused to cry in front of this woman. "There's nothing you can tell him. He's dead."

The woman dropped the cup and no one noticed. "Oh, dear."

For the first time since she'd recognized her mother, Nicki had a glimpse of the woman her mother used to be. "I'm sorry. I shouldn't have blurted it out like that."

"No, no—" Nicki's mother waved the apology away. "I just wasn't expecting this is all. Does Nicki know? Did anyone find her to tell her? She'd want to know."

"She knows." Nicki swallowed. She'd never thought herself to be a coward, but she found that the words to tell her mother who she was wouldn't come without forcing.

"But—" Lester started to speak until Garrett put his hand on the man's arm to silence him.

Nicki looked at both men. There was nothing to do but say it. "I'm Nicki."

Nicki wished her mother had another cup to drop. Anything would be better than the silence that greeted her announcement. The other woman just stared at Nicki.

Nicki reminded herself that she didn't need fairy tales, not even ones that involved mothers coming home again to their daughters.

"Well—" Nicki finally found her voice. The silence was unnerving. "Let me pour you some coffee before you go."

Nicki was proud of the fact that her face didn't crumble. No tears came to her eyes. Even the anger was gone. She would give her mother a cup of coffee and that would be that.

Nicki didn't even limp as she walked toward the coffeepot.

Chapter Three

Garrett was losing his touch. He would have bet Big Blue that Lilly would melt into a puddle of sentimentality at the fact that her daughter was standing before her. Aunt Rose would have been crying into her tissue by now.

But the woman stayed dry-eyed. He thought her hands trembled and her face did grow paler, but she certainly wasn't smiling with joy. She looked over at Garrett. "We're going to have to leave. I didn't know she was here."

Garrett felt a clutch in his stomach at her words. Something was going on here and he had a feeling it was something worse than anybody's sore toes. He took a step closer to Nicki just in case she needed him.

"I'm in the room. You can talk to me," Nicki said as she gripped the handle on the cup she had pulled from the dish drainer.

"Oh, dear. It's just that I'm surprised. Your father's letter said—well, I just didn't expect you to be here," Lillian said as she walked over to the sink.

Garrett knew people didn't always say what they

meant the first time around. He turned to Lillian. "Maybe if you told her why you're here. Surely there's a reason."

The older woman hesitated. "I just came to see Charles, that's all."

The man's question brought Nicki back into focus. Why was her mother here? Nicki turned to face the woman. If you took away the powder and the makeup, you could see traces of the woman she had once been. "You could have come to see him years ago."

The clock ticked and the old refrigerator gurgled.

"And what's he doing here?" Lester finally spoke and jerked his thumb at Garrett.

"I'm Garrett Hamilton. I'm a trucker. I drove Lilly Fern up here."

"And why did you come again?" Nicki turned from the man and addressed her mother.

"I came to talk to your father," Nicki's mother said defiantly. "There's no harm in that."

"You can't possibly think he would want to see you now even if he were alive. You left him years ago."

"He was my husband. I never did divorce him."

"That's it? You came to ask him for a divorce after all these years?"

"Of course not. I don't need a divorce."

"Then what is it—is it money?"

Lillian laughed. "Charles never had any money. All he ever had was this ranch of his."

"He loved this ranch—" *And he loved you.* Nicki almost said the words and then choked them off. What did it matter now?

Lillian wasn't even looking at her any longer. "I know we can't always go back, but I have unfinished business in Dry Creek and I needed a place to stay for a little bit—"

"You're in trouble?"

Lillian shrugged. "In a way, I guess."

"And you need a place to hide?" Strangely enough, Nicki was relieved. Her mother really hadn't come looking for her father because she missed her father or had any fondness for him. She'd just come looking for a safe harbor in some storm she was facing.

"Your father would want me to be here now. He'd feel he owes me that much."

Nicki felt her world click back into place. Everything was as it had been. It felt good to know her way around once again. The fact that her mother had come to her father hoping for comfort in some crisis didn't surprise her. Her father never turned away anyone in need. He might not talk to them much, but he'd let them stay.

"Nobody here owes you anything." Nicki wasn't her father.

"Don't worry. I couldn't possibly stay here now anyway." Lillian Redfern reached out her hand for a cup of coffee. "Once I've had a cup of coffee, Garrett will drive me back to Dry Creek and we'll stay there for a few days."

"Dry Creek?" Nicki didn't like the sound of that.

Garrett wasn't sure he liked the sounds of it, either. He frowned. "No one said anything about days. I thought we were planning to leave tonight." Garrett planned to be in Las Vegas tomorrow night so he could pick up Big Blue and hit the highway.

Lillian looked up at Garrett. "I'm sure you won't mind. It's just going to take longer than I thought."

Garrett did mind, but he didn't have time to speak up before Nicki was talking.

"You can't just stay. Not around Dry Creek," Nicki said.

"No one would deny a widow the right to stand by her husband's grave."

"You're going to tell them you're going to the cemetery?"

"Of course. And I will be. It's the respectable thing to do. I have a black dress with me. I always travel with at least one black dress. And I'm sure someone in Dry Creek will let me stay with them."

"After what you did when you left?" Nicki's hand shook ever so slightly as she poured another cup of coffee into a hardware store mug. "I wouldn't think you'd be very welcome."

Lillian sat down at the kitchen table and took a sip of coffee. "Oh, yes. The money. I suppose they still remember that."

Nicki looked at her mother incredulously. "Of course they remember the money. You stole over eight hundred dollars from the church building fund. I don't know how many bake sales the women of the church had. How could you possibly think they might have forgotten?"

Lillian smiled slightly. "I thought they might have had other things on their minds at the time." Lillian took another sip of coffee and then looked at Nicki. "My leaving was hard on you, wasn't it?"

"No. I did fine."

Nicki could feel Lester looking at her. She glanced up at him. Even now that he was calm, he looked odd. She'd never seen him look like this. His face looked blotched. But he was her Lester. She could count on him. "Haven't I done fine?"

Lester grunted and jerked his thumb at Garrett. "You're sure you don't know him? Jazz at the café said he had a ring and everything ready to propose."

Garrett felt his heart stop. He'd thought the teenager had looked at him strangely when the ring fell out.

Garrett cleared his throat and looked Nicki in the eye. "You did just fine. I can tell."

Nicki was annoyed. Lester should have been the one to say that. "Thank you, but you don't know me well enough to judge."

Garrett grinned. He rather liked the vinegar look on Nicki's face. "It's early. I've got time."

"What's he talking about?" Lester mumbled.

"Oh, for Pete's sake, he's not proposing," Nicki said firmly as she smiled at Lester and glared at Garrett. This was all Garrett's fault. Everything had been fine— until he came up here. Who went around carrying an engagement ring and wearing a tuxedo in the middle of Montana farmland? No wonder poor Lester was confused. "Look at him. He's not even from around here."

Garrett frowned at that. "Good people come from other places, too."

Nicki took a deep breath. "What I meant is that you don't know me and I don't know you so there's no reason to think you'd be proposing. We're strangers."

"I've seen your toes."

"What's he talking about? And what's he doing here anyway?"

Nicki wondered why she'd never seen Lester like this before. What had happened to his hair? She hadn't noticed how his light brown hair was starting to thin and the pink of his scalp showed through, making him look old. And when he squinted like that, his eyes made him look like a ferret. Maybe it was only the cold weather that had scrunched up his face like this. She'd need to get him a warm cap for Christmas. That was what she'd do, she thought. A warm cap would make him look better.

"He brought me here," Lillian said graciously to Lester. "I don't believe we've met. Were you here when I was around? I'm Nicki's mother."

Lillian held her hand out to the man.

Lester had his hand halfway out to meet hers and he stopped in midair. "That's what Nicki's talking about—I remember hearing about you—you're the one who stole the church's money?"

Nicki saw her mother's polite smile tighten. "Is that what they say about me?"

"Yes, ma'am," Lester agreed doubtfully.

"Well, then, I'm getting off easy, I guess."

"Well, I don't know about that—taking money is pretty serious."

"Well, they'll just have to forgive me," Lillian said firmly. She lifted her chin up slightly. "Once an apology is given, it is their Christian duty to forgive."

Lester looked at Lillian, frowning slightly. "I must have missed hearing about the apology."

Nicki could have gone to Lester and hugged him. Now this was the Lester she knew. Unswayed by flattery. Polite and logical, with his feet firmly planted on the earth and no hint of sentiment about him. Not at all like Prince Charming who stood looking at her like she needed some kind of rescuing.

"Well, I haven't given an apology yet," Lillian admitted with a hint of reproach in her voice. "I haven't even finished my coffee." Lillian took a slow sip from her cup. "What do you suppose they'll say?"

"What do you mean?" Nicki felt a small ball of dread starting to roll around in her stomach.

"Why, when I go into Dry Creek and apologize, of course."

"You don't really need to apologize," Nicki said. The last thing she wanted was for her mother's name to again be the primary topic of conversation for Dry Creek. "That's all over and done with."

"I can't do that. You two convinced me of that." Lillian nodded at Lester. She took another sip of coffee. "I can't have people saying I didn't apologize."

"You could write a note," Nicki offered in desperation. People never got as worked up over a letter as they did when someone talked in person. Besides, who knew what her mother would say when she opened her mouth. Nicki could correct a letter.

"What kind of a lady would write a note about something like that?" her mother asked.

The same kind of lady who would steal from the church on the way out of her children's lives, Nicki thought, but she held her tongue.

"No, I'm right," Lillian said firmly. "I'm going to apologize and put an end to all of this. All I need to do is find the minister of that little church. We'll all drive into Dry Creek and find him."

"All of us?" Lester shuffled his feet and looked at Nicki before glancing at Garrett. "You're sure that guy's not proposing?"

"Absolutely."

"Then I'm going to get back to my place. I still have some cattle to feed."

"I could come help you," Nicki offered.

Lester brightened. "You could?"

"She's coming with me." Garrett interrupted them. It was one thing for Nicki to reassure the man that no one was proposing to her, it was another to run off for a cozy drive with her boyfriend while she left her mother with Garrett.

"Nicki and Garrett will take me to Dry Creek," Lillian said airily, as if she was in charge. "They won't need anyone else."

Lester looked at Nicki and shrugged before heading toward the door.

Nicki tried again. "It's early morning. The minister won't be up yet."

"Then we'll wake him up," Lillian said as she stood. "It's his duty to hear confessions."

"You're thinking of priests." Nicki groaned. "Priests hear confessions."

"Priest, minister, it's all the same," Lillian said as she adjusted her skirt and turned to Garrett. "Would you mind bringing the car closer to the door this time? The snow is so slippery and in these shoes—"

Garrett could tell from Nicki's face that her Lester had disappointed her when he made his exit without her. Garrett shouldn't be happy about that fact, but he was. To make up for it, he turned to Nicki and asked, "How about it? Would you like me to bring the car closer so you don't have to walk in the snow?"

"Me?" Nicki breathed lightly. Her Prince Charming was worried about her feet. That's when she remembered she was in her slippers. "Oh, I can't go. I'm not dressed."

Nicki had been searching for a reason not to go, and when she found one she realized she was oddly disappointed.

"Well, I can't leave you here." Garrett didn't want to drive Lillian back into Dry Creek all alone.

"And put on a dress, darling," Nicki's mother called out as she walked toward the kitchen door. "We have time for you to look nice."

Nicki couldn't believe she was hearing those words again. The only time Nicki had worn a dress since her mother left was to her father's funeral. And she certainly wasn't going to wear that dress for her mother's return, Nicki told herself as she limped up the stairs again.

Nicki did have some nice pants outfits that she wore to church. She pulled one of them off its hanger before she reconsidered and hung it back up. No, she wasn't going to fall into the trap of trying to please her mother.

Instead, Nicki put on the jeans she generally used to muck out the barn. They were clean, but they didn't look it. She topped them off with an old sweater of her father's. Her mother might not like it, but Nicki didn't care.

She didn't want to hear what her mother said about dresses and looking good, anyway. Nicki knew she was hopeless. She only had to look in the mirror to know she wasn't princess material. Her mother had been as delicate as the lily that gave her its name. But there was nothing delicate about Nicki's face. She had her father's square jaw and determined forehead. Her hair was plentiful and shiny, but it never took on the styled look that some women's hair had. She just kept it cut and tied back out of her face.

There was never any reason to fuss with her hair. The cows didn't care. Reno wouldn't notice. Even Lester wouldn't care.

Nicki decided her mother would have to accept her as she was.

Nicki felt foolish the minute Garrett opened the passenger door of the limousine for her. She felt like a rebellious Cinderella who had declined her fairy godmother's offer of new clothes but had gone to the ball anyway. The interior of the car was sleek—if it was proper to call the limousine a car. It looked more like an ocean liner to her eyes. Nicki had never seen such a long length of leather that wasn't attached to a cow. And there was a small refrigerator. And her mother.

"Maybe I should drive the pickup in to Dry Creek and just meet you there," Nicki suggested softly as she looked up at Garrett. "I don't really know that I should ride in here dressed in jeans—"

Garrett shrugged. "You can ride up front with me if you'd like. It's not so fancy up there."

Garrett told himself that Nicki was just like any other woman he'd taken for a drive. Any kind of breathing problem he'd had after that kiss had only been because of the freezing temperature.

"I do have a dress," Nicki said when Garrett turned the heater on inside the limousine. The defroster slowly blew a clear space on the front window. "I should have worn it. I imagine all of the women in Las Vegas wear dresses."

Of course they wore dresses, Nicki told herself. Sexy black dresses that pleased men more than mothers.

Garrett grunted. "I'm not from Vegas."

"Oh. I just thought that since Lillian was from there—" Nicki turned her head and noticed the glass window that separated the driver's area from the rear of the limousine was firmly closed. At least her mother and Garrett hadn't been chatting away cozily.

"I don't know your mother. I'm just doing a favor for Chrissy."

"Oh." Of course there was a Chrissy in his life. Or a Suzy or a Patti. Some petite blonde with style. A man that good-looking wouldn't be alone. "I see. Well, good for you."

"I don't know about that."

"Well, of course it's good. And I'm sure she appreciates it."

"She'd better. If she doesn't I'm going to tell her mother about it."

"You're good friends with her mother, too?" Nicki smiled stiffly. The man was practically married whether he knew it or not. "That's nice."

"Well, it's my aunt Rose. Chrissy Hamilton is my cousin."

"Oh."

Nicki decided she should look for something else to wear when she was in Dry Creek. Really, the only store in town was the hardware store, but the stock had changed so much since the minister's new wife, Glory, was doing the ordering that maybe, by some magical coincidence, there were dresses hanging on a rack by the farmer's overalls.

The window separating the front of the limo from the back opened and Nicki smelled a trace of her mother's lily perfume.

"She's getting married, you know. Chrissy is," Lillian announced. "It'll make her mother proud."

"It'll make her mother mad if Chrissy doesn't invite her," Garrett said.

"You can hear back there what we're saying?" Nicki wondered what the point of having a window like that was if it offered no privacy.

Her mother didn't even bother to answer her. "Chrissy said there was no need for anyone to come to her wedding."

Nicki thought about her own mother. "I expect Chrissy has her reasons for not inviting her mother."

Garrett snorted. "Well, if she does, she'd better get them spelled out in a letter or something. And mighty quick. Aunt Rose is a force to be reckoned with when it concerns her family. I should know."

Garrett still remembered the determined look on Aunt Rose's face when she met him at the hospital the day his father's liver finally gave out and he died. Garrett was quickly learning something about the forms that needed to be filled out when someone died.

Garrett hadn't even finished half of the forms before Aunt Rose came to the hospital and took over. She'd told him he wasn't alone in this world as long as she was around and she was going to take him home to live with her and Chrissy. Garrett had already made arrangements to stay in the house where he and his father had lived, but he was touched. Not many single mothers would take on a belligerent sixteen-year-old nephew who knew more about hospital forms than college applications.

"Oh, I'm sure Chrissy will have some pictures taken." Lillian shrugged. "And maybe a video. Some of the chapels include a video with the service. Chrissy's mother can watch that. It'll almost be the same thing."

"Aunt Rose won't think so. She's still hoping Chrissy will go home for Christmas and get married in the living room where she grew up."

Nicki wondered what it would be like for someone to want to be at your wedding that bad. She supposed Reno might be upset if he wasn't invited to her wedding. Of course, he would also be relieved since he hated any public gathering. "Do you think Chrissy will do that?"

"Not likely."

"Well, I think Christmas would be a lovely time to get married. Or even Thanksgiving," Lillian said as she leaned closer to the partition that separated the back from the front. "Too bad she won't be up here tomorrow. Thanksgiving was always my favorite time on the ranch. All those pies we used to make."

"We don't do Thanksgiving at the ranch anymore," Nicki said curtly. Who was her mother trying to fool? It almost sounded as if there was some nostalgia in her voice.

"Really? For the first years I was gone I used to picture you and your father and Reno sitting down to these big Thanksgiving dinners. You know how your father used to like to have the table bulging with food and half the families in Dry Creek coming over to eat with us. There'd be the Hargroves. And the Jenkinses. And, of course, Jacob and Betty Holmes—"

"We don't have company at the ranch anymore."

"Well, you should—the Redfern Ranch is important to this community. Besides, I was sort of hoping to relive one of those Thanksgivings while I'm here," Lillian said as she leaned back into her seat and her face was no longer in the window. "I can almost smell the turkey now."

"Sounds like you have some good family memories," Garrett said after a minute or two had passed.

Nicki looked up at him in surprise. How could they be good memories when they only reminded her of what she had lost? "All that ended."

"I see."

Clearly the man didn't see at all, Nicki thought to herself miserably. "You wouldn't know what it was like. Reno, Dad and I made peace about celebrating Christmas, but Thanksgiving was just never the same. Last year I made meat loaf."

"Nothing wrong with that. The fanciest we ever got in my family was a can of turkey noodle soup."

"Well, at least you had your family with you."

Garrett grunted. The only reason his father had been with him on Thanksgiving was because the bars were closed in the morning and he was too drunk to walk anywhere else by the afternoon. He liked to start his holiday celebrations early. It was Garrett who heated up the soup.

But Garrett didn't believe in telling people about his past. What was done was done. He was doing fine in life now. Of course, he had spent more Thanksgivings in truck stop cafés than he could count, but there was more to living than eating a plate of turkey on some cold Thursday in November.

Besides, he reminded himself, he liked not having the kind of family ties that meant he had to sit himself down to a Thanksgiving table every year. He was a free man.

Chapter Four

Meanwhile in Las Vegas

Chrissy sat up on the edge of her king-size bed in the Baughman Hotel. Today was going to be her wedding day and it would be a good day if she could only stomp down the nausea that threatened her. Now that she had Garrett hundreds of miles north of here and her mother hundreds of miles south, Chrissy was ready to take her vows.

She'd made the appointment with the wedding chaplain for nine o'clock in the morning so that no one would be hanging around the Rose Chapel in the Baughman Casino.

She knew it was bad luck for the groom to see the bride before the ceremony, but she figured her luck couldn't get much worse. Besides, she was too tired to put on her work clothes just to give a loud wake-up knock on Jared's door. Instead, she slipped on the wedding dress Jared had bought for her.

Chrissy hadn't planned to buy a special wedding dress. She had a gray suit that would have worked fine. Besides, a wedding dress seemed a little expensive under the circumstances. They were saving their money to buy a house, and Chrissy didn't mind scrimping on a wedding if they could find a house sooner.

But Jared had showed up with this dress anyway so she slipped it over her head. She turned to look at the hotel mirror. She looked even worse in it than she feared. The dress was short, strappy and it had some kind of iridescent, glittering sequins sewn on every inch of the fabric.

If she had feathers in her hair, Chrissy would look like a showgirl in it. Which was probably why Jared had chosen the dress. Chrissy looked at the material a little more closely. She hoped he hadn't just lifted the dress off one of the costume racks at the back of the casino.

Chrissy had always dreamed of an elegant ivory wedding gown that would sweep the floor and make her look like one of those brides she'd seen on the covers of magazine racks in the drugstores in Glendale.

All of which just went to show that weddings weren't always what a girl imagined they would be. Sometimes there were more important things to consider.

Jared's room was just down the hall from Chrissy's, and she was surprised to find his door was slightly open. She hadn't expected him to be still up. He'd had his bachelor party last night with a couple of friends, and that was why he was staying in a separate room. He said he didn't want to disturb her when he came in late.

Chrissy wasn't happy about the party, but she had smiled gamely. She didn't like the two guys he hung out with, but she never said anything. When they were married, Jared would be all hers. Jared had promised they could leave Las Vegas then and buy a house in some little town somewhere. Chrissy couldn't wait for that day. She hated the crush of people in Las Vegas. She wouldn't even mind waiting tables so much if she knew some of the customers.

"Jar—" Chrissy pushed the door open and stopped. At first she thought she must have the wrong room because all she saw was the back of a woman kissing a man. But then she noticed that whoever had his arm around the woman was wearing one of Jared's favorite shirts.

Chrissy told herself there could be hundreds of shirts in Las Vegas with black spades embroidered on their cuffs. She looked down at the man's shoes.

Then she looked back up at the woman. The woman was wearing Jared's bathrobe.

Shirt. Shoes. Bathrobe.

Chrissy took a step back and stumbled over a high heel that had been left on the floor. Her soft cry made both people turn and look at her.

The woman was one of the casino chorus girls.

"Chrissy!" Jared smoothed back his hair. "You're early."

Chrissy wondered if she should have known Jared had been involved with a woman. She believed in trusting the man she loved. Maybe she'd been too trusting. Had there been signs?

"Just let me get dressed and we'll go downstairs and get married right now." Jared was regaining his voice.

Chrissy held her hand up. "Don't—don't bother. You might as well stay here."

"Don't be silly. You're not going to let a little bit of fun stop us from getting married."

"Yeah, you're all dressed and everything. That's a

great dress, by the way. It looks even better on you than me," the blonde said.

Chrissy wondered if the woman was as insensitive as she sounded. She turned to Jared. "You got the dress from her—no, don't answer. Just give me the keys to my car."

Chrissy had brought her car with her to Vegas. It was her car even though Jared borrowed it most of the time.

"Ah, Chrissy, don't be that way."

Chrissy took a step back as Jared walked toward her.

"Don't touch me." Chrissy hoped the burning in her eyes didn't turn into tears. She wanted to leave with dignity. "Just give me the keys."

Jared smiled. "Ah, don't be mad. Remember, the car's in the shop. They have the keys. It won't be ready until tomorrow."

"Maybe they'll finish early."

Chrissy backed out of the hotel room. She'd talk to the mechanic. She needed to leave Vegas and she needed to leave soon. But where would she go? She couldn't go to her mother's. Maybe she could connect with Garrett and Lilly. Lilly had talked about the people in Dry Creek, Montana. That's where she'd go.

Chapter Five

"The café's open," Garrett announced as he slowly drove down the gravel road that was Dry Creek's main street. It was nine o'clock in the morning and just about time for some bacon and eggs in Garrett's opinion. He hoped the café served a hearty breakfast.

Garrett stopped the limousine in front of the café. He had to park parallel to the road because the limo was so long. The café had been lit up last night, and here it was all lit up again this morning. "Somebody puts in long hours."

"That's Linda Evans and Jazz, well, really Duane Edison. He just goes by Jazz—they're trying to raise enough money to buy the old Jenkinses' farm. They're very responsible youngsters."

Nicki didn't know why she kept spouting off like an old schoolteacher. It must be because, even with the bruise around his eye starting to swell, she'd never met a man so gorgeous as Garrett. He might have stopped sparkling, but he still made all of her frustrations rise to the surface and scream their heads off. Not that she had any intention of letting him see how he affected her.

No, she'd keep her emotions in tight rein. She could do that. After all, her reaction had nothing to do with him personally. She would be rattled by any man who looked as if he'd been sprinkled with gold dust. Not that a man like that would ever be hers in real life. She was destined for a solid plodding man like Lester, who would be useful on the ranch. That was her future. She needed to be practical and stop dreaming about sparkling princes and men like Garrett.

"Is everybody around here so set on staying?" Garrett opened his door.

Nicki looked up at Garrett like he was speaking a foreign language. "Dry Creek is our home."

Garrett grunted. When he was talking to the dog this morning, he'd wondered if all the people in Dry Creek already had their burial plots picked out. He was beginning to think he'd guessed right when he said yes. That kind of certainty made him itch under the collar. How could a man breathe if he knew every step he'd be taking for the rest of his life?

If Garrett was ever fool enough to marry, it would have to be some poor restless soul like himself. He delayed swinging his legs out of the cab of the limousine. "Don't you ever feel the urge to go other places?"

"I go to Billings."

Garrett grunted again. "Why stop there?"

"That's as far as we need to go for cattle sales." Nicki wasn't sure about going into the café with Garrett. He was dressed in his tuxedo and she had on her barn clothes. "You go ahead. I'm really not very hungry."

"Well, I am." Garrett stepped out into the snow-covered road.

Garrett looked down the long gravel road leading

into Dry Creek. For the first time since he could re-member, looking at a road made him feel a little de-pressed. There was something lonely about the thought of one man traveling it all by himself. Garrett decided it must be because he was missing Big Blue. Or maybe he needed to get a dog to travel the road with him so he'd have someone to talk to during the long nights.

Garrett walked around the limousine. Breakfast would make him feel better.

A light sprinkling of snow settled on the front win-dow. Nicki was comfortable in the car watching Garrett until she heard the small window click open behind her.

"I'm glad to see you remember some of what I taught you. A lady never eats breakfast like some ranch hand," Nicki's mother said. "Speaking of which—I hope you're taking care of your hands, too."

Nicki turned to stare at the woman behind her. The woman might be her mother, but Nicki saw nothing of herself in the face that looked through the small win-dow. Her mother's face was like a porcelain doll's. It was flawless, but not real.

"Mother, look at me. I never was the pretty little girl you wanted me to be. I don't have time for lotions and fancy manicures. We need summer help on the ranch, but we don't have money to pay anyone. So, Reno and I do everything. I bale hay and brand cattle. I'm not a lady, I'm a working ranch hand." Nicki opened the door and stepped out. She stood tall and took a deep breath. Nicki knew she was going to order the full stack of pancakes. The morning was beginning to look better.

Garrett already had a foot on the step that led up to the porch that surrounded the café door when Nicki caught up to him. She felt she should caution Garrett about the steps leading up to the café, but she knew Jazz had fixed them all. Maybe it was the door that she should warn him about.

Nicki's heart sank when she heard the woman's voice. Now, *that's* what she should have warned Garrett about.

"Oh, my. Oh, my—" Linda shrieked the moment Garrett stepped inside the café. Nicki and Garrett were both just inside the doorway now and Linda saw them. "Jazz said—but, oh, my!"

Nicki knew it was a mistake bringing Garrett to town without a hat on his head to hide his handsome face, but what could she do now?

"This is Garrett Hamilton." Nicki introduced the man beside her. "He's just in town to—to—"

"I know, I know—" Linda squealed. The teenager had a red streak in her hair and a row of silver earrings circling her left ear. She wore a long black dress with a white chef's apron over it. She had a tattoo of a butterfly over her left eye. She was the last person in Dry Creek who should be making a fuss over how someone looked and, if Nicki got her ear privately for a moment, she would suggest that to Linda. "Jazz said—but I never... I mean, I thought he was mistaken or—well, I just never thought." The teenager stopped to take a breath and reached her hand out to Garrett. "Pleased to meet you."

Garrett was beginning to wonder if Dry Creek might be a little too far off the beaten path. Jazz, the young man he'd talked to last night, looked at him oddly and then this young woman acted as if she'd never seen a stranger. "The pleasure's all mine."

Four empty square tables, each with four wooden

chairs, stood in the middle of the café. Garrett liked the casual fifties look of the place. The floor was black-and-white linoleum and there were red-checked vinyl cloths on the tables. Each table had a squeeze bottle of maple syrup. That was a good sign. He liked pancakes. "This is a very nice place you have here."

"Oh." Linda turned to Nicki. "And he has such nice manners. That's a good thing in a…well, a—" Linda put her head close to Nicki's ear and whispered "—in a husband."

"In a what?" Nicki was glad her teeth were attached. Otherwise, they would have fallen out of her mouth. She had completely forgotten that Lester had gone on about Jazz seeing the ring the man had.

"Oh, I hope I didn't spoil the surprise." Linda put her hands over her lips. "I shouldn't have said anything. I just thought that by now he would have asked."

"Garrett isn't—" Nicki closed her mouth. Garrett was looking at her puzzled. He hadn't heard what Linda had whispered and Nicki wasn't about to tell him. She came as close as she dared. "That was my mother's old engagement ring. Garrett's just passing through Dry Creek and he returned it. Besides, you know I'm not dating anyone."

Linda lowered her voice so only Nicki could hear. "But you want to, don't you? He's the best-looking man I've ever seen around here. You've got to want to date him."

Nicki blushed and shook her head. "No, I—"

Linda winked at Nicki and turned to Garrett. "Sorry about that. Nicki was just telling me about her latest date with Lester. You probably don't know him—"

"Oh, I know him." Garrett turned so the young lady

could see the bruise on the right side of his face. "He gave me this."

"You were fighting." Linda stopped and frowned. "Nicki doesn't like fighting."

"Tell that to Lester."

"Lester started the fight? That doesn't sound like Lester."

Linda moved over so she could whisper in Nicki's ear. "You don't want to marry him if he's always picking fights with people. I don't care if he begs you. Say no."

"I don't need to say no," Nicki whispered back. "He's not asking."

Linda nodded and continued brightly, "Yes, Nicki is almost married to Lester. He's got a big ranch north of here."

"He doesn't care about Lester." Nicki felt her blush deepen. Why didn't Linda just put an Available sign on Nicki's forehead and set her out on the street so every man who drove through Dry Creek could stop and refuse to ask her out?

Linda barely stopped to listen to Nicki. She continued speaking to Garrett. "Lester took her to the Christmas pageant last year. I remember they had the spaghetti dinner here that night, too. Jazz's band was playing romantic music and Lester was very attentive." She shrugged. "It's only a matter of time."

Nicki shook her head. Why did everyone think she needed to be dating? Lots of perfectly fine women didn't date. Of course they were mostly nuns. "Lester doesn't need to ask me on a date. He's a friend of the family. He invited Reno that night, too."

"She's got you there," Garrett agreed cheerfully.

"Sounds like a friend-of-the-family dinner instead of a date to me."

"Family's important to Lester," Linda continued. "That's why he invited Reno."

Nicki frowned. She'd never really thought about why Lester had invited Reno. Now that she thought about it, she realized Lester had talked mostly with Reno. Nicki wondered for the first time if she was as boring to Lester as he was to her. They always did seem to run out of conversation after they covered the weather and the crops. Sometimes cattle prices kept them going longer.

It was depressing to realize that the man you were going to marry had nothing to talk to you about and you were halfway through the dating phase. This was supposed to be the fun time.

"What do you think about the weather?" Nicki looked at Garrett and demanded. "You're a trucker. Weather is important. Do you talk about it?"

"I guess so." Garrett shrugged.

"I mean on a date. Do you talk about it on a date?"

Garrett turned to Nicki. The light was coming in the window of the café and it hit Nicki on the cheek. It gave her a golden Mona Lisa kind of a glow. Something was bothering her and, for the first time in his life, Garrett truly wished he understood women.

"No." Garrett hoped this was the right answer. "Unless you do, that is."

"I was afraid of that." Nicki shoved her hands into the pocket of her coat. She'd forgotten all about her hands until her mother reminded her. They weren't the hands of a dating woman. She didn't wear polish. She kept her nails clipped short. And the skin on her hands was rough and sometimes chapped. She was a fool to think for a moment that Garrett would date someone like her. At least a man like Lester wouldn't worry about her hands or her lack of conversation. "I need to get back and help Lester feed the cows."

Garrett didn't know how one man could be so annoying. "I'm surprised Lester doesn't feed them by himself. Or is it some kind of a date in disguise where you sit and talk about the weather and look at the cows?"

"I don't date," Nicki said.

Linda turned to frown at Nicki. "What Nicki means is that she's been too busy to date very much lately."

"What I mean is that I have to get back and get to work," Nicki repeated.

Garrett grunted. So she didn't date. That meant she'd never go out with him, but it cheered him up anyway. "That's too bad. I don't date much, either, these days."

Nicki stiffened. Who was he trying to fool?

The scent of baking biscuits came from what must be the café's kitchen. Garrett breathed in. "That smells good. Can I put in an order for some of those biscuits with some eggs and bacon?"

Linda thought a moment. "The early rush wiped us out. You're welcome to wait but it will be a few minutes. Will that be a table for two?"

"No, we'll need a table for three."

Lillian was still in the limousine, no doubt writing her apology speech. But Garrett was pretty sure breakfast would lure the woman out of the car. They hadn't had a decent meal since Salt Lake City.

"Three?" Linda frowned.

Garrett nodded.

Linda shrugged and headed back toward the kitchen. "I'll bring out more silverware then."

"How long will it be before you're ready?" Garrett called after her.

"Give us ten minutes." Linda swung open a door to the kitchen and walked into the other room.

Nicki decided disaster had been averted. She didn't know where Linda got such strange ideas, but hopefully Nicki had set the record straight. "Since we have to wait, I think I'll go over to the hardware store and see if the pastor is there."

"I'll go with you."

Nicki hesitated and then decided it was just as well that Garrett didn't stay at the café within reach of Linda's voice. "Good."

Garrett cleared his throat when he opened the door for Nicki to step out into the street. "So you don't date?"

Nicki stopped walking.

Garrett grinned.

"Yeah, I don't much, either," Garrett said as he continued walking.

Nicki hurried to catch up with him.

The morning's light gave a crispness to Dry Creek. A thin layer of white snow coated the road and all of the buildings. Smoke came out of the large building across the street from the café. A dozen or so houses were scattered around the small business buildings. A church with a white steeple was set back off the main road to the east and a barn was set off the main road to the west.

It only took a few minutes to walk over to the hardware store.

Nicki could smell the burning wood as she stomped the snow off her boots on the porch outside the store. Pastor Matthew Curtis was clerking here, and he and his new wife, Glory, kept the potbellied stove in the middle of the large room going all day long when it was snowing. Several straight-backed wooden chairs were usually gathered around the stove and as often as not, a game of checkers was being played beside the stove. Glory kept her art easel set up by the window and painted portraits.

"I don't suppose they sell any jeans here?" Garrett asked as he put his hand around the stone-cold door-knob. He might as well be comfortable for the flight back to Vegas. If Lillian was staying, her chauffeur could come drive her back. That meant Garrett would need to fly back and he sure wasn't getting on any airplane dressed like a butler.

The hardware store door had a half-dozen small panes of glass in it, but Garrett could not see inside the store because of the frost on the glass. He could already smell the flavored coffee brewing inside, though.

"They have overalls." Nicki couldn't picture Garrett wearing them. "Farmer overalls."

Garrett opened the door wide and then waited for Nicki to enter first.

Nicki had known the two old men sitting beside the stove all her life. In fact, Jacob Holmes's wife, Betty, had been her mother's best friend. After Betty died, Jacob spent his mornings at the hardware store.

They both looked up at her with smiles that turned to surprise when they saw Garrett come in behind her.

"Hi. Is Pastor Matthew around?" Nicki asked.

"The pastor?" Jacob was the first of the two men to recover his voice and his manners. He stood up and nodded to Garrett. "Pleased to meet you, young man. Any friend of Nicki's here is a friend of mine." Then

Jacob turned to Nicki and beamed. "Of course, I can see he's more than a friend. We heard you had a fella heading out your way. And here I see he's already in his wedding suit and asking for the pastor. Are you eloping or something?"

Nicki froze. Here was where the thunderbolt reached down from the sky and struck her. Please, let it strike her. "Garrett's not—"

"We don't need the pastor." Garrett frowned and then realized what all the whispering had been about. "I know it looks like I'm in a tuxedo, but it's really just a chauffeur's uniform."

"Looks like a tuxedo to me," Jacob said suspiciously. "You're not just trying to pull the wool over our eyes are you, young man, so you can marry our Nicki with no one knowing?"

The sudden vision of what it would be like to be married to Nicki made his knees shake as if he were heading downhill in Big Blue with no brakes. But his throat didn't close up like he'd have expected. At least he could still breathe. He wondered why that was.

"Garrett is a stranger. He's just passing through. We don't know each other. And we are not dating."

Garrett frowned. She could have been a little less emphatic—just to be polite. She swatted the whole idea away as if it was annoying. Maybe that's why his allergic reaction didn't kick in. Nicki was making it clear she had no interest in even dating him, let alone marrying him. Which should make him feel good. "We're not strangers. You know my name."

Jacob nodded and turned to Garrett. "You wouldn't be the first man to be smitten with a Redfern woman before he knew more than her name. Nicki here is a prize.

I knew her father—shoot, I knew her grandfather before that. I used to work on the Redfern Ranch back in the good old days when it was the biggest ranch between Canada and Texas. I wouldn't take kindly to some man doing wrong by her."

"He's not—" Nicki wondered how many ways a person could die from embarrassment. "He's not doing me wrong. He's not doing anything. He's not smitten with me."

Did Jacob ever look at her? Nicki wondered. She wasn't exactly a femme fatale in her barn-cleaning clothes.

Jacob kept his eyes narrowed on Garrett. "It's a funny thing about the Redfern women and love. Why, I remember hearing that your great-great-grandmother—"

Nicki knew she needed to stop this one. "She wasn't a Redfern. She was an Enger. And she didn't agree to marry Matthew Redfern because she was in love with him, she just needed that gold nugget he was offering up in the saloon so she could take care of those little kids of hers."

"Maybe so," Jacob agreed. "But that doesn't explain what happened with your great-grandmother. Why she—"

"My great-grandfather didn't fall in love with her at first sight, either. He just told that to the ranch hands so they'd stop trying to win her in those poker games and get back to herding the cattle."

"Well, still." Jacob didn't back down. "You've got the same blood running in your veins. The Redfern women always were a passionate lot." Jacob scowled at Garrett. "Not that you need to be knowing about that, young man."

Garrett grinned. "Yes, sir."

Nicki groaned. The thunderbolt was sounding better all the time.

No thunderbolt roared, but the phone did ring.

"Dang it, that phone's been ringing all morning," Jacob complained as he went to sit back down on his chair by the stove. "A man can't get any peace anymore."

"Well, why don't you answer it?" Nicki said as she walked over to the counter.

"It's not my phone," Jacob said righteously. He pulled his chair closer to the stove. "It's not polite to answer someone else's phone. Gotta be for the pastor. But he's been gone. Should be back soon but—"

"Hello," Nicki said into the phone.

"Is this Dry Creek?" a woman's voice asked. She sounded breathless, as if the woman was rushing and worried.

"Yes, can I help you?"

"This is the only Dry Creek number the operator had. I'm trying to locate a Mr. Redfern."

Reno? "I'm Mr. Redfern's sister."

"Oh. Is Lillian Fern there?"

"I can get her for you."

The woman gasped, as if she had seen something she didn't like. "There's no time for that. Just tell her I'm getting gas outside of Vegas and she's to stay where she is until I get there. This is Chrissy."

"Garrett's cousin?" Nicki asked, but the line was dead. The woman had hung up.

"That's Chrissy?" Garrett walked over to the counter. Why would Chrissy be calling the hardware store?

"She said my mot—I mean, Lillian is to stay here until she gets here. Chrissy's left Vegas."

"Chrissy's coming?" Garrett wondered if his cousin had had a change of heart and had decided not to get married after all. "Did she mention any fiancée?"

"No."

"So she's coming alone?"

Nicki shrugged. "Sounds like it."

Well, that's good news, Garrett thought. If Chrissy was just leaving Vegas, she'd be here sometime tomorrow morning. Maybe she'd be willing to stay with Lillian a few days and drive the older woman's limousine back to Vegas so he could fly back. "So she's coming here."

Jacob held his hands out to the heat that was coming from the potbellied stove. "Won't that be nice. We could use some more young women in this town—especially if we're going to be having another wedding. Someone to help throw all that rice."

"They use birdseed these days," the other old man, Elmer, said as he looked up from the wooden stove. He had his shoes off and his legs stretched out toward the stove. "It's the modern way."

"But Nicki's an old-fashioned girl. She'll want rice." Jacob had a satisfied look on his face.

Nicki groaned. "No one's getting married."

"Well, you never know, now, do you?" Jacob drawled as he tipped back his chair. "We've had us a whole lot of weddings ever since last Christmas when the angel came to town."

"She wasn't a real angel," Nicki hastened to add. She didn't want Garrett to think they were completely nuts. "She just played the angel in the Christmas pageant."

"You should have heard her sing," Jacob reminisced. "Almost made me cry. It's a wonder Santa Claus had the heart to shoot at her afterward."

Nicki groaned. "It was a hit man that had dressed up as Santa Claus who tried to kill her."

"I see," Garrett said, appearing bewildered.

"Of course, the reverend risked a bullet to save the angel," Jacob continued.

"That's because he was in love with her," Nicki finished the story for the old man. Everyone knew how the story ended. "Well…and the twins—that would be his young sons—would have been brokenhearted if something had happened to their angel."

No wonder she was having those fairy-tale dreams, Nicki thought to herself. After all of the excitement and romance in Dry Creek lately, it was a miracle she wasn't flying off to enter some dating show in Hollywood. "But all of that romance is behind us now. Matthew and Glory are just another married couple. Dry Creek really is a very quiet little town."

"I see."

Nicki groaned. There was no way a stranger would see that Dry Creek really was a nice sensible place. At least no one had mentioned the rustlers that had kidnapped a local rancher and his girlfriend—well, she wasn't his girlfriend at the time, but she soon came to be. There seemed to be something about danger that made people fall in love around here.

"You know the pastor is going to insist on doing marriage counseling with the two of you," Elmer said thoughtfully as he leaned forward from his chair and cupped his hands around the warmth coming from the woodstove.

"We don't have any need for—" Nicki groaned at the disapproving look on Elmer's face.

"Now, I know you try to hide it, but you've had bad feelings about church ever since your mother left. And I can't fault you for that, but that don't mean you can just wave God goodbye on the most important day of your life."

"I'm not waving God goodbye. I'm not having an important day."

Elmer grunted in disapproval and turned his eyes to Garrett. "And you, young man—are you planning to ditch marriage counseling, too?"

Garrett had forgotten that pastors knew more about marriages than anyone else. They certainly attended more weddings than the average person. Maybe that's where he could get some advice on what to say to Chrissy just in case she hadn't jilted her boyfriend. "Not on your life. If someone claims to have the answers to getting married, I'll sit down and listen."

Elmer beamed. "That's the attitude. The pastor will be glad to know you're open to talking. Now that he's married again, he sure does like to see people walk down the aisle."

Nicki knew her face was getting red. She didn't want to open her mouth because she knew she would sputter. Elmer was the kind of man whose mind ran on a single track. He wasn't going to let go of his marriage idea unless something came along and knocked that idea off his track.

"Lester's been stopping by the ranch, you know."

"Lester Wilkerson?" Elmer frowned. "I know he picks up your mail and has been asking around about what kind of feed you buy for your cattle, but I wouldn't think he'd be the one for you."

"Well, he's asked me out."

"Didn't he bring you and your brother to the Christmas pageant?" Jacob asked with a matching frown.

"He likes to include the family. Family is important to him."

Elmer shook his head. "If he ain't out-and-out asked, you've got no obligation to wait for him. But it does make me think you'd do good to hear what the pastor has to say about getting married."

"I am not getting married," Nicki said through clenched teeth. "What I am going to do is go back over to the café and have breakfast."

Jacob nodded sagely as he leaned back in his chair. "I read in *Woman's World* that people in love eat more. Of course, it's mostly chocolate."

That stopped Nicki. Jacob had ridden the range with her father. "What are you doing reading *Woman's World*?"

Jacob tilted his head toward the small table that stood behind the stove. "Glory says we need to keep informed so she brings in her magazines. That's where Elmer read about the birdseed at weddings."

Elmer frowned. "I didn't know there was so much to know about getting married. It'd make a man think twice about it all if he knew what was involved in guest lists and place cards."

"Well, fortunately, we're not getting married," Garrett said as he started to make his move for the door. Of course, he couldn't go without taking Nicki with him and she was looking shell-shocked.

"We just met," Nicki added for emphasis. "We're just both hungry. We're not even dating."

Garrett stopped. He was forgetting something. "You say those magazines tell you how to do a wedding? With all the trimmings?"

Elmer nodded. "Step by step."

"Save them for me, will you?" Just in case Chrissy didn't stop her wedding, maybe she'd at least do it right and invite Aunt Rose.

Jacob beamed. "You can pick them up when you get back from your breakfast date."

"Date?" Nicki asked.

Elmer nodded. "*Woman's World* would say it was. Eight out of ten readers said a meal alone together counts as a date."

"Then it's not a date," Nicki stated firmly. "My mother's going to be there."

Nicki regretted mentioning her mother the minute she saw the shocked look on the faces of the two older men.

"Lillian's back?" Jacob whispered. His face had turned white.

Nicki nodded miserably as she turned to go. "But she isn't staying."

"She's back?" Jacob said again to no one in particular.

"Yes," Nicki said softly as she started walking toward the door. How could she have forgotten? Jacob used to be her father's best friend just as Betty had been her mother's best friend. Jacob and Betty had been as upset with Lillian as her father had been.

Nicki remembered how withdrawn her father had been after Lillian left. For months, Nicki's father didn't want to see anyone, not even Jacob. Jacob would drive out to the ranch and Nicki's father would send him away. Finally, Jacob stopped coming. The only time the two men had seen each other since then was for Betty's funeral.

Jacob must blame Lillian for the loss of his best friend. He might even blame her for the sadness that Betty had until the day she died.

It seemed that Nicki wasn't the only one who would be upset by seeing Lillian Redfern again.

Nicki and Garrett stopped at the limousine before they walked back to the café, but Lillian waved them on. She had more to worry about than breakfast.

Lillian sat in the back of her limo with the envelope in front of her. No matter how many times she read the papers inside, the diagnosis remained the same. Cancer.

Oh, how she wished Charles were still here so she could talk to him. He'd always been the brave one when it came to facing problems. Her style was to run away. Even coming back to Dry Creek she needed to be sure no one pitied her. The limo was to prove she was some-body now.

Of course the cancer didn't care who she was.

And, before she went in for treatment, she had wanted to make things right with Charles.

Since Charles wasn't here, she'd just have to make things right with the whole town of Dry Creek instead.

Lillian just wished she didn't have to tell Nicki. She couldn't bear to hurt her little girl any more than she'd already been hurt by life. That's why she wouldn't have come back if she had known Nicki was here.

Chapter Six

Nicki swore she was going to walk home and sit in her kitchen where there was no prince, no limo and no mother. This day was so mixed-up, she was beginning to think she needed to start it over. After hearing Elmer and Jacob talk about reading *Woman's World*, nothing should have surprised her.

Nicki only had to open the door to the café to know the day had one more surprise for her. Everything was turned upside down inside the café too. Someone had strewn shiny red paper hearts all over the tables and floors. It looked as if there was something tacked to the walls, but she couldn't see what it was because the lights had been turned off and the window shades drawn down.

Without the morning light, the café was dim. It would be deep dark except for the individual candles burning at each of the tables and on the high shelves that lined the room. The yellow light coming from the candles made the black-and-white floor of the café gleam.

Nicki sniffed. Gone was the smell of baking biscuits. In its place was the scent of raspberries and vanilla from the candles.

"Linda?" Nicki called out.

There was a love song coming from the radio in the kitchen that was so upbeat it would make a man on crutches want to start dancing.

Nicki looked up at Garrett. The candlelight touched his face and made him look like someone in a Renaissance painting. "I'm sorry, people aren't usually this—" Nicki looked around again "—strange."

Garrett smiled. "I have a feeling they're just campaigning for you to date someone other than this Lester fellow." Garrett decided he rather liked the people of Dry Creek. He'd always heard that people in small towns minded each other's business, and it looked as if Dry Creek was no exception. Maybe it wouldn't be so bad to have a whole town filled with dozens of Aunt Roses. Of course, they had *Woman's World* in addition to Aunt Rose. "I'll bet they have something all planned out from one of those magazines. Besides, they're having fun."

Garrett pulled out a chair for Nicki and she sank down into it as though she would really prefer to slide all of the way under the table. "The people in this town need to get a hobby."

"Sounds to me like they have one." Garrett decided the cold air had finally numbed his brain. He didn't even mind that half of the town's population was trying to set him up with the woman in front of him. If he couldn't outromance Lester, he'd have to retire from dating.

Garrett had to stop and remind himself he had stopped dating, at least for a while. He hoped that wasn't a bad omen.

"So what do people do around here for fun?" Garrett asked Nicki as he sat down in a chair opposite her. He wasn't going to give this one up without a fight.

"Besides torturing me?"

Garrett looked over at Nicki. Her cheekbones were high and there wasn't a trace of blush on them. But she sparkled in the candlelight from the melting snowflakes that had fallen on her as she'd walked back to the café.

"Well, there really is only one way to stop them," Garrett said. He waited until Nicki looked at him hopefully. She had the most amazing green eyes. Even in the candlelight, they changed color constantly. A man could get lost just looking into them.

"Yes?" Nicki finally prodded.

"Oh." Garrett cleared his throat. "We have to go on a date, that's all."

"A date?" Nicki squeaked.

Garrett nodded. "And not just any date. A date that would be better than anything *Woman's World* could offer."

Nicki was speechless. "You think they got this from the magazine?"

Garrett nodded and then suddenly remembered something. "And before you ask, your brother can't come."

"I wasn't—"

"And neither can this Lester fellow. Actually, especially not this Lester fellow. Let him get his own date."

Nicki was speechless, which was just as well because she heard Linda walking out from the kitchen.

"All set to order?" Linda held a small pad of paper in one hand and a pen in the other. Linda had changed her clothes so that she was wearing a chef's hat with a red ribbon tied around it and a long white formal dress with shiny red heart pockets. "The special of the day is heart pancakes with strawberries on top. It comes with scrambled eggs, bacon and hazelnut coffee."

"I've had breakfast here before—" Nicki said, bewildered. "You never—" She waved her hand to indicate everything. "Even the dress."

"Left over from Halloween," Linda explained cheerfully. "I was the Queen of Hearts and Jazz was the Joker. We were reading one of Glory's *Woman's World* magazines, and it said people were more likely to eat out if it was a fun experience. So we thought costumes are fun. I wanted something that said good health—you know with the heart and all."

"So it's for health," Nicki said. "And *Woman's World.*"

She looked over at Garrett. He winked at her.

Linda continued. "Well, eight out of ten women rank dining out as their favorite date. Jazz and I have maxed out the lunch crowd. If we want to expand, we need to have another angle. So we thought we'd turn to romance eating—you know, people eat more when they are in love."

"We heard."

"I'd eat here," Garrett offered. "It's a good idea to expand your menu."

"But they used to have regular pancakes." Nicki mourned. The whole world was going crazy around her.

"Nothing wrong with making them into hearts." Garrett defended the café.

Linda looked at Garrett and smiled. "I'm glad you feel that way. I talked to Jazz, and we decided you're the one we are looking for. I didn't think so at first, but you're a good choice. You could teach the men of Dry Creek a thing or two about romance. You've got the tuxedo and the look."

"Me? This isn't a tuxedo. It's a chauffeur's uniform. And it's not even mine. I'm a trucker. I don't have a look. I'm not a romantic kind of guy. I hate poetry. Can't stand the opera."

Linda walked over to a shelf and pulled down a magazine, flipping it open. "Would you buy a woman roses in the middle of winter?"

"Well, yes."

Linda eyed him as she looked over the magazine. "Not just something planted in a pot, but the real thing—those long-stemmed ones."

"Yeah."

Nicki remembered the orchid blossom that Lester had gotten for her. "Roses don't last long in winter." She almost sighed, but she felt she owed it to Lester to defend him. "They're not a practical choice."

Linda waved Nicki's objection aside and kept questioning Garrett. "Question number five. If you were out on a date and a robber threatened to shoot your date unless she gave him her purse, what would you do?"

"Tell her to give it to him."

Linda kept reading in the magazine. "What if she refused and the man held up his gun?"

"Can I knock the gun out of his hand?"

Linda looked up from the magazine. "No."

"Well, where are the police?"

"Not close by. And the robber is counting to three. He's already said two. What do you do?"

"I step in front of her—"

"Excellent choice."

"—and rip the purse out of her hands and give it to the man."

"Oh." Linda looked down the column. "You would be a hero for stepping in front of her, but it doesn't say anything about taking her purse away from her. I think you lose points for that."

"I'm not going to die for some woman's lipstick."

"Not all women want some man to be their hero, either," Nicki said firmly. Where did Linda get this nonsense? "It's better to let the authorities deal with things."

"I asked about the police," Garrett protested.

"That's good. That's the right thing to do." Nicki was getting a headache. "It doesn't matter what the magazine says, people need to use common sense."

"Common sense never made anyone fall in love," Linda said softly as she pulled her order pad out of her hand again. "So, what will it be, folks?"

Nicki hadn't meant to hurt Linda's feelings. A woman Linda's age was supposed to be giddy about love. Nicki gave up. "I believe I'll have the heart special."

"Really?" Linda brightened. "With the strawberries?"

"With extra strawberries, if you have them."

"Make that two specials," Garrett added with a grin. "And I swear I'll take a bullet if someone tries to steal it away from me."

"You're only supposed to take the bullet if they try to steal Nicki's," Linda said softly. "It doesn't count if you're protecting your own breakfast."

"In that case, I'll have a side of bacon with that." Nicki smiled. "Now that I know it's safe."

Nicki should give a man some warning when she

was going to smile like that, Garrett thought. His mouth went dry from the beauty of seeing it. Her green eyes lit up like jewels and sparkled with fun.

"You're beautiful." Garrett wasn't aware that he had spoken aloud until he saw the surprised look on Nicki's face. "I mean, it's beautiful—the café and all."

"Oh, yes." Nicki seemed relieved.

"We need some publicity on this one though," Linda said as she tapped her pen to her order pad. "You know, something that will get the romantic idea across—we can't just advertise heart-shaped pancakes. It needs to be more to make the married folks come out on a cold winter morning and have breakfast together. We've thought of making a poster."

"You don't need a poster. Just take a picture of your breakfast and tack it up on the bulletin board over at the hardware store. All of the men around here go into the hardware store at least once a week. They'd see it."

"Great idea—Jazz has a camera in back, we could take some pictures right now if it's all right with the two of you."

Why did Garrett have the feeling he and Nicki had been led down this path a little too smoothly? Oh, well, let the kids have their fun.

Garrett looked at Nicki. "I don't mind if they snap a picture or two of our plates before they bring them out of the kitchen, do you?"

"Oh, the plates won't be enough," Linda reached over and moved the candle on the table so that it reflected off Garrett's face even more. "To sell romance. We need romance. We need you two in the pictures."

"Us?" Nicki said, then she blurted out what she really meant. "Garrett's great. He's dressed for it. Can't you just use his picture?"

"One man sitting alone and eating heart-shaped pancakes? That's not romantic. In fact, it's kind of creepy." Linda looked more closely at what Nicki was wearing. "Oh."

"I should have worn a dress."

"Don't worry. I have just the thing." Linda started walking toward the back of the kitchen. "The Queen of Hearts costume came with a whole bunch of other costumes. They're made out of paper, but that won't show in the picture. One or two will even go with the tuxedo."

"Uniform," Garrett corrected automatically.

Nicki looked over at Garrett. She had to give the man credit. He seemed to be enjoying himself. She couldn't help but think that Lester would have stormed out of the café by now. Maybe that's why he never talked about anything but the weather. Maybe he didn't allow himself to do enough things in life.

"I've never been in a commercial before—" Garrett wondered how he could get the conversation back to where they'd left off. A photo of romance was fine, but he wanted a date with Nicki before people forgot about *Woman's World* and he lost his excuse. "I wonder what else people do around here to date."

"People in Dry Creek don't date." Nicki frowned slightly. "I know it sounds like they do because of the way everyone's been trying to get you to take me out on a date. But don't worry. There's no place to go on a date anyway. You're safe."

Garrett was beginning to suspect Nicki didn't want to go out on a date with him. "There must be someplace people go."

"Well, there is the café, but we're already here." Nicki wondered if she should suggest that Garrett frown while the picture was being taken. In his tuxedo, the frown made him look fierce. Which was pretty much how most of the men in town would feel about taking their wives out to a romantic breakfast. He might pull in some viewer empathy that way. "The kids go over to the mountains in the summer evenings and party some."

Garrett caught his breath in his throat. "You'd go there with me?"

"It's winter. Nobody goes there in the winter. It's cold."

"Well, where do people go in the evenings around here?"

Nicki shrugged. "Tonight they're having a Thanksgiving Eve service at church."

Garrett heard the sound of boots on the porch outside the café. He didn't want to get interrupted again. "Let's go there, then."

Church certainly wasn't equal to a moonlight evening in the summer, but Garrett wasn't going to quibble at this point in time. He'd told himself he'd have a date with Nicki, and he wasn't going to shy away just because he'd never even heard of a church date before—in fact, he couldn't remember the last time he'd been inside a church. "What's a Thanksgiving Eve service?"

"Everyone brings a candle and they light it and tell something they are thankful for—"

The door to the café opened.

"What happened to the lights?" Elmer asked as he stepped inside. "Something wrong with the electricity?"

"Nothing's wrong with the electricity at the church.

And we're on the same line." Another man stepped into the café.

"Pastor Matthew?" Nicki asked as she looked up.

The door from the kitchen opened again, and Linda came back out with several long dresses draped over her arm. "I've got the costumes. Take your pick. Jazz is looking for the camera."

"We're making an advertisement," Nicki explained to the three men who were now inside the café. Jacob had been the last to enter. "Something to make men bring their wives in for a romantic breakfast."

Elmer grunted suspiciously. "Isn't bacon and eggs enough to bring in the customers?"

"Not according to *Woman's World*," Garrett explained.

"Oh." Elmer nodded.

Linda stopped at the table where Nicki and Garrett sat. She held up the first of the paper dresses. It had a red cross on it in several places and a paper stethoscope in the pocket. "No, that won't do. Jazz wouldn't like to have a nurse in the picture. It'd give people a bad feeling about the café."

The next costume was of a judge. Linda tossed it aside. "Not very romantic."

"But orderly." Nicki wasn't so fast to give up on the judge costume. "And it matches Garrett's tuxedo—I mean the uniform—and it's dignified."

"Dignified's not romantic."

"But it's nice."

"No, this is what we need." Linda held up the last costume.

"Oh," Nicki breathed out.

Nicki heard four men echo her.

It was a princess costume.

"That pink reminds me of the inside of a seashell I saw once when I was a boy," Elmer said. "I've never forgotten it."

The skirt on the dress flared out and had dozens of tiny tucks drawn onto it. The bodice plunged low and the cleavage that was drawn on the paper would have made any prince drool. "I can't wear that. It's—"

"It's winter out, that's why." Garrett hoped they didn't choose the princess outfit. It made his breath stop just to look at the dress and then to think of Nicki wearing it. He certainly didn't want to be sitting in church with those thoughts in his head. He'd be excommunicated for sure, and he hadn't even joined anything.

"Well, we'll take the pictures inside, of course," Linda told him.

"Of course."

"Just as soon as Nicki puts the dress on, in fact."

A bell rang in the kitchen and Linda turned. "Your specials are ready. I'll be right back with them. Nicki, you can just pull that dress over what you're wearing."

"I smell bacon," Elmer said as he pulled a chair over to the table beside Garrett and Nicki. "Mind if I join you?"

"Me, too," Jacob said as he found another chair. "That smells mighty fine."

"Well, I only came over because they said you were looking for me," Pastor Matthew said, but he pulled over a chair all the same.

Garrett was beginning to see why no one dated in Dry Creek. They were never alone long enough.

"It was my mother who wanted to see you," Nicki told the pastor as she stood up. "Maybe she'd like to talk to you in the limousine. There's more privacy there."

Nicki hoped her mother would talk to Pastor Matthew in the limousine. That way her mother could ease her conscience and not be so public about it all. "I'm going to go in the kitchen and put on my dress."

"But it's paper. Stay away from the grill." Garrett saw another reason why people didn't date in Dry Creek. You felt responsible for a person before you even had the opportunity to date them. It wasn't quite fair. It made it hard for a man to concentrate on his moves. "I'd better come with you."

"To put on her dress?" Elmer said as he started to rise.

"It's just a costume," Garrett protested. "It'll go over all her other clothes."

"Oh." Elmer sat down.

Garrett felt all three men watch him as he followed Nicki into the kitchen. Then again, this might be the main reason nobody dated in Dry Creek. There were too many chaperones.

Garrett couldn't remember ever dating anyone who was so protected. He'd have thought it would bother him, but it didn't. He liked knowing there were men who would take care of Nicki and protect her from someone like him. It was depressing to know that he was the kind of man that a town wouldn't want their favorite daughter to date. But he couldn't fault the men for their judgment. They knew he wasn't the kind of man who stayed around for long.

Still, he wished he was sitting back out there with those three men and scowling at the back of some other stranger passing through instead of being the stranger himself.

Chapter Seven

Garrett changed his mind. He didn't wish he was anywhere else in the world right now except inside the kitchen of Dry Creek's café.

The men outside in the dining area didn't know it, but they should have followed him into the kitchen. Garrett was standing so close to Nicki he could feel every curve along her back. He blessed the makers of those paper dresses, whoever they were.

The paper dress didn't just slip on easily. It had to be coaxed over the sweater Nicki was wearing, inch by blessed inch.

Garrett had not noticed the back of Nicki's neck until now. She had reached up and clipped her hair behind her so it didn't get in the way of pulling the dress on. Garrett had already brushed his hand across her hair several times and, if he was lucky, he'd feel its wispy softness several more times before they left the kitchen.

"It's stuck," Nicki said.

Garrett could feel her nervousness and frustration in the way she held her back. "It's just got a twist here."

Garrett reached up and smoothed the hair off of Nicki's neck before he let his hand smooth the paper dress over her shoulder. "We're almost done."

Nicki grunted. "We'd better be."

No one was in the kitchen but the two of them. Linda and Jazz were outside in the other part of the café arranging their breakfast plates.

Garrett gave the dress one last tug. "There."

The dress covered Nicki from her neck to her toes. Even her arms were covered. Still, the whole thing made her feel naked.

"A princess wouldn't really wear something like this, would she?" Nicki looked down at the dress. The drawing showed as much paper skin as it did paper dress. Nicki had tucked the collar and sleeves of her sweater inside the costume so it was just her head sticking out. "It would shock the palace."

While Nicki talked, she had slowly turned around until she was facing Garrett. The morning light filled the kitchen and the air smelled like biscuits and bacon.

Garrett was speechless. No wonder all the princesses he'd ever heard about had become queens. If women dressed like that today, they'd get all the political votes, at least the ones from the men.

"I can't walk in this," Nicki said as she started to move toward the door leading to the rest of the café. The paper dress trailed along with her. "You'll have to carry the train to this thing."

Nicki opened the door to the main room of the café.

Garrett was glad that Linda had covered the windows. Not that it looked as if there was anyone left to peek in the windows from the street outside. All of the people of Dry Creek must have come inside while he and Nicki were in the kitchen.

"Oh, there you are." Nicki's mother was standing at the front of the crowd. Jacob and Elmer were on one side and the young couple who ran the café stood on the other side. "I'm getting ready to say my few words."

"Now?" Nicki squeaked. There wasn't any place to hide. Maybe if she had Garrett lift the train on her dress a little higher she could crawl under it. She might look like a garden slug, but she'd be hidden.

Lillian Redfern looked around and frowned. "No, I can't speak yet. Mabel Hargrove isn't here. She'd never forgive me if she wasn't here when I said what I have to say."

"Good," Linda said as she motioned for Nicki and Garrett to come forward. "We have time to get the pictures taken first then. We don't want the food to be cold for the pictures."

"No one can tell if the food is cold," Nicki reassured her as she sat down.

The table was set for romance. A red napkin was laid carefully across the middle of the table, as if it was an afterthought. Three candles of different lengths stood beside the salt and pepper shakers. A plate of strawberries sat to the right of a small pitcher of cream. Water glistened on the just-washed strawberries.

Jazz, tall and thin, was standing and frowning at the table. "I don't want any shadows hanging over the table." He looked up at the people crowded around the table and lifted an eyebrow.

"I'll go out on the porch and wait," Pastor Matthew offered as he nudged one of the older men.

"And I'll go ask Mabel Hargrove to come over here,"

Elmer said as he reluctantly backed away from the table. "Just don't start anything without me."

"And, Lillian and I—" Jacob looked around for an excuse. "We'll go sit over in the corner. You won't even know we're here."

Jazz had the camera to his eye before anyone even stepped away from the table. "Let's try this angle first." He brought the camera away from his eye and frowned. "No, that's not right. Maybe if we try it from some height."

It took Jazz ten minutes to decide the angle of his first shot. Garrett was sitting at the table and his jaw was beginning to ache from smiling so much.

"I can't hold this much longer," Nicki said through clenched teeth. She sat at the table across from Garrett. Her hand was falling asleep as she held her spoon in midair. "No one eats eggs with a spoon anyway."

"Creative license." Linda was in charge of the staging. She shifted the spoon slightly so it got more candlelight. "Have you ever noticed the way a spoon reflects the light? It's so much more elegant than a fork. Once we start shooting it won't take long."

Linda pulled away from the table and Jazz snapped the picture.

"Look dreamy now," Linda said as Jazz repositioned himself.

"Dreamy?" Nicki wondered if cross-eyed would do.

Linda nodded. "Like you're in love. Remember, romance sells pancakes here."

Nicki had avoided looking at Garrett for that very reason. She didn't want her heart to be out there for anyone who was interested in buying a pancake to see.

Jazz took four more shots before he mentioned the

strawberries. "For the last one, let's do a strawberry shot."

"I'm starving." Nicki thought it might be worth mentioning.

"And she almost fainted once this morning," Garrett added helpfully.

"The food's getting cold." Nicki nodded.

"We'll heat it up for you." Linda sprinkled some pepper on the eggs. "Besides, you'll like the next shot. It involves food."

"We get to eat the eggs?"

Linda shook her head until her earrings swayed. She picked up a whole strawberry from the plate. "You get to split this."

Half of a strawberry didn't look like enough to halt her hunger pangs, but Nicki lifted her knife anyway. She'd be fair.

"No, you don't split it with your knife. You kiss it apart."

"What?"

Garrett was starting to grin. He had a feeling he was going to see more of those green sparks fly out of Nicki's eyes.

"With our lips?" Nicki looked skeptical. "Can't we just each take a bite? That's a lot more sterile."

Linda shook her head and held the strawberry out to Nicki. "Just hold it in your teeth. Garrett will do the rest."

"I—" Nicki was silenced with a strawberry.

Garrett had barely begun to kiss Nicki when Jazz took the first picture.

Nicki wondered why she'd never really tasted a strawberry before. The fruit was warm and soft and sweet with just a hint of something stronger. Maybe the strong part was Garrett's lips. No, they were the soft part.

Jacob had to clear his throat three times before Nicki realized the flashing had stopped.

"Oh." Nicki pulled away from Garrett. She wondered if she had the same bewildered look on her face that he had on his. "Something was wrong with that strawberry. You must have soaked it in something."

Linda grinned. "You liked it, huh?"

Nicki didn't have to answer because the door to the café opened and Mrs. Hargrove walked in.

"Where is she?" Mrs. Hargrove hadn't bothered to put on her coat or take the metal curlers out of her hair. She was wearing a green-checked gingham dress with a white apron over it and clutching a coin purse in her hand. She entered the café and looked in all directions until her gaze settled on Lillian. "There you are."

Nicki felt the blood start to flow in her veins again. It was time someone gave her mother a good scolding and Mrs. Hargrove was just the person to do it. Mrs. Hargrove had taught the first grade Sunday school class for the past thirty years in Dry Creek and she didn't hesitate to speak her mind.

"Hello, Mabel," Nicki's mother said as she stood. "You're looking well."

"I've got baking powder on my face and curlers in my hair. I know I look a fright." Mrs. Hargrove studied Lillian where she stood. "You dyed your hair blond."

Lillian nodded. "I've worn it that way for years now."

"You could have written, you know. I worried about you."

"I didn't think you'd want to hear from me—not after I took the money."

Mrs. Hargrove shrugged. "Charles and Jacob paid it back."

"Oh." Lillian frowned. "I didn't mean for anyone to do that. I meant to sneak into some Sunday service and slip it into the offering plate. At first, anyway. Then I was worried someone would recognize me and I didn't know what I would say."

Mrs. Hargrove nodded. "I see how that could be."

"I want to pay it back now though." Lillian had a purse strap on her shoulder and she swung the purse around to open it. "I could write a check."

"You can't just write a check," Nicki protested. If Mrs. Hargrove wasn't going to scold her mother, someone else would have to do it. "Money can't make up for the hurt you caused the people around here."

"You're right. I did mean to apologize first and ask everyone to forgive me." Lillian looked at the people in the café. "Do you forgive me for doing something so foolish?"

Lillian smiled and blinked as if she were on the verge of tears.

Elmer caved first. "Don't mention it."

Mrs. Hargrove wasn't far behind. "We just worried about you, not the money."

Jacob looked at Lillian, but he didn't say anything.

"Nicki's right, though," Pastor Matthew said, and everyone looked to him. "Money isn't enough."

Lillian smiled. "I meant to include a little extra for the minister of the church, as well."

"I don't take bribes," Pastor Matthew said mildly. "I was just thinking that if you spent some time praying about it, you might think of a better way to make peace with the people of Dry Creek."

"Pray about it?" Lillian covered her surprise quickly. "Why, yes, of course, I can do that."

Nicki felt that someone was finally taking her mother's actions seriously. Good for the pastor.

"Maybe Nicki can pray with you about it," Pastor Matthew continued.

"Me?" Nicki decided the pastor was going too far.

"It'll do the two of you good to pray together," Elmer said.

"We'll all pray about it," Mrs. Hargrove said decisively. "That's what friends and family are for."

Garrett was liking the people of Dry Creek better the longer he was around them. They were an odd group of people, but he could see they were loyal to each other. Kind of like Aunt Rose would be if she was here.

"And, of course there's the Thanksgiving service tonight," Elmer suggested. "We'll all be there, won't we?"

Elmer looked around for nods.

"I'll be there. Nicki and I have a date," Garrett volunteered.

"Really." Pastor Matthew brightened. "You're coming to the Thanksgiving service on a date?"

Garrett nodded cautiously. He wondered if anyone else had ever used church as a dating plan in Dry Creek—he supposed not even Lester had sunk that low.

"I'll have to throw in a few of the love verses in my meditation," the pastor said. "You know the 'love is' ones."

Garrett nodded. He had no idea what the man was talking about.

"I always liked those." Mrs. Hargrove smiled. "'Love is patient. Love is kind.' They are true, true words."

"If you're going to be talking about love, maybe you could mention our pancake heart special," Jazz suggested. "You know just at some break or something."

"I could mention it in the announcements," the pastor said. "Sort of a community service thing."

"Good." Jazz put the cap back on his camera lens. "And tell people to look for the pictures in the hardware store of the guy in the tuxedo."

Garrett felt as if his smile was frozen on his face. He turned to Nicki. "You said the store sells some kind of overalls?"

"We'll go back after breakfast." She was just as anxious as he was to get him into other clothes. No man sparkled in farmer overalls. Once Garrett didn't have the tuxedo anymore, she was sure he'd settle down into looking really quite ordinary.

Nicki sure hoped so. Ever since the strawberry kiss she'd felt her appetite slowly leaving her. She'd never had even the smallest dent in her appetite around Lester. Maybe she was catching a cold or something.

"Do you have more of those strawberries?" Garrett asked Linda as he poured some syrup on his heart-shaped pancake. "They're some of the sweetest ones I've ever eaten."

Linda gave him a strange look. "They're frozen without sugar. Jazz said they were bitter. He wanted to return them to the supplier."

"I thought maybe they had something on them— maybe that's what Jazz thought was bitter." Nicki decided her eggs weren't too cold to eat and looked around for her fork. All she had was a spoon.

"What's in the eggs?" Nicki frowned. She guessed it tasted good, it just didn't taste like eggs.

"Jazz added some grated Parmesan cheese and a sprinkling of dill."

"Humm." Nicki took her second spoonful. They weren't bad. "They kind of set off the pancakes."

Nicki was beginning to see that married people in Dry Creek might like to have a special breakfast at the café. The breakfast would give them something to talk about at home. It might even change the way everyone cooked eggs. A change might be a good thing. How long had everyone in Dry Creek been cooking their eggs the same way anyway?

Chapter Eight

Nicki knew she was wrong about the eggs by the time she finished eating them. They sat in her stomach and protested. Maybe there was a reason everyone made their eggs the same way they always had.

She knew she was also wrong about Garrett's tuxedo the minute she saw him wearing the overalls he was planning to buy over at the hardware store. It hadn't been the tuxedo that sparkled. No, the tuxedo was draped over a chair in the stockroom where she couldn't even see it, and her mouth was going dry just looking at Garrett in the overalls. It was him that sparkled, not his clothes.

Of course, he wasn't making it easy for her.

"You'll freeze to death," Nicki informed him. "Nobody wears those overalls without a shirt."

Where did the man think he was anyway? Venice Beach?

Garrett could pose for the sexy farmer calendar if they had one that went with the sexy firemen and sexy policemen ones. She looked at him closer. What was a truck driver doing with a tan in November? And muscles?

Nicki had seen her share of haying crews, and the sight of working men with muscles was not new to her. She'd even seen those same men shirtless and her only thought had been that someone was saving on the laundry. She wondered if she had been missing something before. Maybe she just hadn't been paying attention or she was too worried about whatever crop was being harvested. Maybe that was it.

"Just give me a minute," Garrett said as he frowned and moved his shoulders. "I don't think this shirt is the right size, either."

Glory had stepped from behind the counter in the hardware store to get Garrett the clothes he wanted. She was walking up to him now with a black shirt in her hand. "Maybe this will fit."

Glory took the shirt and measured it against Garrett's back.

Nicki frowned. She supposed Garrett liked to have Glory smooth the shirt across his back like that. What man wouldn't? Glory was beautiful. She had copper-red hair and skin that was all white and pink. The people of Dry Creek would always think of her as their angel because of the part she played in the Christmas pageant. Nicki thought she looked the part. Yes, any man would like to have someone like Glory fuss over him.

"Glory's married, you know," Nicki offered, just in case their was any question on the matter.

Garrett looked over at Nicki, puzzled. "I know. To the pastor, isn't it?"

Garrett smiled at Glory. "I really appreciate all the time you're taking with me. I would be lost without it."

Nicki frowned.

Glory smiled back. "It's not easy to find things in the store yet. We're working on organization, but we haven't gotten past the bolts. The twins were helping us with them and we got sidetracked."

"Glory's a mother now, too," Nicki added just in case Garrett didn't understand what the mention of the twins actually meant.

"And loving every minute of it," Glory agreed. "They keep me busy."

"I think this one'll fit," Garrett said as he took the black shirt from Glory's hands. "I'll just go in the back and put it on."

Glory watched Garrett step into the back room before she turned to Nicki. "He's a nice man. I'm so happy for you. Jacob and Elmer—" she nodded her head toward the potbellied stove even though the chairs around it were now empty "—they told me how it is."

"I told them a dozen times Garrett doesn't know me. He just drove my mother up here and he's hanging around until she's ready to leave. He'll be back in Vegas before the tuxedo is due back at the rental place."

Glory smiled. "If he's hanging around, that's something. I was only hanging around when I met Matthew, and look what happened."

"Yes, but Matthew—he wanted to get married."

Glory arched her eyebrow. "Not when we first met. He thought I was some kind of a freak because his little boys thought I was a real angel and he thought I told them I was."

"Yes, but it didn't take him long to change his mind when he saw how pretty you are."

Glory straightened a shovel as she walked back to

the counter. "Well, you're pretty, too, so maybe Garrett will change his mind."

Nicki wondered if anyone in Dry Creek ever really looked at her or if they were just all being overly polite. "Well, I'm healthy. And I suppose my teeth are all right."

Glory stepped behind the counter and laughed. "Don't sell yourself short. It's not just your teeth. You could be a striking woman if you wanted to be."

"What do you mean?"

"You've got the bone structure and your eyes are dramatic with all those greens. A little touch of makeup here and there and you could have any man you wanted eating out of your hands."

Nicki sighed. "I've been thinking I should marry Lester. It's the practical thing to do."

"Not if you don't want to marry him." Glory stepped out from behind the counter again. "Let me show you what I mean about that makeup. I've got all my stuff over at the house, but if you watch the store here for a minute or two I'll go get it. It won't take but a few minutes. Everybody's still over at the café anyway so no one will probably even come by."

Glory was right. Nicki could see out the window of the hardware store and into the open door of the café. The café windows were all fogged up from the breathing of the dozen or so people inside. And the people weren't just breathing. Nicki could see them shaking with laughter. "Wonder what they're talking about."

"Matthew said your mother was telling them stories about her Vegas dance days. I'm surprised you're not there listening, too."

Nicki smiled tightly. "I don't think I'd find those days as funny as everyone else does."

Glory nodded and walked over to where Nicki was standing by the window. "You missed her."

"I did fine."

Glory looked out the window toward the café. "I wonder why she left."

"Things here just weren't pretty enough for her." Nicki swore she could hear her mother from across the street. Or maybe Nicki was just remembering her mother's soft pleasing laugh. Her mother had always liked fine things. "I suppose that's what she liked about Vegas. All those dancers in those pretty costumes." Nicki turned to Glory. "Have you ever been to Vegas?"

Glory nodded. "It's not all that pretty. I like Dry Creek a lot better."

Nicki shrugged. "I've never been there. I thought about it a time or two, but it always seemed too complicated. What if I saw her on the street someplace?"

"Well, I'm glad she came back to Dry Creek." Glory gave Nicki a hug. "She should get to know you."

"Oh, there won't be time enough for that." Nicki backed away a little. She didn't want all of Dry Creek to go sentimental on her. "I don't think she's staying long."

"Who's not staying long?" Garrett walked out of the back room with the black shirt all buttoned up.

"My mother."

Glory waved goodbye from the doorway before she left the store.

"I had thought we were just going to be here for a few hours. But now with Chrissy coming—" Garrett realized he wasn't in as much of a rush to get back on the road as he had been. "I know it's an imposition since tomorrow is Thanksgiving, but I'd like to stay another day if that's all right with you? Chrissy should be pulling in sometime tomorrow. Your mother will probably want to stay in the house, but I can stay in the limo tonight."

"It's too cold for that. Reno won't mind if you stay in his room."

Nicki hadn't thought about the sleeping arrangements. Reno truly wouldn't mind if someone slept in his room while he was away, but that meant her mother would have to sleep in her father's old room. Neither Nicki nor Reno had seen any reason to change the room after their father died and her father hadn't given it much thought when he was alive. The last person to hang a picture or pick out a rug had been her mother. It would be like stepping back in a time warp for her.

"If you're planning to have anyone over for Thanksgiving or anything we can be gone for a few hours."

"We're not celebrating Thanksgiving at the ranch this year."

Garrett smiled. "In that case, the turkey soup is on me—if there's a store around here to buy a few cans."

"There's no point in driving into Miles City for that—"

"Well, I'd buy a pumpkin pie, too." Garrett walked over to the window and looked across the street. "Maybe two pies if Chrissy is here and your brother."

"Reno should be back early morning. I guess he'd want to sit down to eat with—our mother." Nicki wasn't sure Reno was any more ready to see their mother than she was, but he deserved the chance to find out for himself how he felt about it. Nicki hoped he stopped at a pay phone on his way back and called, though, so she could warn him about their guest.

"I should go home and dust." She knew it was hopeless to expect her mother to have any good feelings about the home she left, but Nicki wanted the old place to be at its best.

Garrett turned back from the window. "I think it's breaking up over there. I was hoping the pastor would come back so I could pay him for the clothes." He already felt more like himself. The overalls were a little stiff, but they would do.

Garrett heard the sound of footsteps on the porch before the door to the hardware store burst open and a half-dozen people stomped inside. He was glad to see that the pastor was one of them. "I need to pay you for these."

The pastor walked toward the counter. "Before I work up a bill, let's figure out a good time to talk. I understand Jacob and Elmer tried to sign you up for marriage counseling a little prematurely."

"We're not getting married." Nicki wanted to be sure there was no lingering misunderstanding on that point. "I'm not sure I'll ever get married."

"I thought you were interested in Lester," Elmer said as he walked over to the potbellied stove and sat down in one of the chairs. "I was almost going to start looking through *Woman's World* for wedding gift ideas."

Garrett wondered where on the long highway he'd be when Nicki settled down and tied the knot with her Lester.

"She's not marrying Lester." Garrett glared at Nicki for emphasis. He sure hoped she wasn't fool enough to marry that man. Not that it was any of his business. But it did seem a waste if she was. Besides, he just remembered… "He hasn't even asked."

"Well, not in so many words. But when he does I just might say yes." Nicki glared right back at Garrett.

"Good," the pastor said before either one of them could carry the argument further. "Then you're both interested in getting married—just not to each other."

"You can't do marriage counseling with two people who are going to marry other people." Nicki looked over at the stove where Elmer now sat, looking innocent. "Did he put you up to this?"

"Me?"

"Well, I don't see why it wouldn't work." Garrett decided the pastor was on to something. This way he could prove to Nicki that she should not marry Lester. "I'm sure there are times when people go in for counseling and then decide not to marry each other."

Garrett looked to the pastor for confirmation and the man nodded.

"So what's different with us? If we're not going to marry each other, then we just know that up front instead of later. But we still get to think about all the questions."

"Besides," Elmer said from his chair, "your mother is over talking to Mrs. Hargrove and then Jacob wants to talk to her. She won't be ready to go home for another hour. You might as well give the pastor some practice on his counseling technique."

"Oh." Nicki hadn't thought of it that way. She supposed Matthew did need to practice once in a while. "Well, sure. I don't see why not."

"The two of you can sit over here," Elmer said as he got up from his chair. "I need to be getting home to do some chores anyway."

"I didn't think you did chores anymore since you retired." Nicki eyed the chair warily. "Don't leave because of us."

"People should have some privacy when they have marriage counseling." Elmer started to walk toward the door.

"That's only when the counseling is real," Nicki said, but she was too late. Elmer had already opened the door.

"It's a good thing Lester isn't here." Garrett went over and sat in one of the chairs. He liked the way they were grouped around the open stove that had the fire smoldering inside. "He might think it's a little insulting that his bride doesn't care if she talks about their marriage in front of the whole town."

Nicki's eyes started to spark just like Garrett had intended. He held back his smile. He didn't know which warmed him more—the fire to his left or Nicki's eyes to his right.

"I'm only going to be talking about marriage in general."

"Good. That's where we start with the counseling anyway," the pastor said as he pulled one of the chairs close to the fire and motioned for Nicki to take the one empty chair. "We need to talk about what you want out of marriage."

Garrett was surprised. "Isn't that kind of obvious?"

The pastor smiled. "Not always. That's why I have a series of questions that I start the session with."

"Okay. Let's go." Garrett decided he was going to enjoy this. He'd sure like to know what reason Nicki had for even considering marriage to a man like Lester.

"Well, first I'm going to ask which of the following you think is the most important to you in marriage."

The pastor looked up at Garrett and then Nicki. "Common activity interests, common financial values, common family values, or a common faith?"

Garrett was lost already unless you counted sex as an activity interest. He did have a six-figure savings account and he owned Big Blue outright, but he didn't know that that was fancy enough to be called a financial value. He just hadn't had a lot to spend his money on once he had paid off Big Blue.

"Well, what do you think?" the pastor asked.

"For me, it's the land," Nicki said in a rush. "I don't know if that is family or financial or what—but I need to marry someone who understands I always want to be part of the Redfern Ranch."

The pastor nodded. "And that's important to you because…?"

"The land will always be there," Nicki answered without thinking. "It can never leave me."

"Ahh, like your mother did?" The pastor nodded again as he marked something down on the tablet he held in his hand. "Commitment to stay. I'll put that as a family/faith value. I can see that would be especially important for you because of your mother."

Nicki looked around the hardware store to make sure no one else was in the place but the three of them. These questions were a little too revealing for her taste. "I got along fine without my mother."

Garrett had always thought that it was the sight of a crying woman that made him most want to ride in and save a woman from whatever was paining her. But he was wrong. The sight of Nicki fiercely holding back any sign of tears was even worse.

"You've done great," Garrett agreed loyally. "Just great."

"And you? What's important to you?" Nicki turned to him.

"I just want to be able to make her tears go away," Garrett answered without thinking, and knew he had spoken the truth. Maybe that was half of the reason he'd stopped dating. He wanted to be more than a date to a woman.

"So, you want to be your wife's hero." The pastor nodded and wrote something on the tablet just like it was the most ordinary thing in the world. "Again, I'd say that's family values."

"Some women can take care of themselves," Nicki offered. She sure hoped Garrett wasn't going to end up with some whiny woman who didn't even know how to tie her own shoelaces. "Some women don't need a hero."

"Well, I don't need to be a hero everyday. It's just that—when the time comes, I want my wife to look to me for help."

Nicki scowled. She supposed she couldn't argue with that. It's just she had never been the kind of woman Garrett wanted to marry. She relied on herself in life and that was about it. She didn't even tell her problems to Reno. "Isn't that called codependency?"

The pastor chuckled. "It's natural for a man to want to protect and help his wife. I'm sure Lester will want to help you with your problems when you're married."

"Lester?" Nicki couldn't imagine telling her problems to Lester. Maybe that's why they never had any conversation beyond farming concerns. Still, she didn't like the smug look she saw on Garrett's face. "Yeah, sure. He does even now."

Garrett grunted.

"So we have two family value answers," the pastor said as he consulted his notebook. "Not bad."

Garrett snorted. "They couldn't be further apart as answers."

"Oh." The pastor looked up from his notebook. "I didn't know we were trying to match the answers. I thought you were both marrying other people."

Garrett groaned. "That's right. Lester and—Bonnie."

"Bonnie? I've never heard you talk about any Bonnie." Nicki knew she was right to not trust that man. He waited until now to tell her there was a Bonnie.

"Well, I haven't met her yet. But if you've got a Lester in your future, I can have a Bonnie."

"So you do plan to marry someday?" the pastor asked quietly. He didn't even mark anything in his notebook. "I got the impression you weren't really considering it."

"Well, I'm not." Garrett crossed his arms. He'd made that decision years ago. He should stick with it.

"So what does this Bonnie look like?" Nicki decided it was only fair that she know more about Bonnie since Garrett knew all there was to know about Lester.

"How would I know?"

"Well, you must have some picture in your head."

"She wears black spandex." Garrett knew it wasn't much to go on, but a picture was starting to form in his mind. "And her eyes are green—yeah, a real feisty kind of green that flash when she's upset."

"That could be anybody." Nicki crossed her arms.

Garrett didn't even need to look at her to know her eyes were flashing just like his mind was remembering. That would never do. Nicki clearly wasn't describing him as her ideal mate so he shouldn't describe her. "And she likes to ride with me in Big Blue—my truck."

"Where would you go?" Nicki was beginning to wish Garrett was the kind of guy who could put down roots. Not that she had a future with him anyway on account of the black spandex stuff. Black spandex was what men said when they wanted a woman who was exciting in all of the ways that Nicki wasn't. Garrett would probably even meet his Bonnie when he went back to Las Vegas. The city had lots of spandex women who'd like to meet a hero and drive off in Big Blue.

"I just go where my deliveries take me. No place special." Garrett frowned. He hadn't realized until now that he didn't have a special place to go to. One city was pretty much the same as the next one. A man ought to have a place that he longed to reach for more reasons than that he could deliver whatever he was carrying.

"I see." The pastor was thoughtfully looking at Garrett. "I'd say you don't like to be tied down. I hope—ah, Bonnie, is it?—feels the same way. Most women like to have a home."

"I have a home. In the back of Big Blue's cab— there's a bed and a battery-operated television. I even have a small refrigerator." Garrett wondered when his life had gotten so depressingly single. "The bed sleeps two if they're cozy."

Nicki didn't like thinking of Bonnie in Garrett's bed. She turned her attention back to the pastor. "Do you have any questions about how much conversation a married couple need to have for a good marriage?"

"Well, there's no set amount. But don't worry. You two seem to be talking pretty good."

"I mean with Lester."

"Oh." The pastor didn't even look down at his questions this time. "I'd say if you're bothered by the amount of conversation, then there's a problem."

"But if I'm not bothered, then it's okay?" This was the first good news Nicki had heard in this whole time. She was fine with not talking to Lester.

"Well, I wouldn't exactly say that—"

The door opened and a gust of cold air blew into the store followed quickly by Glory. "Sorry it took me so long."

The pastor stood. "That's all right. We were just doing a practice marriage counseling session."

"Oh." Glory raised her eyebrow. "What makes it a practice one?"

"We're marrying different people." Nicki wondered how a woman ever got the kind of polish that Glory had. Her copper-colored hair waved and curled and just generally shone. "So it's a practice for when we do it for real."

"I find it helps people relax for the Big One," the pastor said as he walked over to his wife and gave her a quick kiss. "It'll only take us a minute to wrap up."

"Take your time."

Garrett frowned. Watching the pastor kiss his wife made him realize what he was missing. Those kind of affectionate kisses weren't part of his moves. When he kissed a woman, it was just a rest stop on the road to someplace else. That used to be enough for him.

"Actually, your husband has already given us lots to think about." Nicki shifted in her chair. "We could save the rest for later."

"Yeah," Garrett agreed quickly. He didn't like the feelings those questions stirred up. He'd been a perfectly happy single male a week ago. "I should go check the limo anyway."

Garrett got up from the chair and smiled a goodbye. He would have gone to check the *Titanic* if it would have gotten him out of the store, but no one needed to know that. They didn't even ask what he needed to check on the limo. It was a good thing, he told himself as he stepped out of the store, because he didn't need to check anything.

"I should go check on the twins, too," the pastor said to Nicki. "They're at Mrs. Hargrove's place. Her niece is taking care of them, and they can be a handful."

Nicki waited for the pastor to leave before she turned to Glory. "You don't happen to sell black spandex stuff in the store, do you?"

Glory shook her head. "We have black duct tape that stretches, but that's about all."

Nicki doubted Bonnie would wear duct tape.

"I do have the makeup, though," Glory said as she held up a paper bag. "You're welcome to pick out what you'd like to borrow. I hear you've got a big date coming up tonight."

Nicki nodded. "The Thanksgiving Eve service at church."

"Why, that's a good idea—I've been looking forward to the service ever since Matthew told me about it. I hear it's been a tradition in Dry Creek since the turn of the century."

"That's why people bring their own candles. Back in the early days, the church couldn't afford to buy any candles, and since the service was at night they needed light. The church didn't have electricity back then—actually, the church didn't even have a building.

Everyone just met in the back room of Webster's store for services. I don't know who came up with the idea of people taking their candle to the front of the church and leaving it on the alter when they said what made them thankful."

Glory nodded. "Matthew told me the altar back then was made of a stack of cans set on top of some boxes. I can almost see those first candles in my mind. I've been thinking I might paint a scene of them—Elmer and Jacob told me there were all kinds of candles and candleholders. The cowboys sometimes just brought their candles in their tin drinking cup. That was all they had."

"And Mrs. Hargrove has a silver candelabra that belonged to her mother—she says her mother bought it specially for the Thanksgiving service so she'd have enough candles to represent every member of her family."

"Candlelight can be very romantic," Glory said as she opened the paper bag and rummaged around. "I even put some perfume in here."

"It's only a little bit of a date. He'll be gone after Thanksgiving."

Nicki wondered if going out on a date with a handsome man who was leaving town was the smartest move a woman could make. She'd be forever comparing her dates with Lester to her one date with Garrett.

"Then you'll need a touch of lipstick, too," Glory said as she examined Nicki. "I think with your coloring we need to go with the rose."

"I'm not very good with the lines," Nicki confessed as she peered into the bag of cosmetics Glory had brought over. There were lipsticks and lip liners. Mascara and eye shadow. "What's that?"

"A pot of smudge for your cheeks—it adds some glitter."

"Won't I look kind of funny?"

"Not if you ask your mother to help you with it all."

"Oh." Nicki had almost managed to forget that her mother was here. "She and I don't have that kind of a relationship."

"Who knows what kind of a relationship you can have? Give it some time."

Nicki was going to point out that twenty-two years was a lot of time to give someone when they made no move to contact you, but she didn't get her mouth opened before she heard footsteps on the porch and the door of the store opened.

"There you are," Nicki's mother said as she entered the store and saw Nicki standing at the counter. "Garrett said you were here. I asked him to go into Miles City to buy groceries and wondered if you would go with him."

"We have enough groceries at the ranch."

"Do you have a hundred and ten pounds of turkey and forty pounds of potatoes?"

"No, but we don't need those kind of groceries," Nicki said even as her unease grew.

"We do now," Nicki's mother announced with a flourish. "Garrett said you didn't have plans for Thanksgiving dinner so I took the liberty of inviting guests."

"You mean Mrs. Hargrove?" Nicki hoped that was all her mother meant. That would be fine. She would have invited Mrs. Hargrove herself if they were having more than soup anyway.

"I mean the whole town of Dry Creek."

"The whole town? That must be fifty, sixty people."

"Seventy including me and Garrett. Eighty if we can

reach everyone at the Elkton Ranch. Garth and his new wife, I think it is Sylvia, might have gone to Seattle—Jacob is going to call them and see. Even if they are not there, their ranch hands will probably like to come. I've never known a cowboy to turn down a turkey dinner."

"We can't possibly—" Nicki tried to calculate just how many turkeys that would be.

"Don't worry—everyone's helping. The kids at the café agreed to bake the turkeys for us early tomorrow morning. And Jacob will help them bring them out to the ranch."

"But we'd need pies and sweet potatoes and rolls—"

"We've got it organized. All you need to do is ride along with Garrett into Miles City to buy the food."

"I haven't even dusted yet." Nicki wondered if there might not be something to say for living out of a truck like Garrett did. No one ever expected him to entertain.

"Everything will be fine," Nicki's mother said. "We're not fussy."

"You—not fussy? You made Dad use a coaster when he drank water at the kitchen table. And it was Formica. It was made for water spills."

"That was a long time ago. And it wasn't water he was drinking. I thought if I insisted on a coaster he would think twice before he drank in front of you kids."

"Oh."

"A child's eyes see everything," Nicki's mother continued. "I knew Charles would hate himself if you and Reno didn't grow up to respect him. Next to the land, you were all he had."

"He had you."

Nicki's mother winced. "There's more to the story than you know."

"Then tell me."

Nicki could feel her mother measuring her.

"It's not just about me. But if I can, I'll tell you. I have to ask someone's permission first."

"Is that why you're going to visit Dad's grave? To ask him if you can tell us it was all his fault?"

Nicki wondered if she was too old to run away from home. She had already lost her mother. She didn't want to have the memory of her father tarnished as well by hearing that he had displeased her mother because he drank too much. Even if her father had done that, her mother was probably the cause.

Another pair of footsteps sounded as someone stamped the snow off their shoes before opening the door to the hardware store.

"Everybody ready to go into Miles City," Garrett said as he rubbed his hands together. He'd heard Mrs. Hargrove give the food calculations and he'd joked that he shouldn't have left his truck in Las Vegas. He'd surprised himself when he'd joked. Usually a holiday meal like Thanksgiving gave him a headache. But sitting down with the bunch of people he'd met in this little town didn't seem so bad.

Garrett wondered if something was wrong with him. He'd lived his life by one rule—keep moving in life because then everyone stays a stranger. It was a good rule. That way he didn't disappoint anyone, not even himself. Odd, how that rule no longer sounded very appealing to him.

Chapter Nine

Nicki glittered. She could see it out of the corner of her eyes. She hadn't put on any of the "pot of smudge" Glory had loaned her so she must have gotten sugar on her cheek when Mrs. Hargrove, who had been making pies all afternoon, hugged her. The fortunate thing was that in the darkened church no one cared if Nicki glittered or glowed or downright sparkled like Garrett did.

The day had quieted down and the church looked elegant in the candlelight. The work for the day was done, and all was peaceful except the rustling of little feet in the back pews of the old church. The church walls were white but the flickering of the candles turned the walls golden. Long shadows stretched along the walls as people filed into the church.

Nicki was wearing a plain navy pantsuit with a very ordinary silver pin. She'd looked at the makeup Glory had lent her and quietly set it aside. She could dress up like she was a princess but that wouldn't make her one. She needed to keep her feet firmly planted and, for her, that meant looking the way she always had. She knew there were no fairy-tale endings, and she needed to remember that Garrett was going to leave soon.

The fact that she had dressed plainly didn't mean that Garrett had. He was wearing the tuxedo again and he looked every bit as handsome as he had early this morning.

Even without the limousine, he took Nicki's breath away. But it wasn't just the tuxedo or the limo. She would have found him handsome if he was wearing an old jogging suit and standing beside a bicycle. All of which was why Nicki needed to keep her feet planted in reality. It would be all too easy to let herself become too attached to him. She needed to keep her heart safe.

Nicki and Garrett were on their date. The people of Dry Creek had given them their own pew in honor of the occasion. At least Nicki assumed that was why everyone said hello to them but no one stayed to sit beside them.

The evening had transformed Dry Creek.

All afternoon, everywhere Nicki looked, someone was chopping vegetables or peeling apples or grinding cranberries. She and Garrett had driven to Miles City and returned with enough bags of groceries to fill up the limousine. Nicki's mother had given them a wad of fifty-dollar bills, insisting the Thanksgiving dinner was on her.

By the time they got back to Dry Creek, the work teams were aproned and ready to go. Mrs. Hargrove took the ingredients for the pies and her helpers went with her to her house to bake. Jazz and Linda took the turkeys and the bread for the stuffing. Glory and Matthew were in charge of vegetables and took the bags of green beans, muttering something about hoping the twins liked to snap things.

Even Elmer had been put in charge of the butter when Lillian remembered he liked to carve. He was commissioned to shape the butter into five large turkeys with lines fine enough to show the feathers.

Nicki had volunteered to bake pies, but her mother said she and Garrett were needed back at the ranch to clean the main room in the bunkhouse and put up enough sawhorse tables to seat eighty people.

"We used to get over a hundred people in there when we had guests before," Lillian had said when Nicki had started to protest. "The room can't have shrunk. We get ten to a table and you can fit eight tables in there easy if you put them sideways where the beds used to go."

The bunkhouse had had cowboys sleeping in it for over a hundred years, and the metal legs of the beds left scars that still could be seen in the hardwood floors. Nicki supposed if you matched the bed markings you could get eight tables. There used to be sixteen beds, eight on each half of the bunkhouse.

Garrett drove Nicki back to the ranch in the limousine while her mother stayed in Dry Creek to help with the food.

If everyone hadn't been so intent on their tasks, Nicki would have suspected they had conspired to leave her and Garrett alone. But they didn't give the two of them a second glance when she and Garrett pulled out of town so Nicki decided they'd just paired Garrett with her because he looked strong enough to swing a sawhorse around. She would need that kind of help to set up the tables.

Once Nicki decided she and Garrett were just a work team, she didn't have any trouble talking to him. She'd started out where she'd usually start with a new ranch hand. She'd told him stories about the early days of the ranch. She even told him about the time the cowboys on the ranch had sent back East for a bride and then played poker all winter trying to decide who would get to woo the young woman first.

In turn, Garrett told her about some of the places where he'd driven with Big Blue—how the trees of Tennessee were thick and green and the ocean off the Florida coast was pale blue in the morning.

It wasn't until they opened the closet and found the old pair of children's ballet shoes, however, that they started talking about themselves. Nicki had forgotten about the shoes. Her mother hadn't always been disappointed in her. When Nicki was small, she and her mother had loved to dance together in the kitchen, twirling on the old linoleum until they collapsed in a tangle of giggles. Somehow, after her mother left, Nicki had forgotten there were any good times. When Garrett responded by telling her about his dad dying of liver failure and all of the lonely days he had spent waiting for his father to be a father to him, they both knew they were friends.

Now that they were on their date, sitting in the church that was lit by candlelight, however, the ease of the friendship wasn't the same. Nicki couldn't think of a thing to say. Garrett in overalls was a lot easier to talk to than Garrett in a tuxedo.

"The flowers are lovely," Nicki repeated for the tenth time. She still didn't know when Garrett had slipped away in the grocery store to buy the two red roses. It must have been when she was asking the produce clerk how many yams eighty people might eat if they also had mashed potatoes. "And they're perfect in this vase."

Garrett hadn't stopped with the roses. He'd bought a tiny glass vase that had room for the roses and for a single white taper candle.

His first thought had been to get the biggest vase and the biggest bouquet of flowers that the store had. But then he'd seen the vase that also doubled as a candleholder and he knew he'd found what Nicki would like the best.

"I've never had a prettier candle for the service." Nicki usually followed the old cowboy tradition of melting enough wax in the bottom of a cup to make a candle stick to it. She'd usually just used one of the half-melted, broken candles she kept in a kitchen drawer for when the electricity failed. It might be a white candle or a red candle left from a previous Christmas. But the candle had never been special, and she seldom had anything new to say when she stood up and listed what she was thankful for that year. Over the years she had usually mentioned the ranch or her 4-H calf or something. "I should have gotten a better holder for you."

Garrett grinned. "I'm happy with my cup candle."

Garrett hadn't been to church more than twice in his life and this was nothing like those two other experiences. There were no women in hats and no rustle of important people. People here came in old knit scarves that had been washed until they were all the same colorless gray. Some wore jeans with shiny knees and jackets that were frayed. But they all seemed humbly glad to be together. They smiled and shook hands with each other as though they were longtime friends. Garrett supposed they were.

He wondered why that thought depressed him. He might not have a roomful of friends, but he'd probably seen more different cities than anyone in the church here. That had to count for something. Besides, he could feel Nicki's arm as she sat beside him. He wasn't quite without friends.

Garrett inched a little closer to Nicki. When Nicki had showed him those ballet shoes this afternoon, he had realized that someone else had had a lonely childhood beside himself. Sharing with Nicki had made him feel less of a loner. He supposed it didn't change anything, but he'd realized he wanted Nicki to remember him when he was gone. Usually, he wanted the women he met to forget him as soon as he pulled out of town. But not Nicki.

Nicki wondered if anyone could see her blush in the candlelight. She didn't know if she had moved closer to Garrett or if he had moved closer to her, but she suspected it was she who had done the moving. There was something about the darkness that made her want to be closer to him.

Garrett looked around the small church. "I don't see Lester."

"He'll be a little late." Nicki wondered for the first time why Lester always came to church just as it was almost over. It was as though he wanted points for attending, but didn't really want to be there.

"Oh." Garrett wondered if he could get Nicki to leave the service before Lester arrived. No, he supposed not. Especially not now that it looked like it was going to start.

Mrs. Hargrove stood and walked to the piano beside the altar. The piano playing signaled the beginning of the service and everyone was looking forward as the pastor rose and went to stand behind the altar.

"Each year in Dry Creek, we come together as a community and give thanks for what we have." The pastor looked out over the group of people assembled and smiled.

"We started doing this in the late 1890s when the Redfern Ranch had a harvest dinner that brought everyone from miles around together. Before this town began, we moved the tradition to the back of Webster's store and called it our Thanksgiving Eve service. Today we celebrate here. No matter where it has been held, we have kept the same spirit of thankfulness. Together this community has survived droughts and depressions. Together we've seen good years and bad years. We've seen children born and grow up and move away. We've welcomed strangers and said goodbye to friends. Let's again be thankful for what this year has brought to us. Bring your candle in your own time and share with us what God has done for you."

Garth Elkton and his new bride, were the first to come to the altar. They carried a candleholder made of dozens of old keys. One fat white candle rose from the key base.

"The kids in Seattle made this for us for tonight so we came back early," Garth said proudly. He'd met Sylvia while she was director of a youth center that helped troubled teenagers. "We're thankful that they are doing well and are coming back this summer for a full six weeks. They told us that the old keys stand for old habits they are throwing aside."

A murmur of approval went through the congregation as Garth lit their candle. The Seattle kids had been popular with the people of Dry Creek.

"And what about your new bride?" someone yelled from the back of the church. "What's she thankful for?"

"She's thankful for him," Nicki whispered to Garrett. Marriage had transformed Garth into a man who couldn't stop smiling, but Sylvia still told everyone she was the luckiest one. "She found someone who shared her dream."

"The camp for the kids." Garrett nodded. He had heard about the Seattle youngsters who were putting down roots in Dry Creek even though they had only been here for one month last winter. Many of the kids still wrote letters to the town of Dry Creek and the townspeople took turns writing back.

The next ones to bring their candles to the front of the church were the Curtis twins, the two six-year-old boys that belonged to the minister and his new wife. Their blond heads were bent as they carried two tin can holders to the altar. When they set the holders on the altar, their father reached out to light their candles from the main candle on the altar.

Nicki could see that the twins had made their candle-holders from two identical aluminum cans. They had each cut out a figure in the can so the light from the candle would show through. One figure had wings and had to be an angel. The figure in the other can looked more like a mortal woman.

"We're thankful because we have two mommies now," the first twin boy said.

"And one of them's still an angel," the other boy added eagerly. "Mrs. Hargrove says. Our first mommy is our guardian angel and she flies over us with her supersonic wings that go zoom-zoom."

"All I said was that I'm sure she's watching out for

you boys if there's any way she can," Mrs. Hargrove added from where she sat at the piano. "She knows that we need all the help we can get with that particular task."

The adults in the church smiled.

"And angels don't zoom around," Mrs. Hargrove added indulgently.

"They don't need to," one of the twins agreed. "They have those wings that fly like this." The twins demonstrated how angels fly as they flew back to the pew where they were sitting with their new mother, Glory.

"Those are the cutest little boys," Nicki whispered to Garrett.

He nodded in agreement.

Mrs. Hargrove left the piano and was the next one to bring her candles to the altar.

"Mrs. Hargrove brings candles for all of the Hargroves," Nicki whispered to Garrett as they watched the older woman bring two heavy silver candelabrum to the front. "I think she's up to twenty-two candles that she lights and for each one she mentions a relative by name."

"The Hargroves are grateful," Mrs. Hargrove began. "Two new babies in the family this year and Doris June is coming home next summer to stay for a spell with me."

A ripple of surprise went through the congregation.

"She might even open a business here," Mrs. Hargrove added proudly. "She's got quite a business head on her."

Mrs. Hargrove went on to announce the name of each Hargrove family member as she lit the corresponding candle for them. By the time she had finished, the church glowed brighter inside.

Linda went to the altar next and lit a small green candle standing in a cup from the café. The candle was scented with pine and it started to give off its scent as soon as she lit it.

"I'm grateful for the café," she said quickly as she turned to walk back to her seat. "Business is good."

"And it will be even better with their new romance special," the pastor added from where he stood. "See me later for details."

Linda turned around and smiled at the pastor. "Thanks."

"We're determined to get that Jenkins place bought." The pastor looked over the congregation. "Besides, a little bit of romance will be good for this town."

Everyone laughed and then grew silent.

Garrett watched the candles burn as others in the church brought up their candles. Before long there were candles of every color and size. And the holders were as individual as the people in this town. But almost all of the candleholders looked as if they'd been brought to the altar for many years and had followed the lives of their owners during the good and the bad of that time.

"I'm going to go up now," Garrett whispered to Nicki. "Do you want to come with me?"

Nicki nodded and Garrett didn't know when he'd been as proud. Nicki was willing to walk with him in front of the whole town.

Nicki felt her hand tremble slightly as she steadied her candleholder and took a quick look at the man beside her. The soft light of the candles played on Garrett's face and Nicki decided her first impression of him had been right. He was kind and handsome and—

"She's got flowers," a young girl said in awe when Nicki walked past. "And they're beautiful."

Nicki smiled down at the girl, Amy Jenkins. The six-year-old was clearly writing a story in her head about the flowers and the romance they implied. Nicki almost corrected her and then decided to let it be. Maybe there wasn't as much harm in fairy tales as she'd come to believe.

"You first," Garrett whispered when they reached the altar.

Nicki put her candle on the altar and lit it. Then she turned to face her friends. "This year I'm thankful for—" Nicki stopped. She always said the ranch. But the flowers seemed to promise more than land. She looked out at the candlelit faces around the church. So many of them looked back at her with hope and love on their faces. Why hadn't she seen it before? She might not have had her mother around to help her grow up, but she'd had dozens of mothers and fathers in this church. "I'm thankful for all of you."

"And him," Amy Jenkins whispered from her pew. "You have to be thankful for him."

Nicki knew who the little girl meant. "I'm thankful for everyone tonight."

"I hope she doesn't mean Lester," Garrett said out of the side of his mouth as they stood in front of the altar. "That man isn't good enough for you."

Nicki didn't think he needed to know who made the little girl's eyes sparkle. "It's your turn to light your candle."

Garrett hadn't noticed until he set the cup down next to Nicki's that he was using one of the mugs that advertised the hardware store. He turned around to face the people. "I'm thankful that I get to meet new people and travel to new places like Dry Creek."

A ripple of appreciation went around the pews.

"We're glad you're with us, as well," the pastor said as Garrett reached to light his candle. The pastor also turned to Lillian. "We have two special guests this Thanksgiving."

The warmth of the people in the church made Garrett bold and, when he and Nicki sat back down, he took her hand to hold. It wasn't much of a move. He'd made bigger one's before and never given it a thought. But holding Nicki's hand seemed momentous.

He felt complete.

Everyone stood and, with Mrs. Hargrove playing the piano, sang "Amazing Grace." When the last chord of the song faded, everyone remained standing for a minute as though savoring the evening together.

"Now let's give your neighbors a hug and wish them a happy Thanksgiving," the pastor said. "Then go home and get some sleep. I understand we have ten turkeys waiting for us tomorrow—not to mention Mrs. Hargrove's apple pie."

Garrett was grateful that none of the townspeople had sat in the pew with Nicki and him. Nicki wouldn't have a question about who she should hug since he was the only one sitting next to her.

Nicki's hair smelled of lemon and strands of it gently tickled Garrett's chin while he hugged her. Garrett thought he heard Nicki give a soft sigh of contentment, but he couldn't be sure. Maybe it was just his heart giving the sigh. For the first time in his life, he felt at home.

Garrett kept Nicki in his arms. The townsfolk silently

filed out of the church and soon they were the only two left inside. Still, he didn't want to let her go.

Nicki stirred. She was sinking and she couldn't afford to. She was the one who would need to get on with her life when the fairy tale ended. She looked around the empty church. "Did you see Lester leave?"

Garrett frowned. "I didn't even see him come in."

"Oh, I'm sure he's here. I wanted to be sure he got an invitation for tomorrow."

Nicki stepped back farther so she could breathe easier. "I'll catch up with him before he leaves. People generally hang out for a few minutes outside and talk. He'll be there."

Garrett felt the cold as Nicki walked away from him. Did Lester even know what a lucky man he was? He followed her down the aisle of the little church and out into the cold dark night. There was no snow falling, but small drifts of snow stood at the edges of the spaces where the cars had parked.

"Brrr—" Garrett rubbed his hands together. Sharp tingles of cold ran up and down his fingers and, when he breathed, a white puff of air circled his head.

Clusters of people stood and talked together in the area where the cars were parked. The night sky was clear and as black as velvet. Garrett looked up and saw a million stars twinkling down at him.

"That's something, isn't it?" the pastor said as he came over to Garrett. "I never get tired of looking at all those stars."

Garrett grunted. "Makes the sky kind of crowded."

The pastor laughed. "I understand that when you get close to them, there's lots of room between the stars. Some might even think an individual star might be lonely. I imagine even a star wants company sometimes."

"Yeah, well." Garrett saw that Nicki had found Lester. He was standing over there talking to Elmer. The cold didn't seem to bother Lester and he had his coat open in the front as he talked. The man wore a plaid Western shirt.

Garrett frowned as he thought of the overalls he had waiting for him back at the ranch. All he had was either workclothes or the tuxedo. Neither one showed him off to his best advantage. He needed a sweater. Women always liked a man in a sweater.

"So, how's it going?" the pastor asked a little tentatively.

Garrett turned to look at the pastor square and forced himself to stop the frown. "She's gone to give Lester a personal invitation to Thanksgiving dinner. She didn't give anyone else a personal invite."

A couple of cars had turned on their headlights and the stars were no longer visible. But the people were a lot clearer and Garrett could even see Lester smile.

"Ahh."

"Not that it matters, I suppose. I'm heading out as soon as my cousin gets here anyway." Garrett pulled his eyes back away from Lester and looked at the pastor again.

"I see." The pastor nodded. "Well, then, I guess it's just as well she's inviting Lester. He's a solid man and he'll still be around."

Garrett snorted. "He's too old for her. Besides, she deserves somebody better."

Garrett could see that Nicki had turned and was

walking back toward him. She was smiling so he assumed Lester was coming to dinner.

"Nicki deserves to be happy," the pastor agreed.

"He's coming," Nicki said when she came close to Garrett again. "I wanted to be sure he was coming because Reno should be back. Reno likes to have someone he can play cards with once the dishes are done."

"Oh, well." Garrett felt immediately better. "That's good he can come then."

If Lester kept Reno busy playing cards, Garrett would have even more time to talk to Nicki. He might even convince her to sneak out under the stars with him and dance a waltz or two. If they didn't freeze to death, it would be quite romantic.

"Maybe Chrissy will be here, too, by then," Nicki continued. "Maybe she and my mother can play bridge with Reno and Lester."

Garrett was beginning to like the sounds of Thanksgiving better and better all the time. It was all a matter of planning things.

"Well, I'd better get home and get the twins into bed so we can enjoy tomorrow." The pastor smiled as he turned to join Glory and his sons. He had only walked a couple of steps when he turned and looked at Garrett. "You know, you deserve to be happy, too. Don't sell yourself short. Think about it—we'll talk more later if you'd like."

Garrett almost automatically disagreed with the pastor. He wasn't selling himself short by knowing his limitations. He'd always believed happiness was too much to ask for and he was right. He was no good at things like marriage and forever after. His highest hope had only been to have short-term fun.

"What was that about?" Nicki asked.

"We'd been talking about the stars," Garrett answered with a small smile. He doubted the pastor knew about short-term fun. "I think he's trying to get them to move a little closer together."

"Oh. That doesn't sound very easy." Nicki frowned.

"He didn't say it would be easy." Garrett wondered if the star who stood beside him could be any prettier. The cold had turned Nicki's cheeks red and her eyes sparkled. "Come on, let's go home."

Nicki rode in the front of the limo with Garrett and Nicki's mother rode in the back.

"I never knew this road could ride so smooth," Nicki said as Garrett made the turn onto the Redfern Ranch property. "I wonder if Reno will let us trade the baler in and get a limo." But in spite of her words, she wondered if a limo would be the same without Garrett at the wheel.

"I wish I had Big Blue here so you could take a ride in her, too. She'll show you some smooth riding. Too bad she's back in Vegas at Chrissy's."

"I don't suppose you ever drive by Dry Creek when you're delivering your loads?" Nicki held her breath. She'd wondered about that more than once this evening. "You could stop in."

"There's not much trucking that goes by here."

"Oh." It was probably just as well, Nicki thought. It would be hard to settle down with someone like Lester if she kept remembering Garrett.

"You could meet me someplace when I'm in Vegas or Salt Lake City."

"Sure." Nicki doubted she would ever hear from Garrett after he left. She certainly wasn't going to hang out in either place hoping to catch him when he drove through. It sounded too depressingly like what her mother must have done years ago. Nicki wasn't like her mother, and she wasn't going to make the same mistake of leaving her land for the empty promise of excitement somewhere else.

Oh, well, Nicki thought to herself as she saw the house come into view. She might not have more than a memory, but it would be something to remember that she'd once had a date with Prince Charming. How many ranch women could say the same?

Somehow the thought of it didn't cheer Nicki like she thought it would. Regardless of what moment she had in her past, living a practical life day in and day out was sounding duller with each passing hour. At least things would return to normal when Garrett and her mother finally left.

"We're here," Garrett announced as he pulled the limo under the tree that had become its parking space. The dog, Hunter, seemed happy to share the area once he'd smelled the tires a few times this afternoon.

The kitchen was chilly when they came inside.

"Well, I'm tired," Nicki's mother announced. "If no one minds, I'm going to head up to bed."

No one minded. In fact, no one even noticed the smile Nicki's mother had on her face as she started up the stairs.

"I should be going to bed, too," Nicki said as Garrett helped her off with her coat. "Unless you'd like some tea?"

"I love tea." Garrett hoped no one ever got struck down for lying. His fellow truckers would laugh themselves silly if they saw him drinking a cup of tea. He bet it was even herbal.

"Peppermint okay?" Nicki asked as she walked over to the counter.

"It's my favorite." Garrett figured as long as he was lying he might as well go all the way. And he could convince himself that peppermint tea was nothing but a liquid breath mint and a breath mint was a good dating move. Even a trucker would understand the need for a breath mint.

"Reno doesn't like it, but tea always warms me up on a cold night," Nicki said as she put the kettle on the stove and almost fanned herself without thinking. The night might be cold, but she didn't need warming up. What she needed was something to relax her and keep her sensible. In case the tea wasn't enough, Nicki also turned on the radio and started to move the knob. "How about some news?"

Garrett knew he didn't have much time to store up his memories of Nicki and there were many things they hadn't done together. Listening to the news wasn't top on his list of memories to make. In fact, it didn't even make it to the bottom of the list. "Here, let me find a station."

Garrett stepped over to the radio and turned the knob until he found what he wanted. The sounds of a slow-moving song softly filled the kitchen. "Care to dance?"

"In the kitchen?" Nicki stood with the kettle in her hand. She was ready to pour the hot water into the teapot.

Garrett shrugged. "We're on a date. We can dance anywhere."

Nicki set the kettle back on the stove. "I used to dance in the kitchen with my mother."

Garrett smiled. "I know. You told me."

Nicki knew she shouldn't dance in the kitchen. It was opposed to everything she had done with her life since her mother had left. It spoke of foolishness and dreams of impossible fantasies. It was definitely not sensible. "My dance shoes don't fit me anymore."

"It doesn't matter if you dance barefoot." Garrett held out his arms to her. "You can even dance in your boots if you want."

"I really shouldn't," Nicki said, but her feet betrayed her and she moved toward Garrett anyway. "I haven't danced in years."

Try twenty-two years, Nicki thought to herself as she melted into Garrett's arms. She'd avoided dances in high school for more reasons than because she'd never had a serious boyfriend. Dancing was for women like Nicki's mother, not for women like Nicki.

"I don't know how to dance," Nicki murmured even as she felt her feet giving lie to what she was saying. Her feet were moving in rhythm with Garrett. She hadn't forgotten a thing about dancing over the years. Except— "My mother used to let me lead."

Garrett smiled into her hair. "I'm not your mother."

Oh, my, Nicki thought. She really should have that cup of tea. It would settle her stomach and make the butterflies leave. But Garrett pulled her even closer and she forgot about the tea.

By the end of the second song, Nicki had also forgotten about the ranch and the dinner tomorrow. She'd even forgotten that Reno was out on the road coaxing the old cattle truck home tonight. All she knew was that she was dancing with Prince Charming, and he was holding her like she was a princess to him.

Chapter Ten

Meanwhile, on the open road about ten miles from Dry Creek, Montana.

Reno Redfern cursed turkeys everywhere. Or was it pilgrims he needed to curse?

He was lying on his back on the road embankment somewhere between Miles City and Dry Creek while looking up at the underside of his old truck. The ground was frozen solid beneath his back and oil was dripping on his forehead. And it was all because he was trying to get his truck running so he would be home for Thanksgiving.

Not that Nicki or he would be cooking any turkey. But he knew that it was important that he be home for his sister so that they could ignore the day together.

Before Reno had slid under his truck he had looked at his watch and it showed it was almost midnight. His first hope had been that someone would stop by and give him a ride into Dry Creek. From there he could call Nicki and she could come get him. But there wasn't much traffic on this road at noon during a busy day; he doubted there'd be any passing through at this hour the night before a holiday.

That leaking oil made him think there was engine trouble in the old truck. He wondered if they could find a used truck anywhere for a thousand dollars or so that would have enough power to get their cattle to market. He figured a thousand was as high as they could go unless they went into debt, and Redferns never went into debt.

Reno sighed. It wasn't always easy to have one's ancestors looking over your shoulder, but that's the way it had been for him and Nicki. If they even thought of doing something different, several kind souls in Dry Creek would remind them that the Redferns never did it that way.

The only thing the town had ever let them change was the Thanksgiving dinners the ranch used to hold for the whole community. Reno knew that was because they felt sorry for Nicki and him ever since their mother had abandoned them.

Reno felt the rumble of a vehicle coming down the road before he turned and saw the lights.

Hallelujah! Those lights were too high for a car so they must belong to a truck or at least a pickup. It was probably some farmer coming back from somewhere and that suited Reno just fine. A farmer wouldn't mind the smell of the oil that would hang around Reno even after he wiped the actual oil itself off of his forehead. Besides, Reno always had something to talk about with another man.

Reno heard the truck start to slow and so he figured he might as well try to plug that oil leak as best as he could. No sense leaving an oil spill like that on the ground. He'd already have to dig up the dirt around the oil or nothing would grow there for the next decade. Reno wadded up his handkerchief and jammed it up into the underbelly of the truck.

If Reno hadn't been concentrating on his handkerchief, he would have noticed earlier that the man had an awfully light footstep. And that he made a tinkling sound when he walked.

Not that Reno was in a position to be fussy about his company.

"Nice of you to stop—" Reno began as he slid himself out from under the old truck.

What the— Reno was looking up into the night's darkness and there standing in front of the headlights was a woman who shone and glittered from the top of her low-cut dress to the bottom of its too-short hem. "What are you, an angel?"

Reno was prepared to die right then and there if she was. My, she was a sight to behold, all curvy and golden in the light.

"No," the woman said, and her voice started to tremble. "I'm a bride."

That's when Reno saw the tear that trailed down the woman's cheek. If there was anything that made him more nervous than a woman, it was a woman who was crying. "Ah, ma'am—"

Reno reached for his handkerchief—which was a futile thing to do considering he'd already used it to plug another leak. "Look, ma'am, don't cry. It's going to be okay."

"No, it's not." The woman started crying in earnest now. "He never did love me."

Reno figured he didn't know anything about angels

and even less about crying women, but he did know one thing for sure. He pulled himself to his feet so he could say it square. "The man's a fool then if he can't see who you are."

"That's right," the woman said, and she took a shaky breath. Then she started to cry again. "But he's not the one who got be-betrayed."

Reno usually didn't feel comfortable when he met a new woman. He always worried that he had salad stuck in his teeth or that his conversation was boring or his hair was doing something funny. But this woman was so wound-up, she wouldn't notice if he had a tree growing out of his skull.

"That bad, huh?" Reno asked. He nodded sympathetically. "Then we'll just have to go get him."

The woman nodded a little uncertainly. "Get him?"

"Yeah, we could do a pie in the face. That's always good. Or maybe a kick in the seat of the pants. Or—"

The woman had stopped crying and was smiling just a little. "We could sell his name to a hundred telemarketers."

"That's the spirit."

"Or tell his new girlfriend what a creep he is."

Reno nodded. "Or we could drive into the next town of Dry Creek and get us a cup of coffee if the café is still open."

"Oh—" The woman smiled even wider. "Are we close to Dry Creek? I thought I'd never get there."

"You're going to Dry Creek? Not just through Dry Creek?"

The woman nodded. "Actually, I'm going to the Redfern Ranch near there to visit a friend."

Reno knew every friend Nicki had made since she

was ten years old and none of them could be this vision in front of him. And he'd certainly know if she was a friend of his. That meant the woman was either truly an angel or she was thoroughly confused. Reno's bet was on confused. She probably had the Redfern Ranch mixed up with the Russell Dude Ranch that was located two counties away.

But stopping by the Redfern Ranch wouldn't make her late for seeing her friend whoever the friend was. Not even the cowboys would be up at the Russell Ranch at this time of night.

"What a coincidence! I'm going to the Redfern Ranch, too. Do you mind if I ride along?"

"Would you? I can't figure out where I'm going at night like this. There's not even any signs anyplace."

"I'd be happy to show you the way."

Chapter Eleven

Garrett hadn't slept at all during the night. Instead he had lain on the sofa in the living room of the Redfern Ranch until a faint light started to seep into the windows. He just kept asking himself if what he felt was happiness. He'd never expected to be happy in life and he didn't quite know what to make of it.

The feeling had started last night when he and Nicki waltzed around the kitchen floor. They hadn't talked much; they'd just snuggled together and moved to the music.

It was the feeling of belonging that made him first suspect it was happiness. Garrett had never belonged anywhere, not even when he was growing up with his father. They hadn't had a home; they had only had an address. Garrett wandered the streets and his father drank. His father never acted as if Garrett belonged at home. In fact, he always seemed surprised to see him there.

When Aunt Rose had mentioned taking him into her home when he was sixteen, Garrett had been terrified. A real home with a real family was foreign to him. He'd felt awkward, as though he would be all elbows in a place like that. And he hadn't gotten any better. But here he was. Longing for something that scared him spitless.

It was all Nicki's fault.

He hadn't been happy, but he'd at least been content before he met her.

The one dependable thing about going from place to place as a trucker was that he was safe. There was no one to disappoint him and no one he could disappoint. He didn't have to say any goodbyes because no one ever expected him to stay anyway. It wasn't the best way to live, but it didn't involve any risk to his heart, either.

And now there was Nicki. She had become home to him and he'd never be safe from heartache again.

Well, Garrett told himself, there was no sense in brooding about it. A man didn't break trucking records because he believed in taking the slow route. There was no going back to the way things were. Nicki had danced her way into his heart, and the only way he knew to remove her was to prove to himself that she wouldn't marry him if he were the last man on the earth.

He figured that's pretty much how it would stack up if she chose Lester over him.

Garrett shifted the pillow under his head and eased farther into the sofa. There was no point in getting up yet. He'd lie here and try to figure out how to ask Nicki to marry him so that he could make a quick getaway when she said no.

Knowing he couldn't stay once she'd rejected him meant he'd have to wait until after the dinner to ask Nicki anything. He couldn't leave her with all of those people to feed and it would be uncomfortable for both of them to work together after she'd said no. Lester sure wasn't the kind of guy to stay around and help with the dishes so Garrett had already decided he'd be the one with his hands in the hot water.

Given the number of people coming for dinner and the amount of pots and pans that would be used, Garrett figured he had a good ten hours left of this happy feeling. Maybe he should get out a piece of paper and write down how it felt so he could read it to himself when he was old and gray.

Now that was a depressing thought.

Upstairs, Nicki stared at the ceiling. She'd been afraid to sleep. She knew if she started to dream she would see the real face of Prince Charming in her dreams. Hadn't she read somewhere that if a person died in their dream, they died in real life? Well, it probably wasn't true. But why chance it? The very least that would happen is that her dream would dissolve into tears, and she didn't want that to happen.

Her dreams might have been annoying to her before last night, but at least they weren't self-tormenting nightmares that involved a lot of tears and gnashing of teeth.

The dark in her room got a very little bit lighter. In a few minutes, the darkness would be tinged with pink and Thanksgiving Day would begin. At least the kitchen would be crowded with all kinds of people before too long. There would be no time for quiet dancing with Garrett so she wouldn't have to worry about stopping herself from asking him to dance with her again.

Nicki sat up when she could see the pink of the sun outside her window. Maybe if she got up and fixed some coffee she would feel better. There was no mail today so Lester wouldn't be coming by, but the coffee would settle her stomach anyway.

Nicki tightened the belt on her chenille robe as she tiptoed down the stairs. She didn't want to wake either Garrett or her mother. The day would be long enough even if it started an hour later.

The staircase in the old house went from the second floor hallway to the kitchen and Nicki was grateful for the fact. Garrett was asleep on the sofa and she didn't want him to know that she hadn't been able to sleep. She supposed he was used to nights like last night, but she wasn't.

Nicki almost expected the kitchen to be changed when she got down the stairs and looked up. But there was no golden web covering the room and no sprinkling of fairy dust on the counter. The refrigerator was still old and gurgling. The sink by the window was chipped and the faucet still needed replacing. There was no sign whatsoever that a fairy tale had been born here last night.

At least the coffeepot still sat on the counter by the sink and Nicki walked over to fill the unit with water. Her feet were bare and the linoleum was icy cold so she hurried to reach the rug in front of the sink.

Nicki turned the faucet and the water line hiccuped once before water started to pour out. She put the pot under the faucet before she looked out the window. The night was still dark and no snowflakes were falling like they had been yesterday morning. But—Nicki peered out the window more closely—what was that?

The limousine was parked under the old tree, but there to the side of the limo was a big shadow of something that was as high as the lower branches on the tree.

The pot wasn't full of water yet, but Nicki pulled it away from the stream of water and set it on the counter. She wasn't going to question her sanity again over something strange appearing in the night. She'd just get her broom handle and go investigate.

"Good morning," Garrett said from the doorway that opened into the living room. He had heard Nicki's footsteps and then the sound of running water. "How are you this morning?"

"Well, I'm not crazy," Nicki said firmly as she walked toward the coatrack beside the refrigerator. "I'm going to do what I should have done when you were out there and take the broom to it—whatever it is."

"Okay." Garrett wasn't so sure about her not being crazy. Not that it mattered when she was so cute in that robe of hers. "Chickens get out or something?"

Nicki had wrapped a knit scarf around her neck by the time Garrett walked over to the door. He'd at least had the sense to put a shirt and his overalls on as well as his shoes.

"That broom'll flatten a chicken." Nicki had picked up the broom handle she'd greeted Garrett with yesterday morning. "Maybe you need to take something smaller."

"There's some funny thing out there." Nicki waved toward the window. "Looks like a truck with only its nose."

Garrett took four big steps to the window. "That's Big Blue."

"Your truck? I thought it was still in Vegas."

"It was." Garrett wondered if Nicki would let him borrow her broom. "And the reason it's only the nose is because she's not hooked up to a load. She shouldn't be here."

"Well, do you think someone stole it?"

Garrett nodded. "And she'd better have a good reason."

"I'll let you know," Nicki said as she finished wrapping the scarf around her neck.

"You're not going anywhere." Garrett put his hand out for the broom handle. "You shouldn't be out investigating strange things anyway. What if there was something dangerous?"

"Well, it's no better for you to be out there if there's trouble."

Garrett kept his hand outstretched. "Yes, it is."

Nicki's chin went up. "Just because you're a man—"

"It's not because I'm a man," Garrett said as he looked down at Nicki's feet. "It's because I've got shoes on my feet."

"Oh." Nicki handed him the broom handle. "I forgot you wanted to be every woman's hero anyway."

Garrett grinned as he took the broom handle and grabbed a jacket off the coatrack. Nicki's eyes were sparking again. "Not every woman's hero. Just yours, sweetheart."

Garrett was out the door before Nicki had her breath back. Sweetheart. She'd never thought she liked any of those "darling" names that men called women. Lester had called her Pumpkin once and she'd snapped his head off. But "sweetheart" was kind of nice. At least it didn't call to mind something that was fat and orange.

Nicki decided she'd take some of the coffee cake out of the freezer so she, Garrett and Lillian could have a nice breakfast before they started getting ready for the dinner. It was something she would have done for any other guests.

The fact that she could already hear herself humming while she made the eggs, well, that was just a holiday thing.

Outside, the temperature had to be close to zero degrees. Garrett had put the jacket on the second he walked out the door and he had still felt his breath catch in his throat. The ground cracked beneath his shoes because of all the frost.

Big Blue was darker than the just-dawning sky, but Garrett could easily make out the white letters of Hamilton Trucking on the driver's door. Chrissy had done a good job of parking the truck beside the limo. There wasn't that much room between the car and the fence and Big Blue fit in snugly.

Maybe Chrissy had learned a thing or two about driving since he'd given her those quick two lessons in Vegas in case she needed to move Big Blue while he was gone. Of course, she didn't have a trucker's license. It was a fool thing to just take off in Big Blue.

Garrett put his hand on the door of Big Blue. It was cold enough to give a man frostbite. The windows were all frosted over. He hoped Chrissy had had the sense to turn on the small heater he had in back by the bed. If she had, she'd have been comfortable enough for the night.

Garrett knew Nicki's broom handle wouldn't do him any good in a fight, but he felt better keeping it with him anyway. At least if he had the broom, Nicki wasn't going out chasing something else. So he pulled the broom up with him as he opened the door to Big Blue and stepped up.

The night was still dark and Garrett couldn't see much inside of the truck's cab. There was nothing wrong with his hearing, however, and he definitely heard two grunts of surprise. One of them was Chrissy. The other was from a man.

She's gone and brought Jared with her, Garrett thought to himself as he plastered a smile on his face. He was going to have to be cordial to that man if it killed him.

"Garrett," the wail came from Chrissy, and Garrett saw movement in the bed area.

"Come in and shut the door," Chrissy said as she hugged a jacket to her and moved closer to the front seats in the truck. She was dragging half of the blankets with her. "It's freezing out there."

Garrett sat in the driver's seat and closed the door. He set the broom handle in the passenger's seat and turned around.

"I hope you and Jared had a good night's sleep." Garrett put his smile back on. He could be pleasant.

"I slept like a baby," Chrissy said sweetly. "I doubt Jared slept at all if he heard the things we were plotting to do to him last night."

"We?" Garrett made the connection as he looked at the other form in the bed. Jared didn't have a muscle to spare on his body and the arm that was reaching up to pull the rest of the blankets back had muscles to spare.

"What do you mean 'we'?" Garrett whispered as he took back the broom handle. "Who's here with you?"

"Well," Chrissy said as she yawned, "I couldn't find the place, you know. Dry Creek isn't on any of the maps I got in Salt Lake. I thought there would be signs, but no. I was lucky that his truck had broken down and he needed a ride."

"That's a hitchhiker back there?" Garrett wondered what decade he was in. Any sensible woman knew not to pick up a hitchhiker in this day. Especially on a back road in Montana. Especially at night. "What were you thinking?"

Didn't his cousin watch the news?

"Well, he's not really a hitchhiker. I mean, I know I gave him a ride and all, but—"

Garrett was no longer listening to Chrissy. "Why don't you go in the house and wait for me?"

"But he belongs here. It's not like I just picked up someone," Chrissy protested as she crossed her arms and refused to move.

The man in the bed swung his legs around and put his hand on Chrissy's arm. "That's okay. I want to ask him what he's doing with Nicki's broom anyway."

"You know Nicki?" Garrett frowned. This man looked as if he would be a whole lot more trouble than that Lester fellow. He had a faint smear of oil on his forehead and the air of a man used to taking charge.

The man nodded. "I'm her brother."

"Reno?" Garrett's frown turned to a smile. "Well, why didn't you say so? She's been waiting for you."

The man grunted. "I'm surprised Hunter let you get this close to the truck."

"Hunter's a good dog, but I think he's given up on biting me."

The man grunted again but he didn't smile. "Well, tell Nicki we'll be inside in a minute."

Garrett noticed that Chrissy wasn't making any move to leave with him. He wasn't sure he liked the possessive air that Reno had with Chrissy, but his cousin didn't seem to mind it.

"Well, I'll see you inside then." Garrett opened the door again.

The air wasn't any colder than when he had walked across the ranch yard a few minutes ago, but Garrett noticed it more. Hunter didn't even bother to follow him to the door.

Nicki met him at the door. "Was it Chrissy?"

Garrett nodded as he stepped into the kitchen. "And Reno."

"My brother?" Nicki asked in surprise. "What are they doing together?"

"I don't know, but I intend to find out." Garrett stomped the snow off his shoes as he stood on the mat just inside the door. "It's not like Chrissy to just pick up with some man."

"Reno's not just some man," Nicki protested as she ran her fingers through her hair. She had managed to comb her hair before she came down to the kitchen this morning. "And you don't need to take that tone. Reno's shy with women."

Garrett snorted. "He didn't look shy to me."

"You're sure it's Reno out there?"

"Hunter seems to like him."

"Well, that's Reno then," Nicki said as she moved and stood in front of the sink and looked out the window. The morning had grown lighter and she could see clearly as the door to Garrett's truck opened and Reno stepped out. "Maybe you just missed that he's shy."

Nicki saw Reno turn and offer his arm to the woman who stood behind him. Garrett was right. Reno didn't look the least bit hesitant as he helped the woman out of the truck cab. And she was wearing Reno's jacket.

Nicki didn't know her mother was up until she heard the sound of footsteps on the stairs. She turned.

Lillian Redfern stood in the stairway and she was

fully clothed. She was wearing a red pants suit with matching lipstick and had her blond hair perfectly combed. "Did I hear you say Reno's shy with girls? I can't believe Charles Redfern's son would turn out shy."

"He's not just Dad's son. He's your son, too."

"What are you saying? That Reno's shy because of me?" Lillian Redfern laughed. "I don't have a shy bone in my body."

"Maybe Reno would have gotten to know that if you'd stayed around long enough for him to know you."

"Oh."

Nicki turned away from her mother and opened the door for Reno and Chrissy.

"It's cold out there," Chrissy said as she stepped inside the doorway, rubbing her hands. "Is it going to ever warm up?"

"It'll be warmer by the time everyone comes for dinner," Nicki said as Reno followed Chrissy in.

"People are coming for dinner?" Reno asked as he turned to close the kitchen door. "You invited people?"

"I'm the one who invited them," Lillian Redfern said as she stepped into the center of the room.

"Mom?" Reno asked quietly.

"Lillian is just staying for a few days," Nicki rushed to reassure everyone. "And she wanted to do one of the Thanksgiving dinners like we used to do—you know, where everyone in town comes over."

"Everyone in town?" Chrissy looked shocked. "You invited a whole town for Thanksgiving dinner?"

"Well, a few people are away at this time of year." Lillian kept smiling brightly. "It'll be fun. The only thing we have to do this morning is grind the cranberries and then set up the tables."

"The whole town?" Chrissy still looked shocked. "That's ten times worse than a wedding reception."

"We used to do it all the time," Lillian said. "Charles insisted. He loved to have people around."

"No, he didn't," Nicki said as she turned to get some plates out of the cupboard. "After you left, he stopped seeing everyone, even Jacob." She turned to her mother. "He even stopped going to church. You ruined his life."

"I didn't tell your father to stop going to church." Lillian walked to the sink. "That was his decision. Now, I'm going to have some coffee. Would anyone else like some?"

"You're not even sorry you left," Nicki said tightly.

"I wish you could understand how it was. I couldn't stay here. Not after—" Lillian broke off. "I still need to ask—"

"I know," Nicki said. "You need to ask someone if you can tell us."

"It's the truth." Lillian took a deep breath. "In the meantime, is there anything I can do to help with breakfast? I'm assuming everyone is hungry."

Nicki turned to the coffeepot. The day would be spent feeding hungry people. For the first time, she was glad her mother had invited the whole town to dinner. With all the people around, Nicki had a chance of forgetting her mother was here.

"I'll do the eggs," Garrett offered as he walked to the stove. "Just give me a pan and I'm set."

Nicki wondered how many people would need to be coming to dinner for her to forget Garrett was here.

Chapter Twelve

The inside of the bunkhouse was still musty so Nicki opened both of the doors. "It smells like old boots in here. Let's hope the air's better by the time people are ready to eat dinner."

The wood floor in the bunkhouse had been scrubbed clean yesterday and the windows had been washed.

Garrett had a sawhorse slung over his shoulder and he was walking to the end of the bunkhouse. He was wearing his farmer overalls and one of Reno's plaid flannel shirts. His hair was messy and straw dust had fallen on his neck when he took the sawhorse out of the barn. He looked more like a beggar than a prince.

And yet Nicki had to keep recounting the black scars on the floor where the bedposts had stood. They needed the information to place the sawhorses correctly for the tables. One moment Nicki would have all of the numbers straight and then Garrett would bring in another sawhorse and she'd lose track of her numbers because she was watching him.

It was, Nicki decided, only because everyone in Dry Creek had made such a fuss about them dating that she was distracted like this. It would pass. She just needed some cold air.

"I still say your mother is worried about something," Garrett said as he set down the sawhorse on scars number three and five. "Give her a little bit of time."

"I'm not telling her to leave," Nicki said as she braced herself to push open one of the windows that years of rain had warped shut.

Garrett snorted. "You're not asking her to stay, either."

Nicki tried to force the window open. It stayed shut. "She doesn't want to stay. She just wants some kind of cheap forgiveness and then she'll be on her way."

"She spent six hundred and ten dollars on Thanksgiving dinner. That's not cheap. She could have just sent a card or something."

"I wish she would have."

Garrett walked over and opened the window for Nicki. Cold air blew in. "Well, I can't say as I've done any better with my parents. Sitting in church last night, I wondered if I didn't need to do some forgiving of my own."

Nicki looked out the window. The yard outside the bunkhouse was rough. Reno had driven the truck through this area during the last muddy spell and the tire tracks had frozen in place and were now covered with a light layer of snow. A few stalks of dried wild grass poked through the snow here and there. There was nothing pretty about the ranch or her family. "It's God's fault, you know."

"Huh?"

Nicki turned to look at Garrett. "Our whole family went to church. My father, my mother, me and Reno. It was supposed to keep everything safe. God shouldn't have let this happen to our family."

"I know," Garrett said and opened his arms to Nicki. He didn't know, of course. He'd never given God much thought until last night. He'd never prayed in his life. But now. "Maybe we should talk to the pastor about this."

Nicki had her nose buried in flannel. Garrett's arms were around her. She didn't know why those two facts only added to her misery. "I don't need any sympathy."

"Who said the pastor will give you sympathy?"

"I mean from you." Nicki blinked back her tears and pulled herself away from Garrett's arms. She would do much better with a man who wasn't so kind. "I don't need all this—" Nicki waved her hands "—understanding."

Garrett frowned.

"I really can do fine by myself," Nicki said as she stepped back to the bedpost scars. "I think the next saw-horse goes on scars eleven and thirteen."

Nicki didn't even look up as Garrett walked out of the bunkhouse. She didn't want him to see the tears that were shining in her eyes.

Garrett rubbed his hands together as he opened the door to the barn. The day was warming, but it was still cold enough outside that he should have gloves. He kept a pair in Big Blue so he walked over to the truck.

Once he'd backed Big Blue up a few times earlier this morning, he'd forgiven Chrissy for driving her up here. The truth was he was glad to have the truck here so he could drive her away after his proposal. He figured that if Nicki wouldn't even let him comfort her, she surely wasn't going to agree to be his wife.

Garrett opened the door to Big Blue's cab and

climbed up into her. He'd always liked sitting up high when he was driving down the road. He supposed that someday the fact that he was a trucker would once again be enough for him.

Ah, there were the gloves. Garrett reached into the rear of the cab. As he picked the gloves up off the ledge by the bed, something small and hard fell to the floor.

"What the—" Garrett twisted in his seat so he could lean over and see what had fallen.

He picked up the engagement ring. He recognized it. The last time he'd seen it had been when it was on Chrissy's finger back in Las Vegas.

Garrett knew the engagement ring Lillian had wanted to return to Charles was sitting on top of the refrigerator in the Redfern kitchen, but he would not have confused the two rings anyway. Even with the opals that surrounded it, the diamond in Lillian's ring was modest. Chrissy's diamond, on the other hand, was so large Garrett figured it had to be fake. Chrissy's fiancé, Jared, had lots of flash, but wouldn't have much money until that trust fund he'd talked about kicked in.

Holding the ring in his hand, Garrett realized something. A man didn't just walk up to a woman and ask her to marry him. He had to have a plan. He needed words. And maybe a flower or a strolling guitar player. A man didn't just wring out the dish rag after doing the Thanksgiving dishes and ask a woman to spend the rest of her life with him.

Even if a man expected the answer to be no, his dignity required that he give the matter some planning.

Garrett climbed down from Big Blue. Chrissy and Reno were in the house now sorting through trays of silverware with Lillian. At least Garrett had some time alone to think about a proposal.

The air inside the barn was warmer than the outside air and Garrett flexed his hands for a minute before he picked up another sawhorse. Nicki's horse, Misty, was in her stall and looked over at Garrett hopefully.

"Sorry, I don't have anything for you," Garrett said as he put the sawhorse down and walked over to rub Misty's forehead lightly. The mare whinnied softly and leaned her head closer to his hand. "That'a girl. I don't suppose you have any idea how to propose to someone?"

Misty lowered her head and blew air out her nose.

"Yeah, I don't, either." Garrett ran his hand over Misty's neck and gave her a pat. "It shouldn't be all that hard—I should just walk up and say, 'Will you marry me?'"

Misty nudged at his hand.

"Yeah, you're right—that's too direct. A woman probably wants something more."

Misty nudged his hand again.

"Yeah, you want something sweet, don't you? I suppose that's what a woman wants, too. Something sentimental." Garrett thought a moment. "I was never very good at that kind of thing."

Garrett heard someone open the barn door.

Chrissy stepped into the barn and slammed the door shut. "Men."

Garrett perked up. Chrissy would know more than a horse did about marriage proposals. "Troubles?"

Chrissy folded her arms and grunted.

"Well, I guess no one has proposed today yet, huh?"

Chrissy looked at him as if he'd lost his mind.

"I mean, I was thinking about when Jared proposed

to you. Did he do something special? Something that you remember?" Garrett noticed his cousin was wearing a plaid shirt that looked like it belonged to Reno, too. How many flannel shirts did the man have?

Chrissy scowled at him. "Look, you don't have to find out anything more about me and Jared for Mom. I'm not getting married to Jared. She can relax."

"Well, good. I mean, not good that you're upset, but good that you're—well, anyway, I'm not asking the question about how he gave you the engagement ring for your mom. I'm asking for, you know, general reference."

Garrett knew now why he didn't lie. He wasn't any good at it.

"He put it in a box and gave it to me."

"But did he say anything? Did he get down on his knees or anything?" Garrett would have to remember the knee thing. He might be able to do that.

"He said, 'Here it is,' and turned the television on."

"Oh." Garrett didn't think that would work so well. "But he'd probably said something romantic earlier?"

"He asked if I wanted to order in pizza."

"Well, I see. Thanks." Garrett supposed there was no point in studying the technique of a man who had obviously lost his fiancée anyway.

"The man's a jerk who deserves to be buried up to his neck in an anthill. Nonpoisonous, of course. Reno says the revenge thing can only be something nonlethal."

Chrissy turned as the barn door opened again. Reno stepped inside.

Reno and Chrissy just looked at each other. Garrett cleared his throat then he gave a final pat to Misty's forehead. "I'll be taking another sawhorse to the bunkhouse."

No one seemed to care.

Nicki had opened all of the windows by the time Garrett brought in the sawhorse, and she was dusting the shelves along the side of the bunkhouse.

"Got anything sweet for Misty?" Garrett set the sawhorse down.

"I thought we'd save her sugar for this afternoon. The Curtis twins like to ride her and she always expects a treat for that. Can't say that I blame her—they want her to be a dragon. Besides, if the twins ride her, all the other kids will want a turn, too."

"Sounds like she's going to be busy."

"We're all going to be busy." Nicki stopped dusting for a moment. "I saw you check out your truck. I hope it's okay. I mean, the gears and all."

"It's fine."

"It's just that if there was a problem with anything we'd be happy to help you get it fixed. Between the two of us, Reno and I have fixed almost every kind of engine there is."

Nicki knew it was a long shot that there was trouble with Garrett's truck, but she was hoping he'd have a reason to stay for a few more days, and any kind of mechanical trouble would be enough reason for that.

"No, Big Blue's fine." Garrett leaned against the sawhorse. "But what about your truck—do you need any help with it?"

Garrett didn't suppose help with a truck qualified as a romantic gesture, but it was a start.

Nicki shook her head. "We can't even order parts for

the truck anymore. We'll have to buy something else when we can."

"Oh. Well, if you need anything hauled in the meantime, let me know. I could even haul cattle for you if I got the right trailer to attach to Big Blue."

"There's no more cattle sales this year."

Garrett started to walk back to the door. "Well, I'll go get the rest of those sawhorses. And then I'll start on the plywood tops."

The plywood boards had been cut to serve as tabletops to go with the sawhorse bases twenty-some years ago but they were still sturdy. Nicki's father had wrapped a tarp around them when he stored them in the barn so they weren't even that dusty.

"But we must have had tablecloths when we used those tables before," Nicki said to her mother. Nicki and Garrett had gone into the kitchen to talk to Lillian. "Even I remember white tablecloths."

Lillian shook her head. "Those were sheets. I'd gotten ten extra flat sheets to use."

Nicki groaned. "I wondered why there were so many flat sheets—I gave them away to the church rummage sale years ago. You should have said something when you left."

"About the sheets?"

Nicki nodded stubbornly. "You should have told me things like that that I would need to know. I wasn't prepared."

"I know," Lillian said softly as she reached out to put her hand on Nicki's shoulder. "And I'm sorry."

Nicki turned away without looking at her mother. "Well, we can't just eat off the plywood. We'll just have to think of something else. I think we have four or five sheets. Of course, they're all different colors and sizes."

Lillian withdrew her hand.

"Well, it doesn't have to be sheets," Garrett offered cautiously after a moment of silence. "I have lots of maps in Big Blue. We could use them for table covers."

"But they're your maps. You'll need them."

"I have too many maps," Garrett said and realized it was true. "Besides, most of the places I go these days are clearly marked on the freeways."

When had his life become so predictable? Garrett wondered. There was no more adventure in driving from Las Vegas to Chicago than there was in driving from Atlanta to St. Louis. It was all just following a path of freeways. If a robot could reach the gas pedal, he could drive Big Blue.

The maps were the perfect table covering, Nicki concluded in satisfaction when she stood up and admired the ten tables. She'd just finished taping the last of the maps to the plywood tabletops and they looked good. All of the lines and the tiny blocks of color here and there in the maps made the bunkhouse look happy.

Nicki looked more closely at the map on the table closest to her.

"What's this?" Someone had drawn lines with a red pen.

Garrett came over to look and started to chuckle. "Oh, that was a hurricane from a couple of years ago. I had to reroute myself all over the place."

"And this?" Nicki pointed to something written in green.

"Oh, that was my sunshine route. I was determined

to work my way down to Florida for Christmas that year. I decided I wanted to see an alligator. Had to take loads to five states to do it, but I made it. Pulled into Florida Christmas Eve and met an alligator on Christmas Day."

Nicki looked at the other maps on the tables. The maps were taped together and wrapped around the edges of the table. She walked from table to table. All of the maps had lines drawn on them. "We can't use your maps. They'll get all dirty."

"That's fine." Garrett looked up from the folding chair he was fixing.

"You don't understand—I don't mean just a little dirty, I mean gravy-and-cranberry-sauce-spilled-on-them dirty. They'll be ruined."

Garrett shrugged. "Then we'll throw them away."

"But you can't—these maps tell all about your trips."

"I can get new maps and add new trips." Garrett snapped the chair into place and stood. "You know how it is—new horizons and all."

"I wish I did know how that is," Nicki said. Her voice was glum. She had such a tight hold on the past, she couldn't even see the future. She'd even been a little superstitious about going too far outside of Dry Creek. It was as though she thought that if she went someplace else, she couldn't come back. "The furthest I've been is Billings."

"Well, you could—" Garrett stopped himself. Was he going to say, *come with me?* He cleared his throat. "If you're interested in traveling, I could give you a list of good places to see."

"I've never seen an alligator." Nicki thought a moment. She hadn't realized how much she had missed. "Or a crocodile. Or a whale."

"You'll want to start on one of the coasts then."

Nicki nodded. Maybe she needed to buy an encyclopedia of sea animals. Just in case she ever got a chance to see one.

Someone stomped his boots lightly on the porch outside the bunkhouse door. Then Reno opened the door.

"She—" Reno jerked his head toward the house "—wants to know if you're all set out here. They called from the café and asked if it was time for the turkeys to be brought out."

Garrett snapped the last chair into place. "We're set for eighty people."

Nicki looked around. She'd lit a couple of pine candles and the air in the bunkhouse now had a light holiday scent. The windows sparkled. The wood floor shone. The chairs were neatly lined up around each of the ten tables. "We're ready."

"And we're using paper plates?" Reno stepped over to Nicki and asked quietly. "She's okay with that?"

Reno didn't need to say who "she" was.

"I don't think she knows we have her china packed away," Nicki said. She had shoved the boxes even farther back into the walk-in closet that hung off the side of the bunkhouse. "I thought she'd ask, but she hasn't. She always used to say a lady needed her china."

Garrett was of the opinion that all a lady needed was a pair of emerald eyes, but he doubted Nicki wanted to hear that so he shuffled two of the chairs. "We got the extra-thick paper plates."

Reno nodded. "Works for me. I was just wondering."

"I'm surprised she never came back for the china."

Nicki avoided looking in the direction of the closet. "Dad said she bought that china with the egg money, one piece at a time. It took her five years to get all of the pieces."

"Well, people's tastes change, I guess." Reno shrugged.

"I guess," Nicki agreed, but she wasn't really sure. Her mother's taste had been for pretty things back then and, as far as Nicki could tell, it was pretty things that her mother still wanted. Even this Thanksgiving dinner. It was some sort of pretty fairy tale all wrapped up in neighborhood cheer. Her mother couldn't just make a quiet apology and drive away like a normal person. No, she had to make a production of the whole thing with tears and hugs and cranberry sauce.

"She's not giving any speeches, is she?" The thought suddenly struck Nicki. "I mean the food is the whole thing, isn't it? She's not planning to apologize for stealing the money and leaving and everything again, is she?"

"She apologized for leaving?" Reno frowned.

"Well..." Nicki thought for a moment. "She sort of implied an apology. Then she made it sound all mysterious and said it involved someone else—she as good as said she did it because Dad was a heavy drinker back then. Dad wasn't a drinker."

"He was around the time when Mom left."

"How do you know that? You were only four years old."

Reno shrugged. "He drank some here and there for years. But it used to be worse. After Mom left, he cut back."

"Well, see—then it was because of her. When she left, he cut back."

"He cut back because of us. Without Mom, there was no one but him to take care of us."

She nodded. She wondered what their life would have been like if her mother had been willing to stick with her father in spite of his drinking. She supposed a drinking husband did not fit in with her mother's picture of a perfect life and so she just left.

Nicki looked down. She had a film of gray dust over her jeans. "Now that the room is ready, I guess we should all get ready, too."

Nicki wondered if she and Reno could ever be ready for this dinner their mother wanted.

Chapter Thirteen

"More yams?" Mrs. Hargrove leaned across the table and offered the dish to Nicki. "They're good for you."

Mrs. Hargrove had pronounced every item on the table as good for a person, even the butter in the turkey molds that Jacob had carved and the rolls that had been left too long in the oven and gotten hard and crusty.

"I'm stuffed," Nicki said.

"How about you?" Mrs. Hargrove offered the yams to Garrett, who sat at Nicki's right.

"I've already had two helpings of yams." Garrett wondered why he'd avoided holiday dinners for so long. He kind of liked the friendly chaos of passing dishes and dodging elbows. He even tolerated Lester who sat to the left of Nicki, but who had the good sense to keep his mind on the food. "But thanks. I believe they were the best I've ever eaten."

Mrs. Hargrove beamed. "I put a little pineapple in them this year. It was a new recipe in *Woman's World*."

"I don't suppose you have the magazine with you?" Garrett had wondered how he could get his hands on a couple of issues. They were the experts at this male/

female stuff and they should have an idea or two about how a man could propose after dinner with eighty other people around. At the very least, they should have a strategy for making sure Lester wasn't around when Garrett asked the big question.

Mrs. Hargrove looked over her shoulder. "I think Elmer took it to show to someone. But I don't see him. Unless he's over at table five."

The people at table number five all had their heads down studying something.

"There it is!" a boy whom Garrett didn't recognize said as he pointed. "That's got to be Boston." The boy looked up from the table and called over to Garrett. "Mister, have you been to Boston in that truck of yours?"

Garrett nodded. "I left the truck as close in as I could get at some delivery station and took a bus down to the Commons. I saw a boy skateboarding there about your size."

"The maps were a brilliant idea," Mrs. Hargrove said. "Everybody's been looking up cities and talking about traveling. Seems like everybody has a special place they want to see."

Nicki was proud of Garrett. He'd answered everyone's questions about places he'd been and not made anyone feel foolish for asking anything, not even when Elmer had confused Rhode Island with Washington, D.C., on the map and asked if Garrett had shaken hands with the president there.

"Where would you go, Nicki?" Mrs. Hargrove set the half-eaten dish of yams down. "You haven't said yet."

"She wants to see a whale," Garrett answered for

her. "I figure we should just drive over to Seattle and down the coast until we find one."

"Why would she want to see a whale?" Lester asked from Nicki's right. "There are plenty of animals to see on the ranch."

"I'm thinking of buying a book," Nicki added. "That way I can see pictures of all kinds of animals."

Garrett was wearing his tuxedo and Nicki had decided to wear a green pants suit that she kept for special occasions. She'd even put on some of the makeup Glory had lent her.

"A picture of a whale doesn't begin to do it justice," Garrett argued. He was glad he'd dropped the hint about taking Nicki down the coast. He figured he'd given everyone notice that way. But neither of the women even batted an eye over his statement and Lester just kept on eating. "I could drive you to see a whale in a day or two."

Lester did put down his fork at that.

"How nice." Mrs. Hargrove smiled politely.

Nicki didn't even bother to smile. "You're right. Maybe a video would be better than a picture."

"Are we going to have pie pretty soon?" Lester asked.

Garrett realized no one, not even Lester, thought he was serious about taking Nicki to see a whale. Either that or, he thought with dismay, they knew Nicki so well they were confident she would never go. If that was the case, his proposal was doomed.

Nicki wished Lester would forget about food for just one meal. How was her heart supposed to be happy at the prospect of a future with him when he seemed to care more about a piece of pie than he did about her? It wasn't that she was expecting love from Lester, she assured herself. Her feelings on that hadn't changed. She wanted a sound business relationship with him if he ever did propose. But she'd never expected to be less interesting to him than a piece of pie.

"I think there's going to be a little bit of a program before we have the pie," Mrs. Hargrove said. "It'll give everyone's meal time to settle."

"Oh," Lester said. "Then I think I'll have some more of the yams."

"I didn't know about a program." Nicki tried to keep the panic out of her voice.

"Well, *program* is probably too formal of a word for it. The pastor was just going to say a few words—"

"Oh." Nicki relaxed.

"And then I think your mother was going to say something," Mrs. Hargrove continued.

"Oh." Nicki looked around to see how she could leave the bunkhouse. While all of the tables fit just fine when all of the chairs were pushed under the tables, when the chairs were pulled out and people were sitting in them, it was a different story. But she thought she could squeeze through to an outside aisle if she asked Mr. Jenkins to pull his chair over closer to Jacob's and lifted one of the Curtis twins up while she passed behind his chair.

Nicki stood up at the same moment that the pastor did. He had had the good sense to sit at the end of his table, however, so he wasn't caught in a sea of chairs like she was.

"Since this is truly a community Thanksgiving table," the pastor said, "our long-lost neighbor, Lillian Redfern, has asked me to invite people to share what this community has meant to them."

"Oh." Nicki sat back down.

Mrs. Hargrove was first. Then Mr. Lucas. Then Mr. Jenkins.

Nicki had decided her mother wasn't going to speak after all when her mother calmly stood up.

Lillian Redfern looked over the people in the room before she began to speak. As she looked, the room grew more and more silent. Finally, not even a fork was heard scraping against a plate.

"I came back to Dry Creek to say I am sorry I left twenty years ago. Charles and I were having problems and—well, it's not important what happened. He was angry with me. I was angry with him and swore it was all his fault. In the end, it didn't matter whose fault it was, I was the one who left. I didn't think about how many people my leaving hurt."

Lillian looked directly at Nicki and Nicki lowered her eyes.

"Especially my children. I am very thankful to the people of Dry Creek for taking care of my children in my absence." Lillian swallowed and then continued. "The one thing I regret most in my life is that I lost my children. The one thing I am most grateful for is that I have been able to see them one more time."

There was silence after Lillian sat down.

Nicki refused to look up from her plate. Her mother tied everything up in such a pretty little bow. Lillian might be able to fool the people of Dry Creek, but Nicki wasn't so easily fooled. She knew what her mother most regretted leaving behind.

Nicki looked up and over at her mother. "We have your china, you know."

"The china!" Lillian exclaimed excitedly as she stood up again and walked closer to Nicki's table. "Why didn't you say something? I thought something had happened to it."

"It's in the back closet," Nicki said. It was the only piece of her mother that still remained on the Redfern Ranch. Maybe it was time to let it all go. "I'm sure you'll want to take it back with you."

"Me?"

The surprise in her mother's voice made Nicki look up.

"Why, the china wasn't for me," Lillian said softly. "The china was always meant for you."

"What?"

Lillian nodded. "You were so taken with fairy tales as a child—remember how you used to always make a castle out of hay bales and play princess?"

"I outgrew fairy tales."

"I was sure you'd like those dishes in your own home someday. The rose pattern was so close to the border in your book on fairy tales. I was going to give the china to you when you got married."

"Oh." Nicki remembered the roses. She still had the book on her bedroom bookcase. "I thought it was all for you."

Lillian shook her head and took a step closer to Nicki.

Chairs scraped and people moved until there was a path between Lillian and Nicki.

Nicki blinked her eyes, but she didn't move away. When her mother opened her arms, Nicki let herself be pulled into a hug.

"I'm so very sorry," her mother whispered into Nicki's hair. "Can you forgive me?"

"I can try," Nicki replied. Maybe Garrett had been

right and she should talk to the pastor. Maybe, if she asked for God's help, she could forgive her mother.

"That's all I ask." Nicki's mother held her.

"I didn't open the box," Nicki said as she pulled back a little from her mother's hug. "But Dad packed them away carefully so they're probably still all right."

"We'll wash them up for you and you can start using them." Lillian blinked a couple of times, as well.

Garrett sat at the table next to Nicki's empty chair and blinked his eyes, too. These holiday meals were nothing like he'd expected. He felt warm enough inside to hug someone himself. Garrett looked across Nicki's empty chair. There sat Lester eating his yams. Garrett drew the line at hugging Lester so, instead, he reached across the table and patted Mrs. Hargrove's hand. She took his hand in hers and squeezed it.

"Is it time for pie?" Lester looked up.

"I don't see why not," Mrs. Hargrove said as she stood. "They're on the table in the back, all cut and everything. If someone will help me pass them out, we'll get started."

Garrett helped Mrs. Hargrove pass out the pie slices. In the spirit of goodwill, he even brought Lester a second piece of pie after everyone else had been served.

"They got you trained," Lester sneered as he took the extra pie. "What are you going to do next—dishes?"

Garrett nodded. He figured he could take Lester in a fair fight. Maybe after he did the dishes would be a good time. "You going to stay around for a while?"

Lester nodded.

"Good."

Garrett looked up and saw Nicki leave the room with

the Curtis twins. He supposed it was time for the promised ride on Misty.

Aunt Rose would love all this, Garrett thought to himself as he looked around in satisfaction. People had taken some of the tables down and sat around in small groups talking. A fire was going in the black cast-iron stove at one end of the bunkhouse and an electric heater was plugged in at the opposite end. The day outside was cold, but the sun was shining and someone had opened one of the windows.

"Hey, mister."

Garrett looked down to see the small boy who had asked him about Boston. Three other boys were with him.

"You want to play with us?" the boy asked. "We're going to play trucker."

Garrett smiled. "Maybe you'd like to see the inside of Big Blue."

"Can we?"

Garrett looked over to Mrs. Hargrove. "Don't start the dishes without me. I'll be back in ten minutes."

It was fifteen minutes before Garrett started walking back through the yard toward the house. The boys had been excited about all of the knobs and levers on Big Blue and Garrett had been distracted by the sight of Nicki outside leading Misty around the yard in a circle for the Curtis twins.

Nicki had put a parka over her pants suit and had taken off her shoes and put on her boots. The twins looked as though they were chattering and waving their arms trying to convince Misty to be a dragon. The mare just patiently kept walking. She did, however, obligingly lift her head periodically and blow out a gust of air that turned to fog in the cold afternoon air and could almost be mistaken for smoke. The twins giggled every time Misty did it.

"Hi," Garrett said as he walked up to them all.

"Do you think something's wrong with me?" Nicki looked up from the ground and demanded of Garrett. When Nicki stopped walking, Misty stopped, too.

"No," Garrett answered firmly. Here was his chance. He could say he thought she was so wonderful that he wanted to drive away with her. Or that she was so perfect he wanted to marry her. Or that—

He didn't get a chance to say any of it.

"How can I promise to forgive someone when I don't know how I'll do it?" Nicki asked.

"You'll have lots of help with that. The whole town will help, especially the pastor. He's already offered to help you sort it out. And, of course—" Garrett took a deep breath "—there's me. I'm happy to help."

Garrett didn't know anything about forgiving someone, but he figured he could learn right along with Nicki. Maybe he could even learn about being committed to someone at the same time.

"How can you help?"

The horse nudged Nicki on the back. The twins were waving their arms around and shouting something about swords and fire.

"I could go to counseling with you." Garrett smiled. "I figure we've already aced marriage counseling. We make a good team in counseling."

The horse nudged Nicki again and she started leading the procession away. They'd gone a few yards when

Nicki turned. "We flunked marriage counseling, you know."

"We were doing just fine. We only got through the first question." Garrett decided only a fool would propose to a women who was leading around a dragon being ridden by two little boys. But propose he would. He was working his way up to it. He just needed the right time and some romantic gesture.

Chapter Fourteen

Garrett stomped his shoes on the kitchen porch to make most of the snow drop off of them. He'd scrape them inside, too, after he took his jacket off. The air was much warmer inside the kitchen and Garrett stood in the entryway for a moment after he shut the door.

Garrett saw with satisfaction that a huge stack of dirty pots and pans sat on the counter by the sink. The soft sound of women's voices came from the living room.

He walked toward the voices. "Thanks for not—"

"Oh." Lillian Redfern looked up and quickly snatched her blond wig back from Mrs. Hargrove. She put the wig on her head and looked up at Garrett. "I was just—"

Garrett could see she wasn't finding the words to tell him what was wrong. "You don't have to explain. I just wanted to let you know I was going to go tackle those pots and pans." Garrett smiled. "That was a great meal you ladies put together," he said and turned to go.

"Wait." Mrs. Hargrove called him back. "Lillian, it's nothing to be ashamed of—you're going to have to tell people sooner or later." Mrs. Hargrove put her hand on Lillian's arm.

"You're right." Lillian nodded her head at Garrett. "Besides, you might be able to help Nicki understand when I tell her and Reno about it." Lillian took a deep breath. "The reason I lost my hair is because of the chemotherapy. I have breast cancer."

"And there's no reason to panic," Mrs. Hargrove said firmly. "My niece had breast cancer and she's made a nice recovery." She smiled at Lillian. "Her hair even grew back."

"I plan to tell Nicki and Reno this coming Sunday. I wanted them to get to know me a little more first," Lillian told Garrett. "So if you could keep it quiet for the time being."

"No problem. I wish you'd told me on the way up here though. I could have taken it easier and stopped in a hotel at night or something instead of just driving through like I did."

Lillian shook her head firmly. "Then we wouldn't have made it in time for Thanksgiving. No, the reason I wanted you to drive me is because Chrissy said you'd be able to drive straight through. I wasn't up to flying, but I did want to get to Dry Creek for Thanksgiving."

"I'm glad we made it for Thanksgiving, too," Garrett added softly.

Mrs. Hargrove looked at him. "I'm sure Nicki is happy you are here, too. You two seem to have hit it off."

Garrett nodded. "I'll always remember Nicki."

"Oh. You're leaving?" Mrs. Hargrove looked confused. "I thought you two were—well, maybe my old eyes aren't as sharp as they used to be."

Garrett shook his head. "There's nothing wrong with

your eyes. I plan to ask Nicki to marry me later today. I just don't think she'll say yes."

"Oh." Mrs. Hargrove brightened. "Well, you don't know that until you ask, now do you?"

"I just wish I had some flowers."

"There's an orchid in the refrigerator," Lillian suggested. "In some plastic box."

"No, I think Nicki is more a roses kind of a woman. Even wild roses maybe." Garrett wondered if he could call a florist anywhere in the world and have roses delivered in the next few hours. "I don't suppose anyone grows roses around here and has one left in their garden."

"It's freezing out there. The roses are all cut back." Mrs. Hargrove thought a moment. "You could make her a cowboy's rose though."

"What's that?"

"In the early days of the Redfern Ranch, a cowboy often gave his lady a rose made out of a folded bandanna. They actually found a way to fold them that made them look just like a rose."

"Nicki would like that." Garrett was encouraged. Anything to do with her ranch would please Nicki. "Where can I get a bandanna?"

"I'm sure her father had some," Lillian said as she stood up and adjusted her wig. "Let me run upstairs and check in the drawers. He always kept a package of brand-new ones in the top left drawer."

"Here, let me get them for you," Garrett offered as he motioned Lillian back to her seat.

"See." Lillian turned to Mrs. Hargrove. "That's why I don't like to tell people. Everyone treats me like an invalid." She turned to Garrett. "I'm perfectly able to climb a flight of stairs."

"I'm sure you are, ma'am."

Garrett watched Lillian walk toward the stairs. Why hadn't he noticed earlier that she was frail? That's probably why she'd been so quiet on the ride up here. "Do you think she'll be all right with Chrissy driving her back?"

Mrs. Hargrove nodded. "I'm sure they'll be fine."

"Well, I may as well get some of those pots in the dishwater so they can at least soak a few minutes." Garrett turned to leave for the kitchen.

"Good idea. Clear a place on the table so we can fold those bandannas."

The rose bandannas were easy to make and did look surprisingly like roses. Big, sturdy summer roses. "Now, you're sure Nicki will know what these are?"

Lillian nodded as she tied the roses together in a bouquet. "We used to make them when she was little. She'll remember."

Garrett hoped Nicki's mother was right. He was counting on the cloth roses to give his proposal respectability.

"You're welcome to use the ring, too." Lillian nodded her head toward the refrigerator. "I'd love for Nicki to wear it."

Garrett hesitated. "You know she's given me no reason to think she'll say yes?"

Lillian shrugged. "She seems to like you."

"But she's convinced that Lester is the man for her. And, to give the man his due, he does know about ranching and cattle. I only know about trucking. I don't see how I could make a living for Nicki and me here."

"Nicki would have to love you a lot to be willing to leave this ranch," Mrs. Hargrove agreed.

"That's why I'm saying I should leave the ring on the top of the refrigerator." Garrett felt the collar of his shirt grow tighter. He'd taken his tuxedo jacket off and rolled his sleeves up to do dishes. "What I'm doing is making a statement to Nicki. I don't think we can expect an engagement. I have Big Blue all packed and I intend to take off after she refuses me. To save everyone the awkwardness, you know."

"I see." Lillian smiled slightly. "Off into the sunset."

"The two of us can see to the last of these dishes," Mrs. Hargrove said. There was one last sinkful of pans still soaking. "But if you don't send me a Christmas card from wherever you are, I can tell you I'm going to be very disappointed."

Garrett looked at the two women. Aunt Rose would have approved. "I can do that."

"I saw Nicki go into the bunkhouse a little bit ago," Lillian added. "Reno is leading the horse around now."

"I don't think anyone else is in the bunkhouse," Mrs. Hargrove added. "We've been watching out the window. Last time I looked, I saw Lester talking with Mr. Jenkins over by the barn."

"Well—" Garrett rolled down the sleeves on his shirt and reached for his tuxedo jacket "—I guess there's no time like the present."

After Nicki had given the horse reins to Reno, she had gone into the bunkhouse.

The heat was fast leaving the bunkhouse, but the smell of turkey was still in the air everywhere except in the walk-in closet. The closet had obviously been added after the bunkhouse had been built and inferior lumber had been used. The slats didn't match properly and wind blew into the small room.

Nicki rubbed her arms. She'd taken her heavy coat off and laid it on the floor so she'd have something to sit on. Before that she had stopped to tie a full apron around her waist. She was grateful for the apron because no one had cleaned the closet for years and a film of dust had settled over everything. She'd also noticed water spots on the boxes so the roof in the closet must leak.

Nicki quietly sat cross-legged for a minute after she opened the flaps on the first box of china. Her father had wrapped each piece of china in newspaper, and Nicki slowly unwrapped a cup. It felt like her whole childhood came back to her. Her mother was right. Nicki did think of Cinderella fairy tales when she looked at the roses on those cups.

Last week Nicki would have sworn fairy tales were worthless and that it was best to live as though romance and flowers didn't exist. But now, she wondered if she'd just been afraid love would always disappoint her.

The door to the bunkhouse opened as Nicki took out another cup and unwrapped it. The older men sitting in the barn had come earlier to take a few folding chairs and they must want another one.

Garrett stood in the open doorway of the closet for a few moments just looking at Nicki. The white apron she wore was knee-length and it billowed out around her, as she sat with her legs folded under it. The wind had whipped her hair into disarray and it looked as if it was sprinkled with dust. He'd never seen a more beautiful woman.

"So this is the china?" Garrett walked over to where

Nicki sat and got down on the floor himself. He had the rose bouquet in a brown paper bag that Mrs. Hargrove had given him.

Nicki looked over, smiled and nodded. "Silly, isn't it? What grown woman likes a china pattern because it reminds her of fairy tales?"

Garrett shrugged. "I can't think of a better reason."

"You know that pink dress we saw before—the one I thought my mother used to make me wear. I think I had it all wrong. I loved the dress. I used to pretend I was Cinderella."

"I rather like thinking of you as a princess."

"Oh, I stopped being a princess. All that feminine stuff—it's not me anymore. I gave up being pretty to be useful. I don't wear dresses anymore. It's all jeans. And boots."

"Being feminine isn't about what you wear."

Nicki smiled. "I'm independent, too. I can milk a cow, change a tire, fix a tractor engine, do my taxes."

"I get the picture," Garrett agreed. "And none of that makes you any less of a princess. It's good that you can take care of yourself. I just think you should be cherished like a princess."

Nicki blushed. "You don't have to say that. I'm feeling a little better about my mother."

"This isn't about your mother." Garrett didn't think his proposal was going very well. If he'd learned anything about women from his aunt Rose and Chrissy, it was that he shouldn't get involved in a mother/daughter problem. He needed to turn a corner here quickly.

"Well, I appreciate you trying to make me feel better anyway." Nicki smiled.

"I'm not trying to make you feel better." Garrett felt his voice rise in frustration. "I'm trying to propose."

"Oh." Nicki looked stunned. She jerked her head up so fast, some of the dust even fell out of her hair. "To me?"

Garrett figured a proposal couldn't go much worse. "Of course, to you."

"Oh."

"I didn't mean for it to be so abrupt. I tried to give you a hint earlier with the whales."

"Oh."

Garrett thought Nicki looked a little white. "You're not going to faint on me, are you? If you hang your head down between your knees and take deep breaths, it will be all right."

Nicki closed her eyes. "That only works if you're sitting in a chair. I'll be fine. Just give me a minute."

"I've got all kinds of time."

Nicki took two deep breaths. "You mean marriage. You and me?"

"That was the general idea."

Nicki wondered when her world had gone crazy on her. She'd never expected to meet a man like Garrett. He could be in a fairy tale with all his talk of wanting to be a hero for his bride. A hero was a notch above a prince anyday.

Garrett had to talk. "I made you something—I know they're not real and you deserve ones that are real." He opened the bag and offered Nicki the bouquet of roses. "Your mother assured me you'd remember what these are."

"Cowboy roses," Nicki said softly as she accepted them. "They're perfect."

Nicki put the cloth roses up to her nose just as though she could smell them. "I used to dream about cowboy roses."

"That's good then." Garrett decided things were going a little better. "Well, I just wanted you to know how I feel. I've never met anyone like you."

Nicki smiled. "I'm glad."

"And I want you to remember me," Garrett continued. "Even if you get married to Lester, I want you to remember me."

"I will."

Garrett looked at Nicki. He'd keep the picture of her eyes looking up at him in his heart forever. Quiet glowing emeralds. "I'll remember you, too."

"I'm going to kiss you now, so I don't want you to faint on me." Garrett leaned toward Nicki and she didn't move away.

A kiss can be about a million things, Nicki thought. But not every kiss made a woman feel as if she was a princess. It was too bad that every fairy tale didn't have a happy ending.

"I can't go with you," Nicki whispered finally.

"I know." Garrett drew her into his arms anyway.

"I need to be sensible."

"I know."

Garrett kissed her again. He was beginning to understand why the prince had been willing to search the whole kingdom for his princess. There would be no one else like Nicki in his life.

Mrs. Hargrove looked at Nicki's tearstained face. "Explain it to us again, dear."

Nicki had come running into the kitchen with tears

streaming down her face. Lillian and Mrs. Hargrove had finished washing the last Thanksgiving pot and were having a cup of tea at the kitchen table.

"Life isn't like some fairy tale," Nicki said, and started to cry in earnest. "I have responsibilities. I can't just run off with any man who comes along who thinks I'm a princess."

"He thinks you're a princess?" Mrs. Hargrove said brightly. "That's a good sign."

"But I have chores to do," Nicki wailed. "I can't fall in love."

"Well, someone else can do the chores," Lillian said as she leaned in to hold her daughter. "That's no reason to stay."

Nicki stopped crying and hiccuped. She pulled away from her mother's reach. "I'm not like you. I keep my commitments."

Lillian sat back in her chair. "I see."

"Dear, I hope you're not talking about a commitment to Lester," Mrs. Hargrove said. "I'm not sure he's the right man for you."

"I'm not talking about Lester. Well, not much. I mean the land. I'm committed to the Redfern Ranch. Dad gave it to me and Reno. He meant for me to stay." Nicki dried her eyes and looked at her mother. "I'm not going to leave everything like you did."

Nicki sat up straighter in her chair. She was a strong woman. She had her land. She had her boots. She could do what needed to be done in life.

"Oh, dear, is that what you think?" Lillian finally spoke. "That you need to stay because I left?"

"Dad was never the same after you left. He loved

you and you left him. I've learned a person can't count on love, but the land stays with you."

There was silence in the kitchen.

"Lillian, you have to tell her what happened," Mrs. Hargrove finally said as she rose from the table. "I'll go wait in the living room so you have some privacy."

"You don't need to leave." Nicki smiled at Mrs. Hargrove. "She doesn't need to tell me anything. I know what happened."

"No," Mrs. Hargrove said as she stood up. "You don't."

Lillian waited for Mrs. Hargrove to walk into the living room. "Do you want some tea?"

Nicki shook her head. "What does Mrs. Hargrove mean? You left Dad—that's all there is to it."

Lillian shook her head. "What Mrs. Hargrove wants me to tell you is why I left. I'm still not sure it is a good idea. And I'm not saying that it excuses my leaving. If I'd had as much character as you have, I would have stayed and worked the situation out. But I just didn't know what to do but leave."

"Dad said you left to pursue your dancing career."

Lillian smiled wryly. "That's what I did, but that's not why I left." Lillian looked down at her hands. "Do you remember Betty, Jacob's wife?"

"Of course. The two of them used to be over here all the time."

Lillian nodded. "Betty and your father were having an affair."

"What?"

"I didn't believe it when Jacob first told me, but then I asked your father and he admitted it."

"Jacob knew?"

"He knew. Mrs. Hargrove knew. And Elmer. Except for Betty and your father, that was all. I left the day after he admitted it to me. Jacob asked us all to keep it quiet because he was fighting to save his marriage."

"I never knew. I thought you left because you didn't like me anymore," Nicki said.

"Never," Lillian said as she leaned toward Nicki to give her a hug.

This time Nicki didn't move away.

"Don't give up on love if he's the one you want," Lillian whispered into Nicki's hair. "Don't make my mistake. If you love him, you can work it out."

"But he moves all over and I stay in one place."

Lillian smiled. "You've never heard of compromise? Maybe you could move a little and he could stay a little."

Nicki frowned a minute then smiled. "That doesn't sound so hard."

Lillian kissed her daughter on the forehead. "It won't be. Now go. I heard the truck start up ten minutes ago."

"He's leaving?"

Nicki stood and started walking toward the kitchen door. She grabbed a coat off the rack before she opened the door and went outside. Even when she shaded her eyes with her hand, Nicki could barely see the truck down the road. It was a dot disappearing on the white horizon.

She slipped the coat on over her pants suit and started running toward the barn. The keys were in the pickup. Nicki opened the side door to the barn and stopped. The pickup stood where it always did, right in front of the double doors that led outside. But it wasn't going to be easy to move it. Several of the older men from dinner had set their folding chairs around the truck. Someone—Nicki thought it might be Jacob—was even taking a nap in the back of the pickup.

Nicki turned around and walked out of the barn. It would be easier to take Misty.

"Sorry," Nicki said as she helped the last of the twins down from the saddle. "I'll bring her back in a few minutes."

"She blows smoke in the air," one of the twins announced. "I think she can fly."

The other twin nodded. "She just doesn't want to fly because she's afraid she'll scare the chickens. That's what Reno says."

"You can get the kids to the house all right?" Nicki asked Reno and Chrissy who had been leading Misty around in circles until Nicki came.

"Of course." Reno looked offended. "They're my pals."

Nicki swung herself up into the saddle. Some days it paid to wear boots. She turned Misty around and nudged the mare with her knees.

Misty gave a happy snort and galloped for the gate.

Nicki kept her head down and her collar pulled up. The wind had a bite to it, but it also smelled fresh. A few sprinkles of snow were falling. Nicki watched as the gray and white clumps of ground sped past Misty's feet. Nicki looked up once to see Garrett's truck. She wondered what he was thinking.

Garrett was beginning to wish he'd taken his swing at Lester when the man had stepped out of the barn as Garrett was walking back to his truck. Instead, Garrett had shaken the man's hand and confused him by congratulating him. Not that hitting Lester would change anything, Garrett told himself, but he was itching to do something.

Garrett decided he should have had real flowers. Maybe when he got into Miles City he could stop at a florist and ask them to deliver a bouquet of roses to Nicki. Just so she'd know he wanted her to have them.

From Miles City, he would head out to—Garrett realized he didn't care where he headed out to. He'd already been most of the places he'd ever hoped to see—some of them four or five times.

Still, he had the freedom to go anywhere he wanted.

Yeah, he thought as he turned on his truck's radio, he might be unlucky in love, but he was a lucky man because he could drive Big Blue anywhere his heart desired.

What was wrong with him? Garrett thought to himself. He didn't have the freedom to go where he wanted. The only place his heart wanted to go was five miles behind him and he was headed away from it with every turn of Big Blue's tires. What kind of luck was that?

The road Garrett was driving down was a country dirt road with shallow ditches between it and lines of barbed-wire fence. Cows watched him as he drove by, and the road was narrow. There was no place to turn around until he came to the main road a couple of miles ahead of him.

Garrett pressed a little harder on the gas pedal.

Nicki thought she'd never catch Garrett. Just when she thought she'd make it, he sped up as if he was in some kind of a race. She wondered if he saw her in the rearview mirror. She probably looked a sight, like a madwoman, with her coat flapping about her as she and her horse charged after him. She'd been trying to tell him she wasn't a princess—at least now he might believe her.

Garrett blinked. He saw a flash of green in his mirror and then he hit a bump and the vision vanished. He craned his neck to get a better look. He was catching glimpses of a cape or a jacket flapping in the wind. His best guess was that something was following directly behind him and a piece of cloth was flapping about. He strained his neck even farther. He should be able to see if it was a car. But it was something thinner than a car. A bicycle couldn't go that fast so it must be some kid on a motorcycle.

Garrett slowed down. He had no desire to race a kid on a motorcycle on Thanksgiving Day in the cold and snow. He'd let the kid pass him.

Garrett pulled the truck over to the edge of the road and stopped. He checked the mirror to see how far back the motorcycle was and saw it wasn't a motorcycle at all. It was Misty. And Nicki.

Garrett rolled down his window. The wind was gusty and more snow flurries were beginning to fall.

Nicki reined Misty in. Finally. She and Misty were both breathing hard and their breath was making clouds around their faces. But they were here.

Oh, no, Nicki thought. They were here. She'd concentrated so hard on catching up with Garrett that she hadn't thought of what to say to him when she actually caught up with him.

"You left," she accused him. The wind carried Nicki's words away and she leaned closer to yell inside Garrett's truck. "I didn't know you were going to leave."

"I said goodbye." Garrett wondered if the sun had come out from behind a cloud. Even with the wind and the snow, the day seemed warmer and brighter than before.

"Well, you should have told me you were leaving. And you didn't get any leftover pie," Nicki yelled into the truck, her hands cupped around her mouth.

"Oh." Had he heard right? The day dimmed again. He rolled his window completely down. "You came to bring me pie?"

"Well." Even in the cold, Nicki felt her face flush. She took a deep breath. "No, I forgot the pie."

"That's okay. Tell Lester he can have my piece."

Nicki forced herself to take another breath and then she spoke loudly. "I came about the whale. You said you'd take me to see a whale."

Garrett knew now why a deaf man would sing. He leaned out the door window and felt the bite of snow on his skin. It could have been a caress. "You don't need to go anywhere you don't want to go. I was going to turn around when I got up to the country road."

Nicki wasn't sure she had heard all of that. "You were coming back?" Nicki straightened herself on her horse. "Did you forget something?"

Garrett leaned out the window so he could see Nicki's face. The wind had whipped her hair around her head and put red blotches on her face. "I forgot you. You're my princess."

Nicki started to grin. The man was completely blind. "A princess would have waited at the castle for her hero to come back."

"Not in my fairy tale," Garrett said as he leaned far enough out of his window to kiss Nicki.

Epilogue

Nicki hated to admit it, but her mother was right. Compromise did make everything possible.

When Nicki admitted to Garrett that she had always wanted rose petals to line her bridal path, he swore that's what she'd have even though she had added that she didn't need them. She knew there wouldn't be enough roses in Dry Creek until Mrs. Hargrove's flowers started to bloom in June.

"June!" Garrett had sounded stunned when she told him that. Then he swallowed. "I didn't know it would be that long, but if that's what you want, that's what we'll do."

Nicki smiled. "There's nothing so special about roses. Maybe I could have carnations or something. Then we could get married in February."

"Carnations don't have any smell, but I like the sounds of February. We'll ask Matthew if the church is available."

"Matthew said any time we picked, he'd make sure it was available."

Nicki was surprised how much her feelings about the

Dry Creek church had changed. She'd grown up in that church, but it wasn't until she forgave her mother that she was able to feel God's love wrap around her. Now she felt that love every time she walked into the church. She wouldn't want to be married in any other place.

Garrett seemed to feel the same way.

"If I'm going to be the kind of husband to you that I want to be, I'm going to need God's help," Garrett had told her one Sunday after dinner. They were sitting together on the sofa in the living room at the Redfern Ranch.

He was silent for a moment.

"I had no idea God cared about me the way He does," Garrett finally added.

"I know what you mean," Nicki said. She used to think God didn't care about the Redfern family, but now she saw His blessings everywhere.

Earlier that day, they had walked around the site of the home they were building on the other side of the bunkhouse. Garrett had pulled enough money out of his savings account to pay for the complete three-bedroom house.

Nicki had never thought she could have her own home and stay on the ranch, as well. But then, Nicki was looking forward to many things she'd never thought she could have.

For their honeymoon trip, Nicki wanted to take a trip with Garrett in Big Blue.

"We've got the bed right in back," Garrett reminded her and winked. "In case we want a nap."

"We won't make it out of Dry Creek if all we do is sleep."

Garrett leaned over to hug Nicki. Garrett never

thought he'd know the kind of contentment he had these days. Maybe half of his desire to see new places was just a way of looking for a community. Now that he'd found that community, he didn't need to keep looking.

"But I still want to see the ocean." Nicki sighed as she felt Garrett's arms wrap around her.

Garrett wondered if the compromise he and Nicki had made had flipped them both around. They had agreed that Garrett would make short hauls during the winter months to make money and then help around the ranch during the rest of the year. Nicki had done the financial calculations and figured they'd double the income of the ranch that way. Garrett was happy with the arrangement and was discovering he liked the time best when he was on the ranch.

Nicki, on the other hand, was sending away for travel brochures and making her list of places she wanted to see.

"You promised me the ocean," Nicki whispered with her head snuggled on Garrett's chest.

"That's just the beginning," Garrett agreed as he hugged her even closer.

Their wedding took place on Sunday, February 1, at two o'clock in the afternoon. But the people of Dry Creek swore they would remember the day before even more than the wedding day itself.

"I'll think of that big truck every time I smell a rose," Mrs. Hargrove said. "Why, the whole town smelled like roses."

Garrett had driven Big Blue down to Los Angeles to pick up his aunt for the wedding. While he was there, he'd gone to the flower mart and bought a hundred dozen red roses.

"That's twelve hundred roses," Mrs. Hargrove told the men at the hardware store when she went inside to get out of the cold. "You should have seen Nicki's face when he opened up the back of the truck and those flowers fell out. She's still out there—just standing with Garrett in the middle of the roses."

For once the men were speechless, except for Lester who gave a low whistle of admiration before saying, "He's some guy, that Garrett."

Mrs. Hargrove glanced out the window. "She's going to get cold."

Mrs. Hargrove saw Garrett open his arms and enclose Nicki in them. "Well, maybe not so cold, after all."

Nicki knew it was cold. If was, after all, February in Montana. "You didn't need to do that."

"I know." Garrett smiled as he looked down at Nicki. The cold had turned her cheeks pink and her lips white. She was beautiful.

Nicki swore she could feel rose petals through the soles of her boots. Their perfume drifted up to her as she gazed at her very own prince. She wondered why she'd ever been so set against fairy tales. "You're sparkling."

"It must be snowing."

* * * * *

MORE THAN A COWBOY

Susan Hornick

Deepest gratitude to Sharon, Pam, Janet, Kay, Robin, Peggy, Teresa, Alice and Heidi for their input. Also my husband, who relinquished "our time" so I could pound on the computer keys. And always, my children, Megan and Jon, who are as beautiful on the inside as they are on the outside, and my mom—who said "FINISH THE BOOK."

Remember ye not the former things,
neither consider the things of old.
Behold, I will do a new thing; now it shall spring
forth; shall ye not know it? I will even make a way
in the wilderness, and rivers in the desert.
—*Isaiah* 43:18–19

Chapter One

The rodeo announcer's voice blared over the loud-speaker signaling the day's final events for Cheyenne Frontier Days' rodeo competition. Haley Clayton wiped her sweaty brow and pushed through the crowd toward the bull pens lined up behind the arena.

A whistle from a nearby cowboy quickened her step. She ignored his slow perusal and moved on. The circuit consisted of mostly good, hardworking people with just a few rotten eggs. Today, the latter surfaced like bad pennies, stirring memories she'd locked away for eight years.

The chutes came into view. Haley dismissed her thoughts and focused on the pens. Several bulls bawled from a communal corral, but one stood alone, housed in a corner by thick steel panels.

Resurrection.

The bull that nearly killed her two years before. Haley's heart skipped, jarring a multitude of locked-up emotions. Fear rose from her core, reaching out to suffocate her like a boa squeezing the life from its next meal. The two thousand pound black Brahma fastened his eyes on her. He lifted his powerful head and sniffed the air, tossing his shorn horns as though they weighed a pittance, as though defying her to face him again. She edged closer.

"I remember you."

Her eyes closed briefly, trying to blot out the image of Resurrection's muscled fury battering her into the dirt, his foul breath blowing in her face as his massive head picked her up and tossed her across the arena.

"He looks impressive."

Haley jumped and spun around. The man towered over her like a lodgepole pine. Jet-black hair surrounded a face bronzed by wind and sun. Muscles rippled beneath the western shirt tucked neatly into a pair of Levis. Dark brown eyes scrutinized her with gentle humor and concern. Feminine appreciation stirred; then caution swamped her heart. He exuded power, and power was dangerous.

"He is," she said, stepping back. "You riding today?"

The man shook his head. "No. But my stepbrother is." He leaned against the rail. Resurrection snorted. "He's been away from the circuit for a few years putting his life back together. Sure would hate to see him make a comeback on that one."

Haley relaxed a little but kept a safe distance. She knew all about pulling her life back together. "Maybe he won't. There are a lot of bulls to draw from. Chances are pretty slim to get this one. Besides, some of the best bullfighters in the country are in that arena to watch his back." The man's gaze shifted to rest on her. Haley shivered and broke eye contact.

"I hope you're right."

"Tell him to look fear in the eye and not let it defeat him."

Curiosity and interest lit his eyes. "You talk like you know something about the subject."

She did. In more ways than in the arena, but he couldn't know. She wanted to reach out and reassure him. Fear made her keep her distance. He glanced at his watch and smiled, revealing a set of perfect white teeth. Haley's chest squeezed.

"I'd better get back," he said. "Thanks for talking with me."

"You're welcome. Tell your brother we'll be watching out for him." The man disappeared around the corner.

Haley looked into Resurrection's eyes. "You won't win. I won't let you. I'll see you soon."

She forced her fear into the abyss from where it had risen. This bull was dangerous, unpredictable and as unreadable as a blank page. She would never underestimate him again.

She hurried to her camper parked beyond the grandstands, unlatched the door and flung it open. Her trailer held the July heat like a slow cooker. She opened the window and flipped the switch on the fan above the sink. The scents of popcorn, caramel and hot dogs oscillated in the breeze. Her stomach rumbled. If she hurried, she could make her costume change and still have time to see her daughter compete in the mutton-busting competition.

Haley squeezed into the tiny bedroom she shared with Sarah and donned her clown outfit—ragged jeans, purple suspenders, a patched oversized shirt, and a red-and-blue wig topped with a round-rimmed polka-dot hat.

Her father's picture rested in a wooden frame beside

the bed. An identical costume covered his stocky body. His huge smile sported even white teeth surrounded by wide, painted red lips that stood out against the white face paint. A single black tear was painted near the corner of his eye.

Haley ran her finger over the glass, feeling his loss. Other pictures lined the wall. Pop holding Sarah in the hospital. Pop and Sarah blowing out birthday candles at two years and four. Then the last one—all of them together on Sarah's fifth birthday two years ago, a month before her crash with Resurrection that triggered his fatal heart attack. A soft knock outside drew her attention.

"Haley? You in there?" Hap Jenkins popped his head through the screen door.

"I'm here."

Haley set the picture aside and opened a jar of face paint, then glanced up. Her father's old sidekick leaned against the doorjamb, resting his bum knee on the metal step. His gnarled hand gripped the bent aluminum frame that had seen better days.

"Sarah Rose sent me to fetch you," he said, staying in the doorway while Haley applied the face paint. "Mutton bustin'," he growled. "Kids ridin' sheep. Lot of foolishness if you ask me."

"I seem to remember you cheering me on when I was seven."

"Huh. Thought it was foolish then, too."

She met Hap's gaze in the mirror and slathered the white paint on her forehead. Would Hap and Pop have been so proud of her if they'd known the truth?

"How'd you fare in the competitions today?" Hap asked.

"I'm in the money. Top three for barrels. Should bring in a decent payback."

"How much more you need to buy that land?"

Haley tucked her hair under the wig, rose and stepped into the sunlight with Hap, closing the trailer door behind them. "A few more rodeos' worth. We can't keep traipsing around the country in this portable shack forever. Besides, Sarah wants to go to a real school this year."

She grabbed his arm and headed toward the sheep pens.

His feet shuffled in the dirt. "Resurrection's back."

She pulled her arm from Hap's, hoping he hadn't felt the tremor in her hand. "I know. I've seen him."

"Ain't too late to get someone else to take your place tonight."

Haley slowed her pace, letting Hap catch his breath. The pain, the months of recovery came back in a rush. She concealed her fear behind a forced shrug. "I figured I'd have to face him again someday or at least another like him."

"Ain't another bull like Resurrection."

She brushed her fingers across the costume fabric and felt the raised scars hidden beneath the shirt, constant reminders of her brush with death. "You blame Resurrection for Pop's heart attack," she murmured. "But he wasn't responsible."

"Mebbe not. But yer pop's old heart couldn't take seein' what that critter did to you. I couldn't take it either if…"

The sheep pens came into view. Hap's words trailed into a whisper. Haley stopped mid-stride and faced him, taking his rough hand in hers. He'd been like a second father to her. His feelings mattered.

"You always tell me to face what scares you most, stare it down and use it as a stepping stone." She smiled, hiding her fear under the surface. "Pop called it minimizing the monster without losing sight of the danger. No one thought I'd ever enter the arena again, Hap. But I did. I'll be fine."

"Them cowboys are depending on you to watch their backs."

"Keeping them out of the bulls' line of fire is my job. I'll do it." Haley spotted Sarah straddling the sheep pen fence and waved.

Sarah motioned them to hurry. Her gray-green eyes sparkled with excitement. "Come on. Hurry. I'm next." She spun around and headed for the chute, her black braids slapping against her shoulders.

Haley leaned against the fence, gripping the rail. Her gut twisted every time Sarah rode. A few moments later a gate opened, releasing a black-faced sheep with a jean-clad seven-year-old clinging to its back like a monkey. The animal jumped forward, hunched its back, then sprinted. Haley held her breath as Sarah held on, then slid beneath the sheep's belly. Sarah picked herself out of the dirt. A smile hid her disappointment. Haley released the rail and wiped a bead of sweat from her cheek.

"Tough break," Hap called.

Sarah unpinned the number from her shirt and ran to the fence. "That was wild. Guess I'll be too old next year to compete. I'm going to miss it."

Haley hugged her daughter. "You did your best. That makes you a winner." She ruffled Sarah's bangs and flipped a braid. "Just think of all the new stuff you'll be eligible for next year, because you'll be 'old.'"

"Oh, Mom." The disappointment left Sarah's face.

Haley spotted Sarah's friends pulling their father through the gate. She handed Sarah the backpack stashed beside the fence. "The girls are here. Have fun at the sleepover. I'll see you tomorrow."

"Okay. I love you, Mom."

Haley gathered Sarah close. "I love you, too, Rosie girl." She planted a kiss on Sarah's head, leaving a streak of white face paint in the dark hair. Sarah sprinted across the arena and disappeared. "I love you more than you know."

"She misses not having a father," Hap said, the old unasked questions sparking his eyes.

Haley clenched her fists. "I won't argue with you about this again, Hap. Especially not today. I'm going back to the pens."

"I take that as you don't want company."

"Maybe later," she said. "I need to concentrate on Resurrection."

"Ya might ask God for some help in that direction," Hap said.

"Praying never helped in the past."

Hap's sad smile added a few more wrinkles to his face. "Guess I still got enough prayers for us both. I'll check on the horses and see you later."

He limped toward the stables. Guilt replaced Haley's anger. Hap believed she was keeping Sarah from her father. But Hap didn't know the truth. No one knew. Except God. And the man who'd shattered her dreams. She wasn't faithless. She believed in God, just not in

His ability to protect her or deliver the justice she felt she deserved.

The gift of Sarah didn't erase the violence of that one night or ease her sense of lost security and fear when a man showed too much interest. The handsome features of the man she'd met earlier popped into her mind. She quickly banished it. What she wanted she would never have. God had stolen her chance for a normal life. She couldn't rely on Him.

The truth will set you free. The phrase echoed in her mind, inviting confidences she neither asked for nor wanted. Spinning on her heels, she crossed the arena and hurried toward the bull pens. In a nearby booth, a radio played a familiar hymn. She hurried by before the music stirred memories of happier times, before the world had left its mark on her.

God could have changed the events leading to Sarah's conception. But He hadn't. It was she who had held the choice of life and death in her hands and had chosen life, and she would protect that life with her own, no matter what the cost. Sarah may not have been a product of love, but she was loved. And if God wouldn't protect the innocent, she would, even if it meant forever concealing the truth of Sarah's conception. Nothing—and no one—would ever hurt her daughter.

Jared Sinclair placed the last chair in the circle, then glanced at his watch. The small booth allotted to the Christian Cowboy's Fellowship didn't hold more than twenty people. That hadn't been a problem so far. Volunteering usually didn't take him away from his South Dakota ranch, but this trip was an exception. His stepbrother, Mitch Jessup, had asked him to come, and

Jared arranged his schedule to combine business with spending some much needed time with Mitch.

Mitch's newfound faith was forged in the fires of trials, and Jared wasn't sure it was strong enough yet to handle a comeback into the life that had contributed so much to his downfall. He had to look out for Mitch, keep him centered and on track.

As if on cue, Mitch entered with a handful of old chorus books.

"I wish they hadn't rescheduled my ride. Do you think you'll be back from your business meeting in time to watch me?"

"Hope so," Jared said. "Who'd you draw?"

Mitch's square jaw tightened. "Resurrection. Great way to make a comeback, huh?"

Jared swallowed hard. A vision rose in his mind of the massive bull he'd seen earlier. Fear for Mitch closed his throat. "Maybe you should wait on this one."

"No. I'm ready. Besides, if I win, just think of the extra money I can donate to some worthy cause. I just wish…"

Jared waited.

"I just wish I hadn't wasted so many years."

"They aren't wasted if you allow God to use you with what you've learned," Jared said.

He helped Mitch arrange the music, an uneasy feeling dogging each movement. He'd hated what Mitch's hard drinking and womanizing had done not only to Mitch's body and soul, but to Jared's mother and Mitch's father.

But Jared had faithfully prayed for Mitch, and when his prayer was answered, Mitch was changed so completely that there was no doubt in anyone's mind that

God did indeed answer prayer and transform lives. Still Jared sensed a hidden need—an unshared burden that weighed like a millstone around Mitch's neck.

"You made it back from the edge, Mitch. You can make a difference."

"What about the things I can't take back?" Mitch's voice filled with anguish. His gray-green eyes misted. "How do I make those right?"

Mitch's plea gnawed at Jared's gut. "Is there something you need to talk about?"

Mitch stared at the gravel floor. "I need to fix something, but I don't know how."

Mitch's remorse was so tangible, Jared shuddered. "Sometimes you can't fix what's broken, Mitch," he said. "Those are the things you have to let God fix."

Mitch dropped his gaze. "I've done some awful things, Jared. Can you find someone if…?"

Jared waited, but Mitch grew reflective. "Is there someone you want me to find?" Mitch trembled. What had Mitch done to cause such anguish in his soul? Fear tightened Jared's chest. He'd always been able to smooth things over for his stepbrother. What if this time he couldn't?

Mitch stared at the tent opening, then shook his head.

Jared sensed Mitch's frustration. "I'll reschedule my meeting and stay."

"No. Absolutely not. You go."

"You're more important to me than this meeting," Jared said.

"I know that and love you for it, bro. But I can do this on my own."

Jared hated leaving Mitch like this, but he was right. If he wasn't given a chance to test his new faith, he'd never grow. Jared picked up his jacket, then hesitated. "I'll try to wrap up my meeting fast and see you back here. You sure you'll be okay?"

Mitch nodded, then smiled, relaxing the worry lines along his mouth. "I'll be okay. Promise."

Apprehension gnawed at Jared's confidence, but he headed for the booth entrance, then turned. "One of the bull fighters I ran into gave me a piece of good advice. She said to not let fear defeat you. It's good advice, Mitch. Look it in the eye in your personal life and in the arena. And trust God for the rest."

Mitch slid into a chair and thumbed through Jared's worn Bible. "Say a prayer for me, Jared. I'm a little uneasy about tonight."

"You're in God's hands, Mitch. There's no better place to be."

Jared hurried out of the booth, anxious to conclude his business and return to the rodeo grounds. He was his brother's keeper and Mitch needed him. He should be here. The breath of a prayer whispered on his lips. He lifted his gaze and instantly collided with a clown-clad whirlwind.

The impact knocked the red and blue wig to the ground, loosening a pile of blond hair held up with pins. Soft brown lashes lifted to reveal eyes almost too big for such delicate features. Her feet tottered.

"Clarabelle." He clasped both of her arms firmly. Earlier, he'd been so wrapped up worrying about Mitch that he hadn't appreciated the woman's classical beauty now hidden behind clown's makeup. Her violet eyes locked with his, stealing his breath. "We meet again. Are you all right?"

A startled gasp escaped her over-painted mouth. She

pulled away and stepped back. Picking up the wig, she clutched it between her fingers. "Clarabelle?" she said.

"Seemed appropriate for a lady clown. You're sure you're all right?"

"I'm fine. Did I hurt you?"

He took a deep breath, but his pulse continued to race. "No," he said, offering a smile.

Haley swallowed and stepped back, frightened by the strength in his hands and warmth in his eyes.

"Maybe I should try again," she said, hoping the bite in her voice would deter further interest.

She skirted around him and rushed off. Rounding the corner, she glanced back. He stood where she'd left him, staring after her with a puzzled, almost comical expression on his face. Haley broke contact and entered the arena through a side entrance, but the memory of his eyes stayed.

Someone touched her shoulder. She sucked in a breath and spun around, expecting to see the stranger, but Chester Rawlins, the other clown working the arena, grinned back.

"Girl, you're jumpier than a flea on a dog," he said.

"Nervous energy. I'll work it off."

"Hope so," he said, plopping a baseball cap on his head. "Rodeo's about to start. Let's go."

Tension heightened her anticipation. She reset the wig and purged the stranger from her mind. Her job began when the chute opened, not after the eight-second count.

The announcer introduced the first rider, and Haley waited. Every performance, she put her life on the line for these riders. She mustn't fail. She moved to the side as the first bull leaped from the gate, making short work of the rider. Haley drew the animal's attention while the cowboy dusted the dirt from his chaps and reached for his hat.

The next few hours passed in a blur. She and Chester worked the bulls like a valve and piston. She paused a moment to wipe her damp face, leaving a good portion of the face paint on the towel tucked into her suspenders. Resurrection's name blared over the speaker.

Haley choked back a cry. Fear swirled in the arena dust, settling at her feet, gnawing at her confidence. Sitting behind the barrier protecting the spectators, Hap nodded encouragement. She reset the rubber barrel and waited.

Resurrection stood quietly in the chute, submitting to his handlers as the rider checked the rigging and centered himself, his face hidden behind his hat brim. Haley knew the minute the gate opened the whole arena would be filled with two thousand pounds of raging fury bent on unseating and maiming the man, and her as well.

The cowboy nodded. The gate opened. Resurrection shot out of the chute. Haley kept the bull in her sights. The rider tossed like a doll and but kept his balance. Resurrection bellowed, arched his back and spun around, his leg buckling as he landed.

Haley held her breath as the man tipped sideways and fought to stay upright. The seconds seemed suspended, stretching her nerves to the snapping point. Resurrection ducked his head and twisted.

The buzzer sounded. Moving in front of the crazed bull, Haley and Chester tried to draw Resurrection's attention so the cowboy could dismount, but the bull ignored them and began a series of spins. He twisted hard right, then left.

The cowboy fell over the bull's side, his gloved hand trapped in the rigging. His legs bounced between the massive hooves. Haley's heart hammered against her chest. She reached for the rigging while Chester moved to the bull's other side. His rear hoof clipped Chester's leg. Haley caught a glimpse of two men helping him to the sidelines. She was on her own.

Resurrection's shoulder slammed into her, knocking her off balance. Her wig flew off, and her hair tumbled free. Something warm spurted onto her tongue. The familiar taste of fear rose in her throat. How had she ever thought she was a match for this animal?

Resurrection kicked sideways, catching the cowboy's leg. His bone snapped, pulling a pained scream from his lips. Haley lunged forward, caught the rigging between her fingers and pulled. The man's pain-filled eyes connected with hers. A suffocating sensation tightened her throat. Sarah's eyes.

"You," she gasped. She yanked the rigging free and released him. The force knocked her to the ground. She rose in a daze. Resurrection circled the arena, challenging all efforts to herd him toward the exit.

The cowboy looked at her with eyes full of pain, then recognition, and something else she couldn't quite define.

"I'm sorry," he screamed. "I'm sorry."

Resurrection pawed the dirt. The wild look in his eyes held Haley immobile. The noise dimmed and the world seemed to move in slow motion, sending her back to a place she didn't want to be and a time she didn't want to remember.

"Get him out of there, Haley," Chester yelled.

Haley closed her eyes, reliving in a flash the two incidents that had forever changed her life. Mitch and Resurrection. Two memories converged into one arena.

Resurrection charged. Two feet from her, he pivoted, catching Mitch between his horns and tossing him into the air. Mitch landed with a thud. The bull pounded his limp body.

Haley latched on to her shredded confidence. Ignoring her pain, she grabbed Resurrection's tail and yanked hard, then darted forward and smacked his shoulder. The bull spun around, pawed the ground and charged again. Haley moved in front of Mitch. Resurrection stopped, lifted his head and grunted, then pivoted and trotted out the gate. Mitch lay where he had fallen. Silence hung over the arena.

A new anguish seared her heart. The world spun around her, as though she was viewing someone else's life from a distance and not her own. Her knees buckled. Hap rushed through the gate and caught her before she hit the ground. Her whole body shook with a force that seemed to move the earth.

"I froze, Hap. I killed him. I killed Sarah's father."

Chapter Two

"You're set to go," the nurse said, taking the release form from Haley. "Take it easy, now. You're going to be sore for a while."

Haley slid off the exam table and touched the bandage covering her stitches. Every muscle protested. She stood up and moved toward the door. A call button blinked in the next room. "If you have any problems, don't hesitate to come back," the nurse said, disappearing behind the next curtain.

Little by little, warmth seeped back into Haley's veins, bringing with it a wretchedness of mind she'd never known before. She glanced at the clock. Nearly nine thirty. Barely an hour had passed since she'd agreed to let Hap bring her to the hospital and check her over. The emergency room was almost empty; the halls quiet, except for the steady blip of a monitor and the puff, hiss of the oxygen feed coming from a room down the hall. His room.

She had to pull herself together before facing Hap. The stitches in her forehead throbbed. Her body ached with reddening bruises. But bruises would heal. She wasn't so sure about her spirit.

She should leave and never look back, but the room drew her like an invisible magnet. Not the room. Him. He drew her. She'd put him here. In spite of everything, she couldn't walk away. What if he died? What if he lived? What would that mean for Sarah? If he found out about Sarah...

Her mouth moistened with bile. She inched down the hall and stopped at the glass partition, touching the scrawled name card beside the exam room. Mitch Jessup. She'd never thought about him as a person— until now. He'd been a monster in her nightmares. A name she'd chosen to forget—until now. Fear made her step back, but an unseen hand seemed to urge her forward. She stepped into the room.

Mitch's pale face blended into the pillowcase as though he was a part of it. Several bags hung from a pole, connected to him through IV tubes. The nurse pushed medication into one, then adjusted the fluid drip and looked up.

"Must have been some wreck," she said. "Are you a relative?"

Haley's hand shook. They *were* related. Through Sarah. "Sort of." She looked away. "How bad is he?"

"Stable for now. He's headed for surgery. The doctor's reviewing the X-rays. He'll be back," she said.

"I'll wait if you don't mind."

"It's good that he's not alone."

The nurse checked Mitch's pulse, gave Haley's arm a pat and left. Haley edged closer. A deep gash ran along his jaw. Cuts streaked his arms, some stitched, some held together by butterfly strips. She suspected

the worst injuries lay hidden beneath the sheet. His dark
hair stood out against the pillow. Sunken cheeks gave
his face a death-like appearance. Except for the shallow rise and fall of his chest, he looked like a corpse,
nothing like the man she'd met at the carnival that hot
July night eight years ago.

She'd lied to Pop about where she was going, knowing full well he would refuse to let her go. She'd seen
the tall, handsome cowboy the moment she'd entered
the gate—felt his eyes roam over her. He had a strong
square jaw with full, high cheekbones; crisp dark hair
that curled around his neck and a dazzling smile that
made her heart skip.

He was older, worldly and smooth, and just a tad
drunk. But not so drunk that he hadn't known what he
was doing. He was all the forbidden things she'd been
told to stay away from and everything that enticed an
innocent teen full of curiosity and whimsical dreams.

"I'm Haley," she'd offered.

His grin had turned her knees to Jell-O. "Hello,
Haley." He bowed. "Mitch Jessup, at your service. But
you can call me Lancelot. Seems my Guinevere has
stood me up."

"I'll be Gwen," she'd murmured.

He'd touched her arm. "I'd like that. Wanna ride the
carousel with me?" He'd leaned toward her, his lips
only inches from hers. The flirtation seemed so trivial
then. Not so, now.

The monitor blipped again. Haley jumped, stepped
back, then moved closer to the bed, blocking her
thoughts, holding the past behind the barrier that had
preserved her for so long.

She wanted him to suffer, not die. If he died, it would

be on her head, one more guilt to add to her list of sins. A sob escaped her lips. She closed her eyes and squeezed her head between her hands, unwilling to face him, unable to turn away.

"Haley," Mitch whispered. "It is you."

She opened her eyes and backed toward the door. Reason told her he couldn't hurt her. He was too busted up. But fear didn't know reason. He lifted his arm and groaned.

"Don't go."

Haley's legs shook, but she stopped inching toward the door. "I've hated you for so long." Her gaze drifted over him, avoiding his eyes. "I never wanted this."

His eyes glazed with pain. "I know. Not your fault. None of it…."

Tears welled in her eyes. "You took everything," she said. "My trust, my innocence. All you left in me was shame and fear."

His eyes closed. "I'm sorry."

"Sorry…isn't…enough. I want you to hurt, like you've hurt me."

His head moved back and forth as though her words haunted him. "If I could…change that night… God knows."

Haley clenched her teeth. "Don't you dare drop the God bomb on me."

Mitch's attempted smile ended in a grimace. "Felt that way once or twice." His body spasmed. He caught his breath. "God can heal this. Heal us."

"Us…?" She shrank from the word, from his pleading eyes. "I'll never forgive you for what you did."

"No." He looked incredibly tired. "Forgive yourself." He gasped and looked straight through her. "Give God the hurt. Only way past it." He gasped, then closed his gray-green eyes.

Sarah's eyes.

Haley's breath caught. Whatever else Mitch Jessup was, he was Sarah's father. Something inside her knotted like tangled rope.

Mitch's lips quivered. "Don't let what I did…keep you in darkness."

His chin dipped a tad, rose as though he were struggling to remain awake, then his head rolled sideways. Haley took a step forward and stopped.

Don't you dare die.

For a brief moment his chest stilled, then moved. She released her breath with the movement. Sorry wasn't enough to make up for what he'd destroyed. Mitch Jessup planted her child with violence. She wanted him to pay, not die.

Don't live in darkness. Let God have it.

Anger burned through her. God had abandoned her behind a vacant booth that night, holding a basket full of destroyed dreams. God had left her nurturing a life she hadn't asked for and wouldn't destroy.

The wounds God had allowed denied her all that she dreamed of, leaving her fearful of intimacy, unable to shed the shackles of the past, unable to give Sarah or herself the kind of life they wanted.

And now God had allowed this man back into her life. To what purpose? If God had forgiven Mitch Jessup after what he'd done, she wanted no part of God. There was no way she could ever forgive Mitch.

"Forgive me," he pleaded.

She shook her head. "I can't."

"I'm sorry." Anguish rang in his whispered words.

Haley hardened her heart. "It isn't enough."

She pivoted and rushed down the hall, away from his pleading eyes and wasting body. Someone called to her, but she didn't answer. She shoved the emergency door open and gulped in a cleansing breath, but the tepid air couldn't erase the smell of death any more than the night's darkness could hide what her mind held.

Hap's battered truck waited by the curb, empty. She yanked the door open and slid inside, resting her head against the worn upholstery. A few minutes later, he slid into the seat beside her.

"Somebody light yer tail on fire?" he said softly.

Haley jerked upright. Pain shot through her neck and sides. She wanted to leave this place and all of its memories behind and never look back. But now and forever, they would follow. Sarah was all that mattered. She must protect Sarah.

"Where were you?" she asked.

Hap handed her a steaming cup of coffee. "Looking for you. Didn't you hear me call to you? Ya scared that nice nurse right outta her shoes takin' off like that."

Haley took a big gulp, scalding her tongue, welcoming the pain that drew her back from the past. "I didn't see her."

Hap slanted a look her way and started the engine. His gray eyes filled with sympathy. "Saw the doc. He said you're going to be sore but okay. Not so sure about the other fella." Hap pulled out of the parking lot. "Thought about what you plan to tell Sarah?"

Haley glanced back at the hospital entrance. "That I'm battered but okay."

Hap eased into a turn with the same quiet manner he did everything. Even in the darkness, she could almost picture the well-oiled wheels in his mind rewinding the video, viewing and analyzing each event in detail. A streetlight illuminated his face. He glanced her way. In a flash she saw his hurt, not for himself, but for her and Sarah. Tears stung her eyes.

"You don't have to shade the facts no more. Your pop ain't here for you to protect, Haley. Even if he was, he'd understand. Do you plan to tell Sarah the truth about her father?" he asked without reproof or absolution.

"The truth, Hap? What is the truth?"

He turned the truck again, bringing the fairgrounds into view. "Wasn't sure until I saw you leaving that young man's room. Things never did set right with your story. Didn't happen the way you said, did it?" He reached a hand out and patted her arm. "What do you plan to do about it?"

His face turned toward her, his compassion covered by darkness. Haley's pulse hammered against her throat.

"Nothing. I can't, Hap. And for Sarah's sake, you won't either."

Jared raced into Mitch's room as the nurse injected something into Mitch's IV and unlocked the bed wheels. Tubes and needles poked from Mitch's body. Jared slid to a stop, too stunned to move.

"Jared?" the nurse asked, rolling Mitch's bed toward the elevator.

"Yes."

"He's been asking for you. You can go part of the way to surgery with us."

"How bad?" Jared said.

The nurse poked the elevator button, but didn't look up. "I've seen worse," she said, checking the IV flow.

Jared took Mitch's hand and felt a weak squeeze. "I'm here, Mitch. I understand you rode Resurrection."

"Yeah." Mitch's voice faded. "Rode him. Bull still won. You should've seen it."

"Guess that means you'll have to retire for a while on your winnings until you get better."

Mitch's hand went slack. Jared held on as the elevator ascended to the second floor.

"Won't get…better. Your meeting…" Mitch whispered.

"Went well," Jared said, shutting out the fear gnawing at his throat. "I should have been here."

Mitch's heavy lids opened, revealing eyes that seemed to see into another dimension. "We didn't know my ride would be rescheduled. God did. As it should be…" His voice faded. "Where is she?"

Jared glanced at the nurse. "Who?"

Mitch gulped in a breath. "Haley. She was here."

"There was a young woman here earlier but I think she left," the nurse explained. "She said she was family."

"Who's Haley, Mitch?" Jared asked.

Mitch struggled to stay awake. "I… Don't let her go…" He swallowed. "I…need to forgive…"

The words slurred together, not making sense. Jared bent closer. The connection with Mitch faded.

"You hang on, Mitch." Jared gripped the bed rail. "You hear me? Hang on. I need you."

"Promise," Mitch said.

"Anything. What?"

Mitch's fingers circled Jared's hand. "Haley gets the money." His eyes closed. "I'm so sorry. So sorry."

The elevator doors opened. A male attendant scrambled in to assist the nurse. Jared trotted to keep up as they pulled the gurney toward the surgery's double doors.

"Wait here," the attendant said. "Someone will check in with you later."

Jared's heart pounded against his chest.

Mitch's lips parted. "It's okay. I'm ready to go. Remember...promise."

Jared's gut clamped. "I'll remember, Mitch. But you're going to be all right."

The doors banged shut, cutting off Jared's words. He winced and stared through the glass until Mitch disappeared behind another set of doors. The hall was quiet, dark and empty. He stuffed his hands into his pockets and headed back to the waiting room.

Memories burned his mind—high school rodeos, football games, prom. Their parents had married when Jared was in the fifth grade and Mitch a year behind. Every important event in their lives had been shared. He raked a hand through his hair and glanced around the room. Empty paper cups and wadded tissues lay scattered in the waiting room, remnants from the last occupants. A hardback Bible sat isolated on a table.

Jared sank into the chair and ran his fingers over the gold lettering. For eight years Mitch had been out of his reach. He'd searched and prayed, desperate to keep Mitch out of trouble, but Jared hadn't been able to protect him. He couldn't protect him now. He squeezed the Bible between his hands. He couldn't lose his brother. Mitch had to live.

Jared bowed his head. *Please, God, don't let Mitch die.*

He passed the hours pleading to God on Mitch's behalf. Then the hospital paging system crackled.

"Code blue."

Chapter Three

Six days later, Jared parked behind the Fellowship Booth and headed down the midway. The memory of Walt Jessup's crumpled form at Mitch's gravesite was too raw to revisit. He'd do anything to ease his stepfather's pain. Focusing on the truth about Mitch's accident was a welcome diversion. He'd reviewed the playback tapes and asked Sam McIntosh, the association president, for an investigation, hoping what he believed he'd seen on the tapes was wrong. He paused beside an empty booth and watched the milling people.

"Clarabelle," he murmured to himself. The violet-eyed clown he'd spoken to the day Mitch died formed clearly in his mind. Clarabelle and Mitch's Haley were one and the same. An odd feeling of disappointment punched his gut. "Who are you?" he whispered. "And why would Mitch leave you his winnings without telling his family anything about you?"

He shut out the loud music and joined the flow of people. He'd frozen the replay tape from the moment where it seemed Mitch had recognized Haley, then played the rest in slow motion, right up to the moment

Mitch lay still in the dirt. The more he watched the re-play, the more he felt the tangible connection between the bullfighter and his brother. It was as though for a split second, the screen had come alive.

Something wasn't right. When he'd seen Haley near the bull pens, she'd spoken of facing fear. He'd seen her fear on the replay. Had her fear caused Mitch's death? If so, he couldn't let it go. Mitch deserved justice. Jared needed answers, and he was certain Haley had them.

He pictured her face again. His fingers and nose tin-gled as he remembered her soft skin beneath his steady-ing grasp and the fresh scent of the soap lingering on her flesh. He tensed, the memory surprising him.

The midway sparkled in the afternoon sun. Laugh-ter and music filled the air. The sun half hid behind a cluster of clouds, forming a halo of bright light with de-scending rays that seemed to touch the earth—almost as though the heavens rejoiced in catching Mitch's spirit and carrying it up to God.

God, Mitch made his peace with You. Help me make peace with his death.

He waited for God's peace to ease the pain. But noth-ing came. Only an emptiness left by Mitch's passing and lots of unanswered questions. The arena speaker hummed, announcing the line-up for barrel compe-titions. He shifted direction and weaved through the crowd toward the horse corrals. The announcer's voice echoed between the stands.

"Next up, in third place, a circuit favorite, Haley Clayton, on Spinner..."

Jared drew a sharp breath and edged along the fence toward the gate. A dun horse shot through the open-ing. The woman's face passed in a blur. Horse and rider moved in unison, cleared the first barrel and raced toward the second.

Jared glanced at the clock as the pair formed a cloverleaf around the second barrel. The big gelding tightened the circle around the third, but the woman's toe clipped the barrel edge, tipping it into the dirt. That mistake would knock her out of the big money. She ducked her head, leaned low across the horse's back and raced for the gate.

Jared slipped around the steel panel into the paddock area. If Mitch's death had affected her performance, it certainly hadn't pricked her enough to attend his funeral or send condolences.

Haley dismounted and stood beside the fence, her slender shoulders stooped in disappointment while her fingers stroked the white star on the gelding's forehead. A long braid hung down her back. The gold-fringe on her red shirt matched her hair. A narrow, silver-studded belt emphasized her small waist.

"Haley," he said, stopping behind her.

She turned and tipped her hat back. A pair of vivid violet eyes rounded with recognition. Her left eyebrow lifted a fraction. A tremor touched her smooth lips. Her skin glowed with a beauty previously hidden behind clown makeup. A yellowing bruise discolored her cheek. Bangs partially concealed a flesh-colored bandage on her forehead. She half turned and flipped the stirrup over the horse's back, then loosened the latigo holding the cinch in place.

"We meet again," he said.

A shadow passed over her face and quickly disappeared. "Are you following me?" she asked.

"No," he said, moving toward the horse's head. "I'm Jared Sinclair, Mitch Jessup's brother."

Her eyes flattened and went cold. Her fingers curled around the buckle like a lifeline. She stepped back, catching her spurs in the dirt. Jared reached for her elbow but she pulled away. "I'd like to talk to you about what happened the night Mitch died."

She focused her gaze on his boots. "I'm sorry your brother died, but I don't see how going over it will help you. It won't change what happened."

"Maybe not. But I still need to hear it from someone who was close to him."

"We weren't close." Haley lifted her head, her beautiful eyes focusing on his chin. Wariness darkened them, turning them almost purple.

"I meant close by," Jared said. Suspicion nudged his mind.

"Lots of people were there. Why don't you talk to them?"

Mitch's voice rang through Jared's mind. *Don't let her go... I...need to forgive.*

"I want to talk to *you*. Mitch asked me to find you," Jared said. If Haley was responsible for Mitch's death, there was no way he was going to just let her walk away from it like nothing had happened. "I'd like to know why," he said.

Her face paled. "I can't imagine why."

"I think you do."

She caught her breath, then shifted the reins back and forth in her hands.

Jared felt her fear, sensed deception at work, but if he wanted answers, truthful answers, he'd have to use softer tactics. "Please, Haley. I just need to know what happened to my brother."

Doubt flickered across her face. She dropped her gaze. "I can tell you what I remember. Everything happened so fast, some details are jumbled," she murmured.

She seemed to choose her words carefully. Jared moved to the horse's side, forcing her to look right at him.

"Try. I want to know everything that happened between the time Mitch entered the arena and the time he was carried out. And I want to hear it from you."

Her gaze shifted toward the exit. She buried her fingers in the gelding's mane and combed through the thick hairs. For someone who had nothing to hide, she was acting guilty about something. Disappointment centered in Jared's chest. The sights and sounds dimmed until it seemed the only ones occupying this space were he and Haley—and the mystery surrounding her and Mitch.

"There isn't much to tell," she said. "His ride was normal until the dismount. His hand got caught in the rigging. I pulled it free and we got knocked in the dirt. The impact shook us both." She fidgeted, letting silence fall between them. Her voice caught, then lowered. "Resurrection got to him before I did."

There was more in what she didn't say, in the way her eyes refused to meet his, the way her voice trembled with something more than just sorrow or regret. Mitch deserved to be heard and Jared intended to see this through, no matter how painful it proved to be.

"You knew this bull," he said. "You knew how dangerous he was. That's why you were at the pens that day."

She nodded. Her gaze swept the ground, then glazed as though her thoughts had taken a different direction.

"I knew him. He's dangerous." She murmured so low he barely heard and was uncertain if she was referring to Mitch or the bull.

"You knew Mitch, too, didn't you, Haley?"

Her head snapped up. "No."

"You were with him at the hospital."

"I was there anyway." She touched the bandage on her forehead.

"Why didn't you stay?"

"I couldn't."

"Why?" he probed.

"I just couldn't. Why should I?"

"Did he say anything to you?"

Haley flinched. Fear widened her eyes, touching him in a way that made him regret his harshness but heightened his need for the truth.

The question snaked between them like a whip and struck her. She remembered only too well Mitch's last words. Words that still echoed in her head.

Forgive yourself.

How dare he tell her to forgive herself after what he'd done. She shook the memory loose.

"I think maybe he thought I was someone else."

"He didn't. He was very certain about your name and about wanting me to find you." Jared's brown eyes probed hers.

"I have to go," she said. "If you're looking to blame someone, I can't help you. I did what I could and I'm truly sorry."

"Sorry? Sorry that he died or that your moment of fear may have caused his death?"

Jared's square jaw clenched, giving his rugged face a determined, hard look. Haley's stomach roiled. He was too close to the truth for comfort. If he found out about Sarah, what would happen then? Panic rose to her throat. He emitted the same power she'd sensed the first time she'd run into him outside the bull pens six days ago. How much like Mitch was Jared? *Don't make an enemy of this man*, she cautioned herself.

She finished loosening the cinch, aware that he watched, gauged and absorbed every move. The sun dipped toward the distant mountains. Haley shivered in spite of the heat. She mustn't give him cause to pursue his questions.

Jared's glance sharpened. "How well did you know my brother, Haley?"

She lifted her chin, forcing herself to stare into his eyes. She would not cower before this man or any other. And she wouldn't own Mitch's sins. Heaven knew she had enough of her own to atone for.

"I told you I didn't *know* him. We met briefly several years ago. I didn't see him again until the night he rode Resurrection."

"But you *had* met him before so why did you deny it? You told the nurse at the hospital you were family."

"Meeting doesn't constitute knowing. I was in that arena with him. Two years ago I was laying in the same spot that he was. I needed to know and the doctors wouldn't tell me anything." She shrugged.

"Then why not just say so?" Silence hung between them like dust in an arena.

Her heart dropped. Caught in the deception. She glanced at her watch and moved around Spinner. "I don't know.

"I watched the replays."

Her fist clenched in the animal's mane. "Is there a

point to all this? You weren't in there. You don't know. I have to go."

Jared stepped aside. His hand, large and rough, touched her wrist. She shivered again.

"Don't go far, Haley," he said. "There's more to this than what you've told me. I can find truth in the most unlikely places. You and I are not through."

Haley tugged on Spinner's reins and rushed from the paddock without looking back. Jared had her so confused she didn't know which way was up. Behind the barns, she bent over, rested her hands on her knees, and gulped in waves of fresh air, but it didn't stem the nausea rising to her throat. Spinner nuzzled her neck and nickered.

She led the horse into the barn. When she chanced a look behind her there was no sign of Jared, but she could still feel his power, the air of authority surrounding him, the tingle along her skin that remained long after she'd pulled away from him.

He'd thrown down an invisible gauntlet, and instinct told her he would stop at nothing to discover the truth.

The sun dropped behind the horizon, painting the sky a dark orange. Hap plugged the horse trailer lights into his truck and rechecked the hitch and safety chains, while Haley hooked the camper to her truck.

"Never known you to run from nothing," he said.

Haley placed a finger to her lips and watched Sarah stuff a horse blanket into Hap's truck cab. If she and Sarah could get safely back to Hap's place, Jared would have a hard time finding them.

"There's no reason to stay when there's work waiting at home."

"It's not fair," Sarah said, sticking her lips out. "Why don't you go? Hap and I can come later. After the finals. We never miss the finals."

"We'll go together," Haley said.

Sarah's eyes watered in frustration. "Can I go and at least say goodbye to my friends?"

Haley's heart thudded like a trapped rabbit. "Go. But stay in sight of the truck. I don't want to have to come looking for you. You've got ten minutes."

Hap's silent disapproval cut into the evening air louder than the music coming from the midway. She never should have told him everything.

"Runnin' stinks, don't it?" he said.

Haley moved toward her own truck, which seemed to groan beneath the weight of the camper. "I'm protecting Sarah."

"He's her family, too."

"How do I know he's any different than Mitch?"

"You don't."

Haley locked the camper door and leaned her head against the cool metal. "Don't, Hap. Don't take his side. What if he finds out about Sarah?"

Hap patted her arm, then squeezed her shoulder.

"Sarah's mine. She can't know where she came from. She's too young." Haley turned and leaned against him.

"You didn't do nothin' wrong, girl. You can't run from this."

Haley's eyes misted. "Sarah doesn't need any family but you and me."

"Maybe God thinks otherwise."

"Don't," she said.

Hap's rough hand stroked her hair. "Ain't you forgettin'? Sarah's God's child. There's a reason He placed her with you—a reason He allowed her to come into this world the way she did. And there's a reason this man is here now."

Haley spun around, grabbed the camper jack and rammed it into the truck bed. "Well, I wish God would enlighten me."

"Maybe you ain't listenin'. Wouldn't be the first time," he said.

Haley jammed her hat onto her head. "I suppose you're going to tell me, too, that God had a reason for Mitch being here and a reason that I...played a part in killing him." She brushed away a tear.

"You didn't kill nobody."

"If it had been any other cowboy..."

"What's written is written, honey. And God holds the pen that does the writin'."

She kicked a rock and sent it flying across the parking lot. "I don't want him poking around."

Hap stroked his chin. "Secrets won't stay hidden forever."

Haley caught Sarah's glance, the rebellious look still in her eyes.

Hap motioned Sarah to wait. "Face the man now. Don't wait for him to come to you."

"Tell him what his brother was and seal our fate? Not a chance."

Hap raked a hand through his silver hair and sighed. "Stay and finish this. I'll take Sarah home with me and you won't need to mention her at all."

Haley rubbed her arms, feeling a chill in the warm air.

"You need to make him see that you *are* sorry the boy died." Hap pinned her with his gaze. "You are sorry, aren't you?"

"You know I am."

"He needs to that." Hap tipped his hat back.

"I *do* feel responsible, Hap. Responsible and… relieved. It was an accident, but with Mitch gone, I thought that now it was finally over. I could put an end to all those bad dreams. What does that say about me?"

"That you're human and that you can't do this alone." Hap scuffed his toe in the dust. "Haley, you gotta let God help with this."

Haley glanced at Sarah and swallowed the knot in her throat. Hap could very well be right. But trusting didn't come easy. Especially where God was concerned. She wasn't sure it ever would. "I can't. But I will stay. I'll finish this."

Hap gave a satisfied nod and loaded the horses in his trailer. "I'll get the rest of the stuff from the barn," he said.

The memory of Jared's dark eyes filled her mind, how their warmth the day he'd bumped in to her outside the Fellowship tent had both touched and frightened her, how they'd gleamed like hard shards of rock when he'd questioned her about the accident and knowing Mitch.

She'd backed herself into a corner, and he knew it. If he pushed her too far, he wouldn't like what she had to say. She rechecked the hitch and chains on the camper and fished in her pocket for the keys. Footsteps crunched the gravel behind her.

"I'm almost ready, Hap."

She turned around and stared straight into Jared's flashing dark eyes.

"Going somewhere?" he asked.

She searched frantically for Hap, then saw Sarah wave to her friends and skip toward her.

Chapter Four

Jared watched the child approach. Her movements smacked with familiarity, rekindling old memories of another time and place, memories of a young boy with unruly jet-black hair tagging along behind him with the same bounce in his step and tilt to his head. The puzzle pieces were starting to come together. The first shock wave knocked him like a mule's kick.

Every movement right down to her furrowed brow bore traces of the brother he'd lost. Her black hair refused to be tamed by braids and streamed in a tangled mass around her face. She lifted her chin and darted a look at him. Another shock wave ripped through Jared, pain so intense it stole his breath.

"Hi. I'm Sarah," she said holding his gaze with gray-green eyes.

Jared opened his mouth but nothing came out. This child was a feminine replica of Mitch. She had to be Mitch's daughter. Obviously Haley hadn't expected to see Mitch again. That was the reason he'd seen recognition and shock on the replay tapes, the reason her answers were less than satisfactory. Sarah was the secret

Haley was hiding, the secret that may have cost Mitch his life.

The color drained from Haley's face. Like a bear protecting her young, she moved between him and Sarah. "Sarah Rose. Go to the barn and find Hap," she said.

"But, Mom—"

"Go. Now."

Sarah bounced an uncertain look between them and raced toward the barn. Jared watched until she was out of sight. He wanted to reach out and touch her, make sure she was real. She was so like Mitch it made him ache. Haley had kept Sarah from Mitch, from Walt, from all of them. Why? Anger waged a tug of war inside him.

"She's Mitch's daughter, isn't she, Haley? Did he know?" The question nearly choked him. "What really happened in the arena the night Mitch died?"

He heard the steel in his own voice. She winced, then grabbed his arm and pulled him away from the truck, away from the barns and from Sarah. "She's *my* daughter. Go away. You have no right to hound me."

"Mitch's death gives me that right," he said looking toward the barn. Jared shook with rage. Only God would be able to help her if he was right. "Look me in the eye and tell me that child isn't his and that you didn't deliberately keep her from him. From her grandparents."

She couldn't. She knew it and so did he. "Sarah has a right to know her family," he said. "We just lost Mitch, and Sarah is a living part of him. We have a right to know her." His chest tightened. He fisted his hands against his sides.

Haley flattened herself against the truck. "You have

no rights and neither did Mitch. He lost that the second he left me behind that—"

She covered her mouth with her hand. She wouldn't—couldn't—think about that night or speak of it ever. Not with this man or any other. The fury in Jared's eyes terrified her. The realization of what he wanted, expected, was unthinkable.

She looked toward the barn and saw Sarah pulling Hap toward them, his bum leg sliding in the dirt, kicking dust into the evening air. "I can't talk to you about this now."

He followed her gaze. His eyes narrowed when they rested on Sarah, then softened. For a moment she thought he would refuse, that he would lie in wait, snatch Sarah away and disappear. A hand clenched around her soul.

"When?" he said.

"Tomorrow. I'll meet you at the bull pens in the morning."

His gaze shifted back to her and hardened. "Be there, Haley. If you run, I'll find you."

He spun around without looking back and disappeared into the crowd, his threat hanging in the air like heavy fog. Haley's whole body shook. She gripped the truck and gulped in a breath, felt Hap and Sarah's presence behind her, then Hap's hand touched her shoulder and Sarah's small fingers closed around hers.

"Mom? Are you okay? Who was that man?"

The endless night finally broke, sending a streak of red across the horizon. Haley headed toward the bull pens taking comfort in the familiar surroundings. Meeting Jared felt safer with Hap and Sarah out of

Wyoming and back in Colorado, even if she hadn't answered Sarah's questions to satisfaction. One more strike against Jared Sinclair.

The sounds and smells around the stock pens rose in the morning air. Haley slowed her step, then stopped. Jared stood in front of Resurrection's pen, his profile outlined beneath a wide-brimmed hat. His arms were draped over the top rail, his eyes locked on the bull. She wondered if he, too, had been avoiding Resurrection's pen. Even from a distance, she saw his chin tighten, then his hand brushed over his face.

Her heart squeezed. He was an enemy, a threat to herself and Sarah. She couldn't see him as a man grieving a loss, but she couldn't ignore it either.

"I'm here," she said.

Jared lifted his head, turned and faced her. Shadows lingered beneath his eyes. He hadn't shaved and the stubble darkening his face made him forbidding. She took a backward step.

"I should have been here," Jared said.

His pain mingled with her own. Haley ignored the warning buzzing in her head. "It wouldn't have mattered," she said. "There are no rules with Resurrection. You couldn't have stopped what happened." She hesitated a moment, then added, "Neither could I."

"We'll never know for certain," he said pulling his jacket collar up. "But that's not why we're here, is it? You see, Haley, it's not the beginning or the end that matters most now. It's the space in between."

The space that included Sarah. The beginning did matter, to her, but he loved his brother. Sympathy vanished in a rush of white-hot anger. "Don't presume you know me or anything about me."

His gaze traveled her face, then locked on her eyes. Haley wished she could crawl inside his head and know what he was thinking. This guessing was like falling off a cliff in slow motion.

"That's the whole point. None of us really *know* anything, do we? I'll make this clear and direct. Sarah has a grandfather who feels he's lost everything. The truth is, he hasn't." Tense silence stretched between them. "Mitch isn't here to speak for himself, so I'll do it for him. He deserves justice for what you kept from him. I want you and Sarah to come to South Dakota to meet…"

Haley gasped, certain Resurrection had gut kicked her, but the animal stood quietly, his nose buried in a mound of alfalfa. Her legs threatened to buckle. She shook her head.

Jared lifted a brow. "Is that a no?" he said in a harsh, raw voice.

She looked up, forcing herself to meet his gaze without flinching. "That's a never."

"Mitch made bad choices for a lot of years," Jared said. "In the last few months, he'd turned his life around. He was pulling things together. Trying to right the wrongs."

"And for that he deserves…what?"

His eyes flashed. Haley moved to the corral and stared at Resurrection. Jared moved beside her. "After I left you last night, I thought a lot about everything that's happened. Mitch walked away from you and Sarah. Away from his responsibilities. I get that. I think I understand some things that I didn't before."

Haley's hand fisted. "You understand nothing!" She raised her fist to strike him. He caught her hand, his grip around her wrist powerful and painful. She trembled but stared him down.

If he wanted the truth, she could stomp him into the dust with it. But she couldn't revisit a place that had taken her years to get past. His grip tightened. She struggled, kicking at his legs.

"Haley. Stop it."

He released her. She stepped back. Several people were staring at them. She turned away and gripped the corral panels with shaking hands. The wound that had never really healed ripped open.

"Sometimes people aren't what you think they are," she said. "Sometimes by the time you figure that out, the chute's already opened and it's too late to change the ride. Don't do this." He didn't touch her again, but she felt his hold, like a noose around her neck.

"This isn't negotiable, Haley. You can tell your daughter about her father or leave it to a court. Bottom line is she has more family than just you." He pulled a pen and paper from his pocket and jotted down a number. "It's time to make things right," he said, his tone softening. "If I don't hear from you in three days, I'll come to Colorado and get you."

Haley's throat closed. "You wouldn't."

Jared took her hand and crammed the paper into her palm. "Three days. Call me."

Four hours later Haley pulled into the gravel lane leading to Hap's ranch. She backed the truck and camper under the old pole barn, shut off the engine and leaned back. Gray weathered boards with peeling white paint covered the old house. The outbuildings were ancient and in need of repair, but it was home. The only real home she'd ever known. Her throat tightened. She opened the door and slid from the seat. Across the barnyard, a door slammed. Gravel crunched beneath running feet. Sarah slid to a stop beside the truck, then threw her arms around Haley's waist.

"You're back. I'm sorry I was mad at you last night. Hap said you had to take care of a grown-up thing."

Haley looked into Sarah's gray-green eyes. The innocence and resiliency of her own childhood seemed like a distant memory but one she needed to preserve in Sarah.

How much she had lost. But how much she had gained.

"Hap's in the barn. Annie had her puppies last night. He said he needed to talk to you as soon as you got home."

"Then I'll go see him."

Sarah headed for the house. Haley crossed the barnyard and pulled the barn door open. Bales of fresh hay filled the usually musty barn with a fresh, clean scent.

Hap rose, lifting two squirmy mounds of black and white in his gnarled hands. "Born last night, just after we got home," he said. "Nice pups. Should bring a good price." He set the pups down and avoided looking at her. "Sam McIntosh called."

Air whooshed from Haley's lungs. "Sam?" She managed to choke out the association president's name. "What did he want?"

"Seems someone has requested an inquiry into Mitch's accident. Sam thought you should know."

Someone. Jared.

Haley's legs wobbled. She slid onto a bale and stared at the ground.

"You're on leave until the official inquiry is closed," Hap said quietly.

Suspended. Her livelihood and hard-earned reputation hung in the balance, dangling from a hangman's noose. And she knew who held the rope.

"Sam said it's just a formality and he was sure the ruling would be in your favor. Guess I don't need to ask how your meeting with Sinclair went."

Three days passed like a year. Every day Haley watched the road, waiting for Jared to make good on his promise. He was never far from her thoughts, and she hated the way he'd taken root in her mind and stolen her sense of security and peace. She sent Sarah into town with Hap, knowing full well it would incur Jared's anger if he arrived and she wasn't there, but if he thought she would lie down and play dead so he could issue ultimatums and walk all over her, he could think again.

She drew Annie's pup close to her face, relishing the softness of newborn puppy. Tiny claws flailed against her cheek. The black nose scrunched, then a wet tongue latched around her nose and suckled. The scent of puppy breath lingered on her skin, fresh and new, helpless and innocent. Innocent. The word seemed to taunt her.

Mourning doves cooed in the barn rafters. Haley lifted her head and watched the sun slant through the weathered boards. This place had once been her refuge. As a child she used to come here and pour her heart out to God, just as Sarah sometimes did now. She had faith then. It all seemed like another lifetime. If she sought God's help again, would He hear or turn a deaf ear to her plea like that night so long ago?

"Lord God." The desperate call brought tears to her eyes, remembrances of a time when her faith had been strong floated through her mind. "I haven't asked You for anything for a long time. Please hear me. I love my daughter. Don't take her from me," she murmured.

She sensed someone watching her, twisted around and caught her breath. Jared stood in the doorway, his hair glistening in the morning sun. So this was the answer to her prayer. She set her jaw, but her heart did a treacherous lurch. He was more attractive than she remembered, but that was his only saving grace. His heart was as black as his shadow.

"Do you always make a habit of sneaking up on people?" she asked, placing the pup at Annie's side.

"Only the ones I think might do something foolish, like run away," he said, watching her. "You didn't call. There wasn't anyone at the house and I'm a little surprised that I found you here."

"Sarah's at a birthday party. And where would I go? You made it clear that you'd hunt me to the ends of the earth."

He smiled, transforming harshness to handsome. "So you got the message."

"I got it. You've managed to steal my income and taint my reputation, so tell me, Mr. Sinclair, where would I go and what would I use to go with?"

A hint of compassion glistened in his eyes, angering her.

"You aren't fired, Haley, just sidelined for a while. I want the truth. I want justice. The investigation is my assurance that you won't disappear."

She lifted her chin. "I'm sorry Mitch died. Whatever our differences, I never wanted that to happen." She rose and moved around him, giving her easier access to the door. Her chest pounded, spreading fear through every pore in her body. "Does it make you feel better to sideline me without pay?"

Jared detected no pretense in her voice. Watching her with the pup, he'd caught a glimpse of another dimension to this woman. She was beautiful, but he sensed more depth to her than the women he knew Mitch usually associated with. This one stirred his curiosity.

"No, Haley. I'm not happy about this investigation, but I have to do it—for Mitch. And that brings me to the other reason I'm here."

"There's more than locking us in your trunk and whisking us away?"

Jared ground his teeth, but held his temper. He wasn't at all sure what he was about to do was right or ethical, but the request was the last thing he'd promised Mitch and no matter how much it galled him, he'd see it through.

"Mitch requested that you received the bounty money from his ride," Jared said, gauging her reaction.

Her eyes sparked. "Payment for services rendered? Blood money to salve a deathbed conscience," she said. Pink stained her cheeks. "I don't want it. Find some other cause to donate it to." Her voice simmered with bitterness.

"This $30,000 cost Mitch his life. If you don't want it, think of Sarah." Jared's misgivings increased by the minute. He had no doubt she meant every word. Still, her reactions ran deep enough to justify an act of revenge. A woman scorned thing. He didn't want to wrap his mind completely around that, but he'd promised

Mitch, and that promise must be kept, no matter what. The weight of the investigation settled on his shoulders.

"Look at me, Haley."

Her violet gaze touched him. Her hands twisted nervously. Something flickered far back in her eyes. Jared's chest squeezed. She was afraid of him. The realization left him with a feeling of emptiness. She looked away. The clip holding her hair caught a flash of sun, sending rainbow prisms dancing across the ground, then in a flash of color, they splashed across his shirt.

Their tiny points seemed to stab into his chest. He wanted to know about her—her hopes, dreams, ambitions. Most of all, he wanted the truth and for the first time, dreaded the consequences it might bring. Justice belonged with God. Why couldn't he leave it there?

She whirled around and stepped into the sunlight. Jared followed, pulling an envelope from his pocket.

"This is a cashier's check made out to you." He held it out.

"You have no idea what you're asking me to do."

"Take it, Haley."

She stared at the envelope, then back at him. She took it, holding it away from her as though it were contaminated.

"How soon can you and Sarah be ready to go?" he asked.

Her gaze flew to his face. "Go?"

"I already told you that Sarah meeting Mitch's father wasn't an option."

Haley wadded the envelope in her fist. "She doesn't know about this."

"You've had three days."

"I tried. I just couldn't tell her." The air between them sizzled.

"Three days isn't nearly enough time to explain the last eight years." She lifted her chin. "I won't expose her to Mitch's family."

"Expose her?" Jared swallowed his anger, hating this fine line between righting Mitch's wrong and delivering justice for his brother's death. "You act like we're all a bunch of ax murders or something."

"That would be better than the truth," she murmured.

Jared raked a hand through his hair. "And what is the truth according to Haley? You and Mitch had a relationship that went bad, but you haven't given his family a chance. We just want a chance to know Mitch's daughter. We would never hurt you. I would never hurt you."

Shadows deepened under her eyes. Her face closed, as if guarding a secret. "You already have. How can you ask me to trust that the son isn't like the father?" Her voice broke.

Jared noted eyes filled with sorrow, pain and fear. He saw it, felt it, and it tugged at something inside him. If Mitch used her and dumped her, turning her life upside down, how did he expect her to feel? She hadn't been given any reason to think his family was any different. And he hadn't helped. He'd pushed her into a corner, taken things into his own hands instead of letting God take the lead. He fisted a hand under his chin.

"Walt needs his granddaughter, Haley, as much as I believe she needs him," he said softly. "Mitch's death crushed him. She could give him hope again. A reason to keep on going."

Haley looked away. "You're putting a lot of responsibility on the shoulders of a seven-year-old."

He moved closer, stopping when he saw her step back. She was right. It hadn't bothered him that his demand to come to South Dakota wasn't fair to Haley, but it wasn't fair to Sarah either. That did bother him.

"All right. I have a proposition for you," he said. "You come first. Get to know Walt and my mother and judge for yourself."

Haley pulled her tattered courage around her like a piece of shredded cloth. It was a fair request. Better than the strong-arm tactic he'd been using. A flicker of hope lit her heart then suspicion edged her closer to caution.

"You must have a lot of confidence in your family's ability to change my mind. What's your angle, Sinclair?"

"No angle, Haley."

"If there's no angle, then there's something I want in return."

A hint of admiration lit his eyes. "I'm listening."

"I'll come for a week. And if at week's end I feel Sarah will be hurt by knowing these people, it's my call to make as her mother and you'll let us both go."

Haley could have milked a cow in the silence that followed. His gaze never left her face. She held it, challenge for challenge, in spite of her fear.

He gave a curt nod. "You're a hard woman."

"When the well-being of my daughter is concerned, I am."

"All right."

"How do I know you'll keep your word?" she asked.

"How do I know you'll keep yours—or be fair in your judgment?" he countered. "It seems we've reached a point where we have to trust each other. At least a little." He hesitated a moment, then held out his hand. "We have a deal?"

Haley felt the envelope bunched in her left hand. She took his hand with her right and felt a shudder run through her body. Sarah mustn't know the truth. Tainted blood money or not, Jared had given her the funds to disappear with Sarah, if it came to that. Accepting his invitation to go to the ranch would buy her time. That was enough because the truth was, she would never, ever subject Sarah to Mitch's family.

Chapter Five

Two days later, Jared sat in the kitchen of his South Dakota ranch watching his mother, Adele, vigorously scrub a plate that he suspected wasn't all that dirty. His mother's response concerning Haley and Sarah had been guarded. He hadn't told Walt yet, more at his mother's insistence than anything else.

"I'm not sure what you hope to accomplish having Haley come here, Jared. This could get ugly."

"Or not," Jared said. That he was very aware of Haley as a woman was undeniable, but maybe that's what had gotten Mitch into trouble. "You don't think this could be good for Walt?"

"Maybe. But until Haley is done judging us, I'd rather Walt not know who she is or why she's here." Adele dried her hands and turned around. "Keep your friends close but your enemies closer? If that's how you're viewing this, son, you're doing it for the wrong reason. If you're going to press this issue of incorporating Haley and Sarah into this family, you need to be looking at what's possible in Haley, not what's lacking."

Jared swirled the cold coffee around the mug and

shifted uncomfortably. He was looking for a reason to blame Mitch's death on something other than God's timing. It was easier to blame someone else than accept that God would take Mitch when he was finally at a place he could do the most good. One day, it would be okay. Just not today.

Adele crossed the room and touched his shoulder. "Whatever happened between Mitch and Haley, he left her to raise a child on her own. Jared, that's devastating."

Jared dropped his gaze. He hadn't looked at it in that light. His mother was right. It's what his father had done. If anyone understood Haley and her reasons for doing what she did, his mother would.

"I don't doubt Haley loves Sarah," Jared said, remembering her whispered prayer in the barn. "I just think there's more she hasn't told us. The rest of us deserve to love Sarah, too."

Jared's conscience nudged. Was God using Haley to force him to deal with his own judgmental spirit? He'd seen something while watching her with the pup. She'd been vulnerable, raw with hurt. He didn't want to believe she was the calculating monster he'd made her out to be in his mind. Indecision divided his loyalty. He fisted his hands.

How could he lead others to faith if he placed his need for justice above Haley's need for God or above his trust that God would make all things just in His own way and time?

"Haley needs to see that we're not bad people."

"I agree, but I'm worried how all this is going to affect Walt," Adele said.

Jared patted her hand. "I would never do anything

to hurt Walt, you know that." He placed his hands on her shoulders. "All of us need to heal."

"Even Haley?" Adele asked.

Jared nodded. "Even Haley."

"Then I trust that what you're doing is honorable, Jared. *If* it's the real reason you're doing it," Adele said. Her dark eyes probed his. "Have you examined your own heart and prayed hard about this?"

Jared's conscience pricked. He'd made this deal on the tail of a whim, because he'd glimpsed Haley's pain, but his mother had given him a lot more to think about. No matter which way he looked at bringing Haley here, it still felt right.

"She'll see we're good for Sarah and Sarah's good for us. Walt can have a piece of Mitch to hold onto, and maybe Sarah can help Walt through this dark place he's in right now."

Adele pressed her lips together. "You speak of Sarah. But who will help Haley, Jared? You seem to forget that God doesn't renovate, He recreates. A child is easy to love, but if you find out you're wrong in your assumptions about Haley, are you prepared to support her instead of antagonizing her?"

Jared's mind floundered. His tunnel vision hadn't broadened to include that, but if helping Haley face her monsters is what it took for Sarah to come...

"I guess I will."

"Then you might start by dropping this investigating." Adele crossed back to the sink and folded the dish towel. "Walt isn't well, Jared. I don't want him hurt. I want it clear that I don't want Walt to know about Sarah yet. Not until we know for sure what Haley plans to do. Do you really plan to let them go if that's what she decides?"

Jared looked away. "I hope it won't come to that."

Adele shook her head and sighed. "I expect we'll be doing a powerful lot of praying in the next week. What time is she coming?"

"Late this evening."

Adele's brow wrinkled. "I guess I'd better get busy." She headed toward the stairs, then turned. "Jared. You're certain about this?"

"Given the information I have to work with, I'm as certain as I can be." He watched her leave and brushed a hand across his eyes then picked up the phone and called Sam McIntosh. This could all backfire and hurt the people he loved most. All because he hadn't let God take the lead. Jared bowed his head.

Lord God. I should have asked for Your guidance. I'm sorry. You said all things work together for good. Please work this out for good.

A half hour past Hot Springs, South Dakota, Haley pulled onto a narrow two-lane road. She set Jared's directions on the seat, saw her hand shake and swallowed hard.

"Pull it together, Haley. It's just a week."

She'd banked the money and researched an escape for Sarah and herself. She had a plan. After they were settled, somehow, someway, she'd get word to Hap.

At the end of the road, a huge barn surrounded by a white fence came into view. A low-roofed bunkhouse was attached to one side of the barn. Not far away, a sprawling two-story log house nestled in a clearing of towering pines that resembled castle guards. Potted plants swayed in the breeze caught by the wide veranda.

Haley sucked in a breath and swallowed down a feeling of homecoming. If this had been any place other than Jared's she would have loved it—and so would Sarah. Sarah assumed that Haley had taken a quick job that required her to leave immediately. While the assumption wasn't entirely true, it wasn't a lie.

Hap wasn't happy either, but he knew why and where she was going and had once again told her to be up front with Jared about Mitch. The truth hurts, he'd said, but it's the lie that leaves the scars. It seemed her whole life revolved around half-truths. She hated it. But the alternative was much worse. What had happened to the level-headed young woman of yesterday?

The truth will set you free. The words whispered from deep in her memory.

Anger knotted inside her. The truth would destroy Sarah. Haley stopped the truck, shut off the engine and got out. Jared opened the front door and stepped onto the veranda, followed by a slender elderly woman with a riot of silver curls framing her striking features. She walked off the porch with a spry step that defied her age. Jared followed.

"You must be Haley," she said. "I'm Adele Jessup, Jared's mom." Her dark eyes mirrored Jared's.

Haley gazed uncomfortably from Jared to Adele. "I hope my being here isn't an inconvenience, Mrs. Jessup."

"Call me Adele, dear. Everyone does. And you're welcome here as long as we're clear that I don't want my husband hurt any more than you want your daughter hurt. Walt doesn't know. He just thinks you're a friend of Mitch and Jared and you're here on a short stay. Unless you plan on letting Sarah be a part of our family, I don't want him to know anything else."

Blunt and to the point, just like Hap. Adele's warm smile took the bite out of her words.

"I don't want anyone hurt, either," Haley said.

She felt Jared's hands on her shoulders. For a brief instant, a feeling of being protected consumed her. She clawed her way through the ridiculousness of that emotion and pulled her suitcase from the truck bed, shying away from Jared's touch. The chill of loneliness followed. Jared reached for the handle, his hand brushing hers.

"I'll take that," he said.

"Afraid I might bolt?"

"Yes." He smiled, softening the words.

He seemed more relaxed than she'd ever seen him. But why wouldn't he be? He was in home ground. She was the intruder.

Haley bit back a retort. She didn't want to make a scene in front of Adele. Instinctively, she liked Adele Jessup, though that feeling hadn't been tested. Could she believe Jared? He was a man, and men lied. Mitch had lied. Look where that landed her. But Jared wasn't Mitch. They didn't share blood.

Adele's watchful eyes held questions she was too polite to voice. "Walt wanted to be here, but he's had a bout with his blood pressure again. His medication makes him sleep, so I doubt you'll meet him tonight."

Haley released a breath. Pardoned. Reprieved. Stayed. She didn't have to face Mitch's father tonight. The reason didn't matter.

"I've got some things in the barn to finish up," Jared

said. "I'll just be a few minutes." He set the suitcase on the porch.

His gaze caught Haley's. She couldn't look away. He turned and disappeared, swallowed up by the deepening shadows.

"You must be hungry," Adele said. "I have turkey sandwiches and tea ready."

"You shouldn't have gone to so much trouble."

"No trouble. It's nice to have another woman in the house. All this testosterone gets a bit overwhelming at times."

Haley's pulse jumped, throbbing like an old wound that ached on a rainy day. The vision of Mitch abandoning her behind the carnival booth rose to the surface. She stumbled on the step, let go of Adele's arm and gripped the handrail. Coming here was a mistake.

Adele swung the front door open. "Welcome to our home." She ushered Haley inside.

The focal point from the doorway was a massive moss rock fireplace. Family pictures encased in traditional Western frames graced the halved log serving as a mantle.

Haley focused on a picture of Mitch. One arm was linked with Jared's, the other with an older man she guessed was Walt Jessup. She stopped and stared at the pictures. She was doing the one thing she'd vowed never to do—walking into Mitch's world of her own free will.

Adele's gaze followed Haley's. "This was taken a few weeks before Mitch died," she said.

Haley's heartbeat drummed in her ears.

A few months before I killed him.

That infernal voice refused to be silenced. She wanted to crush it between her hands and push it away.

She hadn't wanted Mitch to die, but she hadn't wanted him to live either. She just wanted him to leave her alone.

"I'm sorry for your loss," Haley said. "My Pop died a few years ago. It's hard to lose someone you love."

Adele touched the frame, then she turned and smiled. "We did love Mitch, but he wasn't perfect. We know that, Haley. I'm sorry he hurt you."

Like Hap, Adele inspired confidences. Haley longed for a woman to confide in, to trust. Her chest tightened. She waited for the bottom to fall out of her world, much like it had when she knew she was pregnant with Sarah, but she remained oddly grounded. Her confidence rose a notch.

"If you ever want to talk, I'm a good listener," Adele said.

Haley smiled. Would Adele feel the same if she knew about Mitch? Would any of them? The answer shouldn't matter, but it did. Guilt poked her like a hot iron. She hated Mitch for what he'd done. She should hate his family, too. But she didn't.

She followed Adele to the kitchen, her eyes sweeping the wide ceiling beams. A huge wagon wheel light fixture hung from the center beam in the great room. In the adjoining dining room, an antler chandelier hung over an antique oak table. Western art graced knotty pine walls and bronze sculptures adorned hand-carved end tables. Recessed light gave the room a cozy, relaxed feel.

Even the kitchen was done with a modernized version of an antique stove and refrigerator, much like the ones she'd seen at the log home show she and Hap had attended a few years ago in Denver.

"You have a lovely home," Haley said. "Did you and Walt design and build it yourself?"

Adele smiled and motioned toward the breakfast nook where the table was set for two. Warmth tugged inside Haley. She shoved it back. Feeling homey about this place was something she couldn't afford. She sat down while Adele poured tea into the glasses. The kitchen door opened, drawing their attention.

"Actually, Jared did," Adele said.

"Did what?" Jared said, setting Haley's suitcase on the floor and closing the door.

"Designed and built this house," Adele said.

"Oh." He glanced at Haley.

A smile lit his eyes. Her breath hitched. "You never said this was your house." It hurt to breathe. She thought she was coming to Sarah's grandfather's house, not Jared's.

"The place is a family project," Jared said, avoiding Haley's eyes. "We all worked on it."

Adele motioned to the chair next to Haley and Jared slid into it. "Eat, you two. I'm sure Haley's exhausted and needs rest."

Jared offered thanks. Haley bowed her head, uncertain what to make of this man. When he was finished, Adele busied herself at the sink.

"Jared sank everything into this place. He just keeps us here because he thinks we're too old to take care of ourselves," she said, laughing. "He did the same with Mitch, always looking out for him, fixing things."

Haley met Jared's gaze across the table. If his intent was to fix her, too, he could think again. She wasn't broken.

"So this is a what's mine is yours thing," she said.

"Is that so bad?" Jared asked. "It's important to have family close." His gaze challenged her.

"I suppose that depends on the family," Haley said, picking the crust off her bread. "This is a beautiful place. You do good work."

"Thank you," he said, breaking eye contact.

Adele finished at the sink, then brushed a kiss on Jared's cheek. "If you two don't mind, I think I'll check on Walt and turn in. Tomorrow's going to be busy. Jared, don't forget the afternoon riding session."

"I haven't forgotten," Jared said. "Maybe Haley can help."

"I'm sure the children would like that. If you don't mind," Adele added, smiling at Haley.

"I don't mind. You'll have to tell me what's expected," Haley said grateful for anything that would occupy time.

"Jared can fill you in, dear. Good night, Haley. I'll look forward to getting to know you better." She headed out the kitchen and up the stairs.

Haley finished her sandwich and took a sip of tea, holding the chilled glass between her hands. Jared watched her, but she had no idea what was going on behind those dark eyes. The room was more confining with Adele gone. Jared seemed closer, more intimidating.

"So what is this riding session about, and what do I have to do?"

"A friend of mine cares for handicapped kids during the week. Once a week they come here and we let them ride and brush the horses. Does wonders for their sense of independence and accomplishment. Mom's been helping, but with Walt not well and taking a lot of her time, your help would be appreciated."

Haley swallowed hard and fingered the condensation on the glass. This was a side of Jared she'd never expected. She wished she'd seen it first. "I'd be happy to help. I think what you're doing is wonderful," she said. "Pop and I used to clown-up and go to the children's ICU and cancer wards and put on a little act." She smiled at the memory. "It's amazing how little it takes to get a child's mind off their troubles."

She lifted her gaze and found him watching her. The glass slid from her fingers, shattering as it hit the table.

Jared reached for a dish towel, sopping up tea before it spilled to the floor. "Are you okay?"

"I'm fine. I'm so sorry," Haley sputtered. "I must be more tired than I thought." She reached for the shattered pieces, cutting her hand on a jagged edge.

Jared pulled a handkerchief from his pocket and wrapped the cut. She stared at the blood soaking through the white cloth.

It was impossible to steady her erratic pulse. "I should have been more careful," she murmured.

Jared covered her hand with his, applying pressure to the cut. Her soft skin brushed against his. He had the feeling she wasn't referring to the broken glass but rather letting him glimpse into her life. He'd wanted her vulnerable so she could see she wasn't the only one who had suffered by Mitch's actions. He'd expected toughness. He hadn't expected her fragility to affect him so much. He pulled the handkerchief back and looked at the torn skin. Jared's breath solidified in his throat.

Weariness replaced the spark in Haley's eyes. Morning would make her more guarded—harder to reach. He had to reach her, now, tonight, for Walt's sake.

"Let's go to the bathroom and clean this up," he said.

He led her to the half bath near the laundry and eased her onto the toilet seat, then pulled out peroxide and bandages. He flushed the wound with warm soapy water, pinched the skin together and patted it dry. She didn't flinch once, almost as if physical pain stanched the emotional.

"This might sting," he said picking up the antiseptic bottle.

He squirted a liberal amount of liquid onto a cotton ball, dabbed the wound and gently blew on the damp skin. Her hand, so small in his, trembled. Her eyes misted, but not a tear fell.

His vow to not become emotionally involved shattered. "I know Mitch hurt you, Haley. I know you don't want to be here or talk about what happened. I was wrong to jump to conclusions, but I'm not sorry you're here." He secured the bandage and stepped back, irritated that he could be drawn to her in spite of everything he thought he knew, yet driven by the Spirit within him to help. "Letting go doesn't hurt as much as you think—not as much as holding on."

She stood in a flash and walked into the kitchen. "What would you know of letting go?"

"More than you think." He leaned against the bathroom door, arms crossed. "I've walked that path. Like you, I've already seen yesterday, and it gave me a glimpse of what I want for tomorrow. Someday, if you want to listen, I'll tell you my story. Looking inside ourselves is the toughest thing any of us will ever do, but at some point, it's something we all have to face."

"Is that what Mitch did?" she said resentfully. "Did he look inside himself?"

The spark of challenge was back in her eyes. Jared welcomed it.

"I wonder what he saw." she said, lifting her chin.

"I've wondered that myself." Jared leaned against the sink. "Whatever it was, it brought him back to the God of the second chance, and the third and the fourth. God never gives up on us, Haley, and more often than not, He's the only one who can really help us."

"Sometimes it isn't enough." She picked at the bandage. "Thank you for taking care of this. I'll help with the kitchen."

Jared shook his head. "Not this time." He picked up her suitcase sitting near the door. "It's getting late. Let me show you to your room. Tomorrow's a big day."

Her lashes dropped, hiding her eyes. "You mean tomorrow I have to meet Mitch's father."

Jared nodded. His chest tightened. How impulsive he'd been to put his own plan first. It was too late for regrets. Too late to go back and do it right.

Jared moved through the great room to the stairs. "Walt's a good man, Haley. I hope you'll give him a chance."

They walked up the stairs. Voices murmured in a room at the end of the hall. Jared stopped before they reached it, opened a door and set the suitcase inside.

"I'm across the hall if you need anything," he said, knowing she would die before asking.

She stepped inside and turned around, the haunted look back in her eyes. "How much does Walt know about why I'm here?" she said.

"Only what Mom told him. That you're a friend of

mine and Mitch's, and you're here as my guest. I'll see you in the morning."

He headed for the stairs. The patch on Haley's hand was an easy fix for a simple problem, but the one on her heart.... He could see it, knew who caused it, but had no idea how to fix it. He paused to listen for the sound of her door closing. He didn't hear it until he reached the ground floor. His chest pounded. His misgivings increased by the minute. From here on, he would have to guard his own feelings as well as Haley's actions.

Chapter Six

Haley rose from the bedroom chair and massaged her stiff neck while the sun was still a thought on the horizon. She would have gone to bed hours ago but for the driving need to keep torturous nightmares at bay—the darkness before the dawn. Not even her phone call to Hap and his usual optimistic words of wisdom eased the worry.

A sliver of gray light signaled the long night was ending. She released a sigh. A low burning lamp cast her shadow on the wall. The scent of freshly mowed hay drifted through the open window. Outside, a door banged, a gate creaked and a horse nickered.

She had actually prayed for the darkness to linger, but the morning dawned in spite of her prayer. She hadn't expected Him to answer, but she'd hoped.

She inhaled, relishing the brisk morning air. The day was here, and like every day since her fateful meeting with Mitch, she would embrace it and try to find what was good. A soft thump outside her door made her jump.

"Haley?" Jared's voice squeezed through the heavy

oak barrier. "I saw your light," he said. "I know you're up. If you're game, I could use some company with chores this morning."

Haley glanced toward the door, then the bed. The clothes she'd slept in were rumpled. Her unpacked suitcase, still waiting to be relieved of its contents, lay on top of the coverlet she hadn't slept under. Her stomach knotted.

"Haley?" His voice was quieter now, almost a whisper.

"I'm here," she said. "I haven't escaped down the trellis."

He chuckled. "Good. Do you want to help me milk some cows or not?"

"Not." She concentrated on the silence beyond the door, hoping he'd gone.

"Is there a reason we have to talk through the door?" he said.

Laughter danced in his voice. Haley could almost picture the ends of his mouth lifting into a smile. A clear vision of his face forged in her mind. Her pulse jumped.

She caught her reflection in the mirror and groaned. Yesterday's clothes clung to her skin. Smudged mascara emphasized the sleepless circles under her eyes. Her hair hung to her waist in tangled waves from the braids she'd worn yesterday.

"I'm not presentable, Jared."

"I doubt that's possible," he said. "I think you're just hiding."

She stormed across the room and yanked the door open. "Get over that, will you?" she snapped. "I'm here, aren't I?"

"Yes. You are." His sharp assessing gaze darkened, touched her briefly and shifted to include the room.

"You haven't changed," he said. "Good. You're just perfect for doing barn chores. Splash some water on your face and brush your teeth. If we hurry, we can watch the sun rise."

She stepped back, one hand on the doorknob, ready to shut him out. She shouldn't go. One minute he hounded her, wanting justice for Mitch's death, and the next he treated her like she mattered. Who was this man, anyway? Good grief, last night, he'd even apologized, and she didn't have a witness to prove he'd actually done the deed.

"Haven't you had enough of these four walls for one night, Haley?" Jared's low voice sent a shiver down her back. "There's a gorgeous day starting out there. You don't strike me as the kind of woman to miss a minute of it." He leaned against the doorjamb and crossed his arms, watching her in a way that reawakened feelings she didn't wish to explore.

"You have no idea what kind of woman I am," she said. "I'm no slouch."

"Then show me."

The hall shadows deepened his dark eyes to obsidian—eyes that held an earnestness and honesty that she saw when she remembered Pop, or looked at Hap. She swallowed with difficulty and found her voice. "Give me five," she said.

"Three," he countered, "outside the back door."

A few minutes later, she hurried down the stairs to the kitchen, her ponytail bouncing against her back. The fresh scent of lilac soap lingered on her face. Jared waited on the back porch. She stepped outside and caught her breath. Dawn was breaking, bathing the horizon in a red glow. The scenery and colors changed every second. The world was waking up. Much as she hated to agree with Jared about anything, he was right. It would have been a shame to miss this.

He handed her a jacket and motioned her toward the barn, whistling a happy tune. A lively spring lifted his step. She caught his light mood and changed a little, too. Haunting memories faded. For this moment, this instant, she was free. She wanted to bathe in the glow of that freedom. Caution blinked in her brain.

Remember where you are and who he is.

The lightness left her heart, leaving an ache for its absence. She followed Jared into the barn, hanging back a moment to watch a rabbit nibble grass near the fence. Barnyard hens clucked as they pecked for bugs. In the surrounding paddocks, playful foals reared and nipped at each other while their mothers grazed.

"So, which cow do you want?" he asked, coming close behind her. "Gracie or Claire?"

Unnerved by his nearness, Haley sidestepped him, putting distance between them. "Whichever one you don't want," she said, eyeing the two Jersey cows munching hay in their stalls.

"I'll take Claire. You take Gracie." A mischievous smile curved his lips. He handed her a bucket. "I'm warning you, she's ornery."

Haley lifted her chin. "I face bulls for a living, why would one cow intimidate me?"

A shadow crossed his face, then disappeared. "There's a difference between the he's and she's," Jared said.

"Really," she said, refusing to let him goad her.

"She's kick."

"And he's don't?" Haley countered.

Jared nodded toward Gracie's stall. "Okay. We'll see," he mumbled.

"Say again?" Haley gripped the bucket handle.

"I said, we'll see."

"Is there something in particular that sets this cow off?"

Jared shrugged and grinned. "Doesn't take much."

Haley grabbed a milking stool from the corner and eased into the stall, placing one hand on Gracie's rump. The animal mooed and glanced back. Her large brown eyes seemed calm enough, but looks could be deceiving. Gracie's velvety ears twitched back and forth, then she ducked her head into the manger. Haley paused long enough to shoot a look at Jared.

"You gonna stand there all day?" she asked. "Don't you have your own cow to milk?"

His grin widened. "I do. Holler if you need help."

"Not likely," she muttered.

She set the stool beside Gracie's hind legs, placed the bucket in front of the stool, and slid one hand down the cow's hind quarter. She rubbed in slow circles until she came to the soft flank where the leg and thigh met, the juncture where her forehead should rest while her fingers did the work. Gracie mooed and lifted a leg in warning.

Haley smiled. Jared had given her a ticklish cow. This could be tricky, but if that were all she had to contend with, she'd manage. She settled on the stool and glanced over at the other stall. Jared's dark head rested on Claire's flank. His deft hands worked a steady stream of milk from the udders. Each squeeze pull made the muscles along his shoulders ripple. A wild flutter settled in Haley's stomach.

Jared glanced over his shoulder. "Everything okay?"

"Just peachy," she said, resettling on the stool.

It was too easy to get lost in the way he looked at her. She adjusted the bucket, cupped her hands and blew warm air onto her chilled fingers. Gracie continued to munch, one eye rolled in Haley's direction.

"Behave yourself, Gracie, and we'll get along just fine," Haley said.

She massaged the cow's belly, careful to make each move precise while she eased her hand back until she made contact with the massive milk bag. Gracie's warm, soft skin melded into Haley's fingers. She tugged at the udders and kept her head out of Gracie's flank.

"Done," Jared called five minutes later. "Mom's making butter today so I'll run this to the shed and put it in the separator." He paused beside her. She chanced an upward glance. "I'm impressed," he said. "Gracie's usually dumped her pail and mashed a few toes by now."

Haley smiled in spite of herself. "I take it this was a test, and I passed."

"With flying colors."

"Good for me," she said, returning to the task at hand.

Heat crept up her neck, radiating warmth through her body. She liked the way he made her feel right now, but didn't trust it. He seemed oblivious to the effect he had on her. She needed to keep it that way.

"I'll be back in a few minutes," he said, moving toward the door.

"Don't hurry on my account," she called.

The pail was half full when the barn door opened. Footsteps shuffled through the fresh shavings scattered on the barn floor. Haley's fingers froze. This wasn't

Jared. Jared didn't shuffle. She doubted the hired hand did either. That left Mitch's father. She wasn't ready to see him. Not yet.

"Jared?"

The unfamiliar voice sent a tremor through her body. She stilled her hands and held her breath. If she didn't move, maybe he'd think no one was here. She closed her eyes. Her head shifted, bumping Gracie's flank.

The cow hunched her back and kicked out, spilling the pail. Haley jumped sideways. The tip of the cow's hoof caught her shoulder. Gracie settled and let out a long, low call, then plunged her head back into the manger, content that she'd done what she set out to do. Haley's world spun like a lariat. A man's feeble hands pulled her from the stall.

"Are you all right?" he asked.

Haley looked into Mitch's father's face. He bore little resemblance to the man she had seen in the photos. His shoulders carried an invisible burden, giving him the stooped appearance of a much older man. Worry lines creased the corners of his eyes. His mouth drooped, as though he seldom smiled anymore. His deep gray eyes were flecked with green and reflected sadness laced with concern. Her first instinct was to comfort and reassure him.

"Are you all right?" he repeated. "What was Jared thinking, letting you milk Gracie?"

Haley slumped against the stall post and winced as pain shot through her shoulder. "In all fairness, Mr. Jessup, Jared did warn me. I was proving a point and doing quite well until a few seconds ago."

"I startled you, didn't I?"

Walt's concern was genuine. She forced the tense

muscles to relax, then turned toward the sound of a bucket clanging at the other end of the barn. Jared entered looming larger than life in the rising sun's shadow.

"Haley?" His voice, strong and sure, resonated through the barn. In the space of a heartbeat, he was there, lifting her up and setting her on a hay bale. "I'm sorry. I shouldn't have left…."

"I'm okay." She moved away from his arms and scooted to the far side of the bale. "This isn't the first time I've been knocked in the dirt. I'm sure it won't be the last." She rubbed her smarting shoulder. "I have a job to finish."

Walt's bushy brows pulled together. "Absolutely not," he said, glowering at Jared.

"I agree," Jared said. "Shorty can finish."

Pride waged a war inside her. She never left a job unfinished, even one as simple as milking a cow, but Walt's worried face halted her protest. She picked at the hay. Why should it bother her to worry him? This was Mitch's father, Mitch's family. By all that was fair and just, she shouldn't be here.

Jared nodded toward her shoulder. "May I?" he asked. He knelt before her on one knee, his gaze probing hers. Panic shot through her. She broke eye contact and looked over his shoulder.

Jared's touch made her feel strange, almost needy. The last thing she wanted was to need a man, especially one as potent as Jared Sinclair. He was twisting her emotions into a wad of snarled twine. It was getting harder to define what was happening inside her.

"I'd rather you didn't," she said, wishing herself anywhere but here, at this time, with this man. "Jared, I think coming here was a mistake," she murmured. "I need to go."

"Leave?" Walt asked, disappointment filling his eyes. "But you just got here. Jared said you knew Mitch. I was hoping we'd have time to talk."

Ice spread through Haley's stomach. She pushed her fist into the bale, drawing Jared's attention.

"In due time, Walt," he said.

Jared's gaze held her, the agreement between them bouncing silently between them. She'd promised to be fair, but she felt ill-equipped to handle any time with Walt, especially if it meant talking about Mitch.

Walt moved a few stalls away. "Please stay, Haley. Jared's never brought a young lady home before and I'd like to hear about Mitch." His plea twisted Haley's gut. He thought she was Jared's girlfriend. He thought she and Mitch had just been friends. Bile rose to her throat and with it, a choking fear that now she was here, there was no escaping the inevitable. When the time came to talk about Mitch, and it would, what could she possibly say that would comfort this man?

You could share Sarah.

Haley stiffened. Not Sarah, not yet. She needed to keep Sarah safe—untouched by Mitch's dirty act. Her gaze roamed over Jared's face. "You promised," she said.

"So did you. Be fair."

Warmth and warning filled his eyes, almost as though he willed his strength into her. Every emotion inside her floundered—anger, fear, hope, all caught in a whirling vortex, leaving her unable to discern anything for certain, except the strength he offered and she needed, but could never accept.

"I don't know what to do," she murmured. "I need Hap."

The hushed words sounded far away, like a lost child searching for something familiar. Jared doubted her voiced need was meant for his ears, but rather a thought she hadn't realized she'd spoken.

Their gazes locked, but hers seemed to look beyond the connection. He was losing her again to that place she never let anyone else go, the place that held the key to the woman behind the clown makeup and the pain she thought no one else could see. For the first time he really saw it, and it ripped him in two.

"If you need Hap, I'll bring him," Jared said, resting his hands on her shoulders. "Just say the word."

Her surprised gaze pulled back to include him. "You would do that?"

He brushed a piece of pine shaving from her hair, letting his hand linger on the silky strands. She didn't pull away. "Yes," he said. "I would do that."

The bell outside the kitchen door tinkled, blending with the song of waking birds.

"Breakfast. Come on." Adele's voice called from the porch.

Jared took Haley's hand and pulled her to her feet. When she looked at him again, her face was unreadable, shutting him out.

She brushed the dirt and straw from her jeans. The emotion of the past few minutes dissolved, annihilating all traces of the vulnerable woman he'd seen, as though within that space, she'd determined something in her mind. She hurried toward the barn entrance, passed Walt and offered a half smile.

"Thank you for saving me from Gracie," she said before stepping into the sunlight.

Jared rammed his hands into his pockets and joined Walt. Together they watched Haley climb the porch steps and disappear into the house.

"There's a lot of hurt locked up in that gal," Walt said, fastening the barn door. "Whatever on earth caused it?"

Jared placed a hand on Walt's shoulder, giving it a gentle squeeze. "I suspect Mitch did."

Walt's shoulders slumped. "Mitch? But I thought Haley was your girl. Whatever could Mitch have done?"

Jared urged Walt toward the house. He didn't know for sure what Mitch had done, but he planned to find out. "Mitch was a mess when they met several years ago," Jared said, avoiding any reference to the Cheyenne incident. "Only Haley knows what happened." Until he knew what Haley planned to do, silence seemed the better part of valor. "It was a bad time for him and for us. I'm sure it was for Haley, too."

Walt shielded his eyes, hiding the worried look Jared had seen so often during Mitch's runaway years. "Mitch fixed his mistakes," Walt said. "How could he have missed this one?"

It was a question Jared had asked himself many times in the last few days and with no satisfying answer. He stopped at the porch steps. "Maybe he didn't know what to do about this one. Maybe he was trying to figure it out when God took him home. Whatever happened, Haley's hurt is real. We have to make it right."

"You haven't told me everything, have you, son?" Walt said.

Jared sighed. "I don't know everything and the story isn't mine to tell. Trust me on this."

Walt nodded. They climbed the steps and entered the mudroom off the kitchen.

"Hope everyone's hungry," Adele called, handing Haley a bowl of gravy. She set it on the table. Jared wished he knew what was in her heart. Walt deserved the truth, but if Haley chose to take her secret and leave, she would remove forever the last living part of Mitch that Walt would ever have. Jared couldn't let that happen.

A cold knot formed in his stomach. The cost might be more than he'd anticipated, but he'd put her in God's hands, and God was faithful and just. He'd have to trust. And wait.

Walt's eyes softened. "There's more to it than just helping her, isn't there?" Without waiting for a reply, he entered the kitchen.

Jared took a minute then followed. There was more, but to tag it with a definition at this stage would be crazy.

Breakfast seemed to go on forever with Jared and Adele carrying most of the conversation. Jared watched Haley's troubled face. For a long moment, she looked back at him, then pushed her eggs around the plate. Once the meal was finished, she rose and stacked the dirty dishes.

"Leave them, dear," Adele said. "I'll pop them in the dishwasher. There's a nice spot near the stream beyond the paddocks. Why don't you take a blanket and enjoy the scenery for a couple of hours? The quiet and fresh air will do you some good."

"Mom naps in that spot lots of times," Jared said, stacking more dishes near the sink.

Adele waved him away. "I don't nap. I meditate."

"You snore when you meditate?" Jared asked. His comment pulled a smile from Haley, softening her features.

Adele smacked his arm. "Behave yourself," she said.

Haley relaxed. The love in this family reminded her of Hap and Sarah. It was real, not put on for her benefit. Adele's love for Walt manifested in every move, every word. He returned it action and word, with a touch or a smile. What would being loved like that be like? She looked up to find Jared watching her. Dreams disappeared in a wave of fear.

"Haley?" Adele said. "I can show you the trail if you want to go."

"I think…" She pulled her gaze from Jared's. "I think I'll just clean up and make a few phone calls before the kids get here."

"Holler if you need anything," Adele said. "Walt and I will be down here making butter."

"And I'll meet all of you in the barn in a couple of hours," Jared said.

Haley hurried upstairs and cleaned up, then called Sarah. Tears stung her eyes. She should be home, not here. By the time Sarah handed the phone to Hap, Haley couldn't speak. She listened as Hap assured her of his love and prayers. The miles seemed to drift, bringing him closer.

He'd signed off with, "This is your chance to make somethin' good out of somethin' bad. Take it." His voice was gruff with emotion leaving her as raw as the skin on a newly branded calf.

The truth will set you free. The phrase taunted her, ringing in her ears until she wanted to ram her palms against the sides of her head and squeeze them out.

She wanted to close her heart, but the shadow of truth held, letting a sliver of light into the darkness. A car door banged outside, followed by squeals of excited children. She pushed off the bed and headed for the barn.

Chapter Seven

Charity, a six-year-old with Down syndrome, latched on to Haley as soon as she crossed the barnyard. Haley put her arm around the child, knelt down and introduced herself.

Jared smiled at them and Haley's chest tightened. She'd have to examine the feelings Jared dredged from her at some point but not now.

"I expected you a half hour ago," he said. "What kept you?"

"Phone," Haley said, swallowing hard.

"Everything okay?" He lead the last horse into the barn and tied him to a stall.

Haley nodded and touched the picture of Sarah she'd tucked into her pocket. Having it close made her daughter seem closer. "What do you need me to do?"

"Line the kids along the fence. This is a one-on-one deal. Soon as Mom and Walt get here we'll let the kids into the stalls and just supervise their work. They know the drill."

Haley rose and Charity slipped her hand into Haley's and smiled, her eyes sparkling. Haley caught Charity's excitement. This wasn't much different from what she and Pop had done in the hospital wards, only these kids weren't bedfast or terminal.

Walt and Adele joined them, each taking sole responsibility for a child. Jared handled each one with care and tenderness tempered with enough firmness to keep them safe. Almost as though they belonged to him. Haley was conscious of him watching her with dark eyes that held a spark of some indefinable emotion. She concentrated on Charity, but every time his eyes compelled her to look at him, her pulse would jump, then another memory invaded the warmth, leaving a coldness in her chest and a longing for something always beyond reach.

The afternoon passed too quickly and soon they were loading the kids back in the van and waving them off. Walt looked exhausted. Adele hurried him off to the house.

"I'll help with dinner," Haley called, setting the last saddle on the rack.

She closed the tack room door feeling invigorated and more aware of Jared than ever before. She liked this new side to him and so far hadn't seen anything in Walt and Adele that raised warnings concerning Sarah. She relaxed her guard a little.

"You were great today," Jared said. "We make a pretty good team." He headed toward the grain shed, leaving her standing in the warmth of his praise.

Dinner was subdued, the afternoon's physical exertion taking its toll on everyone. Haley helped clear the table and load the dishes, conscious of Jared's closeness. She needed to get away from him for a while, away from feelings that were better left buried, feelings she feared and didn't want to explore.

"If we're done here, I think I'll take a walk," Haley said.

"Good for you, dear. It's a beautiful evening for one," Adele said. "Oh. By the way, Jared, I almost forgot. A Sam McIntosh called. He said to call him. Something about a snag on the investigation you requested?" The question in her voice was reflected in her eyes. "Did we have a problem with something?"

Jared's gaze flew to Haley. The comfortable atmosphere shattered like glass.

"The problem was mine," Jared said. "I'm handling it."

Haley gripped the chair and waited for the bomb to drop. Her nails pressed into the hard oak. Sam hadn't called her with good news, so what kind of snag was there? Certainly not one that would benefit her if Jared was handling it. Had Jared finally gotten her kicked out of rodeo? Circuit life was all she'd known. She couldn't imagine herself in any other livelihood. Maybe that's what Jared wanted—her and Sarah depending on his family. Fatigue faded in a rush of adrenaline, replaced by searing anger.

"Excuse me," she said, heading out the door. "I'll take that walk now." She reached the bottom of the porch steps and bent over, fighting waves of nausea. For a moment the world circled, then stilled. Behind her, the porch door squeaked. Panic welled in her throat.

"Haley, wait." Jared's footsteps plunked on the board steps. Her stomach clenched so tightly she couldn't move. He stepped around her, blocking her way.

"Are you all right?" he asked.

"No," she said, straightening. Her stomach lurched and settled. "I'm not all right. You got what you wanted."

"And that is?"

"The chance to gloat on home territory. Well, go ahead. If you've finished destroying my life, can I go back to whatever is left?"

"Look at me, Haley." She refused, focusing instead on some invisible spot to his left. "Look at me," he commanded, lifting her chin with his finger. She transferred all her anger into one look. "I'm not gloating," he said. "And I am sorry about this. At the time I requested the investigation, I needed to know about Mitch. I didn't know about Sarah."

She raised her chin higher. "But you still needed vindication."

Her arrow hit its target. Jared felt the barb. He had wanted vindication in the beginning. But this was now and things were different. He knew about Sarah and the affect of jumping in where angels fear to tread and not allowing God to lead him had messed up everything.

"Stopping the investigation is out of my hands, Haley. I'm sorry. That's the snap Sam was talking about. We're still working on getting it dropped."

"How big of you. Do it for Sarah, not because it was an accident." Her eyes darkened like storm clouds. "Don't you see what will happen by dropping the investigation now?"

"If it's any consolation, Sam told me from the beginning that the ruling would most likely go in your favor," Jared said, confused by her anger.

"And you went ahead with it anyway. I'm still guilty by assumption. I want my name cleared. Unless you're willing to make a public apology and reinstate my reputation, whatever happens won't be enough. Would you do that? For me? For Sarah?" Her words came faster, her panic more pronounced.

A knot rose in Jared's throat. She was right, but he still wasn't ready to take it that far. He dropped his gaze, ashamed of the doubt still clouding his mind.

"I didn't think so," Haley said. "If they fault me, will you take it further? Send me to jail? It was an accident, Jared, and this is the last time I will defend myself to you."

Watching her unravel pained him. He should have left things in God's hands, but no, he'd jumped the gun and made a mess before he had all the facts. He'd done this too much lately, and God forgive him, he was still doing it.

"You don't have to worry about supporting Sarah, Haley. We'll take care of you both."

Her eyes blazed. "I have a life. It's mine and it doesn't include you. I don't need you or any man to take care of me or my daughter. That's what you were hoping for, wasn't it? You're sorry for lots of things. So am I. Does that qualify you for redemption?"

Jared's anger rose. "No. Does it you?"

Rage shook her. She'd glimpsed parts of Jared that stirred a yearning for things she thought she'd never have. Things that stirred a hope in spite of her circumstances. Reality punched her in the gut. What a fool she'd been to let those feelings creep in. She wanted to hurt him like his doubt hurt her.

"It doesn't qualify either of us," she said lowering her voice. "The truth is you're not sure I didn't let Resurrection kill Mitch, even if you want to believe I didn't. You'll never be certain, will you?"

The truth hit her like a steamroller. Disappointment throbbed like a painful knot inside her. It mattered that Jared believed her. Why, she didn't know. And it mattered more that she believed in her own innocence.

She would always feel responsible, but accepting the truth in her heart as well as her mind released the doubt and some of the guilt. Her own vindication had been a long time coming. She'd never meant to physically hurt Mitch. If anything good had come from being here with Jared, this was it. Maybe, someday, he would believe it, too.

"Tell me about you and Mitch, Haley. Make me understand how all this fits," he said so softly she almost missed it.

The shame of eight years ago rose to the surface, tearing open old wounds, leaving her raw and vulnerable. "Mitch was a wrong turn I made a long time ago," she said in a low voice. "If I'd wanted to destroy him, I could have done it eight years ago. I didn't."

Jared's tense jaw betrayed his frustration. "Isn't Sarah proof that your relationship wasn't all bad?" His look translated as disappointment. "Most people don't have a child with someone they don't care about."

"Mitch wasn't most people." Haley's heart pounded so hard she was sure he could see it move beneath her shirt. He thought she'd slept with Mitch, then kept the news of Sarah from him. How wrong could he be? She couldn't hold his gaze. If she did, he would see her shame, not Mitch's. Carrying her own cross was so familiar she'd miss it if it wasn't there. Oh, what she wouldn't give to share the load, but not with this man, her enemy's brother.

"You want to know what Mitch gave me," she said,

hearing the bitterness in her voice. "I'll tell you. He gave me the gift of looking over my shoulder for the rest of my life." Without waiting for his response, she turned and fled toward the paddocks.

Jared let her go, but her words hung in the air, haunting him, leaving an insinuation that he never knew Mitch at all. Why would she need to look over her shoulder, unless...

Something inside him died. The reflection taking seed in his mind was too awful to contemplate. Mitch at his worst would never do such a thing. He couldn't. Yet Mitch's pained cry came back in a rush of memory.

I've done some awful things.

Every move Haley made said Mitch could have and if he had... Jared fisted his hands. He had wrongly judged Haley in the department of keeping Sarah from Mitch, but not in the incident with Resurrection. If the roles were reversed, how far would he have gone to protect his child? His stomach roiled. There was no way to know for sure what really happened or why. More than ever, in spite of his doubts, he needed to stop judging her at every turn.

Jared shoved the darkness from his mind and headed toward the small office building beside the barn, his troubled thoughts hounding his heels. His mother met him at the door.

"Is Haley all right? She seemed upset about the call."

Jared sat down at his drafting board and stared at the blueprints for the ranch expansion. "I'm afraid I started something I can't undo."

"I'm sorry. I was afraid stopping the investigation wouldn't be so easy."

He studied his mother's face. Her earnest eyes, filled

with life and unquenchable warmth, asked questions she wouldn't voice. For the first time it dawned on him that maybe the key to helping Haley lied with his mother.

"Is there something I can do?" she asked.

"Maybe. What do you see when you look at Haley?"

Adele frowned. "I'm not sure I know what you mean."

"What do you see inside her, Mom?"

"I don't have X-ray vision, Jared. I'm not sure a few hours gives me the right to make any kind of assessment."

"Try, Mom. You're a good judge of character. It's important."

Adele grew quiet. "I see a woman in a lot of pain who thinks she doesn't deserve to be loved."

Jared slid a pencil between his fingers, surprised by her answer. "Why do you think she believes that?"

"Just a hunch. Her movements, reactions. Women see these things, but I could be wrong. You've known her longer. You should know better than me." She stepped in front of the desk and stopped. "Jared, if this is related to Haley's relationship to Mitch, this might be something you can't fix. I don't want to see you or Walt hurt."

"I don't want that either."

"You can't rescue the world. Sometimes people have to find their own way."

Jared reflected on his mother's words. "And maybe God puts certain people in our path so He can use us to help them find their own way," Jared said, believing more and more that was what had happened in spite of the circumstances. "Maybe God is using us now to make Haley see that in spite of everything, she is important. If that's the case, then I haven't allowed Him to use me in that way. I've failed."

She patted his arm, then opened the door and stepped outside. "Or not. Just be careful."

After she'd gone, Jared fisted his hands under his chin, then bowed his head. "Lord God," he murmured. "Help me. I'm lost in this and I don't know what to do. Show me the truth."

A sense of God's peace washed over him, renewing and offering hope. He turned back to the drawing board and finished the sketch.

Night settled over the valley, the full moon reflecting on the shimmering stream. Cold settled around Haley's heart. She'd seen enough of Jared to know he'd backed her into a corner, again. The wind whispered through the pines, touching her cheek like Jared had done not so long ago. He'd put a brand on her, not like Mitch, but a mark just the same. She knew the danger of instant attraction and wouldn't fall into that trap again.

Still, the truth lay closer to the surface than ever before. She'd rather face a rank bull again than the ghost of Mitch. Everything she'd done had been to protect those she loved. If the truth were known, would people look at her and Sarah differently?

Would Jared?

Of course he would. Whatever path she chose, someone would lose. She rose and brushed the tears from her face, then turned toward the house and saw Adele making her way through the brush.

"I was afraid you'd get lost," Adele said. "Beautiful, isn't it?"

Haley nodded.

"I always find such peace here. There was a time I never thought I would."

Haley knew that feeling well, but it surprised her that this calm, together woman would, too. She plunked a rock into the water and edged toward the path. "What happened to make you feel that way?"

"Jared's father." Her quiet voice held no malice, only acceptance for what had been and was no longer.

"I was young. We eloped. Six months later, the reality of being married to a man with a cruel streak sank in. But I was pregnant with Jared." She paused as if looking back was something she rarely did. "I wish I'd listened to my parents. They saw what I didn't or wouldn't. I would have done anything to get away and spare Jared growing up in that atmosphere."

"How did you make it through?" Haley slowed her step.

"Life got better when I decided God could carry the load better than I could."

"Maybe some people are more deserving of God's favor than others," Haley said.

The touch on her shoulder was gentle. "God doesn't play favorites, dear. If He did, how would anyone trust Him? He loves us all and desires all to come to Him, but the final choice to trust and follow are left up to us."

"Sometimes we choose to follow but bad things still happen," Haley said.

"The world is what it is, Haley. We have to live in it for the present. It's good that we don't see the beginning and the end. We'd evade anything remotely difficult and never grow."

Haley closed her eyes, clearly seeing Sarah's face. "I'm sorry for what you went through," she said. She opened her eyes to find Adele still watching, warmth and understanding in her dark eyes. "What did you tell Jared about his father?"

Adele smiled. "The truth. It's shaded a bit differently when a little boy is five than when he's thirty, though."

"What if…" Haley swallowed. "Why doesn't God stop the bad things before they happen? What if He's responsible for our predicaments and there's no way to fix what happens or make it better?"

Adele's gaze was reflective. "You can always make it better. God isn't in the business of placing His children in predicaments, Haley. We manage that quite nicely on our own. The journey may be rough, but He promises a safe landing."

Haley brushed a hot tear off her cheek. "What if I can't make it through the journey?"

Adele took her hand and squeezed it. "If you're truly God's child, that's impossible. What's troubling you? Can I help?"

"No. No one can. Nothing is right—anywhere."

Haley freed her hands and ran them down her jeans, then stepped onto the path. Adele waited for her to continue, but Haley knew she wouldn't. She longed for someone to share her burden with, someone who could explain what was happening inside her—anyone but Jared's mother, whose warmth and quiet manner encouraged confidences that, if the truth were known, would only tear apart and destroy both their families. The house came into view and she quickened her step. When they reached the porch, Adele stopped.

"There's more to life than surviving, Haley. There's joy and love. You deserve that. Everyone does. I'll see you in the morning."

Haley slipped into the house and hurried up the stairs to her room, avoiding the den where Jared and Walt were bent over a chessboard. Fear and shame clawed at her insides like an old enemy. She didn't want Sarah to know the truth or be torn in relationships or worst of all hate her for Mitch's sin. She didn't want to be here where reminders of Mitch constantly bombarded her and feelings of hearth and home and Jared invaded her thoughts.

The truth will set you free.

She opened her bedroom window and lifted her gaze to the heavens. "Will it set me free?" she whispered. "How can You make this right?"

Haley rose at first light and entered the barn. She grabbed a clean pail and headed for Gracie's stall. The cow was munching hay, which meant Jared must be up, too. She quickly washed the cow's udders and sanitized her hands, then sat on the milking stool and closed her eyes.

She'd never been so tired. Against her better judgment, she asked God for help last night, wrestled with Him for some time with no resolution. Why should He listen to her? She'd abandoned Him, just as He had her, but she'd hoped He would feel some of her desperation and take pity on her.

Instead, exhaustion had riddled her sleep with nightmares of Mitch and visions of Sarah being taken away. She didn't doubt Walt and Adele would love Sarah, as well as materially offer her more than she and Hap ever could. What would happen if she let Sarah come and Sarah didn't want to leave?

Gracie stomped her foot as Haley yanked a little

too hard. She eased her grip. It could happen. If Sarah came. Haley ground her teeth. She'd stick with her plan—finish out the week and use the money Mitch had left to take Sarah somewhere safe. Away from the truth about him. Away from Jared.

Away from Sarah's family.

Haley's chest squeezed. She sidelined the voice in her head and finished milking, carried the milk to the mudroom and poured it into the separator, then stepped into the kitchen.

"You're up early," Jared said. "Gracie give you any trouble this time?"

Her heart lurched, then settled back into its natural rhythm. "No. She was fine." Jared was reason enough not to stay. He confused her with memories of the life she'd dreamed of before Mitch. A life lost. There was no future in lost dreams.

He downed a glass of juice, rinsed and set it in the dishwasher. "Thought we might take a ride, if you're interested. Have a bunch of spring colts I'd like you to see."

"I'd like that." She heard Adele and Walt shuffling around upstairs. So far, Walt hadn't cornered her to talk about Mitch. She suspected Jared was responsible for the reprieve. Still, it made her anxious every time Walt was close. "I'll go saddle up."

"Aren't you hungry?" he asked.

Haley shook her head. "Show me which horses you want and I'll get them ready while you eat," she said.

Disappointment shaded his eyes. His lips tightened a fraction. "Who are you running from, Haley? Me or Walt?"

"Both," she challenged. "Do you have a problem with that?"

"Yes," he said, joining her by the door, "I do. Come on. I'll show you where everything is."

A few minutes later, Haley tied the saddled horses to the fence and headed for the house. She entered the mudroom and grabbed her hat from the hook.

"Ready when you are," she said stepping into the kitchen. To her dismay, Walt and Adele had joined Jared.

Jared looked up from the sink and smiled. "Give me a minute."

"You two go on," Adele said, shooing Jared away.

He placed his cereal bowl in the dishwasher. Haley's chest tightened. This could have been her life, or something similar, if only Mitch... She shook the memory loose.

"Morning, Haley," Walt said, pouring a cup of coffee. "You better eat. Jared has a way of making a short ride into an all day thing."

"I'm not much on breakfast," she replied, backing into the mudroom. "I'll be fine."

Walt challenged her comfort zone, but the fault was hers, not his. She could feel the love in this room and wanted to be included, but Mitch made that impossible.

"I'll bring the horses up," she said.

Jared's black brow arched, mocking her desire to run. She hadn't fooled him. "Right behind you," he said. "Think you could go a little faster?"

Haley ignored the jibe and pushed the porch door open as the phone rang. Adele answered. Silence followed. Then Adele's choked, "Sarah, is everything all right?" made Haley spin around. She pushed past Jared and rushed toward Adele, who cradled the phone like it was something precious.

"Your mother's right here," Adele said, her voice hushed. "Just a minute."

Haley resisted the urge to yank the phone from Adele's hands. Hap would never give Sarah this number. They'd call her cell. Except she'd forgotten to plug it in last night. Something must have happened. Fear twisted her heart.

Adele handed the receiver to Haley with shaking hands. Her stricken gaze bounced from Walt to Jared, then a tear slid down Adele's face.

"It's Sarah," she said in a choked whisper.

Haley grabbed the phone then sank into a chair, her knees shaking.

"Sarah, it's Mom. Are you okay? Is Hap okay?"

She felt Jared's hand on her shoulder, strong, reassuring, and welcomed it.

Haley heard Sarah's muffled, "We're fine," and released her breath. Sarah's panicked voice kept talking, but Haley barely heard. Sarah was all right. Nothing else mattered.

Sarah explained that Haley had forgotten to fill out the insurance form for the gymkhana entry and she couldn't ride in the horse competition without it. Hap couldn't find the information and wouldn't call the emergency number Haley had left, so she'd called instead. Haley gave her the number and had her repeat it. She held the phone close, wishing it would bring Sarah closer than just the sound of her voice.

"I thought something bad had happened, Sarah. Don't ever scare me like that again," Haley said. "I love you," she murmured. She hung up, then raised her head to find three pairs of eyes watching her. Her pulse raced, feeling like she'd just been roped and yanked from the saddle.

Adele was dabbing tears from eyes that held a trace of panic as they passed from Jared, to Walt, to her. Jared's face was grim. Walt's puzzled look passed between the three of them. He placed an arm around Adele, studied them all for a brief moment, then looked at Haley. His intense stare made her want to run.

"Haley. Who is Sarah?" he said, breaking the silence. "And why would talking to her upset my wife like this?"

Chapter Eight

Haley lifted her chin, letting her gaze rest on each person.

"Sarah's…my daughter," she said, feeling the noose tighten around her.

"I get that," Walt said. "But why didn't you bring her with you and why would talking to her make Adele cry?"

Haley's gaze bounced between Adele and Walt, then rested on Jared. No help there. Omitting the truth had worked until now. But this was too big to shade over. Walt's eyes seemed to look right into her soul to the secret she'd kept from him.

"Jared?" Adele said. "I don't think…"

"It's time," Jared said, shaking his head. He took Walt's elbow.

Haley backed away. She was the outsider, the one who didn't belong, but Sarah's call had opened the gate and there was no turning back now.

"There's something I need to tell you," she said. "It's about Sarah."

She caught Jared's warning look, Adele's worried

frown. Walt edged forward. His face flushed. "What am I missing here?"

Haley's insides shook. She leveled her gaze on Jared, then Walt. "It's about Sarah and Mitch," she said.

For a moment Walt seemed suspended, then his face turned red. Words formed on his lips, but he couldn't get them out.

"What about Sarah and Mitch?" he finally choked.

"I… Mitch…" Her voice warbled. "Sarah is Mitch's daughter. Mitch's and mine."

A strangled cry escaped Walt's mouth. His arms lifted, then dropped. He was getting more and more agitated. Blurting it out like this wasn't what she'd wanted. But few things in her life were what she'd wanted. Walt didn't deserve to be hurt any more than she deserved what his son had done. She looked to Jared but he was concentrating on Walt's blotched features and shaking legs.

"Mom, why don't you get his meds?" Jared said.

Walt waved them both away. "No. I can't think when I take them. I need to think."

Haley waited for him to blast her.

"I have a granddaughter," he said, awe filling his voice. His eyes misted. "Mitch's girl." His gaze met hers, accusing. "Why didn't you tell us?"

The shame of that day overwhelmed her. "I couldn't. Mitch was… He was… I wanted him out of my life. And Sarah's." She ran her hands across her jeans, then reached inside her shirt pocket and pulled out the picture of Sarah that she'd kept close to her heart since coming here. "I'm sorry," she said, holding it out.

"Haley, I don't think he's ready," Adele began. Her dark eyes flashed a warning.

"It's too late for that now," Walt said pulling away. "Are you all in on this? Am I the only one who didn't know?" He reached for the photo, then gasped. "Spitting image of her daddy." He inhaled sharply, then grabbed Jared's arm and pitched forward, crushing the photo to his chest.

Jared lifted him and carried him to a chair, Adele right behind.

Haley felt more alone than she'd ever felt in her life. Her stomach lurched. She'd watched Mitch die and lived with the knowledge every day that had it not been Mitch, she may have acted faster. Jared was right. She was in some part responsible. But Walt… She'd never forgive herself if something happened to him. Neither would Jared and Adele. How could she face any of them again? She rushed to her truck, pulled the keys from under the seat and drove away.

It was dark when Haley pulled back into Jared's drive and cut the engine. A single, low burning light came from her bedroom window—a beacon in a storm. Walt's crumpled body and Adele's stricken face brought back vivid memories of Mitch lying in the arena. She needed to make sure Walt was all right, to somehow explain without causing him any more hurt.

She got out and rushed for the porch, then caught sight of a huge shape looming along the fence beside the house. Anxiety swamped her. She reached for the doorknob, hoping it wasn't locked.

"Haley, wait."

Jared's voice stopped her cold. He urged the horse into the light and paused beside the porch.

"I shouldn't have run off," she said retracing her steps.

"No. You shouldn't have." His gaze bored into her, stretching her nerves like barbed wire to a post. "Walt asked for you all afternoon. He's afraid you're going to take Sarah and go into hiding. Is he right?"

Heat crept up Haley's neck. She was grateful that her back was to the light so he couldn't see the truth in his words.

"Walt's okay then?"

"Yes. Are you going to answer my question?"

"No."

She could feel his agitation. "I think you just did. So is Walt why you came back?"

She nodded.

Jared crossed his arms on top of the saddle horn and leaned forward. "Are you prepared to answer his questions without putting any more stress on him?"

"Do I have a choice? You're the one who forced me to come here, so don't put all the blame on me. You wanted him to know. Now he knows."

"I wanted Sarah to come with you. Look, Haley, we can play the blame game all night and never resolve it. Walt knows, so you know what comes next. And I'm warning you, it isn't running."

She moved to the horses side and absently stroked the powerful neck. "I don't want to hurt Walt any more than you want to see him hurt. I don't think I can finish this."

"I will never be finished, Haley. Not now. You closed the door on that."

She met his gaze and backed away. "You have a right to be angry with me, but my first consideration is still my daughter. And she doesn't know."

Jared heaved a sigh. "Then it's time she did." He shifted his weight.

"You messed things up." Her voice sounded small, even to her own ears.

Jared's eyes softened. "And your method of delivery is a little unorthodox."

"I'm sorry." Panic rushed to her throat. "I thought something had happened. I should...talk to Walt and Adele now." The horse lowered his head. She rubbed the sensitive pressure points behind his ears wishing Jared would dismount and not tower over her like a lion waiting for a meal.

"When you do, do you think you could manage to be a little less diplomatic?"

Her eyes flew to his face. He smiled and she realized he was trying to lighten the tension. She relaxed a little, then scuffed her toe in the dirt. "I failed Tact and Diplomacy 101," she countered.

Jared chuckled. The sound stirred her heart. "Wait until morning. The doctor gave Walt something to help him sleep and Mom won't leave him tonight."

"She must think I'm awful."

"She thinks you've been hurt, but her first concern is about Walt."

"They must really love each other," Haley said, shifting her gaze to the house. "They're lucky to have that." Longing stirred her heart. She heard Jared dismount, then move behind her, the connection between them so tangible she could barely breathe.

"Ride with me," he said.

It wasn't a question. Uncertainty and fear tightened her chest. She stepped around the horse, putting the animal between herself and Jared, then moved toward the barn. She didn't want to ride with Jared, but the alternative of being alone with her thoughts wasn't appealing either.

"Mitch didn't know about Sarah," she said quietly. "I could have found him. I didn't want to."

"Why not?"

The horse nickered, adding to the sounds of crickets, hoot owls and cattle mooing. The scent of Adele's rose garden filled the night air. "Because he was in a bad place and didn't deserve her. I wanted her in my world. Not his."

She rushed ahead, needing space. Jared wasn't Mitch. But the mocking voice of doubt wouldn't be silenced. Nothing good could come from this. She needed to hold Sarah tight and feel the love between them and lay to rest this want for something more. Something she wasn't able to give. Sarah was enough. Whatever this thing was between her and Jared, she had to stop it.

She spun around, nearly smashing into his chest. He dropped the reins and placed his hands on her shoulders, then stared into her eyes for what seemed an eternity. She stepped back. The warm night air separated them.

"You don't have to do everything by yourself, Haley. And it isn't wrong to want something more for yourself either." No anger filled his eyes, only endless questions and a desire to know the truth.

"I'm doing the best I know how, Jared. I know better than anyone that how a girl feels about herself is tied to how she feels about her father," she said, steering the conversation back to Sarah. "All I know about Mitch are things that I don't want Sarah to know."

"Maybe that's why God put us in each other's paths."

Haley bristled. "You hunted me down. I don't think God had anything to do with it."

"I'm sure He did. If you can't find anything good about Mitch, then let us help. You only saw the bad. We saw both. We saw him straighten his life out. Don't deny Sarah the good things."

Haley brushed away an escaping tear. Words stuck in her throat. Jared wasn't saying anything Hap hadn't said already.

"To know what is right and not do it is as bad as doing wrong," Jared said. His low voice took the sting out of his words. "You know this is right."

She turned back to the barn, flipping on the light inside the door. She quickly saddled a horse while Jared watched. They'd gone through a gamut of emotions this day, shock, anger, compassion, longing, yet she sensed something new, like a door opening, an unseen opportunity, but the what and why were shaded.

"What are you afraid of, Haley?"

She mounted and joined him outside, letting her horse fall into step on the gravel road. "I'm afraid of not ever being normal." She regretted the words as soon as she said them.

A smile tugged at his mouth. "I got the feeling you think normal is highly overrated. You're a bullfighter. Not exactly a job you'd look for in the classifieds."

The laughter left his eyes as the last light from the barn faded and the ranch house disappeared from view.

"Mitch was a fool to let you go," he said.

His voice was soft as the summer breeze, his words a vivid reminder of the normal life she wanted and would never have—all because of Mitch. Mitch hadn't let her go. He'd used her and cast her aside. She could never come to any man pure and undefiled. Not now. She let the night wash over her, the darkness covering her shame. The ride was a silent one, both she and Jared lost in their own thoughts. It ended much too soon. When they returned to the barn she unsaddled her horse and tossed some feed in the stall.

Jared ran a brush over his horse and latched the gate. "I appreciate the gift you're giving Walt—and what it's costing you."

She ducked her quivering chin. "I haven't agreed to bring Sarah yet. I'm still not convinced it's the right thing."

"It's the only thing," he said, a hint of anger back in his voice. "Don't take this from him."

Haley stepped out of the barn into the moonlight. Hap would know. She'd talk to Hap, then decide.

Jared's hands guided her in a half circle, his face inches from her own. She felt the pull toward him in spite of all that had passed between them. It had been so long since she'd been alone with any man but Pop and Hap. She wanted the fear to go away. She wanted back all that Mitch had stolen and destroyed. She wanted normal—to be here, drinking in the scent of earth and horse, with Jared—free from the chains that had bound her for so long.

She wanted to not be alone, to love and be loved, to be that special someone like Adele was to Walt, and feel protective arms around her and know the brush of a man's lips without knowing the terror that followed. If she could do that, with Jared of all people, maybe there was a chance she could grow whole again.

She lifted her gaze from his shirt button, following the line of his throat to his lips, then his eyes. Something smoldered in their depths. She caught her breath, forcing back her rising panic.

His calloused hand brushed a wisp of hair from her face and lingered on the pulse throbbing in her neck. She steeled herself for his head to dip, for his lips to touch hers. Instead, he planted a well-placed kiss on the top of her head.

"Good night, Haley. Dream well. I'll see you in the morning."

He walked back into the barn leaving her uncertain whether to be disappointed or pleased.

Ten days later, Haley arrived back at Jared's with Sarah in tow. She hoped he'd kept his word in seeing that Walt and Adele were gone a few hours before this meeting took place.

Haley's discussion with Walt and Adele after her outburst about Sarah had been tense—the most difficult interview she'd ever had, but she'd managed to answer Walt's questions, leaving his memories of Mitch in a favorable light.

There was no doubt both Adele and Jared suspected her feelings ran much deeper than she was willing to voice, but they'd both kept silent. She sensed Adele's protectiveness of Walt had shifted their relationship in a different direction.

Haley pulled into the drive and glanced at Sarah. So far Sarah had taken everything in stride, but Haley knew her daughter well enough to notice the unusual quietness that had settled over her the last few hours. How she wished Hap had accepted Jared's invitation, or better yet, let her take Mitch's money and run, but he'd left her with a whispered, "You start runnin' now, you'll never stop, and Sarah's the one who'll pay. I ain't goin' anywhere. I'll be right here when you need me."

Jared shut the barn door and walked toward them as the truck rolled to a stop. Late afternoon sun cast a long shadow before him. Haley's heart skipped. She had missed him more than she'd realized. That in itself didn't bode well for her.

"Is he really my uncle?" Sarah asked, craning her neck to see over the dash. A hint of excitement returned to her voice.

Haley nodded. Telling Sarah about Mitch without putting him in a bad light had been hard. Telling her that her father had died in a rodeo accident was harder. She'd expected a barrage of questions about Mitch, but Sarah's only reaction was joy that now she had a real family with relatives like her other friends.

"He looks like Superman," Sarah said. "'Cept his eyes are dark. He's got nice eyes, Mom. Don't you think?"

"I suppose he does," Haley said, trying not to remember how they glistened in the moonlight, then softened before his lips burned the kiss into her forehead.

Jared left her wanting more of the one thing she feared she'd never achieve—a relationship unfettered by pain and bad memories.

Sarah opened the door and jumped out, her wide-eyed gaze absorbing everything at once. Haley followed, grateful that Sarah was such a well-adjusted seven-year-old in spite of her apprehensions. If only she, too, possessed the same resiliency.

Sarah's gaze lingered on the house. Haley sensed it draw Sarah, just as it had drawn her. Fear jabbed into her heart.

"Is this where my dad lived?" Sarah asked.

Haley winced at the word choice. Mitch had never been a dad. "I suppose he did for a while," she said.

Jared joined them and squatted down to Sarah's level. He extended his hand and she took it. "Welcome to the Silver Quarter, Sarah. Your grandparents didn't think you'd be here until later. They went into town to take care of a few things."

Haley relaxed a little. Jared had kept his word.

"Would you like to see your room?" Jared asked Sarah.

"My room? My very own room? Here?"

Sarah's face lit up. Haley shifted uncomfortably. This place offered more than she could ever hope to give her daughter. When the time came to leave, what if Sarah didn't want to go?

"Sarah and I can share my room," Haley said.

Jared's black brow lifted. "You don't have to do that." He rose, his face only a foot from hers. "There's plenty of room for everyone."

Haley's gaze fastened on his lips, suspending the breath in her lungs. "I know that," she murmured.

"Hey, you two. I'm here," Sarah said, pushing them apart. "I feel like the middle of an Oreo cookie."

Jared threw back his head and laughed. The sound went straight to Haley's soul and settled. To an outsider looking on, they could have been a loving, happy family. She wanted that—to share her life with someone. How could she fix what Mitch had taken away?

Jared pulled the suitcases from the pickup bed. "I take it Hap decided not to accept our invitation."

"He thought it would be easier for Walt if he wasn't around," Haley said, feeling his absence.

"But not easier for you."

Haley shrugged her shoulders. "I'm used to not easy." His perception unsettled her. She pulled her purse from the truck and shut the door.

"Let's get you two settled," Jared said. "Which is it, Sarah? You want to room with your mom or not?"

"Not," she said, wrinkling her nose. "Mom talks in her sleep and has nightmares. Sometimes she screams. Hap has to go and wake her up."

Sarah glanced up at Haley. She felt Jared's curious gaze, but couldn't bring herself to look at him. He was part of the reason for her restless nights.

"Is it okay if I have my own room?" Sarah asked.

"Sure," Haley replied, her voice shaking.

"Then follow me," Jared said, heading toward the house.

He hadn't missed the range of emotions racing across Haley's face—surprise, hurt, but mostly anxiety. The nightmare revelation was something new. Jared swallowed, then tightness closed his throat. Nothing was certain, but his suspicions about the life Mitch led before he'd repented and accepted God's forgiveness hounded him.

Sarah's chatter filled the hallway. He led the way upstairs, trying to imagine Haley's fear of walking into Mitch's home territory, of losing Sarah to all the things Walt and Adele could and would shower on her, things she couldn't provide. She wanted to protect Sarah and herself. He wanted that, too. They'd come a long way since that first meeting at the Cheyenne rodeo grounds. If he'd relied more on God's leading than his own actions, would things have been smoother for Haley and his doubts about Mitch's death put to rest?

He paused at the bedroom across from his, the one Haley had occupied ten days ago, then moved to the room right next to it and opened the door. "These rooms have a connecting bath between them. Mom thought you might want your own rooms, but with this one, you can be together and still have your own space." He set the suitcases down. "I'll leave you to settle and will be back in about fifteen minutes to give Sarah the grand tour. That work for you?"

"Works for me," Sarah piped up. She grabbed her suitcase, the wheels leaving a trail on the plush burgundy carpet as she raced through the bathroom to the opposite room.

Jared faced Haley. "You and Sarah have nothing to be afraid of."

"I want to believe that," Haley said.

"Then believe it."

Her chin quivered. "Prove it."

"I intend to," he said, resisting the urge to touch her cheek. "You've done a wonderful job raising Sarah, Haley. She's a great kid."

"Sometimes she's seven going on twenty."

Jared watched Sarah investigate each corner of the room, then bounce on the bed and run her hand over the bedspread. "She wouldn't be who she is if she'd been raised any other way by any other person. You gave her that. Be confident in it."

"Sometimes love isn't enough," Haley murmured so softly he almost missed it.

Anger at Mitch pulsed through Jared, surprising him. So far, he'd laid most of the blame at Haley's feet. But Mitch was guilty, too. "Love is enough if it's the right kind," he said, shifting his gaze back to Haley. "Does this room work for you?"

Tears welled in her eyes.

"It works fine," she whispered. "Thank you."

"You're welcome." He tipped her chin and saw fragility reflecting in her eyes. Too many fears gripped her. He wanted to be the one to wipe away the mistrust and pain—the pain that Mitch had caused. He owed her that. "I'll see you at the barn in fifteen."

An hour later, they exited the chicken house on the final leg of the grand tour. Walt's Jeep pulled into the drive. Jared glanced at Sarah, but she was busy arguing the diet of molting chickens with Haley. Neither had noticed the vehicle nor Walt's stunned look of disbelief as he gazed at Sarah's animated face.

For a moment Jared feared Walt would rush forward and frighten Sarah, but his mother's firm grip kept Walt grounded. Jared saw her lips move with one silent word.

Wait.

Sarah turned and looked up. A curious gleam lit her gray-green eyes. She smiled at Walt and waved.

Haley tensed. Before she turned around, she knew this was the moment she had dreaded.

"Is that him?" Sarah asked. "Is that my grandad?"

Haley placed a hand on Sarah's shoulder. "Yes." She couldn't meet Jared's eyes, but heard him move beside her in a protective gesture that she found oddly comforting. Walt walked toward them, his uncertain steps checked by Adele's more steady ones.

Sarah pressed close against Haley's leg. "What should I do?" she said. "What should I say?"

Haley bent close to Sarah's ear. "Don't be afraid to be yourself."

Sarah took a few steps forward. "Mom, I'm not scared, but what if he asks about my dad? I don't know anything. You never told me."

Sarah's accusation hit Haley like an arrow. "You never asked. You had me and Pop and Hap. I didn't think you needed anyone else."

"I didn't. But it's different now."

Haley rubbed the tight muscles along her neck. As if she needed to be reminded. Walt crossed the grass between the drive and the barn and stopped. Tears filled his eyes. He knelt to Sarah's level.

"Hello, Sarah. You look just like your dad."

Sarah didn't flinch. "Really?"

Walt nodded. "He would have loved to have known you."

Sarah cocked her head sideways. Her practical side overrode any uncertainty. "You think so? I never got to meet him." A heavy sigh escaped her lips.

Panic rose to Haley's throat. This was harder than she'd anticipated. She felt Jared's hand on her shoulder and pulled away. What did he think she was going to do, yank Sarah away and run or blurt out something awful about Mitch? She would never do that to Sarah. Walt and Sarah walked toward the house as Adele looked on.

"It'll be okay, Haley," Jared murmured.

"You don't know that," Haley said, watching Sarah laugh at something Walt said.

Sarah stopped and called back. "Mom, Grandad Walt is going to show me some pictures of my dad. Is that okay?" A worried look crept over her face. "I won't go if you don't want me to."

"You go ahead. I'll be in shortly."

Tears choked Haley's voice, but Sarah didn't seem

to notice as she threw her arms around Walt and gave him the same impulsive hug she used to give Pop, then slipped her hand into his. Walt's feet seemed to float across the yard. Haley imagined Sarah's past memories emptying, being replaced with ones of her "new" family. She turned away from Adele's compassionate gaze.

"You're not losing a daughter, Haley," Adele said. "We hope you'll see this as gaining a family. I'll be in the house if you need anything."

Haley gulped in a breath. That Adele could be so generous after all that had transpired overwhelmed her. One look, one word from anyone right now and she would fall apart. She was losing pieces of herself and Sarah. She could sense it, feel it and was powerless to stop it.

"You and Sarah are safe here," Jared murmured.

Safe, maybe, as long as she kept the truth to herself. *The truth will set you free.* The truth was she wasn't safe at all. Haley gripped his arm, unaware of her fingernails pressing into his muscle until he flinched.

"I'm sorry." She patted the red marks and flushed. "I didn't mean to hurt you."

"You didn't. You couldn't."

She wasn't sure what he meant and didn't want to ask, but a flutter of wanting brushed against her heart. The staggering realization that she wanted this man in her life made her step back. She couldn't afford to care. He loved his brother. His faith was strong. Those two things created a huge chasm between them.

"I could hurt you, Jared. You have no idea."

His near black eyes seemed to grow darker. She squirmed. Jared faced her, his hands resting on her shoulders. She didn't have the energy to move away. Truth was she wanted his support—needed it—and hated herself for it. But maybe, until the shock of Sarah's acceptance of Walt wore off, she could lean on him just a little.

"Sarah said you were having bad dreams. I know being here has you spooked. How can I make it better?"

She pulled away. "You can't."

She couldn't tell him the truth. She cared what he thought. If he knew, he would look at her differently. She was tainted, used. Not by her own choice, but by the will of a man stronger than her and a God that had refused to hear her cry. What could she ever offer any man that Mitch hadn't already sullied?

Love. The word teased the corner of her mind. *You could love him. You could trust him with the truth.*

"Don't do this, Jared," she choked out. "Don't confuse me."

A smile tugged at his mouth. "I want you confused. Whatever Mitch did, I want you to see the opposite."

The breath left her body, leaving a crushing feeling in her chest. His eyes never left her face. She felt herself being pulled in two, as though someone had stretched her out on one of those medieval racks and her body had lost its give. She stepped back, breaking contact.

"I don't think that's possible," she said.

His gaze deepened. "Then you don't want it bad enough."

"How would you know? I'm here. I'm trying. You always get what you want, don't you?"

"Not always," he said, his look serious.

"Don't hurt us," she whispered. "I couldn't stand it if you hurt us." His genuine astonishment made her regret her words.

"Hurting you and Sarah is the furthest thing from

my mind. I'm not so clouded by love for Mitch that I've forgotten what he was like before God changed him."

Haley broke eye contact and stepped back. A steel weight of fear pulled her away from him.

"Don't limit Sarah's capacity to love because you're afraid of it," he said.

Anger ripped along her spine. She lifted her gaze. "How would you know what I'm afraid of? Don't you dare judge me, Jared. Sarah's welfare is first. I'll allow her your version of Mitch's life, but don't ask me to sit around and listen to stories about a man I will always despise." Her voice rose a notch, unraveling that dark place in her mind. "I won't have her destroyed by things she doesn't need to know and wouldn't understand."

"*Destroyed* is a pretty strong word. You're hurting her and you don't even realize it. And what about you? You'll never have what you want as long as you're afraid. You don't show fear when you face the bulls. I don't understand why you choose to hide behind it now. Make me understand."

"You can't understand. You aren't a woman or a mother."

"Thank the good Lord for that. I like being a man, but it doesn't mean I don't feel any less," he said.

"If this is going to lead back to the forgiveness speech again, save your breath."

"What's forgiveness got to do with it? I thought we were talking about being afraid." Jared shook his head. "Regardless of what you believe, Mitch learned to give his fears to God and he learned the importance of forgiveness."

Haley's hands fisted. "And who did he forgive in the end, Jared? Me? For what?"

"I'm still trying to figure that out," he said, his eyes flashing like hot coal. "Mitch couldn't figure it out alone and neither can you or I."

Her breath burned in her throat. "Don't tell me what I have to do and stop trying to fix me." The hair along her neck tingled. "My life was just fine before you and your brother messed with it."

Hurt burned in his dark eyes.

She felt him shudder as he drew a deep breath.

"All right," he murmured, throwing up his hands. "You win. It doesn't really matter whether it's you or Mitch that needs to forgive or be forgiven, it doesn't change what is. It doesn't change your value, Haley. Someday you're going to realize you're worth fighting for, and you'll let go of all that misery you wrap around yourself like a winter blanket. Does it keep you warm or only make you realize how cold and empty your life really is?"

Chapter Nine

Walt and Sarah looked up from the great room table as Haley entered the front door. She caught a glimpse of Adele in the kitchen, then crossed the hardwood floor and stopped next to Sarah. Excitement radiated from her face.

"Look, Mom. Grandad Walt's right. I do look like my dad. How come you didn't tell me or have any pictures?"

Haley glanced at the photos on the mantel, the boxes of snapshots strung out across the coffee table. Pictures of an abundant life, minus the struggles and poverty she and Sarah had experienced.

Her gaze darted around the room and came to rest on Walt's hands draped over Sarah's shoulders, hugging her close to him, pulling her away from Haley and Hap and their old familiar way of life. Panic bubbled through her.

"Can you excuse us, Walt? We need to clean up."

"But Mom," Sarah protested.

"Now, Sarah."

Walt's gaze softened, pinning Haley to the spot near the stairs. "Go and do as your mom says. We'll have plenty of time to talk."

Sarah heaved a sigh. She sprinted across the room and up the stairs. Haley leveled her gaze on Walt. She didn't want to hurt this man, but she had to protect her daughter.

Protect Sarah or herself?

Both. Was there anything wrong in that?

"I want to thank you for bringing Sarah here," Walt said. "She's a gift. I know this has been hard for you." He shuffled uncomfortably. "Whatever happened before, we're here now. We're family. We can make things easier."

Easier? For whom? Haley couldn't have moved if she'd wanted to. Walt glanced at the floor, then back at her.

"I know it's probably too soon for me to say this, but Adele and I talked while you were gone. We would love it if you and Sarah would think about moving here."

"We have a life. In Colorado," Haley choked out. "We're just here for the next two weeks."

"Sarah's Mitch's daughter, too," Walt said.

She flinched. Did he think she would ever forget, especially when reminders of Mitch lingered at every turn? She shoved her arm out, palm forward. "Don't. Please don't put my daughter in a situation where she has to choose one of us over the other," she said, swallowing down rising panic. "I agreed to two weeks. Nothing more."

Walt's eyes softened. "I didn't mean to be hurtful. Sharing Sarah is new for you. I understand that. Take your time, Haley. We want this to work for all of us. In families everyone loses if everyone doesn't win." He offered a smile and a nod, then turned and went into the kitchen.

She heard him quietly talking to Adele and sank onto the bottom step. Walt's understanding and acceptance confused her far more than if he'd gotten angry and railed back.

"Mom," Sarah called from the stairs. "Come on."

Haley rose, the heaviness in her steps matched only by the heaviness in her heart. Sarah washed up and raced back down to find Walt. Hope of spending time with Sarah hit the ground.

During the next few days it seemed like Jared avoided her, but at dinner she'd find him studying her, an intensity in his brown eyes that both thrilled and terrified her. She wasn't immune to him any more than he was to her and his absence left a void she didn't understand.

Jared said she had value. That fear kept her looking back instead of ahead. He didn't know the consequences if she looked too far ahead and allowed herself to act on her dreams and hopes only to find she wasn't emotionally whole enough to sustain a relationship that might lead to something more serious. She wasn't the only one who would be hurt if she tried and failed.

Sarah wanted a home and family—a father. Being here made that painfully clear. Haley's gut twisted. She wanted her soul to heal. She just didn't think it was possible in this house, with this family. She couldn't shatter the images of Mitch that Walt continued to share with Sarah, even though his memories were light-years away from what she knew. Yet there had to be more for her own soul than emptiness and lost dreams.

Restlessness dogged her steps. She wandered out to the corral, saddled the three-year-old gelding Jared had asked her to work and led him to the round pen. She put the colt through some lead changes and side passes, then introduced him to a new movement. As always, he was quick to respond and eager to please. Grateful for the diversion, she let the horse's rhythm and the soft breeze carry her troubled thoughts away.

Jared set a piece of broken harness inside the barn and made a mental note to repair it later, then paused to watch the horse and rider move across the arena, their movements graceful and fluid. A whisper of admiration stirred his heart. Haley had a gift with horses that few people were given. He wished she recognized the value in it—and in herself. Had Mitch so crushed her that she didn't feel worthy of anything good?

She stopped the gelding and leaned over his neck, then scratched his ears and offered an affectionate hug. The animal bent his neck and nuzzled her boot.

Jared stood still, unwilling to break the moment. Her relaxed, easy manner transformed her face, making her radiant. He wanted to see that look on her face again. He wanted to be the reason for it. The thought stunned him. He missed a step, drawing the horse's attention. The moment was lost.

"I thought you'd be with Walt and Sarah," he said, trying to cover the lapse.

She dismounted and walked toward him, stopping at the fence. He got the feeling she felt safer for the barrier.

"I tried a few times, but they're so wrapped up in each other they hardly notice I'm around. I don't like being a third wheel."

"This is new for her, but she'll settle and come back to you. You're still the most important person in her life, Haley. She loves you."

"I know."

"Did Walt tell you that he'd like you and Sarah to stay longer?"

"More like indefinitely," she said. She ran the reins through her fingers. "How do you feel about that? It's your house."

"It's our home," he corrected. "It belongs to all of us. And yes. I'd like you to stay, too."

Her eyes challenged him. "I can't. I have to make my own way."

"Have you heard anything more?"

"You're referring to the investigation," he said.

"I am."

Brave words. Frightened words. Jared's chest tightened, but he held her gaze. "I told you, Haley. It's out of my hands now. I'm sorry. We'll both have to wait."

She rubbed one hand against her jeans, then gripped the reins so hard her knuckles turned white. She opened the gate and led the horse out of the round pen. She didn't like being pushed. Neither did he.

"I want things to be the way they were before Mitch walked into that arena and you found me."

"You can't go back, Haley. Neither of us can."

Her shoulders drooped a fraction, but her head remained high. "Fix what you took away," she murmured. "Give me back my life, Jared."

Her plea knifed through him. "Your life is tied to ours now. Through Sarah. That isn't something either of us can change," he said, drinking in the sheen of her golden hair. Unshed tears made her eyes sparkle like amethyst stones. "I don't want it to change."

Her chin quivered. He reached for her hand, but she pulled away and hurried to the barn, her back as rigid as a fence post. She slammed the door behind her. It creaked open. He saw her slumped against the horse, her shoulders shaking with sobs she refused to utter.

His chest squeezed. It was as though God had taken her pain and placed it on him. The need to comfort her welled inside him, but she wouldn't welcome him. Maybe not ever. He went to his office, closed the door and sat down.

Heavenly Father. The prayer lumped in his throat. He stopped, then rested his elbows on the desk and put his face in his hands. He'd been so impulsive. He'd left God out of his decision to request an investigation, and everything since then had had a domino effect, each fallen piece landing directly on Haley. He'd been unfair and selfish.

His mind raced with memories, foremost all the things Haley hadn't said about Mitch, but all the things her mannerisms did say. Silent rage at his brother nearly unraveled his control. He'd told Haley she couldn't face her fear alone. Well, ditto. He couldn't face his fear about Mitch alone either. He swallowed, then fisted his hands under his chin.

Lord God. I'm not sure I can forgive Mitch, let alone expect Haley to. I care about her, Lord, and she refuses to let You into her life. Help her find her way back to You. And help me forgive Mitch and find a way to help Haley forgive him, too. In Jesus's name.

Sunday morning, Haley put the last ribbon in Sarah's long black hair. "You look lovely," she said. "Have fun at church."

"You should go, Mom. It's rude to not go when someone asks you, especially if you're staying at their house."

"And it's rude to speak to your mother in that voice,

too. I taught you better manners," Haley said, meeting Sarah's gaze in the mirror.

"Going won't hurt. It's only once." Sarah turned around, her gray-green eyes wide and beseeching. "It would make me and Grandad Walt so happy. Even Uncle Jared said he'd love for you to come."

Haley stiffened.

"Pleeeezzze." Sarah ran to Haley's closet and pulled out a lavender blouse and white jeans. "You don't have to wear a dress. Hap says God doesn't care how you come. He just wants you to come."

Haley dropped her gaze. Shamed by a seven-year-old. Hap had always been there to smooth over the church issue, but he wasn't here. Even if he were, Haley knew what he'd say. "'Bout time ya faced yer issues with yer Maker, girl." Problem was, those issues were so monumental that if she were inclined, she didn't know how or even where to begin.

Sarah rummaged through her suitcase and pulled out Haley's amethyst earrings. "I brought these. Hap says a girl just never knows." She cocked her head sideways. "What did he mean?"

"Someday I'll tell you," Haley said, her voice too choked to say more. She ran her fingers over the earrings, remembering the day she'd admired them in a gift shop in Calgary. After seeing the price, she promptly put them back. These were Pop's last gift to her and she knew the sacrifice he'd made to buy them.

"Sarah," Adele called from downstairs. "We're going to be late if you don't come on."

"Please, Mom. Come. We'll wait."

Haley pushed her hair back. Going might make her feel closer to Pop. Right now, she needed that. "All

right. Give me five minutes," Haley said, already re-
gretting the impulse.

Sarah hugged her tight and skipped down the hall.

Walt and Adele looked surprised and pleased when
Haley hurried downstairs. Sarah's huge smile lifted the
heaviness in her heart, but it was Jared's response that
held her captive.

He wouldn't take his eyes off her and the light in
their dark depths stirred something inside her she
thought would never live again.

"I'm glad you're coming," he said, clearing his throat.

Twenty minutes later they arrived at a small white
country church much like the ones she and Pop had
attended throughout her childhood years. Memories
played like an old movie through Haley's mind. There
was a time she'd blindly trusted God. Why did He abandon her? She hesitated at the door and felt Jared stop
behind her.

"You can sit out here if you're too uncomfortable.
I'll stay, too."

Haley shook her head. "I have to do this. It's important to Sarah."

"Don't do it for Sarah," he said, his voice inches from
her ear. "Do it because it's important for you."

She felt the love inside as soon as she stepped
through the door. Jared introduced her to several people. As the service began, she was surprised to hear his
deep baritone voice lift in song. She closed her eyes and
listened, trying not to be so aware of his arm brushing
against her shoulder.

She was determined to not listen to the minister's
sermon, but the title intrigued her from the start and
when he spoke about faith that stands the test, the words

rooted in her heart. What was wrong with her that her faith floundered when others remained strong regardless of their circumstances? Why was she different, and why did it matter?

All the way home, Sarah chattered about the new friends she'd made. Haley sat quietly in the back seat with Adele and Sarah, catching Jared's eye every so often in the mirror. Heaviness weighted her heart again. Going today was a huge mistake. Church was one more reason she couldn't stay here. If people knew…if Jared knew.

As soon as Jared shut the engine off, Haley pleaded a headache and went to her room. She phoned Hap, just to hear his voice and be closer to the one place she felt safe, but peace eluded her. Hap signed off with "I love you, Haley"—something she always knew but he never said. He was worried, and she'd done nothing to relieve him of that burden. If she tried talking to God again, would He hear her or just drop another bomb like every other time she'd taken the plunge?

"God," she whispered. "I trusted You once. Now it's broken and I can't fix it. I just can't."

It is better to take refuge in the Lord than to trust in man.

The verse came out of nowhere, echoing in her mind like a call in the canyon. She ached with an inner pain. She had disobeyed Pop and trusted Mitch and in that disobedience, she tied God's hands with her choice. Was it fair to completely blame God? Hap said God wouldn't go against a person's will to choose. Did that mean she must live with the consequences of her choice to disobey Pop and go with Mitch? She'd been so young, so trusting.

"Why, God? I just need to know why."

She waited for something else to pop into her head, a verse, a voice, anything to assure her God was there, but nothing happened. He was gone, and she was alone.

The next morning Haley stopped outside the kitchen and listened to the sound of Sarah's laughter. She stepped into the room. Walt, Sarah and Adele hovered around the stove, steam rising from a pot hidden from view. Canning jars stood upside down on the counter. The kitchen was littered with colanders, boxes of pectin and sugar. A huge basket filled with end-of-season peaches sat on the floor.

Sarah looked up and smiled. "Hey, Mom. How's the head?"

"Doable."

"Good morning, Haley," Adele said. "Coffee's on and there are eggs in the microwave if you're hungry." Walt pulled a cup off the shelf, filled it with steaming coffee and handed it to Haley.

"Thank you," she said, her gaze darting around the kitchen. Jared was nowhere to be seen. Some of the morning brightness evaporated. She lifted the cup to her lips, hiding her disappointment behind the rising steam cloud.

"It's supposed to be jelly," Sarah said, lifting the spoon from the pot. "You promised to help, remember?"

"Must have been a brain lapse," Haley said, her thoughts turning to the last time she, Pop and Sarah had hovered over a boiling pot of Colorado peaches. "It doesn't look like jelly," she said. "So what are we making?"

Walt smiled and Haley realized she'd referred to

them as a unit for the first time. We. Heat crept up her neck.

"We are making peach butter," Walt said, mashing more peaches in the colander, then removing the skin and seed.

"Let me stir those in," Sarah said, turning back to the stove. "This is going to be so good. We haven't done this since Poppy died."

Haley stared into the mug, then blinked back a tear.

"Sarah's been telling us about your dad," Adele said. "He sounds like a very unique person."

"He was one of a kind," Haley said.

Adele handed Sarah a bigger spoon and began measuring sugar. "I'd love to hear more about him sometime." She dumped the sugar into the pot and instructed Sarah on the importance of not letting the bottom scorch.

A surge of envy ripped through Haley. She should be doing this with Sarah. How could they ever go back to the way it used to be? She could never give Sarah the things that Mitch's family offered.

"You best eat, Haley," Adele said. "I'm afraid Jared got a little carried away with the peach buying. There're two more bushels on the porch."

Tears stung Haley's throat. She stepped into the mudroom to collect herself. This scene mirrored the one when Pop was alive, but the situation and the people were different. No matter how many memories it stirred or how much it hurt, she had to see this through. For Sarah—and like Jared had said—for herself, too.

Someone behind her slipped a bib apron around her neck. Haley jumped and scrambled to steady the mug, then felt two arms slip around her waist. A gentle tug on the apron strings pulled her backwards. She landed against a rock hard chest and tried to bolt sideways, but the pressure held.

"Family efforts require all hands. Can't have you getting your clothes all messed up with peach juice," Jared said. He stepped back, letting a rush of morning air settle between them, then tied the strings.

"There's something wrong with this picture of you and me in aprons," Haley said, wishing her awareness of him didn't make her so jumpy.

"Another news flash. I can cook," he murmured, his breath fanning her hair.

She kept her back to him, wanting him to pull her into his arms, but he didn't. That was just one more pipe dream, close yet unattainable. She wanted to belong here with Jared, but by the end of the week she and Sarah would be safely back in Colorado, and he would become just another memory—a pleasant one for the most part, but a memory just the same. It had been a long time since she'd allowed herself the luxury of a pleasant dream. Even a temporary one. What harm would a little dreaming do?

"I'm glad you're feeling better," he said, stepping closer. His chest nearly touched her back as he adjusted her shirt collar over the bib strap. "I missed you."

The urge to lean against him overruled her instinct to move away. A flash of the fear that always kept her on the fringe of happiness ripped through her—God dangling the carrot in front of the horse only to pull it away. He'd helped create the problems in her by shaping the events in her life. Why wouldn't He remove the fear?

Why hadn't she asked?

The question hammered against her heart. She stiffened her back and felt Jared's amused chuckle. She wouldn't be toyed with, yet she had the distinct feeling neither God nor Jared were playing games. Both wanted something she couldn't deliver. They stepped into the kitchen together. Adele, Walt and Sarah seemed oblivious to the tension, but she knew Jared felt it, even seemed to find her discomfiture amusing.

"Welcome back to the land of the living, Haley," he murmured.

"What do you mean by that?" she asked.

"I think you know." He pulled her heavy hair back and fastened it with a piece of string. Walt and Adele glanced their way, smiled and returned to their tasks. "You're a stubborn woman, Haley Clayton."

"I have to be. Remember, I make my living in a man's world."

"I can't argue with that. I think we'd better pitch in and help before I give in to the urge to kiss more than your forehead," he whispered.

She stepped away and glanced at him, certain he was jesting, but the tenderness in his expression knocked the air from her lungs and threw her off balance. He moved around her and joined Walt, who was slicing more peaches near the sink. What would it be like to be loved by a man like Jared Sinclair? What would it be like to love him back?

"Come on, Mom," Sarah said. "If you don't help, we'll be here all day. Grandad Walt said if we got done in time, we could go down to the pond and swim."

"Okay, what do you want me to do?" Haley asked, glancing at Adele. Light banter sidelined Haley's doubts, at least for now. But she knew they'd come back in full force when she least expected it. She wanted to go on living this dream, but nothing good would come of riding a fine line between what reality was and what she wanted reality to be.

"You and Jared wash, slice and pit," Adele said. "Then pass them on to Walt to mash. Sarah and I will do the rest. With any luck we'll be finished before supper."

Jared tossed Haley a peach pit. "Come on, partner. We're behind. The rest of the crew is waiting on us." He offered a dazzling smile that made her heart jump. "I promise to be good."

For the next several hours, the kitchen filled with laughter. A warm camaraderie that Haley hadn't felt for a long time kept even Mitch's shadow at bay. It was good to smile, to feel part of a family again. She craved to belong to something, to someone, to be complete and happy without her secret threatening her happiness.

"You have wrinkles in your forehead," Jared said.

"That will win you points," Haley replied.

"I said the wrong thing."

"Men usually do," she said.

"Is it something I did?"

She shook her head. "I was just thinking." She grabbed another peach and concentrated on slicing out the pit.

"There's a Dutch oven cooking contest over at the dude ranch tomorrow night," Adele said. "You and Haley should go, Jared."

"Wow. A date," Sarah piped up, her eyes lighting with mischief. "Mom never goes on dates."

"Really?" Jared said, sliding a sideways look at Haley. His eyes darkened. "Then we'll have to do something about that, won't we? Will you do me the honor of escorting me so we can show the 'dudes' how real western cooking is done?"

"Mom can't cook," Sarah said, sniffing the boiling peach pot.

"You're kidding," Jared said. "She grew up on a ranch and can't cook?"

Sarah shrugged. "Hap tried to teach her, but he said every time he eats something she's made he has to stock up on antacids."

"Out of the mouths of babes." Walt chuckled.

A flush crept up Haley's neck. She shot Sarah a warning look. "Is everyone done having fun at my expense? I didn't exactly have time to learn. I was too busy keeping our heads above water," she said, hating the defensive ring in her voice.

The room grew quiet. Haley pressed her hands against the counter and dropped her head.

Jared faced her, forcing her to look up. "I'm sorry things have been so rough for you and Sarah. It's time you had a little fun. I can use a Dutch oven. I even have a few tricks for making the job easier. Would you like me to teach you?"

Haley couldn't breathe. She locked gazes with Jared and couldn't pull away. The warmth of his shoulder against hers, the scent of his aftershave, the tilt of amusement on his lips that lit a twinkle in his eyes filled the empty space in heart. The moment lasted an eternity and sizzled with a connection she didn't want to end yet feared to continue.

"You have a peach peeling on your nose," Jared said softly. He plucked the fruit from her skin with a touch so light she thought she'd imagined it. "Will you go with me? I promise to bring Rolaids and not make any comments about charred biscuits."

"Better take some Alka-Seltzer, too," Sarah piped up, drawing a laugh from Walt and Adele. It pulled Haley back from the space where, for just a few seconds, only she and Jared had occupied. Sarah seemed oblivious, but the moment hadn't gone unnoticed by Walt and Adele. Adele's worried look offset Walt's pleasured smile.

"Come with me," Jared persisted.

Haley threw up her hands. "Do I have a choice?"

"With me, you always have a choice, Haley. Don't ever forget that."

Her heart lurched. Being with Jared, sharing the things that made him laugh, was what she wanted. Even if nothing could come of it, she'd have something pleasant to think back on when she left here.

"All right," she said, dropping her gaze. "I'll go."

Sarah climbed down from the chair, gave Jared a high five and hugged Haley. "Way to go, Mom. You've got a date. It's about time."

Haley was too mortified to look at anyone.

"You don't think she'll back out, do you?" Jared asked, addressing Sarah.

"She better not."

"Promise," Jared said, lifting Haley's chin with his finger, "you won't back out."

She hesitated a second. "I won't back out."

By the time they'd finished the peaches and cleaned up, it was too late to swim. Haley had worked herself into emotional exhaustion weighing the pros and cons of her upcoming "date." Whatever had possessed her to agree? She pleaded a return of her headache and hurried Sarah off to bed.

Seconds after Sarah's head hit the pillow, she was sound asleep. Haley watched the girl's chest rise and fall with each breath. She fingered a silky strand of Sarah's dark hair, then Sarah's eyelid cracked open.

"I love you, Mom," she murmured, opening the other eyelid. "Uncle Jared likes you a lot. I hope we can stay here longer."

Haley's chest squeezed. "Don't you want to go home? Home to Hap, and Spinner and our old life?" Mitch's picture mocked her from Sarah's bed stand. Haley resisted the urge to throw it against the wall. She tucked the sheet around Sarah.

"Hap would come here if you asked him," Sarah said yawning and burrowing deeper into the pillow. "We belong here. Grandad Walt said so."

She bent and kissed Sarah's cheek. "We'll talk about it later. Get some sleep. I love you," she whispered, but Sarah's eyes had already closed. Haley slumped in the chair and spent a restless night watching her daughter sleep, more uncertain about their future than ever.

Chapter Ten

The next day passed far too quickly for Haley. It was nearly five when Sarah skipped into the barn.

"Come on, Mom." She wrinkled her nose and flicked a piece of manure off Haley's shirt. "Uncle Jared's been inside for the last half hour getting stuff ready. You've gotta take a bath and start getting ready." Sarah pulled her toward the house.

Haley dragged her feet. What had possessed her to agree to this? If she could make it to the weekend, her two-week obligation would be finished. She and Sarah could go home and hopefully get back to their lives. She rammed the pitchfork into the hay and headed for the house. Who was she kidding? Nothing would be the same again. She'd still have to share Sarah, though not quite as much.

A few hours later, Jared placed a large Dutch oven filled with cowboy stew and topped with biscuits into the back of his SUV. He ushered Haley into the front seat. She could still find an excuse to back out. She fidgeted with the seatbelt and refused to look at him.

Jared hadn't been able to take his eyes off her from

the minute she'd walked down the stairs. Her golden hair hung in loose waves to her waist, fastened to one side with a comb of German silver hearts that matched the belt around her slender waist. Lavender accents on her white blouse deepened her eyes. The familiar scent of honeysuckle filled the vehicle. Underneath her nervousness, he sensed a hint of reserved excitement. It wasn't all he'd hoped for, but it was a start.

"You look beautiful tonight," he said.

"Thank you. You look pretty nice yourself," she stammered.

"Just nice? I spent hours getting ready," he said, grinning.

Her tense smile relaxed. "You did good. Sarah's impressed."

He chanced a quick look at her profile. "Sarah's not the one I want to impress."

She clasped her hands in her lap and pressed herself into the seat. Thirty minutes later they pulled up at Martin Davis's dude ranch. The double barn doors stood open. Straw bales and ropes outlined a huge wooden platform where dozens of couples were already tapping their toes in time with the music and taking advantage of the games Martin had placed at tables around the room.

A dessert table stood in the corner with a huge punch bowl in the middle. Japanese lanterns lit the interior with an intimate glow. Opposite the barn, a trench of hot coals sent steam rising from assorted pots hanging from hooks.

Jared lifted his pot from the car. He greeted several people and introduced Haley to a few, conscious of the speculative glances following them as he led her to the cooking pits. Let them speculate that he'd finally been caught. He glanced at Haley, finding the prospect appealing. If only he knew where she stood with her faith.

Haley crowded close behind him. "I don't think I can do this, Jared. I'll burn everything and embarrass you in front of all these people."

"That'll never happen. I'll talk you through it. The contest requires one of us prepare the dish, which I've done, and the other to cook it. That's your job."

"You should have let me do the prep work."

"Your fault. You were hiding," he said. "Just follow my instructions and you'll be fine." He grasped her hand and headed for the entry table, took his number then pointed to a vacant spot near the fire pit. "Come on. There's no way you can mess this up."

Haley laughed. "Obviously you weren't listening when Sarah tried to warn you. I can't cook over a stove. What makes you think I can do it over a campfire?"

He bowed slightly. "The difference is I'm here to help you. Together we can do anything." He hadn't thought about his impulsive quest for justice in a long time. There was definitely value in allowing God to use him instead of following his own agenda.

A flush crept into Haley's's cheeks that he suspected had nothing to do with the heat from the pits. She was downright gorgeous when her eyes weren't shaded with doubt and fear. One more step toward the healing process he'd prayed for. Tonight her eyes sparkled, and he'd made it happen. His heart was full.

"What do I do?" she whispered.

"Hang the pot over that medium hook, leave it for twenty minutes, then come back and put one scoop of hot coals on the top of the pot and cook it for another ten or until the biscuits are brown on top."

Her eyes widened. "That's it?"

"That's it." Jared smiled back.

"What do we do in the meantime?"

"I play a mean game of checkers. Wanna give it a go?"

"You bet," she laughed. "I play an even meaner game. But better set your watch so I know when to come back and stir the pot."

Lively country music greeted them as they headed for the tables. For the next few minutes, Jared watched her concentrate on beating him, then his watch alarm sounded.

"You're a tough competitor," he said. "I knew it that day I saw you on the barrels."

Haley grew quiet. Jared could have kicked himself for the reminder. Truth was, he remembered every moment in her presence, the good and the bad. They headed back to the cooking pits. Haley scooped coals onto the Dutch oven lid and glanced at him.

"That enough?"

"It'll do."

"Ten minutes more?" she asked.

"More or less. All we have to do is brown the biscuit tops." Jared took her hand and led her to a table. "We'd better stay close."

"Where did you learn all this?" she asked.

"Mom. She's a remarkable woman. There were times before she met Walt that a pot of stew was all we had for a week."

Quiet settled between them. Several times, Jared caught her watching him, curiosity in her eyes. Several minutes later, Haley checked the biscuits, then removed the pot and set it on the judging table. The quick-paced music echoing from the loft ended. A slow tune blared over the speaker.

"We've got some time before the judging starts. Walk with me," Jared said, leading her toward the rear door.

"I don't think…" she hedged.

"My intentions are honorable, I promise. You can't come to Martin's place and not see this view of the Black Hills on a moonlit night. You're safe with me, Haley."

Her doubt pricked him like a thorn. He led her out back, stopping near the corrals. She lifted her gaze to the sky, the light dancing off her hair and shimmering off her face like snow crystals.

"You're right. It's incredible," she murmured, placing her hands on the fence rail. The music shifted and the distinct sound of Patsy Cline's "Crazy" echoed through the night. He moved behind her and touched her shoulders, felt her resistance even though she didn't pull away. He closed his eyes and rested his face against her ear, murmuring the words along with the vocalist.

The tremor racing through her body touched him. Right now, this minute, her past with Mitch was unimportant. He was a man, and, God willing, she was the woman he wanted in his life. He brushed his face against hers and heard her breath catch. Jared wanted the moment to last forever. He murmured the next phrase.

Haley turned into his arms. She was powerless to draw away. Didn't want to. Whatever lay ahead, she would have this moment, steal it, cherish it, hold it close, because all too soon, it would be gone. She'd be alone again. Jared's lips nuzzled her temple. She held tightly to his arm, afraid if she let go, her weakened limbs would collapse.

I'm falling in love with you, Jared. The silent admission didn't generate fear, only a sadness that what she'd finally found she could never have. The vocalist began the last round of the song. Jared whispered along with her.

Haley's velvet skin invited his touch. Her heart pounded against his. He spanned her waist with his hands, drawing her close, then dipped his head and claimed her lips. It was the sweetest thing he'd ever experienced. When he broke away, the look of wonder on her face made him smile.

"I don't want you and Sarah to leave." Haley's shallow breathing stopped for the space of a heartbeat. Tucking his chin, he looked into her beautiful eyes. "Say you'll stay."

Her eyes closed and opened again. This couldn't be real. Good things like Jared couldn't happen to her. Walt's words echoed through her mind. *Jared's always fixed Mitch's mistakes.* Adele had said the same thing. Even Jared had voiced something to that effect. She was a mistake that Jared needed to fix because he loved Mitch, not her. She looked into his eyes, wanting desperately to believe what she saw in their depths, then shook her head.

"I can't."

The strains of the music faded as the vocalist finished the last lyric. Jared's shoulders slumped a little. He stood motionless in the moonlight, his dark eyes shimmering with disappointment. Another lively tune began. The moment was lost. He took her hand and led her back toward the refreshment table.

"It was a mistake coming here," she said, not meeting his eyes. "Would you please take me home?"

"Which home, Haley?"

Confusion clouded her face then a slow blush pinked her cheeks. "Take me back to the house. Please."

"Is that what you really want?"

"Yes."

One look at her face told him it wasn't. Sadness shadowed her eyes. Whatever damage Mitch had done, he'd done well. It was too late now for a lot of things. Emptiness hollowed the place in his heart where hope had sprung. He spoke to the woman behind the entry table, then led Haley to the car.

"We can stay long enough to find out who's won if you want," she said, staring at the ground.

He already knew who had won, and it had nothing to do with the cooking contest. "Maddie's got it covered," he said. "Haley, I would never hurt you."

Her eyes clouded. "You already have."

She slid into the seat. The drive home was silent. She exited the car and ran into the house before he had turned the engine off, leaving him with the feeling that he'd just lost the most precious thing to come into his life.

Morning came too soon to suit Haley. She splashed water onto her face, then pressed her fingers into her temples. Sarah slipped into the bathroom and closed the door.

"Mom, some cows broke through the fence. Uncle

Jared needs us to help him. Grandma and Grandpa left already."

Haley moaned, slid a washcloth under the water, then wrung it out and put it over her eyes. "They're gone? Where?"

"Don't you remember?" Sarah huffed. "They're helping with the bake sale at church today. They're supposed to come back and get me later." She grabbed her hat off the bed. "Come on. We need to help."

Haley looked into the mirror. Her pale reflection stared back. She couldn't face Jared after last night. And especially not after her own awareness of how important he'd become to her. She straightened and turned away from the reflection.

Sarah's face scrunched. "What's wrong?"

"I don't think I can help. My head is spinning."

Sarah looked doubtful. "You're mad at Uncle Jared, aren't you? That's why you came home early last night. Uncle Jared told Grandma we weren't staying. Is that true?" Her voice rose a notch.

Haley's heart twisted. She'd hoped to break the news a little more gently. "Were you listening at doors again?"

Sarah shrugged and dropped her gaze. "How else am I supposed to find out what's going on? Why are you mad at Uncle Jared?"

"I'm not mad at Jared." Haley bent to Sarah's level. *How do I make her see?* She took a deep breath and pressed her fingers against her temples. "There are some things you won't understand until you grow up, Sarah. You knew this visit was temporary. It is what it is. A visit. Not a move. This isn't our home. It isn't our life."

Tears filled Sarah's eyes, spilling down her cheeks.

"But it could be. You, Hap and me, we could be happy here. And Uncle Jared wants you here. I know he does. You won't come. I heard him say so. If this was my dad's home, doesn't that make it mine, too? Grandad Walt said so."

Walt. With all his good intentions, he wasn't above manipulation after all. Haley gathered Sarah close, savoring the feel of her daughter's warmth and cursing the abnormal childhood that had made her as comfortable in an adult world as one made up of her own peers.

Walt wouldn't have to threaten to take Sarah. She'd willingly stay if Haley gave the word. And maybe even if she didn't. All of her worst fears were becoming reality.

"Why can't we stay?" Sarah cried. "It's not like my dad was a bad person because he couldn't take care of us. I want to be where he was and know about him." Sarah's shoulder's shook. Her bottom lip quivered. She sucked it into her mouth.

Oh, God. His name was a mere thought in Haley's mind, a silent plea on her lips. A sense of His presence surrounded her, something she hadn't felt or allowed herself to feel for a very long time. The lump in her throat grew too large to swallow, the tears behind her eyes impossible to stay. She let them roll down her face and tightened her grip around her sobbing child.

"We can't stay, Sarah. It's a grown-up thing that I can't explain to you right now, but someday I will. Besides, Hap needs us and you have school soon, and your friends…"

"I can change schools. This is our family, Mom. The only one we have. You're going to ruin it because you're scared of Uncle Jared." She released her hold on Haley's neck and pushed away.

"Where did you get that notion?" Haley said.

"I may be a kid, but I'm not dumb. He likes you a lot. I think you like him, too, but you're scared to be around him. It's silly to be afraid of boys, but that's why you made him bring you home, isn't it?"

"That's not true, Sarah. I'm not afraid, and I do like Jared."

Far too much.

"You were crying last night," Sarah said, her gaze challenging. "I heard you."

Haley's chest tightened. "I'm sorry. I never meant for you to hear. Leaving here is about you and me taking care of ourselves, making our own way. It doesn't mean you can't come back and visit. I would never take that away from you or your grandparents."

"But I want to *stay*, always," Sarah pleaded.

Haley stifled her agitation. This was what she'd feared all along. Now it was actually happening. Now she had to do the one thing she'd vowed never to do. Hurt her child. Loving Jared was just an added complication she hadn't counted on, but would deal with, later.

"Sarah, the hardest part about growing up is learning that we can't always have and do the things we want."

"You go home and come and get me when it's time for school."

Haley's patience snapped. She rose and leaned against the sink. "No. I can't keep going back and forth. I have to find work, and that may not be easy right now. We're leaving Saturday. I don't want to hear any argument about it."

Sarah's lips quivered, but her chin lifted. She

stomped to the door. "Okay, but I don't have to like it," she said. "I'll tell Uncle Jared you can't help. We'll get the cows ourselves." She banged the door behind her.

Haley winced, then followed. "Sarah. Wait." Sarah paused at the top of the stairs but didn't turn around. "You know I love you. I only want the very best for you."

"That would be staying here," she said, half turning.

Haley rested her head on the doorjamb, too weary to argue. "I love you, too," Sarah said, dropping her gaze.

"Tell Jared I'll come."

"Okay," Sarah said, brushing tears away. "You're not going to change your mind about leaving, are you?"

Haley shook her head. "No."

"I can keep hoping 'til Saturday, can't I?"

"You can hope," Haley said, feeling her daughter's hurt, "but my decision stands. I'll be down in a minute."

Sarah disappeared down the stairs. Haley closed the door. A knot of fear rose to her throat. Sarah was thriving here. What child wouldn't with a loving set of grandparents, a doting uncle, a mother close by and un-biased memories of a father she wanted to believe in?

She pulled a light jacket from her suitcase, catching her finger in the zipper, welcoming the physical pain. Leaving was in her and Sarah's best interest.

Jared's face formed in her mind, then the image disappeared and she saw Mitch, as clearly as if his physical presence stood before her. Nausea rose to her throat. She closed her mind, forcing back the memory of what followed. She and Sarah had to get home, back to Hap and the life they knew. Back on safe ground. She raced for the barn, the sun beating on her head, memories of Mitch nipping at her heels.

Jared led the horses from the corral as Haley stormed off the porch. Something had sent her over the edge. He sensed it in the way she moved, the way she glanced behind her as though something or someone followed.

His pulse accelerated. She's running again. *Help me understand what she needs, Lord.* Leaving things in God's hands was proving harder than he'd thought, but it's what he should have done in the first place instead of trying to take matters into his own hands.

Haley pulled her hair up and tucked it under her hat. Sarah exited the barn, leading a smaller horse behind her. She glanced at Haley and frowned, then gripped the saddle strings and pulled herself onto the horse's back.

"Thanks for coming," Jared said. "Sarah said you didn't feel well. You don't have to do this."

"You can't do it alone," she said, not meeting his gaze.

"I could," he said. "It would just take a lot longer."

Haley accepted the reins. Their fingers touched, and she pulled away. "I'll be okay."

"Suppose you will if stubbornness has anything to do with it," Jared said, hoping for a smile that never appeared. "How about Sarah? Is she comfortable doing this?"

Haley nodded. "Hap and Pop ran cattle. She's been on horses since before she could walk."

"Good. The cows aren't too scattered, so it shouldn't take long. Once I get them started toward the main gate, Sarah can bring up the rear and push them forward, not too fast, though, or they'll scatter into the brush. Haley, keep them between you and the fence and follow the fence line to the gate."

"We know what to do, Jared," Haley said, mount-

ing her horse. "Just show us where you want them to
end up."

Jared checked his cinch and joined Haley and Sarah.
"We've got a twenty-minute ride before I can do that.
Any questions?"

Sarah and Haley shook their heads. Side by side,
they rode down the road toward the hills beyond the
house. Minutes later, they entered the tree-lined ridge
bordering public grazing lands. Haley gazed across a
land uncluttered by fence posts and barbed wire. Her
thoughts centered on the beauty and freedom of place
and time. All the troubles of the past few days evaporated into the landscape.

Scattered cattle grazed in the distance, looking much
like dots on a page. The scent of pine and sage filled
the air. She shook her rope loose and coiled it again,
then glanced at Jared and Sarah riding a comfortable
distance ahead. Jared sat tall in the saddle, confident
and disturbingly handsome. Sarah chattered comfort-
ably at his side, small and innocent and totally trusting.
This felt right. But feelings were deceptive and untrust-
worthy. Still, how could she take Sarah from a life that
she seemed born to live?

Jared broke off and pointed at Sarah to head down
the draw. "Wait there," he called. "Once I've got them
going, keep a good distance so you don't rush them."
Sarah turned her horse around. "You sure you're up for
this?" Jared asked.

"Yup." Sarah smiled for the first time today.

"Good girl," Jared grinned back.

Haley guarded her heart. She was proud of Sarah's
capabilities at so young an age. Proud, too that Jared
recognized them and wasn't afraid to utilize them. But

it hurt to feel the closeness between Jared and Sarah and be the outsider looking in. *You don't have to be outside. You could let him in.*

Or not. Haley rested her arms across the saddle horn. She wouldn't add to the day's difficulties. Her fingers tightened around the reins.

Jared smiled. Haley's chest tightened.

"I'll drive them towards that tree grove," he said. "There's an orange gate about two miles down. You can't see it from here, but that's where they need to go. Just head toward those rock formations and go a little to the left."

Haley nodded and moved behind a line of trees until the cattle came in sight, then closed in to guide them along the fence. Jared kicked his horse into a gallop and flushed four heifers from the brush. He moved with grace and speed. It was obvious he belonged to the land and the life. Haley tucked the scene into her memory, then concentrated on the cattle.

By the time they reached the gate, the sun was high in the sky. Haley rode ahead. Jared herded the last of the cattle from the trees and pushed them toward open range. Leaning over, she reached for the gate latch, but it held firm. The cattle drew closer. Haley dismounted and leaned her shoulder into the rusty spring, then pulled the gate wide and remounted. The cattle passed through, bawling loudly and kicking up a dust cloud.

"We make a good team," Jared said, closing the gate and brushing a sleeve across his sweaty brow.

"Wow," Sarah said. "That was so fun. We haven't done that since Hap quit running cattle last year. Can we do it again?"

"Maybe," Jared said, turning his horse around. "I'm

glad you had fun. How's the headache?" he asked, addressing Haley.

"Fine." In truth it was pounding, but the atmosphere was so relaxed she didn't want to break the spell.

"We'd better head back," Jared said. "I did a temporary fix on the fence earlier, but I'll need to come back and do it right."

"Is it okay if I ride ahead?" Sarah asked, looking at Jared. "Grandma was coming back to take me to the bake sale at church."

"That's up to your mom," Jared said.

Haley nodded. She didn't want to be alone with him, but she didn't need another excuse for Sarah to be angry with her. "You sure you know the way?"

"Yup. Go through the third gate, catch the road and look for the barn."

Haley waved Sarah on. She kicked the horse into a gallop and rode ahead. Haley fell into an easy jog beside Jared.

"I take it you haven't reconsidered," Jared said.

Haley shook her head. They veered off the main trail and headed down a gulch. This wasn't the way back. She stopped the horse.

Jared circled back. "There's something I want you to see," he said.

They followed the gulch, exiting into a huge open valley. Charred trees pointed to the sky, others lay in burnt clumps across the lush valley floor littered with wildflowers. A gentle breeze tickled her cheek and the piercing cry of a hawk echoed across the blue sky.

"It's beautiful," Haley said. "So peaceful."

"It wasn't a few years ago. It's easy to forget the

beauty when you witness the devastation of a fire. You think the land will never recover."

She stood in the stirrups and shaded her eyes.

"It's more beautiful now than before," Jared said. "Kind of symbolic, isn't it?"

"What do you mean?"

"You've been through a wildfire, too, Haley, and like this canyon, you've come back, stronger and lovelier."

She sat back down, tears welling in her eyes. "You didn't know me before."

"I know you now. Beauty comes from ashes. Like you and Sarah. You deserve to be happy. Don't convince yourself you don't."

The hawk's shadow passed over them again. Haley wished she could latch on to the tail and for a little while, soar above her problems and feel free. The sympathy in Jared's eyes was more than she could stand— one more reason not to stay. She loved him. She could handle his anger, even his pain and blaming her for Mitch's loss, but never his pity.

"We'd better get back," she said, turning the horse around.

Jared followed. "Someday, you have to stop running," he murmured.

His words followed Haley all the way to the main road.

"I need…" both began together and stopped.

"You go first," Jared said.

Haley lifted a rein, cuing the horse to pick up his pace. "I need you to know how much I appreciate your hospitality."

"But…" Jared said, looking straight ahead. "You're still leaving."

"We have to get back to our lives, Jared. I need to know I have a job to go back to, a job that hasn't been… compromised by…" This was so awkward. She hated it.

"The investigation," Jared finished.

"Have you heard anything more?"

"Sam called this morning. You've been reinstated and cleared," he said. "I already sent letters to the people who matter most."

Haley's gaze flew to Jared's. "You wrote letters before you knew the outcome? Why?"

"It was the right thing to do. You're exonerated, Haley. Free."

Exonerated. Free. Not likely. There would always be some who looked at her and wondered, just like Jared. She looked up to find him watching her. "Were you going to tell me?"

"Yes. But I'll confess, I thought if you had nothing to go back to, you would stay."

"That wouldn't have been fair," she murmured.

"Nothing about meeting you has been fair." They rode to the sound of hooves against gravel and birds chirping in the pines. "I wish I'd met you first," he said.

She closed her eyes swaying with the horse's rhythm. *So do I, Jared. So do I. But you didn't and we're here and this is the way things are.*

"Thank you for the endorsements," she said. "I'll set up times for Sarah to come and visit Walt during school breaks."

"Will you come, too?"

"Probably not." She paused a moment, then continued. "There's something else I need you to answer."

"Ask," he said.

"Do you believe I hate that Mitch was killed?"

"Yes," he said without hesitation.

She stared into his eyes and saw truth. It didn't change the fact they had no future, but it lifted a huge weight from her heart. "Thank you. You have no idea how much this means to me."

He looked away. "I think I do." He moved his horse closer. Their legs bumped. "I'm not sorry for last night, only sorry that it made you uncomfortable. If I could, I'd do things differently from start to finish."

Start to finish. She didn't want to think about start or finish. She nudged her horse ahead, breaking contact, but Jared persisted, easing his animal into a matching pace.

"I'd like your opinion on a project I'm working on when we get back to the house," he said.

Longing pulled like a wire stretcher across her heart. She wanted to be part of his life, but she could never be what he deserved. Even if he loved her, Mitch would always stand in the middle. She couldn't stay and let her heart be stomped all over again. The cost was too high for everyone. They rode into the barnyard and put the horses away. She paused beside a box stall housing the most beautiful paint mare she'd ever seen.

"That's Calliope," Jared said. "Pretty, isn't she?"

Haley stroked the velvety nose, then ran her hands along the muscular neck. "She's beautiful. She wasn't here before or I'd have seen her." Haley looked at the mare's heavy sides. "She's in foal."

"Walt must have brought her in off pasture before they picked Sarah up," Jared said. "She's carrying the last of a long line of cutting horses. You might say next to Sarah, Calliope is the apple of Walt's eye."

Haley gave the mare's neck a final rub and turned away. "What did you want to show me?" she asked.

He held his hand out. She hesitated a moment, then took it. He led her toward the small office where she'd seen him sequestered for hours on end.

"What do you do in here?" she asked. Blueprints were scattered across a wide corner table.

"This is the bones of the ranching operation," he said. "Breeding and sales records, feed bills, supply lists. You know the drill. Come here. This is what I wanted to show you."

Haley looked at the blueprints. "Are you expanding the ranch?" It would be a shame to blight the land with more buildings, but this was none of her business. It wasn't her home.

"They're plans to expand the riding program," Jared said. "This is the new barn and arena. Animal programs can reach a lot of kids that people can't. This has been a dream of mine for a long time. It's a much needed ministry, Haley. These kids need to experience God's love as much as the rest of us, perhaps more because of their disabilities. If I can be a tool to show them the way…give them some hope and healing."

His voice choked.

Hope for the soul. Healing for the mind. Was there such a thing? Haley wasn't sure anymore. Jared turned a few blueprint pages and found the one he wanted. "What do you think?"

Haley stepped back and fingered the table edge. "I think it's a beautiful and noble cause, one that you'd be very good at, but you can't fix all things for all people, Jared."

"I can't, but with God's help, I can do something."

He lifted his dark eyes to hers and studied her face, as though weighing whether he should say more. "I couldn't fix Mitch either, but God did."

The brightness of the day disappeared beneath a cloud of anger. "Why does nearly every conversation come back to Mitch? Maybe if you'd stop trying to fix everyone and just try to understand them, we'd all be better off." She backed toward the door, powerless to stop the flow. "Did you bring me here to share this dream of yours or to defend Mitch and make me see him differently so you could fix me, too?"

Jared laid the plans aside. "I didn't have an agenda. The plans were important to me and I wanted to share them with you."

She wanted to believe him.

"Your plan won't work. I'm not broken, Jared. That's something Mitch tried and failed at." Suspicion guarded her words.

"I want you whole and happy. That's all," he said.

He took a step toward her, but she retreated. One hand rested on the door knob, ready to yank it open if he got too close.

"I wasn't unhappy before coming here. I'm not the one whose soul was sick. Mitch was," she snapped.

"I'm not going to defend Mitch. I can't." He crossed the office floor and put his hands on her shoulders. Her skin was warm beneath his fingers, but her eyes were flat and cold.

"It doesn't end there or you would never have looked for me. You always fix and finish things. You said so yourself. So did Walt." Jared's features hardened. Doom settled like a cloud inside the building.

Jared didn't really care about her welfare. She was

only another object to add to his list of accomplishments. Another one of Mitch's broken toys that needed a crutch until they could walk again. The pain of it was unbearable. How many others were there?

"You have to have a cause to work on, don't you, Jared? Well, I am not a cause," she said, leashing her anger with short, controlled words. "Neither is my daughter."

His dark eyes softened, inviting her in. "No, you're not a cause," he said. "But I don't expect you to believe that. We could be partners, helping others. I see you disappearing, Haley. That would be a waste when I also see glimpses of the woman you are inside. The one who wants to come out but is afraid."

His words ripped into her soul like talons. "I..." The word trailed off, taking the thought with it. She wanted her life whole, not left in the fragments of Mitch's waste. Wholeness lay within reach. All she had to do was grasp it. But not here. Not with Jared who looked at her as an unfinished project. She wanted his love, his heart, and wanting that was selfish in itself when she couldn't come to him pure and undefiled.

Dreams. A million little scenes flashed by in a split second, filled with joy, hope, sharing, but the final memory was so poignant she opened the door to escape. Mitch. He was the reason Jared saw her the way he did. Mitch had ruined any chance for her to be happy with any man. She would never be free and she couldn't be repaired.

"Don't waste your time on me, Jared. You can't help me. Mitch saw to that."

She saw her despair reflected in his eyes. "Dreams

can be reshaped," he said. "Not every man is Mitch. I'm not, Haley. I would never hurt you."

She snapped inside. "Stop saying that. That's what Mitch said just before he raped me." She recoiled at voicing the word she'd danced around for eight years. Speaking it brought a release, however minor, but didn't lessen the vileness. "He used me and threw me away. The only good thing he ever did was leave me with Sarah. He killed a part of me that will never live again," she said with quiet fury. "Only Sarah matters."

Shock siphoned the blood from Jared's face. He gripped the desk chair, the horror of what she'd revealed written all over his face. He didn't see her anymore. He saw through her. The ugliness of Mitch's act would forever stand between them, now. Nothing would be the same again.

A scuffle outside the window made her jump, then the door yanked open. Haley's stomach lurched to her throat. Walt stood behind the screen door, his face as white as the hair on his head. He wasn't supposed to be here.

"Jared," he whispered. His stricken eyes turned on Haley. "Mitch," he said softly. "Sarah." Anger flashed across his face. "You're lying." His voice cracked, then his feeble legs buckled. Haley reached for him, but he pulled away and stumbled. It was Jared who broke his fall.

Chapter Eleven

"What have I done?" Haley whispered. Her face turned chalky, her eyes deep pools of misery. "I never wanted this. Never wanted anyone to know."

Jared lifted Walt in his arms, but even his slight weight felt like a sack of boulders. Walt mumbled something and opened his eyes. Shock dulled his reflexes. "Not true," he muttered. Jared managed to pull the screen door open and carry Walt into the house.

"I'm sorry," Haley said, closing the door. Tears streamed down her face. "I'm so sorry. I never meant…"

"It's done, Haley," Jared said. One look at Walt's face made him wish it could be undone. But Walt's devastation didn't hold a candle to the pain he saw in Haley's eyes. "You didn't do anything wrong. Let's deal with one thing at a time." He laid Walt on the couch.

"She lied," Walt moaned, his head thrashing from side to side. "Why would she do that?" His angry gaze impaled Haley. "We wanted you to stay here. Why would you do this?" He closed his eyes and whispered, "Sarah. You came because of Sarah."

"Walt, stop it," Jared said. Haley looked like she was

about to collapse. Her shaking hands cupped her cheeks, but retaliation sparked her eyes. This was not the time for a showdown. "I'm sorry, Haley. He doesn't realize what he's saying."

"I do know," Walt said, falling back against the couch cushion.

If it had been anyone but Walt making the accusation, Jared had no doubt Haley would have used any means possible to defend herself. But it was Walt, and no doubt his frail health held her in check. She cast a fleeting look at Jared, then ran up the stairs. He should have defended her without hesitation. Now it was too late.

Mitch raped me.

She never wanted anyone to know.

Jared didn't want to wrap his mind around those words, but they kept repeating over and over like an old horror flick. In his heart he'd known, just hadn't wanted to conceive of something so ugly being done by someone he loved so much. He eased Walt back onto the couch and put a pillow behind his head.

"Stay here," Jared said. "And don't move."

"You're going after her?" Walt cried. "You know she's lying. Mitch wouldn't do such a thing."

"We don't know what Mitch was capable of before he came back, Walt," Jared said. "He was pretty messed up."

"But you can't believe…" Walt turned his face away.

Jared remembered the fear in Haley's eyes, the choked-off hurt and anger. He understood all of it now. Any doubt lingering in his mind dissolved. "I do believe, Walt. Have you taken a good hard look at her? There's no way she's lying about this. We should have helped her. All of us." He wished he'd conveyed that to her from the start. "I'll be back. Haley needs me."

He rushed up the stairs and twisted Haley's doorknob. It held. Heartrending sobs echoed under the door crack. "Haley, let me in." The crying quieted. He suspected she'd buried her face into a pillow to muffle the sound. "None of this matters to me."

Liar. It does matter. But we can deal with it.

"We'll work through this," he pleaded. "Open the door. We have to talk."

His stomach lurched at the thought of what more talk would reveal, but this wasn't about him. It was about the brother he'd never lost faith in—until now. It was about the vile act that had destroyed hope in the woman he'd come to cherish. It was about a future that had held a sliver of hope, and now seemed bleak and unattainable, tainted with memories that shouldn't matter, but did.

"It's too late, Jared. Go away. There's nothing left."

She sounded so close yet unreachable. Two inches of door separated them. Those two inches seemed like a canyon span. He had to see her, hold her, take away the bad memories and give her new ones. *Please Lord God. Help me.*

He moved down the hall to Sarah's door and slipped inside to the bathroom that joined Sarah's room to Haley's. Haley hunched against her bedroom door with her legs drawn tight against her chest. Her cloud of silky hair hid what he knew was a face as ravaged as her soul.

He was losing her. If he didn't draw her back, he'd lose her forever. She'd disappear into her circle of pain and be lost.

"Haley?"

She jumped to her feet, her agony so tangible it stole

his breath. "Get out," she choked. "I don't want you here."

"I'm not leaving you like this." He stepped into her room. The late-afternoon sun was hot on his back, casting a long shadow as he passed in front of the window. She watched the shadow approach with panic-widened eyes, then flattened herself against the door, groping for the lock, watching his shadow creep before him.

Jared backed off. He was bigger than her, stronger, and the last thing he wanted was to appear threatening. He stopped, hunkered down on his ankles and looked up. "I'm not going away until we talk this through," he said, softly, evenly.

"I said no. I don't want you here," she repeated. "I don't want to talk. I just want to go home." Hysteria bubbled close to the surface.

He suspected her mind had flashed back. He felt her helplessness, her rage. He had to make her see him for who he was, not who she saw in her mind. "Haley. It's me, Jared. I'm not going anywhere."

For a split second, the shadows lifted from her eyes, then tears rolled down her cheeks. "I have nothing to give you."

"Then I won't ask for anything." He rose and hesitated a moment. Nothing in his entire life was more important than making her see him. If he bungled this, he'd lose her forever.

She wrapped her arms around herself. "I don't want to feel this way. I want to be normal."

Her eyes held a plea he couldn't ignore. He crossed the room in three strides and gathered her close. "Haley, Haley. We'll get through this. Let me help you."

For a moment, she yielded. He savored the feel of

her in his arms. He would protect her forever, love her, help her heal. Her heart pounded in unison with his. Then she pushed back and beat clenched fists against his chest. Shadows haunted her eyes again. Her sobs grew louder.

She ducked around him, bolting like a green filly. "You can't help me. Don't you see? It's no good, Jared. I'm so sorry that Walt overheard. I'm so sorry about everything. I hadn't thought about Mitch in years until he showed up." She cast her gaze to the floor. "Since then, I've thought of little else."

She was pulling away and there wasn't a thing he could do to stop her. "Haley." This time he heard the plea in his own voice.

"Let's not do this," she said. "I'll see that Walt has time with Sarah, but I won't come back here, Jared. Don't ask me to, don't call. Just let it be. Let me go. Please."

He'd lost her. That stubborn pride that he so admired had aligned with her fear and defeated him. That she asked him to let her go meant he still had a minor foothold if he chose to press the matter. The thought tasted like gall. He looked deep into her eyes and saw years of hidden anguish culminated in this one moment. She'd suffered enough. He wouldn't add to it.

"This is what you really want?"

A tear rolled down her face, followed by another. "It's what I have to have. It's what I need."

What you need is someone to love you through this. Let me love you, Haley.

Longing, sadness and loss scattered from her like broken crystals. He knew in his heart that her decision was final. He could argue until the chickens roosted.

Perhaps it was God's plan for him to be the instrument of forcing her to face her pain to move ahead without anything more. He swallowed hard, then nodded, accepting defeat. He crossed the room, opened the locked door and walked toward the stairs. A hollow echo followed his steps. Haley's door closed quietly behind him.

The sun rose like it did every morning, bathing the late-summer day with hues of orange and red. Jared found no joy in it. He smoothed the tattered letter on his desk, its edges a testimony to how often he'd poured over the words. His office door opened and he lifted his head.

"I can't believe they're gone," Adele said, closing the door behind her. "You look awful, Jared. Have you been in here all night?"

Jared nodded. "I couldn't sleep." The final scene in Haley's room had kept him pacing the floor for hours, his heart as empty as the room where she'd slept. "I came out here to work, but couldn't even do that."

"What is this?" Adele said, coming around the desk.

"A letter Mitch wrote. Carl Martin sent over a box of stuff Mitch left at the Fellowship Booth in Cheyenne. This was in it. It's postmarked six months ago." Jared set his elbows on his desk, then dropped his head into his hands.

"The letter doesn't mention Haley by name. Only what happened the night he met her." His voice hitched. He swallowed hard and continued. "I remember him saying that he'd done some awful things. Things he couldn't make right." Jared banged his fist on the desk. "Everything Haley said is true. I suspected. I knew, but I'd hoped. It's all here. Mitch's regret and sorrow, his need for forgiveness and fear of owning what he'd done." Tears stung Jared's eyes. He refused to let them fall. "I don't know what to do with this."

Adele moved to the other side of the desk without reading the letter. Her quiet strength filled the room, settling some of Jared's pent-up rage.

"You have to keep it, Jared. Put it away for now. At some point, Haley may need to see it to move past where she is. I don't know when that time will be, but you'll know."

Jared picked up a pencil and snapped it in his hand, the sick feeling inside him returning, along with anger he didn't know he was capable of.

Don't go to that place. Not yet.

He shoved Mitch from his mind. Mitch wasn't important. Haley was, and she'd made it clear she didn't want to see him again—ever.

"You saw Haley and Sarah before they left. Were they okay?" he asked.

"Sarah's angry and doesn't understand what all the tension is about, but she loves her mom. She will work through this and be okay. I'm not so sure about Walt. Or you and Haley." Adele's warm hand penetrated the coldness in his body. "God's healing happens in His own way and in His own time. Don't lose faith."

"She won't be back," Jared said. The knowledge twisted and turned inside him.

"You don't know that. She needs time. What happened with Mitch isn't eight years ago for Haley. In her mind, it's yesterday."

Jared's throat closed. Yes. And now he was supposed to do the same thing he'd once told Haley to do. Give this mess to God. That day seemed like a lifetime ago.

He thought he'd done that. He hadn't appreciated the magnitude of his request until now. How did a person give violation to God and forge ahead? He tried to shut out the picture.

"I saw Walt drive off early this morning," he said. "Where did he go?"

"To see Pastor McDonald."

Jared nodded. "That's good."

"Maybe you should go, too," Adele said.

"Not now."

She reached across the desk and patted his hand. "I'm sorry. It's awful to watch someone you love suffer and not be able to do a thing to make it better. You do love her, don't you?"

Jared nodded, then leaned against his desk and cradled his head in his hands again. The place Haley had filled in his heart was ravaged and empty. Her voice echoed in the dark chamber.

Go away. I can't give you what you need. I never should have come here. I don't want to see you again.

He processed every reaction and word, every look and piece of body language, from the time he'd run into her in Cheyenne outside the Fellowship Booth to last night. Finally he understood the depth of her despair, the source of her hopelessness.

It was the legacy she'd left him. He pressed his fingers deeper into his temple, trying to squeeze from his mind the horror of her confession, erase the picture of what Mitch had done to her and the terror she must have felt, the sounds of her anguished cries as she'd sobbed her misery into the darkness. The thoughts circled in his mind, chasing the flat words of Haley's confession.

His mother's hand breached the coldness in his body. "Does she know how you feel?"

Jared shook his head. "She knows I wanted her to stay."

"And how did she respond?"

"She left and didn't look back. I think that pretty much says it all."

"This isn't about you, Jared," Adele chided gently. "You matter. That's part of why she's so hurt. She isn't in a place to really hear you right now." She tapped his hand. "She will. You did the most important thing. You left Walt and went after her. That's what she'll remember. Not right away, but when the pain settles. Give her time to recognize that you see *her*, not what Mitch *did* to her." She gave his hand a final squeeze and walked to the door.

Jared lifted his head. Letting go would require every bit of grit and prayer in him, but it was what she wanted. He'd do it, with God's help. "I love her enough to let her go, but I'll never give up on her," he said, the weight of the decision heavy on his heart.

"I'd be very disappointed in you if you did. Let me know if there's some way I can help," she said, her smile reaching her eyes.

"You already have."

"Haley may be out of our reach, but she's never out of God's. He doesn't give up on any of us." She rose and slipped through the door.

Jared watched her walk to the house then picked up the phone and dialed Sam McIntosh's number. He'd already taken the necessary steps to reinstate her reputation and secure her livelihood, but it wouldn't hurt to go above and beyond.

If Haley wouldn't let him be a direct part of her life, he'd stay in the background and watch from a distance. He could live with her loss, as long as she was okay— as long as her wounds healed and she was happy again.

September sneaked in like a baby's sigh, bringing cooler nights and shorter days. Haley usually looked forward to fall and a lighter travel schedule, but this time, she coveted work. Anything to keep Jared's memory at bay. Even Hap seemed at a loss to know what to do with her. He tiptoed around her as if uncertain what might set her off.

Every few days, flowers arrived from Jared with cards she refused to read. Never in her life had anyone given her flowers. She pretended not to care, telling Hap to throw them away and threatening to refuse further deliveries, but a warm glow flowed through her that Jared hadn't forgotten or tossed her away.

She would touch the petals, drink in the rich fragrance when no one was around, and when blooms wilted and the stems turned brown, Hap would toss them in the trash. Her heart would break all over again, which was stupid. They were just flowers and they were dead. Sarah caught her once lifting an unopened card from the trash.

"You're upset all the time because you love Uncle Jared," Sarah had said. "He loves you, too. I know he does. He asks about you all the time. Why can't we be a family?"

Haley couldn't tell her why without destroying her small world. She'd fought back tears, and Sarah had stormed away. Haley had plucked a yellow rose that hadn't yet died, carried it to her room and pressed it between the pages of *A Tale of Two Cities*.

Collecting a fading bloom from each bouquet had become a ritual now, along with the message cards she still couldn't bring herself to read.

Once, when Jared had called Sarah, Haley picked up the extension just to hear his voice. Sometimes she thought she'd caught glimpses of him at a few rodeos, but it had to be an illusion, a figment of her imagination, and when she searched for him, she never found him.

The truth was, she loved him. If she had any doubts before, they'd vanished after her rushed flight home and the magnitude of telling him to leave her alone settled in. The ugliness of rape would always stand between them. How could Jared move past it if she couldn't? He deserved better.

You can move past it, but you can't do it alone.

The thought stayed with her while she parked her old camper near the Rangely rodeo grounds, waved a greeting to a few familiar faces and set about securing her campsite. Local rodeos didn't pay as much as the bigger ones, but the work was steady and the partici-pants like family. Work was what she needed now. She was more than grateful Sam had called.

She'd traveled alone before, but this was the first time that it gnawed at her like a mouse on a rope. The days were busy and exhausting, but the nights… The nights were endless.

Sarah had refused to come. The distance between them hurt almost as much losing Jared. She remem-bered every whisper, every touch, from the day they'd first met until now.

"Stop it," she whispered. "It was over before it even started." The ache in her soul seemed endless.

Sunday provided a lull in activity. The last events were scheduled after lunch and ran into early evening. She wandered restlessly around the campsites, then strolled over to the area where Cowboy Church was set up. She hadn't been to a service since going with Jared and she didn't really want to go now, but the thought of being alone with herself in her present state of mind wasn't appealing either. If the service made her uncomfortable, she'd leave.

The sun dipped below the horizon. Campfires filled the air with the smells of coffee and bacon. Laughter and the sound of strumming guitars surrounded the camp. People milled around, some joining other campfires, others heading toward the area set aside for the service. A few called and waved to her, but still, she'd never felt lonelier in her life.

She jammed her hands into her jean pockets and followed the crowd. Soft music played inside the makeshift tent. She recognized the old hymn, "Amazing Grace," Pop's favorite. Memories rushed back of rodeos past, before Jared or Sarah or Mitch. Her faith had been simple then, happy and filled with contentment.

She'd confessed herself a sinner in need of the saving grace of The One who died and rose again to redeem her, believed that the goodness of God dwelt in those who believed. She'd trusted with her whole heart and soul in a jealous God who protected His own. Right up until Mitch, the trial by fire where she'd disappeared in the ashes along with her faith.

The strains of music surrounded her, the old hymn pounded into her mind.

Why couldn't she think of Jared without remembering that Mitch had stolen the one thing she had to offer the man she loved, herself, her purity? *Lord God, I needed You. Why weren't You there?*

"You going in?" someone murmured from behind.

"I'm not sure," Haley said, stepping aside to let him pass. A few moments later, she edged into a back row and sat down on a folding chair. Pop had been disappointed when she'd quit attending church and the rodeo tent meetings. He and Sarah had gone without her. She felt like she'd lost a part of him. Now she felt his presence along with something more, Someone more. Someone higher.

The music stopped and a young man stepped to the front. He smiled at the small crowd and welcomed them. Haley fidgeted, dipping her chin to let her hair hide her face. The song service began but she didn't join. She studied the profiles of those caught up in the worship of music, their joyous faces lifted in praise. They looked content, peaceful.

The young man ended the song. A hush fell inside the tent. He began slowly, "Elizabeth Elliott once said that in the hard lessons of life, God wants to give us Himself."

The words drew Haley in spite of her resolve to not take anything he said to heart. His next words hit her like a gut punch.

"I had intended to speak on the greatness of God's love this morning, but He gave me another message instead. I'd like to share with you about the groaning of God. There is an appointed time for everything, and God notes our sufferings. His Spirit prays for us with groaning which cannot be uttered."

Haley tried to stem a rush of hurt. If God noted her suffering, why hadn't He done anything about it?

The young minister glanced around the small gathering, his warmth and energy filling the space. "Many of us have been in tough spots—heartrending situations that have tested our faith. I want you to know that it's okay to struggle. What we have to recognize is that searching for an escape doesn't leave us any strength to endure what God is asking us to go through."

Haley edged to the end of her seat as he talked about suffering being only for this present time and how people's sufferings are not wasted.

"Glory will come," he'd said. "But until the glory, we groan."

He talked about staying focused on the glory as people groan over the suffering in this world and how the Spirit of God focuses on the glory, yet groans, praying for them because they don't always know how—feeling with them—and groaning with uttering too deep for words.

A gentle urgency stirred in Haley's heart. The man encouraged everyone who suffered to not abandon their walk with the Lord to join the enemy of their souls, but to focus on the glory awaiting them.

His eyes seemed to look straight into Haley's soul as he quietly ended his message with, "It's okay to groan and grieve 'in hope.' Allow the Spirit of God to comfort you. Trust His prayers on your behalf, prayers that are too deep for words."

Haley barely moved as the final song stirred the faith she'd buried with her innocence. The song talked about all things working for good and trusting God's heart when one can't see His hand. Just what was in God's heart for her?

The music ended. People shuffled out of the tent. For the first time in a long while, she wanted to be alone. She wanted time to think. Time to test the shaky ground the message had encouraged her to explore. Haley pushed back into the chair. If she were invisible, the world would go away and leave her alone. But that wasn't what she wanted or needed. She needed to think about what she'd heard. Really think. She tucked her chin, listening to the sounds of people shuffling outside the tent.

"Is there something I can help you with? Anything I can do?"

The young minister's voice forced her to lift her head. Compassion radiated from his eyes.

Haley's eyes welled. "Pray for me," she murmured.

"I will," he said quietly.

Unnerved by his words as well as her request, she rose and hurried into the cool night air. A man studied the bulls near the pens, his chin resting on the rail. She'd lost count of the nights she'd stood in the same spot, studying the bulls before competition, vowing to keep the riders safe no matter what.

The man shifted, the sun outlining his profile, then he pushed his hat back with a familiar gesture that stirred her memory. She watched a moment longer, then walked slowly back toward the camper, wondering if images of Jared would always haunt her in how others carried themselves. She hadn't realized what a powerful opponent love could be.

Chapter Twelve

Sleep was as elusive as happily ever after, but one picture stayed in the foreground of Haley's mind through that night and the next. It wasn't Jared, Mitch, or the events of that disastrous night eight years ago, but an image of the Spirit of God praying on her behalf because she couldn't believe enough to pray for herself anymore.

A sliver of the old faith she'd held as a child stole into the darkness, drawing her toward the light. She pulled Pop's Bible out of the drawer and laid it beside her unable to remember the last time she'd turned the pages. Maybe it was time. Maybe the questions she needed answered lay within these pages. As soon as she finished her work, she'd search for some answers.

She flung the sleeping bag aside and padded to the door, shivering as her bare feet hit the floor. She readied herself for the day's events, then flipped the lock and pushed the door open. A mist hung over the rodeo grounds, the sun beginning to tease the skyline. The bull pens and campground buzzed with activity. A morning chill nipped her skin. She rubbed her arms, grabbed some jerky and trail mix from the truck, then saw two familiar figures crossing the parking lot. Her chest tightened.

Walt and Adele. How had they known where to find her?

Hap.

Please, God, don't let there be another scene like before. None of us could bear it.

Her pulse ceased to pound. Anxiousness evaporated in the morning mist, leaving only a sense of wonder. Her plea was sincere. Had God actually heard and calmed her anxiety? Would He hear again?

Help me protect Sarah without hurting Walt and Adele any more than I already have.

Haley drew strength from the quietness of spirit that remained. She half expected this newfound calmness to disappear, but it didn't. She lifted her chin and waited for Walt and Adele to reach her campsite.

Adele rushed forward, gathering Haley in a welcoming embrace. Her first instinct was to back off and keep her defenses up, but the emotion Adele generated was warm and loving.

"I've missed you," Adele said. "I'd be lying if I said I haven't been worried. How are you?"

"I'm good," Haley fibbed.

She stepped away, avoiding Adele's gaze that saw far more than Haley wanted. She looked directly at Walt, refusing to cower behind the pain of their last encounter.

Before her stood the broken man she'd seen when she first arrived at Jared's ranch—before Sarah's presence penetrated his grief and gave him hope. She remembered the day she'd seen them bent over a chessboard, Sarah's dark hair contrasting with Walt's snowy crop.

Sarah hated chess, but she'd played to please Walt, and the two were in stitches over some silly move Sarah had made. Walt's eyes had sparkled with joy.

Now he looked years older. She'd brought a permanent sadness into his life with her ill-timed confession. He hadn't deserved that.

"I'm sorry I hurt you," she said. "There's nothing more I can say to make the truth easier."

"I wish you could tell me it never happened, but I know better," Walt said. "Jared made me see. He's always looked out for Mitch, but this time…"

Haley flinched. Walt didn't voice the rest of his thoughts, but Haley knew what he was thinking. Jared fixed Mitch's messes. This was one he couldn't do anything about.

"Is Jared with you?" she asked.

"No," Adele said. "He's at a cattle buyer's meeting."

Haley's heart deflated. She was one of Mitch's messes and since she wouldn't see him, he'd sent Walt and Adele in his place.

Oh, Jared.

She closed her eyes and felt his touch, heard his laugh. It hurt to think of him. In retrospect, she knew he'd stood up to his family on her behalf because she'd had no one else. He felt responsible for her.

He wanted to right what Mitch had wronged even if it meant bringing her to his ranch and making her a part of his life—a partner. She wanted more than that. What she wanted and what she could deliver were worlds apart. Jared would martyr himself for her and Sarah. That's the type of man he was. She loved him for it, but would never accept it. She opened her eyes.

Walt watched her, his gray gaze filled with sadness. She had to say something.

"You didn't need to come all this way to tell me you believe me." Silence hung like the morning mist. "Sarah is your granddaughter, Walt. You don't have to be afraid that I'll keep her from you. I would never use her against you. I know you would never use her against me."

Walt stepped forward. "I know. What I came for doesn't concern Sarah. It's about you and me." He gripped his fingers, pulling nervously at them. "I need to say this in person and it couldn't wait any longer." He looked straight into Haley's eyes. "I accused you, doubted you, blamed you because I didn't want to see my son the way you saw him." He let his hands fall to his sides. "There is no excuse for the things I said." He paused a moment, catching his breath. "I talked with my pastor. Adele and I spent hours praying for God's peace. I believe you, Haley. And I want you to know how very sorry I am for what my son…" His voice choked. "Can you forgive me?"

Tears flowed down Walt's face. Shock wedged words in Haley's throat. She touched her own cheeks, surprised to find them wet. Walt opened his arms. She hesitated a moment, then followed her instincts and embraced him. The warmth of forgiveness flooded her like whitewash on an old fence, rejuvenating, renewing.

"Thank you for this," she whispered. "I do forgive you."

Her heart released a pocket of pain. Walt needed her forgiveness as much as she needed his. She admitted the truth with grace and hope. When she let him go, part of the hurt she'd carried like a shield left, too. For a moment, she felt as if she'd sprouted wings and could fly. Tears filled her eyes again.

So this is what it feels like to forgive.

"Will you stay and have breakfast with me?" she said, her voice choking. "I'll try not to burn it."

Breakfast was serene. Haley wanted it to last. The only people missing were Hap, Sarah and Jared. She must mend the rift with Sarah. And Jared, too, but she couldn't, wouldn't think about him right now.

Walt approached her while Adele started to clean up. "There's one more thing I'd like to ask you," he said, his head humbly bent. "It concerns Sarah."

She nodded. "Okay."

"The mare, Calliope. I'd like Sarah to have her. And the foal, too. She was Mitch's horse. I realize you might not want any reminders of him around, but Calliope's wonderful, and the foal is the last of its line." Walt hesitated. "If you'd rather not, I understand."

Haley looked into his eyes. He did understand, and oddly, the discomfort she expected to feel wasn't there. Maybe there was hope for her after all. "I think Sarah would love that. Thank you, Walt."

"Thank you, for Sarah. She's a rose, Haley. Seems we always thank God for the roses, but we never thank Him for the thorns that come with them. I never saw the value in the thorns before." Adele joined him and they turned to go. "I'll make the arrangements for Calliope as soon as she foals."

Haley leaned against the camper long after they'd driven out of sight. So much had happened in so short a time. She couldn't think about Jared without feeling

his loss. She headed for the rodeo grounds with Walt's
words ringing in her mind.

I never saw the value in the thorns.

Haley threw herself into facing bulls and racing
barrels but nothing eased her restless spirit. At night,
something tugged inside her, a gentle plea, beckoning,
offering something more than a lonely fire on a chilly
evening. Mitch was her thorn, and she didn't want to
see any value in him. But the truth was, without Mitch
there would be no Sarah.

The thorn and the rose.

What would it cost her to forgive Mitch? Her body
shuddered. She stoked the fire. Jared's face danced in
the flames, then twisted in the smoke and disappeared.
She loved him beyond a shadow, but he wasn't in love
with her. He was cleaning up after Mitch. But for Mitch,
what might have been? But for Mitch, she would never
have met Jared. But for Mitch, she would never have
had Sarah.

*Oh, God. Why couldn't I have met Jared first? Why
couldn't Sarah be his?*

Only the snap of the logs and the singing crickets answered. She separated the coals and entered the camper.
Her father's picture smiled down at her. The photo wavered in a watery gaze.

Her heart shattered. She climbed onto the bedspread
and curled up in a ball, sobbing her misery into the pillow. Pop's worn Bible lay unopened on the bed where
she'd left it a few days ago. Outside, a rumble of thunder threatened. She felt the coming storm deep inside
her and her heart skipped.

It was as though two people struggled inside her,

each wanting her to go in a different direction. If she wanted peace, she must confront the issues warring for her soul. She must confront herself, her anger at Mitch and most of all her feelings for Jared.

Outside the window, gray clouds swirled. Thunder shook the camper. She pressed her fingers against her temples. Sarah was born on a day much like this; a day filled with anguish and joy; a day that sometimes led to darker thoughts. How she craved peace in her soul, for an answer to the why of Mitch and the ache of Jared. She opened Pop's Bible and flipped a page, memories dropping like rain. Did God feel her turmoil? Was he praying for her, like the young minister had said? She fanned the pages and found a card stuck in the center.

She pulled it out and laid the open Bible on the bed, noting the tattered edges of the page. Pop must have sought comfort here often. Maybe she would find some, too. An underlined passage stood out.

"I am fearfully and wonderfully made." She whispered the words.

Sarah's face formed in Haley's mind. She closed her eyes, then sought the page again and continued reading.

"My frame was not hidden from You when I was made in secret and skillfully wrought in the depths of the earth."

The sense of terror she'd felt so long ago flashed through her. God had seen. All these years she'd thought God had shut out her pleas because she'd disobeyed Pop in going to the carnival and flirting with Mitch.

She'd felt she'd brought misfortune on herself as well as Pop. She knew what happened wasn't all her fault, but part of it was. She'd called for God then. He hadn't answered. Why hadn't He rescued her from the thorn?

Her eyes darted back to the page, needing to understand, needing to let go of the burden always weighting
her down even when she thought it didn't.

"Your eyes have seen my unformed substance and
in Your book they were all written, the days that were
ordained for me, when as yet there was not one of them.
How precious are Your thoughts to me, O God. How
vast is the sum of them. If I should count them they
would outnumber the sand."

Her voice faded in a clap of thunder. She sat up like
a lightening bolt and hugged her knees. The truth of the
written Word lit the darkness in her heart.

*In Your book they were written, the days that were
ordained for me.*

For Sarah. For Mitch.

She picked up the card she'd pulled from the center of
Pop's Bible and turned it over. A sticky note with Pop's
handwriting brought tears to her eyes. She held it close.

"My beautiful Haley. I trust you will find this in
God's time, and that it will bring you the healing of
soul I have long prayed for and fulfill the purpose God
ordained for both you and Sarah. I love you both so
much. Pop."

The words wavered through her tears. She opened
up the envelope. Pop had underlined a quote, noting
the words came from *The Purpose Driven Life*. Haley
whispered the words, letting them settle in her soul.

"You were conceived in the mind of God. He thought
of you first. It is not fate nor chance nor luck nor coincidence that you are breathing at this very moment. You
are alive because God wanted to create you."

Haley's eyes widened. Sarah was here because God
wanted her here. And He wanted her here in the very

fashion He had ordained for both of them—for a bigger purpose that she had chosen to bury beneath anger and pain. Reality hurtled her back to earth. Two giant teardrops rolled down her cheeks. But what purpose? She hadn't bothered to try to find out.

"I'm sorry, so sorry. I missed it. Everyone else saw, but I missed it. Oh, Lord God, I'm ready to see the value of the thorn."

The peace she'd known as a child washed through her, then Mitch's plea echoed in her memory.

Forgive me. Forgive yourself.

She tucked Pop's note and card back into the passage and closed it. She wasn't ready to wrap her mind around forgiving Mitch, not yet. But the anger and pain were gone, leaving her free to explore the possibility. All that needed closure was Jared. No matter where she was or what she did, he was never far from her thoughts.

"I love you, Jared," she whispered. The patter of rain beat against the camper. Haley's tears fell, too.

Be my partner, he'd said.

If she was to find God's purpose in the trials He'd placed in her path, she must let go of Jared and free him of his need to rescue her. She had to see him again, talk to him one more time. Release him. For Sarah's sake and her own.

Three days later, Haley arrived at Jared's house long after dark. A sense of coming home swamped her. She gripped the steering wheel, determined to see this through. She parked away from the house and stepped into the chilly night air. The porch light was on, but the house appeared dark and deserted.

She hadn't told anyone but Hap about her plan to see

Jared again. She'd sworn him to silence, leaving less time for questions from Sarah and rehearsed speeches on Jared's part. She needed to gauge his reactions without prep time. Now it appeared no one was home.

She walked toward the barn. Surely someone was holding vigil with Calliope. Jared wouldn't leave the mare alone for long, especially this close to giving birth. She opened the barn door and entered. A low moan rose from Calliope's stall. Fear squeezed Haley's heart.

She hurried down the aisle as fast as she dared. The mare lay on her side, the hair along her flanks and sides heaving with each labored breath. Thin flecks of sweat formed around her eyes. How long she'd labored, Haley could only guess, but the window of time between safe and critical was slipping away. The mare couldn't last much longer. Where was everyone?

"Easy, girl," she crooned, rubbing her hands over the mare's side. "We'll have to do this together."

She'd never delivered a foal on her own before, but everything she'd watched Hap do came back in a flash. She moved around the mare's head along her back to her hindquarter and saw one tiny foot covered in a thin bluish-white sac. Haley swallowed hard. There should be two.

Panic gripped her. *Think, Haley. What would Hap do?*

Calliope struggled to rise, then fell back into the straw. If the foal's other leg remained hung-up, both would die. Haley reached for the emergency kit outside Calliope's stall and slipped her arm into a set of elbow length plastic gloves. Her experience stopped here. If she did something wrong, the mare would die. If she did nothing, they'd die anyway. And she'd be responsible.

"Help me, Lord. Send Jared. Send anyone."

Calliope groaned, her sleek body slippery with sweat. The window of safety closed. Haley waited for the contraction to end, then felt for the foals bent leg. She had to untangle it. She had to do it now.

A door banged outside.

"Jared. Shorty. Anyone. I'm in here. I need help," she called. The barn door slammed open.

"Haley?" Jared's quick steps rustled the barn shavings.

"Here." She shifted in the straw. "Calliope's in a bad way."

In an instant, he was there, standing behind her.

A cry of relief broke from her lips. Jared was here. Everything would be okay. "The leg is hung up," she said. "What do I do?"

"Follow the leg line with your hand. Feel where it's bent back."

Jared's calm voice didn't settle her fear. Haley pulled back. "I can't. Where were you? If she dies…"

"She won't die." His certainty bolstered her courage. "You have to finish this. There's no time. Feel for the knee."

"It's here. I feel it. It's bent."

"Follow it to the end of the foot. See if you can free it and straighten it out."

Haley gritted her teeth and felt for the tiny hoof. Heat penetrated the thin plastic glove. The mare's body contracted and tightened. Haley panicked.

"Wait it out," Jared said calmly. "Then push back and straighten the leg."

She waited. The pressure around her arm subsided. She pushed on the leg, moving it a fraction. Calliope moaned again, a deep wracking sound that brought tears to Haley's eyes. "Easy, girl," she crooned. "It's going to be okay." She pushed again. The leg gave. "I got it."

"Good girl." His voice held a faint tremor. "Now ease the leg out, grab them both and pull with the next contraction."

She grabbed the tiny hooves and waited, then pulled with everything inside her. The foal slid into the straw. Calliope moaned again. The foal was silent.

"No. Oh, no," Haley murmured.

Jared knelt in the straw. Using his sleeve, he wiped the sac from the foal's nose, then breathed air into the lifeless body. The small chest rose. Once, twice, three times.

Calliope staggered to her feel, pawing the ground. Haley pulled the glove off and stroked the mare's quivering body. Her gaze fixed on the foal's still, small form.

"Please, Lord. Let him live," she murmured.

She watched Jared work, and dared to hope that God would answer her prayer. One tiny hoof moved. Then both front feet twitched. A hesitant snort vibrated the small nostrils. Calliope nickered. The foal answered. Haley let the tears fall. "Thank You," she murmured, lifting her eyes toward heaven.

Jared waited a few more seconds, then swirled iodine around the navel area. Calliope nuzzled her baby, licking him, encouraging him to stand with short, low calls. Jared's arm slid around her waist.

"You did it. You saved them both," he said.

Haley rubbed her hands down her jeans. "Oh, Jared. I was so scared. Why wasn't someone here? Where were you?"

"The generator on the well pump went out. Calliope

was fine when Shorty and I went to work on it. Then I decided to come back and check on her."

"Where's Walt and Adele?"

"Rapid City. They'll be back later tonight," he said, pulling her closer.

Haley realized she was trembling.

Jared guided her toward the stall door. "Let's give mother and son some time to bond before we move them to a clean stall."

Haley gripped his hands. "I don't want to leave. Can't we just sit in the corner and watch them for a while?"

He turned her around, lifting her face with his finger, then erased her tears with his thumbs. She leaned into his chest, letting his strength flow into her.

"I thought they were both going to die," she said. "It would have been my fault. Like Mitch."

Jared held her tighter. She melted into him, wanting to stay, knowing she couldn't.

"Mitch wasn't your fault," he said softly. "Mitch wasn't anyone's fault. It was just his time."

She knew he was right. "It's hard to let go of it." She felt his dark eyes watching her, probing for answers she wasn't sure she had.

"Why are you here, Haley? Why did you come back?"

A tremor ripped through her straight to his heart. He'd hoped she'd returned because she'd come to her senses and realized she couldn't live without him any more than he wanted to live without her. She ducked her chin and backed away, dashing that hope. Her gaze flew to his. The air between them crackled.

"I came to see you."

His heart nearly stopped. Had God finally answered

his prayers? He took her hand, led her to a corner of Calliope's stall and sat down. She kept enough distance so their bodies didn't touch.

"Why? Why did you need to see me?" he asked.

She broke a piece of straw between her fingers. "Because I want you to know that I understand why you asked me to move here and be your partner."

"What is it you think you understand, Haley?"

Her eyes turned to deep amethyst in the shadowed stall. "I know that family is important to you. The most important thing in your life next to God." She hesitated, watching Calliope and the foal. "I know that you've spent a lifetime looking out for Mitch, fixing his mistakes, cleaning up his messes. Walt said so."

She looked straight at him. "You said so, too. I want you to know that you don't need to fix Mitch's mistakes. God has taken care of that for me. I just have to trust Him for the rest. I still have some things to work through, but I release you, Jared. You have no obligation to either me or Sarah."

Jared shifted to face her. His heart soared, then anger flashed through him, the storm before the calm. "Obligation. Is that what you think? That I wanted you here so I could fix what Mitch screwed up?"

"Isn't it?" Her luminous eyes shimmered with tears.

Jared scooted closer, taking her cold hands in his. "You don't know me very well at all, do you, Haley Clayton?"

She shook her head, dropping her gaze. "That's just the point. We don't know each other."

"I know that I love you for who you are, not because of what Mitch did or what you've endured because of it. I know that you're a warm, loving woman and mother with a heart as big as a Colorado mountain. I know I want to give you all the things I think you've longed for and you think you don't deserve. You are God's gift to me. I don't want to lose you, Haley. Ever." Her hand shook in his. "Look at me."

She raised her downcast eyes. He saw a shimmer of hope and her fear of reaching for it. He cupped her face in his hands.

"I love you. It doesn't matter to me what it took to make you into that person. I love you." He brushed his thumbs against her soft skin.

Her heart dropped. The tangy scent of his cologne filled the stall. She wanted nothing more than to believe, to have the right to claim his arms around her, to feel his protection along with the love shining from his eyes. He lifted his hand, gently pushing her hair from her shoulder.

"I prayed," she whispered. "It's taken me a long time, but I prayed for God to show me a purpose for the pain. I still can't see it, Jared."

"Sometimes we're so busy banging our head against a closed window we don't see the one that's opened across the room."

She closed her eyes. Jared said he loved her and she'd run away from him, but she'd come back. Was it really for the reason's she'd stated? *I love you. I see you*, he had said. Panic rose to her throat along with the shadow of memory. This was Jared. He wouldn't hurt her. She could give him anything but what he wanted most, herself.

"You deserve more than I can give you," she said.

"I deserve what God has put in front of me. So do you. It wasn't chance that brought you into my life. Yes,

I sought you out for all the wrong reasons. But God brought you back to me for all the right ones."

He touched her face. "You said you don't see a purpose for the pain. I believe God's purpose was us, working together as one to show others the way to His saving grace."

The veil lifted from her eyes, letting her see what God had put before her from the beginning, His work, His way, with the man of His choosing.

"You've told me why you came," he said. "I have a question for you." He took her face in his hands again. "Do you love me, Haley?"

A draft teased her hair, blowing strands across her face. He captured them, caressing them between his fingers. She leaned into his touch.

"This isn't a trick question," he said, a smile pulling at his mouth. "Do you love me?"

"Yes," she murmured, looking down. "I love you. I have for a long time. I was just so afraid."

"Do you trust me?"

She gazed into his eyes and saw all the dreams of the future reflected back at her. Their future.

"Yes," she murmured. "I trust you." The admission released Mitch's final hold. *The truth will set you free.* So this was God's plan all along. She'd been too blind to see.

Jared crushed her to him. "I know you have fears. We'll work through them. Don't ever leave me again, Haley."

He claimed her lips. She surrendered not just her fears, but her heart and all that lay within.

"This isn't going to be easy," she said, wanting him

to be sure. "I have...lots of issues. You can still walk away."

Jared smiled. "Not a chance. Everyone has issues. Isn't it amazing what God allows us to go through so that one person might come to know His grace and love?"

She'd never looked at her life in quite that fashion until now. Jared was right. She had a lot to offer. She'd been to the edge and back. She could show others the way to find the light hidden by the darkness. She searched Jared's face. The love in his heart reflected in his eyes, erasing all doubt.

"I'm not going anywhere, Haley." He fished into his pocket and pulled out a small black box. "I've been carrying this thing around for weeks, afraid to put it in a drawer for fear that I wouldn't have it when you finally came to your senses. Will you marry me, Haley?"

"You never said you wanted to marry me before."

"I couldn't. I had to let God do His work in your life first. It was the only way." He pulled the ring from the box. "I think it's about time this found its rightful place in the world."

He took her hand. "Haley Clayton, will you honor me by being my wife, sharing my life and helping me build our dreams for the rest of our lives?"

She didn't hesitate a second. "Yes, Jared. I will."

He slid the amethyst on her finger. She belonged to him. He belonged to her. She had only God to thank for this precious gift, this miracle of love. She shifted, leaning against Jared's chest. Calliope's foal inched closer. Haley reached out, touching his velvety nose. The solitaire sparkled in the dim light.

"So what are you going to call this bundle of curiosity?" Jared asked.

"Miracle," she whispered. "Because God performed a miracle in my heart, and I'll never forget it. Every time I look at him, I'll remember." She stared at the ring, not wanting to break the moment. "Didn't you think you were taking an awful big chance that I might not come back, or say no?"

She felt him chuckle. "With God on our side, how could you say no?" He folded his arms around her and nuzzled her ear. "How do you think Sarah will feel about changing her name to Sinclair?"

"I think she'll be thrilled."

"Then let's phone Hap and our daughter and tell them the news."

Epilogue

Spring. The time of new life. New beginnings. The smell of wildflowers drifted in the air. Haley drew in their scent and let Spinner cross the field at his own pace, the letter Jared had given her crumpled in her hand. She'd come full circle.

The past two months being married to Jared had been the happiest of her life. Sarah was ecstatic. Hap was content in the guesthouse, sharing chores with Jared's foreman. Jared was adding a wing onto the house for Walt and Adele. Life was good, and she was grateful to God for His gifts. So why did the issue of Mitch have to come into play again now?

She lifted her eyes to the sky, half wishing God would speak in an audible voice and make it plain and clear, but she already knew the answer in her heart.

Because to completely forgive herself and be free of the past she had to forgive Mitch. Because forgiveness was a choice she had chosen to place on the back burner.

Months of praying, counseling and soul-searching had shown her the importance of forgiveness. So had Jared, in the way he never pushed but let her come to terms in her own time. She trusted him—trusted he would never do anything to harm her. That's why he'd given her Mitch's letter. Because he knew it didn't have the power to hurt her anymore.

She dismounted and settled in the grass, then pulled the letter from the battered envelope. The words leaped from the page, Mitch's anguish touching her in a way she'd never expected. She'd wanted him to suffer, told him so that day in the hospital. Now she knew how deeply he had, and it brought no satisfaction. She'd have been worried if it had.

A huge tear splattered on the page. She closed her eyes.

"I'm sorry, Mitch. Sorry for both of our pain. I do forgive you."

The final burden lifted from her heart. She was free and the issue of what to tell Sarah about her father was settled. As far as she was concerned, the matter was finished. She rose, put the letter back in the envelope and picked up Spinner's reins. She turned toward the house and saw Jared making his way toward her. She broke into a run, Spinner trotting alongside.

Jared met her halfway through the meadow. She threw her arms around him and held him close.

"It's over," she whispered. "I love you, Jared. I'll love you forever."

He looked into her eyes, all the love in his heart shining there for her to see, then his head dipped and he claimed her lips. The shadow of a hawk sailed above them and Haley was certain God smiled.

* * * * *

Dear Reader,

Truly living for others requires daily dying to ourselves. At some point, forgiveness becomes an issue that confronts us all, whether it is a need to be forgiven or whether we are the ones who must do the forgiving. The wounds on our souls can be deeply emotional and devastating or relatively minor. In either case, we must choose whether to embrace a bitter spirit or experience the release forgiveness brings. Whichever path we choose will change us.

During our darkest times we tend to push God away. We feel He has abandoned us and we blame Him for our troubles, when in truth He is as close as He was to Jesus when Jesus hung on a cross to pay for our sins. Forgiving is never easy and doesn't happen overnight, but the release that comes with the action is well worth the effort.

My prayer is that anyone who embraces an unforgiving spirit will reap the benefits of or from forgiveness, no matter what the wrong, no matter who is right. May you seek God and find Him a willing advocate for a weary soul.

God bless each of you,
Susan Hornick

QUESTIONS FOR DISCUSSION

1. What was the truth that finally set Haley free?

2. Why do you think Haley chose the profession of rodeo clown, and what significance, if any, do you see from her clown makeup and costume?

3. What do you think prompted Haley to keep a child conceived from rape rather than give that child away?

4. At what point does Jared let go of his need for justice and allow God to use him to help Haley? What areas can you let go of in your own life for God to use you more effectively?

5. The Bible says perfect love casts out fear. How did Jared use his love for Haley to deal with her fears and how did it change him? How can God's unconditional love change us?

6. At what point did Walt realize the damage Mitch had done and how did this realization change how he viewed Haley? How do each of us handle the disappointments with friends and family and still honor God by our reactions?

7. Bad things happen in life to people who don't seem to deserve them. Why is it so easy to lose our faith during those times and why do you think we

blame God instead of the one who is the destroyer of our souls?

8. Why do you think God measures our trials by His strength, not our own?

9. What do you feel is the lesson behind the rose and the thorn?

10. At what point did Jared realize that praying for people was more important than "fixing" them? How can we change our prayer life to help others instead of "fixing" them, which is God's job?

11. What finally brings Haley to the realization that she is worthy of being loved and giving love?

12. If your child was a product of rape, how would you deal with the issue of telling your child without destroying his/her self-image? Do you think Haley's choice was the right one?

WE HOPE YOU
ENJOYED THESE TWO

LOVE
INSPIRED®
BOOKS.

If you were **inspired** by these

uplifting, **heartwarming**

romances, be sure to look for

all six Love Inspired® books

every month.

Love Inspired®

www.LoveInspired.com

Get 2 Free Books,
Plus 2 Free Gifts—
just for trying the Reader Service!

Love Inspired®

Love Inspired®

Save $1.00

on the purchase of any
Love Inspired® book.

Available wherever books are sold, including most bookstores, supermarkets, drugstores and discount stores.

✂

Save $1.00

on the purchase of any Love Inspired® book.

Coupon valid until July 31, 2018.
Redeemable at participating retail outlets in the U.S. and Canada only.
Limit one coupon per customer.

52615199

Canadian Retailers: Harlequin Enterprises Limited will pay the face value of this coupon plus 10.25¢ if submitted by customer for this product only. Any other use constitutes fraud. Coupon is nonassignable. Void if taxed, prohibited or restricted by law. Consumer must pay any government taxes. Void if copied. Inmar Promotional Services ("IPS") customers submit coupons and proof of sales to Harlequin Enterprises Limited, PO Box 31000, Scarborough, ON M1R 0E7, Canada. Non-IPS retailer—for reimbursement submit coupons and proof of sales directly to Harlequin Enterprises Limited, Retail Marketing Department, 225 Duncan Mill Rd., Don Mills, ON M3B 3K9, Canada.

5 65373 00076 2   (8100)0 12313

U.S. Retailers: Harlequin Enterprises Limited will pay the face value of this coupon plus 8¢ if submitted by customer for this product only. Any other use constitutes fraud. Coupon is nonassignable. Void if taxed, prohibited or restricted by law. Consumer must pay any government taxes. Void if copied. For reimbursement submit coupons and proof of sales directly to Harlequin Enterprises, Ltd 482, NCH Marketing Services, P.O. Box 880001, El Paso, TX 88588-0001, U.S.A. Cash value 1/100 cents.

® and ™ are trademarks owned and used by the trademark owner and/or its licensee.

© 2018 Harlequin Enterprises Limited

LICOUP0318

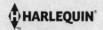

Save $1.00

on the purchase of any

Harlequin® series book.

Available wherever books are sold, including
most bookstores, supermarkets, drugstores
and discount stores.

Save $1.00

on the purchase of any Harlequin® series book.

Coupon valid until July 31, 2018.
Redeemable at participating retail outlets in the U.S. and Canada only.
Limit one coupon per customer.

LOVE
Harlequin romance?

Join our Harlequin community to share your thoughts and connect with other romance readers!

Be the first to find out about promotions, news, and exclusive content!

Sign up for the Harlequin e-newsletter and download a free book from any series at
www.TryHarlequin.com

CONNECT WITH US AT:

Harlequin.com/Community

 Facebook.com/HarlequinBooks

 Twitter.com/HarlequinBooks

 Instagram.com/HarlequinBooks

 Pinterest.com/HarlequinBooks

ReaderService.com

ROMANCE WHEN YOU NEED IT

Inspirational Romance to Warm Your Heart and Soul

Join our social communities to connect with other readers who share your love!

Sign up for the Love Inspired newsletter at **www.LoveInspired.com** to be the first to find out about upcoming titles, special promotions and exclusive content.

CONNECT WITH US AT:

Harlequin.com/Community

 Facebook.com/LoveInspiredBooks

 Twitter.com/LoveInspiredBks

LISOCIAL2017